Praise for
At Summer's

"I loved everything about this book: the richly drawn characters, the evocative setting, the very heart and soul of the story within the pages. It's everything you want in a novel for these times we are in. A sparkling debut from a new author we're all going to want more from."

—Susan Meissner, bestselling author of *The Nature of Fragile Things*

"Readers will be captivated by this stirring debut of love, family secrets, and human frailties. Told with wit and tenderness, this story is as unique as its characters, Bertie and Julian Wakeford, an earl like no other. Ellis deftly captures the devastation of war and what it means to be comfortable in one's own skin."

—Renée Rosen, bestselling author of *The Social Graces*

"Ellis's lyrical, emotional writing brings the beauty of Braemore alive while revealing the complexity of the richly drawn characters as Bertie pursues artistic recognition alongside her emotionally charged love affair with Julian. Historical fiction fans will appreciate this."

—*Publishers Weekly*

"The lush setting and vivid characters are utterly captivating in Ellis's lovely debut."
—*Booklist*

"Superb. . . . Readers will be filled with suspense, sometimes even anxiousness, but also cheer for Bertie's boldness, her sense of accomplishment, and the decision she makes at summer's end."

—Historical Novel Society

THE
FORGOTTEN
COTTAGE

Courtney Ellis

BERKLEY
NEW YORK

BERKLEY
An imprint of Penguin Random House LLC
penguinrandomhouse.com

Library of Congress Cataloging-in-Publication Data

Names: Ellis, Courtney, 1992– author.
Title: The forgotten cottage / Courtney Ellis.
Description: First Edition. | New York: Berkley, 2022.
Identifiers: LCCN 2022003026 (print) | LCCN 2022003027 (ebook) |
ISBN 9780593201312 (trade paperback) | ISBN 9780593201329 (ebook)
Subjects: LCGFT: Novels.
Classification: LCC PS3605.L4646 F67 2022 (print) |
LCC PS3605.L4646 (ebook) | DDC 813/.6—dc23
LC record available at https://lccn.loc.gov/2022003026
LC ebook record available at https://lccn.loc.gov/2022003027

First Edition: August 2022

Printed in the United States of America
1st Printing

Book design by Daniel Brount

"I found it not inappropriate that the years of frustration and grief and loss, of work and conflict and painful resurrection, should have led me through their dark and devious ways to this new beginning."

—VERA BRITTAIN, *TESTAMENT OF YOUTH*

THE
FORGOTTEN
COTTAGE

Prologue

AUGUST 1920

There was a beauty in the calm serenity of morning chores—the strength in her fingertips, the rhythm in each pull, the drumming of milk in her pail. The weather was cooling off after a particularly hot summer, and she found herself smiling absently at the gooseflesh on her forearms. Autumn was her favorite time of year.

Suddenly, the dogs sounded off from across the yard, making a frightful racket. She cursed as the cow kicked the pail of milk, sending it across her boots. With a sigh, she abandoned the milking and spotted her daughter toddling after the dogs toward the front of the cottage. She never would have thought a baby could move so fast on stubby legs.

She hastened her pace, leaving the barn to cut across the garden, which needed seeing to, but she quite liked the wild nature of it. So different to the sculpted gardens of her youth. Birds called from the trees nearby, a pair of larks leaping and flying across to the nest she knew they were keeping under the nursery window. They went up, and she watched them dance together in the sky before disappearing into the tree once more.

The dogs were still going when she turned the corner. It was not a bark for rabbits or squirrels, but the one reserved for the rare occasion when they were out of doors to see the postman or the grocer, trying desperately to protect their domain from the smiling intruders. She could finally see her daughter up ahead, bent over the lavender that lined the flagstone path. She had taught baby how to brush her little hands across the stalks to scare up the soothing scent that reminded her of bath time. She smiled and moved her attention to the end of the path, where the three dogs were circling their victim.

The man must have been passing, or had gotten turned around; no one from the village came this far up the road. He wore simple linen trousers and a flat cap pulled down over his eyes. From afar, she could not make out the words, but he was certainly talking to the dogs, and whatever he was saying had quietened them.

On instinct, she scooped the baby into her arms and made her way down the path, lifting two fingers to her lips to whistle for the dogs. One of them looked up, the others still enamored with the new smells of a stranger.

"For heaven's sake," she said, "let the poor man be! Enough, chaps. Here!"

Two of them trotted in her direction, then past, having caught some other, more thrilling trail to follow. The last still wiggled at the knees of the man at the end of the path. She approached him from behind, sighing as though excitable dogs were the sole problem in the world. Why had she bothered with them anyway? Was it not enough that she was running a small holding on her own, without these little terrors making such chaos?

"I am terribly sorry, sir," she said. "They are pests, these dogs, but clearly rather good for security. Have you lost your way?"

The man turned, at the same time lifting his cap from his head. Her eyes took a moment to focus, or so she thought, for what she was seeing was certainly a trick of the mind. But the hair was the same, the nose, the eyes, and when he spoke with a familiar voice, she fell to the grass.

Beneath her, the earth was swaying. Baby had landed firmly in her lap, giggling about the silliness of Mama's sudden drop. Her daughter grabbed at her necklace and she let her tug it, holding her close to her chest. The sun blocked her vision until the man went to a knee in front of her and she could see more clearly the curve of his jaw beneath his beard, the wear of war.

Tears were coming steadily now, and it was difficult to breathe. She was shaking all over, and it began to worry the baby. She let go of the necklace and tucked her face into her mother's neck.

"Steady, now . . ." he said.

When he grasped her arm, she flinched. She stared down at the impossible hand, not a scratch on it, and waited until the heat of his palm soaked through to her flesh.

What had begun as another sunny afternoon had turned into a daydream. In an instant, she was drawn violently back, away from the present, by an unseen tether, back to the grief and the arguments, to the dark and bloody years of war, and further to the bright and tumultuous days before.

One

Audrey

APRIL 2014

Stepping out of the taxi in Langswick, North Yorkshire, it became clear why I had never heard of it. I'd suffered eighteen hours of flights and layovers between Philadelphia and Manchester Airport, only to discover I still had a three-hour train journey and twenty-minute taxi ride ahead of me. My grandmother's birthplace would certainly not be found by anyone who didn't already know about it.

My shoulders, sore from toting an oversize backpack, slumped as I watched the taxi rumble down the narrow road, stranding me in the middle of a county in England I had never considered before Gran died. But now, thanks to her generosity, I owned a piece of it. She never spoke to me about her past, and if my mother knew anything, it had died with her when I was a little girl. I only knew Gran was British from the line she repeated each time someone asked about her heritage. *My father was a lord, you know.*

The cool spring air smelled of earth, woodsmoke, and manure. I swayed as I gazed around, trying to get my bearings. There wasn't much to the village but a hodgepodge of stone terraced houses crawling down a gentle hill, where a quaint chapel and village hall rested at the bottom. On my other side, the sun was setting over a wonky white building that was both the village shop and post office, strung with pastel bunting. Straight across the cobbled road was the local pub, gold lettering labeling it THE CROSS KEYS INN. Overflowing flower baskets hung beside each of the leaded windows, which glowed with dim light.

My mouth went dry.

Before crossing, I looked down at my phone to check the time. I had arrived in England at 12:40 P.M., and thanks to immigration lines and the time I'd spent figuring out the British railway system, it was already nearing seven o'clock. There were no texts—my phone plan didn't include the UK, so I would continue avoiding calls from my dad and sister. I had taken care of Gran in her final year, and perhaps that was why she left this hitherto unknown property to me, of all people. But that didn't stop the family from voicing their strong opinions on what I should do with it. It would be some time before they could trust me again.

Beth, my sister, would have been the obvious choice. She was a top real estate agent in New Jersey, and was married with two kids. If there was anyone who could have handled this quickly and cleanly, ensuring we got the most money from Gran's assets, it was Beth. And she made sure I knew that.

An older gentleman in a tweed newsie cap had come up the road, and eyed me curiously before touching his brim in greeting. I supposed they didn't get many strange faces in a place like this—especially ones that looked as swollen as mine. I'd cried on the plane, on the train, and in the taxi, and was feeling the urge again. I missed my grandmother, felt unworthy of her gift, and was directionless without her need of my help.

God, I wanted a drink.

With a grunt, I heaved my backpack off the ground and slipped my hand into the pocket of my jeans to feel the cool metal of my AA medallion. It hadn't been easy, but with Gran's help, I had earned it after remaining sober one year. Now, I needed the reminder that I was strong enough to have earned it. That I could do it without her.

I took a deep breath and headed inside the Cross Keys Inn.

The pub was close and dim. Three walls were half-paneled in the same oak the bar was built of, while the fourth was all stone, housing a fireplace big enough to sit in. Candles flickered at each of the four tables and over the mantelpiece. The only electric light came from a small gambling machine in the corner, and lamps used sparingly around the bar, which accommodated four stools. Three of them were empty, the last occupied by a hunched figure.

Immediately, my senses filled with the familiar yeasty scent of spilled beer. I told myself it was nothing I hadn't handled before, though after the day I'd had, it was tempting. I tightened my fingers around the strap of my backpack and tried to keep my mind from falling into the familiar spiral of excuses: *It's just one beer. You've had a bad day. It'll help you beat the jet lag. If you eat a big meal, you won't even feel it.*

"'Ow do, love?"

It was the barmaid who had spoken, standing with one hand resting on a brass tap. She looked to be about my age, with a silky black bob pushed behind her ears, a septum piercing, and perfect winged eyeliner. She didn't look at all like she belonged in the quiet countryside.

"Can we get you summat?" she asked.

I warmed to the charming flat vowels of her thick accent, and stepped away from the drafty door, letting my backpack fall to the ground. My fingers found the surface of the bar and began to tap nervously. It'd been a long time since I'd allowed myself to step up to one.

"The taxi driver said you would have rooms available?" I said.

The barmaid raised her cleanly threaded eyebrows. "Did he now? Well, that were presumptuous of him."

I opened my mouth to speak, but nothing came out. The man on the stool chuckled. He was young compared to the other patrons, with overgrown dark hair and a short beard. In front of him was a pint of beer still filled to the brim, and a smaller glass of what looked like orange juice.

"I'm having you on, love," said the barmaid with a wink. "Only, we don't get many American tourists round here—mostly locals for walking holidays—and unfortunately those locals have filled all four of our rooms."

I sighed, slumping against the bar. Already, my throat was tightening, tears threatening for the tenth time that day. I was so tired and hungry, I wanted to collapse to a heap on the floor. Where was I going to find another place to stay, when there was nowhere else for miles?

"Not being funny, but you look like you've been through the wars today," said the barmaid, waving me over. "Come, set yourself down. I'm Namita."

"Audrey," I said, gratefully taking the stool in front of her.

"How 'bout a pint, then, Audrey? First one's on me."

"Sure. Uh, no—" I had spoken without thinking, an instinctual answer. I put my hand up to stop Namita at the tap. "No thank you. I don't drink."

I found the declaration helped me to refocus. Saying no wasn't enough. Not after how painful it had been to crawl my way back from the depths I'd found myself in a year ago.

Namita gave a short laugh and pointed her thumb over her shoulder. "Neither does Leslie there. I keep the orange juice in for him, don't I, Les?" The man on the stool lifted his face to scorn her playfully. "Lucky for me, really; I get to drink that pint once he's through glaring at it."

It was strange to see such familiarity between them, when the bars I was used to in Philadelphia were places of anonymity. Here, locals gathered around the tables, leaned over to speak and joke with those sitting on the other end of the room.

I turned back to Namita, hoping she would show me the same kindness. "Do you have a phone I could use? Mine doesn't work here."

Leslie pushed his iPhone across the bar toward me, keeping his gaze on that full pint. He looked up only when I hesitated, deep, rich brown eyes reflecting the warmth of the dim light.

"Go on," he said, "it won't bite ya."

I gave him a quick smile of gratitude and picked up the phone to open the map. I needed to find a bed and stay in it until the walls stopped spinning around me. Gran's house had apparently been shut since the 1940s, so wasn't inhabitable. It was already dark outside, and it had been over twenty-four hours since I'd slept properly.

"You won't have any luck looking nearby," said Namita as she pulled a fresh pint for one of the older patrons. "There's a food festival on this weekend in the next market town—brings holidaymakers in droves. Why I'm full up. Is that not the reason you've come?"

I let my head fall into my hand, staring down at the bright screen of Leslie's phone. I opened the map application and tried a quick search for hotels. She was right—everything within a short drive was full, and there were no more buses running tonight.

I set the phone down and squeezed my eyes shut, thinking of Gran in her final days, looking so fragile in the hospice bed. In that moment, I would have done anything to speak to her again and ask her why she had planned this for me. Why she trusted me when I was such a disaster. Why she had kept this massive secret from me at all.

"You might try York." This was Leslie, still facing front. "You can get there in forty-five minutes by taxi."

"York, Les?" said Namita. "At an hour? The taxi will charge her up the nose, and besides, it's Friday—it'll be nowt but stag dos and tourists."

I put the phone back down, and finally losing all my composure, let my head follow it. The scuffed bar was sticky and cool under my forehead, smelling of a thousand pints. I wondered, briefly, if Gran had ever found herself inside of this pub as a girl, if she had ever sat on this stool. If this was what she had in mind for me when she put me in her will.

But it couldn't have been. She knew I struggled with alcohol; it was the reason I had moved into her house a year ago. After rehab, there was no job to return to, no apartment, no going back to the city that had broken me. My dad was tired of my antics after a turbulent adolescence, and I couldn't stand to be under Beth's judgmental glare. So Gran had taken me in, given me the unconditional love I was craving. In return, I took care of her after her stroke, returned as much of the love as I could until we ran out of time. She had left me her family home, trusted me to do the right thing with their legacy.

True to form, I was already screwing up. I hadn't even made a plan. I had taken the first flight available, with its crappy timing and two layovers. After Gran's funeral, I had needed to get far away from my mess of a life and figure out what to do next.

"I can give you a lift wherever you need to go," Leslie said.

I almost didn't hear him, as the small space was beginning to hum with voices loosened by alcohol. When I lifted my head, he was looking straight at me for perhaps the first time, waiting with a look of mild annoyance, as if he regretted coming to the pub on the one night a helpless American decided to walk in.

"You don't have to do that," I said. "Thank you, though."

"He can do you one better," said Namita. "Leslie has got a guest room. I've just finished telling him he ought to be letting it out in tourist season."

Again, Leslie turned his eyes on her, lips pressed together in a line, and again, she found the look on his face to be giggle-worthy. She must have been joking. Using his phone was one thing. Shacking up with a foreign male stranger was another.

"I'll just call a taxi to York," I said, "or go back to Manchester if I have to."

Namita's eyes widened. "Oh no, don't do that, love. What about Whitby?"

"Where's that?"

"Just up the coast. Lovely seaside town, is Whitby. Spent summer holidays there as a girl. Best fish and chips in the country."

Leslie's mouth quirked at Namita. "You missed your calling as a travel agent."

"Not really the corporate type, am I? Much prefer drinking on the job."

I felt another rush of grief. Sleep deprivation was a lot like being drunk—it smashed inhibitions, made you brave, sharpened every emotion.

"I need to be here," I said, pointedly enough that I got both of their attention. "I came all this way to be *here*, in this village. It's where my grandmother was born and it might be all that's left of her now . . ."

That seemed to touch them both. Namita slid her hand across the bar to lay atop mine, bracelets rattling against the wood. "Don't you fret, love," she said. "Surely there's someone in this place who can get you sorted." She gave Leslie a pointed look.

He put his hand in front of me, palm open. I took it as an invitation to return his phone, and set it in his grasp. I expected he was ready to get out of there before he got roped into helping me any further. Instead, he stood, shuffled to the stool nearest me, and sat again with the gentlest sigh.

"Look; I *have* got a spare room," he said.

I blinked up at him, at the tightness in his brow. He was certainly rough around the edges, but there was a softness to his face that made me comfortable—made me want to trust him.

"That's really kind, but I couldn't inconvenience you like that."

"Oh, you've got to," Namita said. "Leslie's is swish. Trust me, the roll-top tub is an absolute dream."

So they were dating—or had dated. I didn't think his current girl-friend would be encouraging another woman to bunk at his place. In that case, could I trust her judgment? They had been nothing but kind to me. And the last thing I wanted to do was get into another taxi . . .

I looked at Leslie, his kind eyes, his hair that was long enough that he had to push a lock of it behind his ear when it fell forward. There was something about him. Maybe it was that he was sober, too. Maybe it was because he lived here, where Gran's life began.

"Maybe just for tonight," I said. "And I could pay for the room."

He shook his head. "There's no need. I'm up early for work; I'll hardly know you're there, and I won't be under your feet. And I'm not a murderer, if that's what you're thinking. Namita has known me since I was small; she can keep me honest. In fact, ask anyone. Bernard isn't here to tell you I used to piss in his hedges when I was seventeen. That's true, I'm afraid."

Namita winked. "He's one of the good ones, our Leslie. Piss notwithstanding."

I looked back at the man in question. I was so tired that I began to feel a little nauseous, and if I stayed at the bar any longer, I was going to drink myself under it.

"Okay," I said, slipping off my stool. "Let's go before I change my mind."

Two

Audrey

I managed to nod off for the five minutes we spent in Leslie's car, so I didn't get to ask what he did for a living, or why he had ordered that pint if he was sober, and he didn't get to ask me why I had found myself in his country without any plans for where I was going to stay.

The answer to that was simple. I needed to get away from my family, from the FOR SALE sign on Gran's front lawn, from the radio silence I got from coworkers I used to call friends, from my jobless, hopeless future. So I got on the first flight to Manchester without thinking of my next step.

When we arrived at Leslie's house, I was too tired to register what it looked like, or how it smelled, or even whether or not the sheets were clean. He spoke to me gently, handed me fresh towels, pointed out the bathroom and the guest room where I was to sleep. Something cold touched my hand and I looked down to find a wiggly, pointy-eared dog smiling up at me. I managed to use the bathroom and peel my jeans off before falling into bed. I closed my eyes and didn't open them again until I blinked awake at five o'clock in the morning.

That was when I was conscious enough to take note of the luxurious quality of the bedsheets (which smelled freshly laundered) and the plush duvet that cocooned me. For a moment, I was dizzy with the realization of where I was and how I'd gotten there, what I'd done in the long hours leading up to my decision to stay.

I sat up quickly and my aching head spun. Looking around, I noticed the fine details of the room for the first time: the thick magnolia walls with beams peeking through; the low, slanted eaves; the pine wardrobe and bedside table. Two small curtained windows could have been painted on for how stunning the vistas were—perfectly green, patchwork countryside rolling up and down as far as the eye could see. A river glittered in the valley, and beyond, a wash of color where wild heather bloomed between swaying grasses.

I stood at the larger window, squinting in the light, momentarily struck by the untouched beauty.

Leslie's Land Rover was still parked out front, so he hadn't left for work. I would have to be quiet if I was going to slip out without having to speak to him. At least I had had the wherewithal to lock the door last night. I lifted the latch and opened it slowly to avoid making noise. Creeping to the bathroom, I spotted the tub Namita had been raving about. I would have liked to sink into it, but wasn't planning on staying any longer than necessary. I brushed my teeth, washing away the sickly, sour film left in my mouth, and scraped my hair into a messy bun, cringing at the long-grown-out highlights that revealed the dull brown at my roots. Once I was changed into a fresh pair of jeans, I grabbed my backpack and headed out.

My plan was to leave and never see Leslie again. But as I stood at the bottom of the narrow staircase, drinking in the charm of his idyllic, if worryingly clean, English cottage, I heard my conscience telling me to wait. It sounded a lot like Gran, voice shaky with age but full of brass: *A stranger showed you kindness. Don't take that for granted, love.*

I sighed, letting my backpack fall to the ground. Gran was right, of course. She had shown me that kindness when she took me in. The least I could do was pay it forward. I took my wallet out of my backpack. The village shop was near enough to walk. Leslie had given me the bed, now I would give him the breakfast. That's what Gran would have done.

Fifteen minutes later, I was trudging back up Leslie's gravel drive with a grocery bag in each hand. The house was a perfect rectangular stack of grey stone. Charming French windows sat in timber frames, and a squat, split door was nestled in the middle. I followed a flagstone path around the back of the house to where the garden continued to stretch its legs. Beyond the short fence was nothing but the pure hills and undulations I had seen from my window. The vast grassland was divided by drystone walls and squat trees. Sunlight poured over the earth, broken up by the slowly moving shadows of cotton candy clouds.

As the wind whipped loose hairs over my eyes, I started to feel better. This place was astounding, enchanting, and as I breathed the earthy, floral scent on the breeze, nostalgia pinched at my stomach, like I was homesick for this place, though I had never been here before. I wondered if Gran's house was as beautiful. I wished she could be by my side and see this place again. Wished she could tell me what to do next, here, and in my life.

The grocery bag rustled, and I looked down to see the pointy-eared dog from last night poking it with his nose. His bottom wiggled as his tail went back and forth, and his lips drew back in a grin.

"Hi, there," I said. "What's your name, handsome?"

"Jim."

I turned to find Leslie standing on the threshold of a glass door that led into a conservatory attached to the back of the house. He wore a T-shirt and grey sweatpants. One hand rested in his pocket while the other gripped a ceramic mug. His hair was pushed to one side, messy from sleep.

"That's not a dog's name," I said.

"He likes it well enough," Leslie replied. "It was the first name I thought of when I found him."

Jim ran off to sniff in the raised vegetable beds, and I took a cautious step closer to Leslie. He looked completely at ease—happy, even, to find me lingering.

"He was a stray, living in the barn when I bought it," Leslie said.

"Just a bag of bones, bless him. I started sharing my bacon butties, and the rest is history."

I looked around me. "What barn?"

Leslie nodded his head toward the house. "This one. It was full of cow shite and dead cats when I bought it three years ago."

My gaze trailed upward. The house was even more impressive to me, knowing what it had once been. "You did this all yourself?"

"Much of it, but I brought on a couple of mates in the end. It was my first project. Now I use it as a sort of portfolio for clients. I make my living working on houses—barn conversions are quite popular hereabouts."

"I can see why. It's so beautiful. Are those your sheep?"

"They belong to a neighboring farm. It's great; I get to enjoy them without any of the work." Leslie's eyes crinkled in the morning sun, and I stiffened as he studied me. Even with a clear head, I couldn't deny an attraction to him, and wondered if he felt the same. "Been round the shops?"

"I thought I could cook for you, to say thanks for rescuing me last night. The guy at the store showed me what to buy for breakfast."

"Keith, was it?"

"Do you know him?"

"Oh aye. It's a small village."

Seeing as he didn't voice any objections, I joined him in the conservatory, standing close enough to notice the wrinkles in his T-shirt, which he'd obviously slept in. The thought heated the back of my neck. This situation was far too intimate to be in with someone I had barely spoken to, though he seemed unashamed to be caught in his pajamas.

"Would you remind me of your name?" he asked. "I'm a bastard for forgetting, but as I recall you only said it once."

I was foggy enough last night myself; I could hardly blame him. "Audrey."

"That's right—Christ. I swear that's the first time that's ever happened." He shook his head and sighed at himself. I decided not to read too far into it. "Shall I fix you a brew?" He raised his own mug of tea.

"Sure . . . Thanks."

He shuffled over limestone floors on bare feet to flick the electric kettle on. I set the grocery bags on the counter and began to unload. I expected the kitchen to be sleek and modern, considering how new it was, but he'd designed it to remain in keeping with the age of the barn, with exposed stone and white cabinets with wooden knobs. Though it wasn't completely vintage—there were shiny, state-of-the-art appliances, one of which Leslie was firing up.

"I'll fry these up for us," Leslie said, unwrapping the bacon and sausages. "There are some eggs in the fridge, I think."

"I'm supposed to be cooking for *you*," I said.

Leslie scratched at his beard, smiling a little more deeply than before. At least he was easy to get along with. I had been imagining sitting awkwardly across from him at the long farm table, searching for anecdotes for polite conversation. I was never good at that sort of thing, not until I had a few drinks in me.

I stuck my hand in my pocket to grip my medallion, feeling guilty.

"You can do the toast, then." Leslie placed two sausages in the pan with a sharp sizzle. The kettle clicked off and he crossed the room to pour the water into a fresh mug. "Milk? Sugar?"

Gran was the only person I knew who drank tea with milk and sugar. I nodded, and Leslie let it steep, returning to poke at the sausages before adding the fixings. When he handed it to me it was golden brown and the perfect temperature, sweet, and surprisingly strong and earthy.

"I like this," I said.

"Good job, too. That's Yorkshire Tea, that."

While he worked on the meat, I made the toast. Jim came running through the door when he smelled the hot pork, and Leslie obliged his busy nose with bacon. Once everything was ready, we piled it all on two plates and sat at the table. I could feel heat coming from the old cooker behind me, and thought how cozy it must be in winter.

Looking down at my plate, I tried to decide where to begin. Keith at the shop had advised me to buy bacon, sausages, black pudding, tomatoes, mushrooms, and beans—all of which were steaming fragrantly in front of me. My stomach was turning inward, refusing to accept. I set my utensils down and leaned away.

"You okay?" Leslie asked, pausing with his fork under his chin.

For a moment, I couldn't answer, only closed my eyes and waited for the floor to stop swaying beneath me. Then I decided the truth was far better than what my stomach had in mind.

"I'm really hungover," I said.

Leslie blinked at me. Clearly he had heard *something* last night. "Did you not say you were sober?"

"You remembered that, but not my name?"

He cringed. "My head was in my ass when you walked in."

That was relatable enough. "I *was* sober," I answered, "until Gran . . ."

I'd been doing well that week until the crying. From the time we reached cruising altitude, I had sobbed until the flight attendant asked if I was going to be all right, and I caved. I had started with a tiny bottle of merlot, and then another, and then it was vodka, running smoothly over my wine-soaked throat. I had woken still drunk upon landing, and continued with cans of Carling on the train to York. Ironically, it wasn't until I had reached the pub that I'd actually stopped.

I waited for Leslie's expression to shift to something sour and judgmental. Instead, he looked concerned. I didn't want pity either, so I laughed. "Do you really think I would have agreed to stay in a stranger's house, in a foreign country, if I hadn't been under the influence?"

Leslie allowed a smile and swallowed a gulp of his tea. "You'll want to tuck in, then. Nothing sorts a hangover like a proper fry-up."

Taking his word, I fought my screaming stomach for three bites of bacon, and like magic, my headache began to recess, and I could sit straighter.

"Thank you for having me last night," I said, pausing to butter my toast. "I know it probably wasn't what you had planned for your evening, having a stranger in your guest room."

He gave a little shrug. "That's okay. I'm glad to see someone put the room to use. Last person to sleep in it was Namita, when her place was renovated."

"I thought you two might be together."

"Just old friends."

Strangely reassured, I took a bite of toast.

"What do you do, back at home?" he asked.

The question shook me, and I reached for my tea. He couldn't have known, but I hated answering it, hated trying to meander my way around the truth of the situation.

"I was an RN," I said.

"Must be intense work, that. Are you on holiday?"

I dipped my toast into runny yolk. "I inherited a property nearby from my grandmother."

"You must have been close."

I nodded. "My mom died of breast cancer when I was six, and Gran took up all of the mothering duties. She's the reason I stayed sober for so long."

"I'm sorry," Leslie said, and I smiled my thanks.

My sister and I had stepped off the school bus at Gran's house every day, spent every afternoon and dinner with her. Dad traveled a lot for work, so we stayed whole weeks at a time until Gran's house started to feel more like home than ours. It was Gran who bought us our first bras, explained about periods, and took us shopping for prom dresses. Maybe it was because she was so devastated to lose her daughter, or because she could see my dad had no clue how to raise two girls on his own, but she was always happy to step in.

"Whereabouts is the house, if you don't mind my asking?" Leslie asked.

"I'm not sure. I didn't even know it existed until after she died. You probably know it, though . . ."

I took my phone out of my pocket to flick to the email I'd saved with the house's address. It didn't have a number, just a road and a name: Sparrow Cottage.

I slid the phone across the table to Leslie, and a peculiar look came over his face. I thought for a moment he was going to tell me that the place had already been demolished, or burned to the ground, or didn't exist at all. But when his face came up, his dark eyes were glittering, as they had last night at the pub, and his lips bent in a boyish smile.

"Know it? I've only been obsessed with Sparrow since I was small. I broke my arm falling out of an oak tree in the back garden when I was ten."

The idea should have tickled me. Instead, it gave me an odd burn of jealousy. This man, whom I had only just met, got to live his whole life in the village where Gran was born, had spent summers running through the garden of Sparrow Cottage, a place she chose never to mention to me when she was alive. I should have had those memories, too.

"What do you plan to do with it?" Leslie asked, returning my phone.

"Sell it, I guess. I keep thinking that's why she must have left it to me. She knows I need the money more than anyone else in the family. But it's weird, right?"

Leslie folded his arms over his chest and sat back in his chair, listening.

"Gran kept this massive secret her whole life. To leave her home so suddenly on her own, something must have gone wrong with her parents. But I can't figure out why she kept the house all this time, or why she always boasted that her father was a lord."

Leslie furrowed his brow, poking at his beans. "The people who lived at Sparrow weren't nobility."

I wasn't completely surprised. The way Gran said it—*my father was a lord*—often got a laugh as if she was joking, and her expression gave nothing away. A little part of me hoped I was inheriting Pemberley, but I knew enough about history to understand that places like that didn't normally pass to daughters.

"I'm guessing Sparrow doesn't come with a stately manor, then?" I said.

"It's a pretty humble cottage on a small holding. Four bedrooms maybe. From what I know, these guys were commoners, making a living."

It made sense. If Gran had owned a manor, she wouldn't have clipped coupons in the morning while drinking her tea, or splurged on only tattered paperbacks at the library for fifty cents apiece. Imagining her working on a farm wasn't too much of a stretch. She was never afraid to get her hands dirty.

"Likely, you'll learn more about them whilst you're going through the house," Leslie said.

"I'm sure it's empty," I answered.

"Not from what I've heard."

I sighed, rubbing my eye. This had the potential to be a bigger undertaking than I thought. "Apparently there's been a caretaker looking after the place for all these years . . ."

Leslie's eyes widened. "Shit. Bernard."

"The piss hedge guy?"

"Yeah . . . The old man hates me 'cause I used to break into the garden and outbuildings as a lad."

"And because you pissed in his hedges."

"We have a history, though he's miserable at the best of times. I hadn't thought of him until you said *caretaker*. He must be at least ninety years old now."

"At that age, he can't be doing much caretaking."

"It's a good old stone house—it's been standing for centuries, and will do for another hundred years."

"You think so?"

"It's my livelihood, rescuing historic properties, and Sparrow is Grade II listed. You can rest assured, it isn't going anywhere."

"What does that mean, listed?"

"It's protected by the government. You would need special permissions to alter the building."

I sat forward, wrapping my hands around my mug, which had gone cold. It was a lot to process. I had come with the idea that I would find a condemned manor, and then someone who could sell it for me, returning home with a few photos of what was left of it. But if what Leslie said was true, this was going to take more work.

"I could walk over there with you, if you like," said Leslie. "It isn't far, and my boss won't mind if I'm late to work." Of course, he worked for himself. "You might need a bit of a hand with Bernard, the old codger."

"You've done enough already. If you could just point me in the right direction, I'm sure I'll be able to find where Bernard lives. Apparently, the attorneys called to let him know the owner passed away, but he'll have the key."

Leslie leaned his elbows on the table. "Honestly, it's no trouble. I've been dying to see the inside of that place. It's—" His eyes drifted off, as he seemed to be checking himself. "It's the reason I became a builder, you know? As a child, I was thrilled by the mystery of it, but in time I began to hate seeing such a lovely house all dark and shut; I wanted to bring it back to life, to make it a home again. You'd be doing me a massive favor by letting me tag along."

There was no way I could argue with that, especially not when Leslie's eyes were so full of emotion. I knew what it felt like to love a vocation that way, to wake up and go to work with a smile, and even on the hardest of days, know I was exactly where I wanted to be. It made me like him even more.

"Well," I said. "I *do* owe you a favor . . ."

Leslie smiled as his phone buzzed in his pocket. He apologized and brought it out, his brow furrowing as he read whatever had come across the screen.

"It's Namita. Apparently someone's been ringing for you at the pub. A woman called Beth?"

I set down my fork, sure I was about to finally be sick. "That's my sister. But I didn't tell her where I was staying."

"She probably googled the village; Keys is the only local accommodation."

I let out a long sigh and closed my eyes. Clearly, Beth wasn't going to let me continue to ignore her texts and emails. With the way she fought for control in every situation, I knew she wasn't above hopping on a plane and coming here herself. I was going to have to call her.

"Do you not get on?" Leslie asked, reading my distress.

"Not since we were kids. And she doesn't know that I drank." Beth was not going to be pleased.

Thanking him, I brought my plate to the sink before retreating to my room, armed with his Wi-Fi password. As I connected to the internet, texts came flying in from Beth, asking where I was staying, asking about the Cross Keys Inn, and letting me know that the "girl at the front desk" told her I'd been there. I supposed that was the downfall of staying in such a small village. There was certainly only one American Audrey staying in town.

Steeling myself, I began to pace and tapped on Beth's number. She answered on the first ring, her voice making me grate my teeth. "Would it have been *so* difficult for you to text me when you landed?"

I rolled my eyes, glad she couldn't see. "I don't have an international phone plan."

"That excuse doesn't really hold up anymore, Audrey." Beth sighed, crackling the line. "You didn't even tell us what airport you were flying into. We had no way of finding you if something happened." A pause. "You're not drinking, are you?"

I refocused my attention out the window, taking deep breaths. "I'm sorry I didn't text you. I was going to call you tonight."

"You didn't answer my question, Audrey."

She was using her Mom Voice on me now. I'd heard her use it

dozens of times when her kids were misbehaving; her wife was a total contrast of her, too laid-back to discipline. When I didn't answer, there was rustling on her end, and a door closing. She spoke more quietly. It was late there. "I found empties at Gran's."

I let my head fall against the wall beside the window. I'd been in such a hurry to leave that I hadn't thought to check my usual hiding places. They were all from the week between Gran's death and the funeral, but Beth would never believe that.

"How long has this been going on?" she asked.

"I had a few bad days."

"And have you had any since?" she asked. I bit my lip. "Audrey?"

"On the plane," I answered quickly.

Another sigh made me hold the phone away from my ear again. "I think I need to come over there and bring you home."

I leaned away from the wall, bracing one hand on it to steady myself. That was the last thing I wanted—I needed space from her, from all of them.

"Beth, no," I said. "I haven't even been here for twenty-four hours. Let me take some time to figure this out—"

"Dad and I agree this is not something you can handle on your own."

I rolled my eyes, resisting the urge to lash out at her the way I had in the past. "I promise you I'm okay now. I just need a week or so to make plans for Gran's house, and then I'll be on a plane back home."

"I should be there. Selling houses is what I do best."

"This house is different," I said, somehow believing it wholeheartedly, though I hadn't even set foot inside the cottage yet. "It's all that's left of her now . . ." The thought of her home back in New Jersey, emptied except for the sugar cookie–scented candle Beth always used for open houses, made my throat tighten.

"Gran left you with more responsibility than you can handle right now," Beth said. "Especially if you're drinking. You need to come home and get yourself to a meeting."

"I'm *not* drinking. I drank."

"What is the difference?" Her voice was tight now; cold. "You are on extremely thin ice as it is. Do you want all that money we spent on an attorney to go to waste, or do you want your goddamn job back?"

I closed my eyes, sinking to a seat on the floor. The stability of the ground was always a comfort when my heart began to race, when my lungs forgot how to fill, and my vision tunneled. A panic attack was the last thing I needed right now. I tried to slow my breathing, to focus on five things I could see, four I could touch, three I could hear—

But all I could think about was the too-tight blazer I'd worn to the hearing, its lining damp under my arms, the potent smell of my attorney's floral perfume, and the White Stripes song that was playing on my drive home. The Board of Nursing had decided not to revoke my suspended license, which should have been a relief. Instead, I'd spent every moment of my one-year probation period dreading the day I had to return to a career that I loved, but that had my mental health in shreds.

"Audrey?" Beth's voice sounded far away on the other end of the line. "Did I lose you?"

I shook my head before realizing she couldn't see, and tested my voice. It was weak, but proved I was still breathing, and with that, my pulse evened. "I'm here, sorry." Beth huffed, and I imagined her running her palm from the roots of her hair and up to her perfectly arranged bun.

"Call me later," Beth said. "Or whenever. Call me if you feel like drinking, okay? Promise you will."

"I promise," I answered, and drew a full breath that made the room come into view again.

"Just because Gran is gone doesn't mean you have to do this on your own."

My hand went to my mouth and I hung up before she could hear me break.

Three

Audrey

It was a short walk to Bernard's house, but by the time we reached it, I was already thinking about the Cross Keys Inn. I always wanted a drink after a panic attack, even though drinking sometimes led to them. But it was instinct for me to reach for one anytime my mood shifted. Luckily, Leslie didn't slow as we passed the pub, and I was able to refocus my attention on keeping pace with him. I let my eyes sweep back and forth, and focused on my senses again, grounding myself back in reality.

Bernard lived in a semidetached stone house at the bottom of the hill and across the village green. As we approached, his neighbor, a woman about my father's age, waved to Leslie as she lifted a watering can to her flower boxes. "Now, then, Leslie Whiting," she said, "we don't see enough of you. How's your nan? Good health?"

Leslie smiled and leaned an elbow on her gate. "She's well, cheers. Your loo holding up?"

The woman rolled her eyes. "Oh aye. Harry still owes you a pint for coming round on short notice. What was the ruddy point in marrying the man if he can't even do the handiwork?"

They shared a laugh, and she winked at me as if we were in on the same inside joke. Then with another wave, she lowered her watering can. "Bye, then, lad. Say hello to your nan for us!"

Leslie waved back. "Mind how you go."

When we turned again, I looked up at him curiously. "You seriously do know *everyone*."

All I got was a timid shrug. It seemed what Leslie said to me at the pub last night was true. I was sure anyone in this village would vouch for his good nature, especially if he was in the habit of doing the neighbor's plumbing for free.

Another few paces, and we were in front of Bernard's hedges, which I eyed with particular apprehension. Though it made sense why Leslie chose them; they were halfway between his childhood home and the pub.

At the door, Leslie lifted his fist to knock and stepped back to look at his shoes. An exaggerated sigh told me all I needed to know about how this interaction would go.

When Bernard didn't answer, Leslie knocked again, this time with the side of his fist. "Oi, old man. It's Leslie Whiting," he shouted, his accent suddenly prominent. "Open up."

Again, nothing. I leaned over to look into one of the front windows, but the net curtains were closed. Leslie crouched to lift the letter slot, and shouted through it.

"I'm here about Sparrow."

Straightening, Leslie winked at me, and sure enough, I heard heavy footfalls on the other side of the door. Bernard muttered words we couldn't decipher, then the door unlocked and swung inward. He looked his age, though he had strong, broad shoulders and appeared well fed. He wore a cable-knit sweater and slacks, and what was left of his hair was combed over with care. His face was large and liver-spotted, but most of his wrinkles kept to the parts of the face that bent when he scowled.

"What the hell do you want, Whiting?" he growled, making himself larger. "I bloody told you the cottage i'n't for sale."

"I don't want to buy it, you daft bugger," Leslie said.

"Then get off of me property or I'll call the police."

The door began to close, but Leslie stopped it with, apparently, a much stronger arm than Bernard's. "We're here for the keys. This is Audrey Collins—Dorothy's granddaughter. She owns Sparrow now, and she'd very much like to see inside."

It was then that he took note of me before refocusing his attention on Leslie. Bernard wrinkled his chin, looking for all the world as if he was about to blow smoke out of his hairy ears. Then, something fractured his resolve, and his guarded eyes turned on me again. "You the Yank who's been ringing me all day and night?"

My eyebrows went up, but I was too amused to be offended. Grumpy or not, I already liked Bernard. "No—sorry. That was probably Gran's attorney. She, um . . ." He blinked, and I found it suddenly difficult to formulate the words. If he hadn't answered the phone, did he know that she was dead? Would he even care? "She passed away last month."

For a moment, the old face showed no reaction. And then, only briefly, he dropped his chin to rub his nose and fixed another look of scorn on Leslie.

"I know you would hate to see a window broken as much as I would," Leslie said. "So if you wouldn't mind?"

Bernard huffed, then let his hand drop from the door handle. "Wait there."

We did, standing in the threshold as he used his cane and waddled away into the house. When he returned, he held an envelope and set of keys, but handed me only the latter.

"I've not been up there in a few weeks, mind," he said. "I er, had a fall . . ."

I saw in him the same hesitancy to speak of his ailments as Gran used to have. In her final months, there wasn't much at all she could do on her own. I'd washed her, taken her to the bathroom, fed her, until she finally went to hospice. My aunt had suggested hiring a nurse, but Gran had refused, saying, *My Audrey will look after me.*

My heart ached, and I gave Bernard a full smile, holding the keys to my chest so he knew how much they meant to me. "Thank you for taking such good care of it."

"Everything's as she left it, save a few boxes here and there. Didn't want anything important lying about. And er, I'm meant to give this to you."

I stared at the envelope for a moment before taking it from his hand. It was still sealed and was addressed to me at Sparrow Cottage. But nobody had known I was coming.

"Who is it from?" I asked Bernard, even as the hair was standing up on my arms. I knew before he answered, felt my throat closing at the notion.

"It's from your gran." Before I could thank him, his eyes moved under wiry brows to Leslie. "I'd not throw your lot in with this one, lass, I were you."

Leslie, taking no offense, smiled and stuck his hand out. "Many thanks for your help, Bernard. See you round the pub?"

Bernard ignored the offered handshake, and growled. "Piss off, you cheeky git."

SPARROW COTTAGE WAS A mile walk in the opposite direction as the village center. We stopped at Leslie's on the way to get Jim, who ran ahead of us off-leash. The dog bounded from the road, zipping in and out of the hedgerows, sniffing and offering the occasional bark at a bird. Leslie took me down a footpath that led up to the farm from behind. The earth was well saturated, and where there weren't puddles, there was thick mud.

"We have got to get you a pair of wellies," Leslie said, looking down at his own rubber boots. He had dressed in jeans and a fitted T-shirt, even though it was breezy enough for me to wear my jacket. There was an easiness to his gait, to the serene expression on his face, to the way his hair moved in the wind. To look at him, one would never doubt that this was where he was from, where he belonged. That Yorkshire was in his veins.

I did wonder why his accent was different when he wasn't speaking to locals. And the Rolex he wore on his left wrist had definitely raised an eyebrow. But what did I know? Maybe there was big money in barn conversions.

"Are you going to open it?" he asked.

I was clinging to the envelope Bernard had given me, feeling a bit nauseous at the thought. Whatever was inside would truly be the last of the Gran I had known.

"I'll wait until we're inside," I answered, and took another quick glance at my name in her handwriting. For courage.

Tall grasses blew at our knees, and before long there was nothing in all directions but swathes of fields and wild moorland. I was breathing easier suddenly, like until today, I had been filling my lungs only halfway. In the distance, the church bells rang on the hour, a sound I was already beginning to love.

Up ahead, two chimney stacks came into view behind blossoming trees. Leslie showed me how to pass through the kissing gate, and on the other side of the fence the grass was growing with abandon, broken up in some places by tall wildflowers of red, yellow, purple, and white. They swayed as Jim pushed his way through them, and we followed.

"Looks like Bernard hasn't been tending the garden very closely," Leslie said. "Cor, she's gorgeous though, ain't she?"

Leslie's gaze was up on the house, stacked stones now coming into view. There was a fire in his eyes, a little smile fixed on the corner of his mouth, the tiniest bounce in his step. He was so excited. Maybe even more than I was.

To the left of the house was a cattle barn, skirted by a drystone wall that continued around to the front of the house. I looked behind me at the acres of grazing land.

"When was the last time this was a working farm?" I asked.

"Second World War, according to my nan."

"She knew the people who lived here?"

"She would have been only small at the time, but I'm sure she has stories."

My pulse quickened. It was odd, to think there might be people in this little village who knew more about my family history than I did. But the more I learned, the more I craved information. I clearly wasn't going to get much out of Bernard. It would be much easier to speak to someone willing to talk.

"Would you introduce us?" I asked. "I mean, if you think she'd talk to me?"

"I can do." Leslie chuckled. "If I'm honest, Nan would be offended if she knew you were here and didn't go round hers for Sunday lunch. You're welcome to join me when I go tomorrow. It's just the pair of us up here—all the other grandchildren have moved on."

Leslie whistled for the dog and he came bounding up to his heel. We weaved our way through the garden, where patches of roses clung to life, but most of the other plants had been overtaken by ivy and weeds. The house was built of stone, grey with lichen. Its tiled roof bowed slightly in the middle, and the windows were placed with perfect symmetry. The back door was wide and shorter than Leslie, with a little square window I couldn't see much through.

Leslie stepped away, gesturing to the lock for me to do the honors. I took a deep breath, brought out the ring of mismatched keys, some old, some modern. I chose the one that looked about the size of the old lock, and sure enough, it turned easily and the door swung away as if by its own volition.

Inside, the air was thick and stale, smelling heavily of mothballs. I wondered if it had been more than a few weeks since the caretaker had stopped by. The floor was solid stone, gritty under my leather boots. Sun followed me through the door, shining a triangle of light onto a storm of floating dust spores.

I gathered we were standing in a mudroom—a narrow space with exposed stone and pegged hooks. Covered in a fuzzy film of dust were hats, coats, basket totes, scarves, still hanging like they had just been used.

"They dashed out in a right hurry, didn't they?" Leslie said, reaching for a fedora hat from one of the shelves. He brushed off the dust and turned it over to look at the label.

"This is like a time capsule," I said breathlessly. "There's no way Gran's parents were still here when she ran away. Whatever happened, they all left at the same time."

I found a cupboard against the other wall, holding rusting tin cans with vintage labels—dried milk and eggs, corned beef, lima beans, coffee, and jam. There were preserves, too, pickled eggs and plums in massive cloudy jars. I opened one of the drawers to find a ration book. In my excitement, I lifted it without remembering how old it was. Some of it began to crumble in my hands, but I could make out the surname: *Smith*. The next two lines on the book were clearer.

OTHER NAMES: *Emilie R*

ADDRESS: *Sparrow Cottage, Hilltop Road, Langswick*

I'd never known Gran's maiden name, but this must have been her mother. The hairs stood up on the back of my neck. Had they left her here on her own? And if so, why?

Jim barked on the other side of the open door, making me look up to see Leslie duck through the door and into the next room. I set the ration book carefully back into the drawer for safekeeping. At five foot two, I easily passed under the low doorframe, but imagined anyone a few inches taller would need to watch their head.

The kitchen had equally low ceilings, and timber beams made the space feel cozy and dim. Copper pans, ladles, and open shelves lined the walls, cluttered with mismatched Wedgwood plates, teacups, and ceramic jars. The butler sink was skirted by a floral curtain, above which hung a clothes dryer, still draped with white linen napkins. Beside the tap was a vintage portable radio, and I imagined swing music pouring out of it, and a young woman dancing around the kitchen. An enormous inglenook fireplace housed an old woodstove against one wall.

I drew out one of the chairs at the heavy farm table and sat down, smoothing my hands over the worn surface. In the stillness of the room, I could almost hear the clinking of plates, scraping of forks and knives, sizzling of a pan of bacon. With everything left as it was used by the family, it was easy to imagine the lives they led. I could see their tastes, what objects they cherished, and even what was unimportant, banished to a dark corner. The cottage was eerie, but at the same time, it felt like a home somehow. It felt, impossibly, like *my* home.

The next room was formal dining, with a Victorian cast-iron fireplace, striped wallpaper, and a long table, still set with doilies and silver candlesticks. Beside it was a snug living space, cluttered with so much mismatched furniture of various patterns that I could barely move around it. Brass horse medallions were tacked to the mantel over the fireplace, and even the windowsills held small trinkets of glass and porcelain. A sewing machine sat in one corner under a floor lamp, with a basket of knitting things beside the bench. I bent to take up a ball of yarn, enjoying the familiar roughness, wondering if Gran's mother had taught her the way she'd taught me. Books cluttered the wall on either side of the fireplace from floor to ceiling. A bowl of lavender hearts sat on one of the end tables, and so I picked one up to sniff, finding the scent had long gone.

I sighed. There would be a lot to sort through, like there was at Gran's New Jersey house. Beth was probably there now, throwing things into a dumpster without stopping to consider what might be precious. I wouldn't have had the strength to take on the job myself. I wasn't sure how I would handle it now.

I found Leslie in the small foyer, where I was met with more timber beams and worn stone floors. To one side were a narrow table, mirror, and umbrella stand.

"I expected the place would be a tip, if I'm honest," Leslie said.

"Needs some work doing to it, but otherwise, it's in good nick, this house. It must have been split into two workman's cottages originally."

"Do you know when it was built?"

"I would have thought early eighteenth century." He ran his hand lovingly along the exposed stone wall, eyes aglint. I was glad to be able to repay him for his kindness the night before.

The narrow stairs were housed behind a small door, and curved sharply to the right. Most of the latch doors at the top were shut, but one was cracked. Leslie pushed it in and crossed the room to open the curtains. I gasped. I had thought there was nothing that could surpass the view from Leslie's house, but this put it to shame. In the frame of the window, there was everything that made this part of the world so magnificent, all in colors so intense they seemed artificial, like a work of art, or a photograph enhanced by editing.

"See why I always wanted to get inside?" he said. "Best view in the village, this—in the county, maybe."

This was definitely a bedroom once belonging to a little girl. The faded wallpaper was pink peonies, visible even through the layer of dust, the iron bed nestled under the eaves covered in a simple quilt. Books leaned on shelves along one wall, beside a set of binoculars, a doll, a wooden duck, and a bone china Victorian lady whose style I recognized. I picked it up, and sure enough, ROYAL DOULTON was stamped on the base.

My skin prickled, hairs standing on end. "My gran had tons of these. I used to crochet little scarves and capes for them when I was just learning."

Leslie lifted a brow at me. "You're a *knitter*, are you?"

"Don't let my steely facade fool you."

"I wouldn't say steely . . ." He moved his attention to checking the floorboards for cracks.

"No?" I asked curiously.

"Well, you were"—his eyes came up—"sort of crying at the pub last night."

I filled with heat and spun away to grasp the cool iron footboard. Apparently there were parts of the evening that the plane vodka had erased from my memory. I tried to recover quickly, smiling at Leslie as he crossed the room again. "I'll crochet something for you if you're nice to me."

"I've never found reason to argue with a proper wool jumper."

Leslie moved on to inspect the next room, leaving me alone. It was as quiet as a chapel, except for the birds chirping outside, and Jim barking at the wind in the trees. I closed my eyes and imagined the room as it might have been—warm, clean, lived in. The air maybe laced with the smell of perfume and hair spray. I opened the door of the wardrobe, but it was empty; only hangers remained. I imagined a young woman in victory rolls, throwing dresses and skirts into an open suitcase.

Now that I was here, had seen the charming and comfortable place she had grown up, I couldn't stop wondering: What had Gran been running from? What took her to America?

There was a cedar chest at the end of the bed, and I knelt to brush the dust off. This was a piece of storage built to protect whatever was inside—Gran had bought me one when I was a little girl, hoping it would one day hold my wedding dress. Wishful thinking, on her part, but I cherished it. My pulse raced as I saw it wasn't locked, and carefully lifted the lid.

On top was a plain patchwork quilt. I lifted it out and set it gently aside, searching for more. Underneath was a pale blue cotton dress with buttons down the front. It was faded from overwashing, and the seams were stained yellow from sweat. I bent again, finding a few white handkerchiefs and an armband. This, too, was discolored from age and wear, but there was no denying the bright symbol stitched onto it. The Red Cross.

At the bottom was a flat jewelry box, the corners worn away. I opened it curiously to find what looked like a military medal, with a red-blue-and-white-striped ribbon and a silver medallion. I touched the cold medal, in dire need of a polish, and wondered whom it could have belonged to.

Keeping the uniform and medal with me, I shut the chest, leaving the rest for later. It was time to read Gran's letter.

With a huff, I sat on the chest and carefully opened the envelope while dust motes danced in the sunbeam coming through the window. My hand was unsteady as I slid the folded paper out, noticing it was still crisp. It must have been written recently—but Gran was hardly coherent in the end, and would have had trouble even holding a pen. How did she manage it?

I felt a sharp pain in my chest as I began to read.

My dear Audrey,

I do apologize for all the fuss. You will not have been expecting this, but I'm afraid I couldn't find the words to tell you what I've been planning of late. You know as well as anyone that I do not speak of my past, and that is why I am writing this instead. I hope you will understand, and forgive me for being brief. I woke this morning with a clarity I have not felt in quite some time, but I fear it will be lost with the sunlight.

You know by now that I have left my mother's home to you. Our little family was built on secrets, a series of them that led us to Sparrow Cottage. Many of those secrets remain within its walls, for one to find should one choose to go looking. I leave that choice to you, my sweet. The pain of my past was too much for me to bear, and I suppose that's why I've kept my eyes to the future. You are my future, Audrey, and you are made of stronger stuff than your grandmother. I am aware that I am leaving you with a burden, and I hope you will forgive me for what you find.

*Remember what I have always told you: It is never too late to
start again.*

*All my love and hope,
Gran*

I sniffed, and quickly dried my cheeks with the back of my hand.
My own laughter surprised me, but helped me to recover. Of course
the letter explained nothing at all—as coherent as her writing was,
she was no match for dementia. But that didn't matter to me, not in
that moment. It was enough just to have her words in front of me.

I replaced the letter and left the room to find Leslie. There were
two other bedrooms of equal size, one tastefully furnished in the same
cluttered, British way as the last, and a third which was half the size,
with a writing desk, typewriter, and more bookshelves. It then became clear to me that something rather important was missing.

I found Leslie downstairs in the dining room, studying the frame
of a window.

"There's no bathroom in this house," I said.

Leslie smiled at the horror on my face. "Cottages out here were
the last to modernize. I suspect there's an outdoor privy, and an old
copper tub lying about."

I shuddered, imagining trudging out into the rain to piss, and
sharing cold bathwater with my sister and dad.

"Find anything else interesting upstairs?" he asked. I raised the
armband to show him. Leslie reached up to pinch the fabric. "Looks
like a VAD's uniform."

"What's a VAD?"

"Voluntary Aid Detachments. They were volunteer civilians who
nursed soldiers during the wars. Loads of famous ones—Vera Brittain, Agatha Christie . . ."

"How do you know all this stuff?"

"I'm a bit of a nerd, really."

I looked at the clothing with a newfound wonder. A nurse like me. A *war* nurse. Whoever had worn this uniform must have possessed unfathomable courage. Could this have belonged to Gran, or her mother, Emilie? And what about the medal?

I brought my head up, trying to refocus on the moment. "Is something wrong with the window?"

"It's running with damp, I'm afraid," Leslie said. "As is the one upstairs. We'll get a tarpaulin to cover it first of all, until we can replace them, perhaps install double glaze . . ."

"We?"

He hung his head and looked up at me from under dark lashes. "Sorry, I've got carried away, haven't I? But if you'll have me, I'd like to be the one to bring this place up to date. I'm quite sympathetic with my restorations—I maintain all the original charm of a place—and I would hate to see a listed house so well preserved fall into the wrong hands . . ."

It was a lot to take in at that moment. I couldn't afford to renovate. I'd come here to liquidate the property into something I could utilize. With Gran gone, I had nowhere to live. I needed the money for a deposit on an apartment, to support me while I looked for a new nursing job.

I put my hand in my pocket to feel for the cold comfort of my sobriety medallion. But it was gone. I'd forgotten I'd left it back at Leslie's house, feeling I no longer deserved to carry it.

The emotion must have been present on my face, for Leslie backed away from the window. "I can see I've overstepped the line," he said. "I know you've got a lot of decisions to make, so I'll leave you to it."

He started to go, and for a few seconds, I let him. Then I looked down at the dress and the armband. There was so much history locked away in this cottage, so much that might help me understand what this all meant. Did Gran leave me the cottage so I could discover the history she had preserved so carefully inside of it for all these years?

"Wait," I said. "I can't make any promises—I don't have the money to do that. But if you're willing, if you love this place as much as you say you do, I could really use your help figuring out what to do next."

Leslie's face remained somber, but he nodded. "All right, then. Let's have a chat."

Four

Audrey

"Are you sure your nan won't mind that I'm tagging along?"

"Course she won't," Leslie answered as he locked the front door behind us. "She'll be thrilled to see something besides my narky mug."

I chuckled at both the word choice and the way his face melted into soft creases. There was no denying the man was handsome, with his overgrown hair, his slim physique muscled from manual labor, and a face that was serious but kind. If we had met under different circumstances, I might have fallen for him the moment he opened his full lips to reveal that charming accent.

Yesterday, I had agreed to stay in his guest room for a few more nights while I came up with a plan for Sparrow Cottage, but I needed to keep things platonic. The counselors at rehab talked about the importance of knowing oneself first—these new, strange sober people we become. We are different beings now, wanting different things, needing different things. The objects of our desire have been turned upside down. It's important to learn who we are *sober* before getting into anything—emotional or sexual—with another person. Now that I was starting over with my journey, I had to keep my feelings in check.

"I'm looking forward to meeting your grandmother," I said to Leslie. "She sounds like a spitfire."

"You'll like her, my nan. She still drinks her afternoon cuppa with a nip of brandy."

His mouth flattened almost as quickly as it had curled. Being so open about my sobriety, I wasn't unaccustomed to the reaction. People had a difficult time knowing what to say about the situation, too concerned they might hurt my feelings. Though I hadn't expected Leslie to have such a hard time, considering what Namita had said.

"It's okay to talk about it," I said. "I won't be instantly triggered into relapse."

"No, that was—" Leslie slid his hands into the pockets of his jacket. "I've put my foot in it; I'm sorry."

"There was a lot that happened before I showed up here, okay? And you're right, anyway—your nan sounds extremely cool."

That seemed to ease him. I put my hand in my pocket where I'd been keeping the military medal in place of my sobriety chip. Leslie had told me it was a medal of gallantry, and though the inscription on the sides had faded over the years, I thought the owner might let me borrow some of their courage.

"How long have you been sober?" I asked. Leslie's brow furrowed into a wince, or it might have been in defense of the cool, late-afternoon breeze. "If that's too personal, you don't have to answer . . ."

"Er, I dunno, actually. I can't say I've ever been bothered to keep track."

I nodded, though he was studying his boots. "I just—I thought you might be in the program. Do you have AA here?"

"No, yeah—we have, but—I'm not . . ." Leslie looked up at me, face gone pink. "I'm not in the program, I'm just—I'm not drinking at the moment. Namita likes to take the piss . . ."

That was accompanied by a little laugh, and I decided to let the conversation fall away. Whether or not he had a real problem was none of my business, and I certainly wasn't one to pass out copies of the Big Book to anyone trying to cut back. It had taken me years to accept that my relationship with alcohol was unhealthy, that it was a danger to my body and mind, that I needed to go into treatment for what was a serious addiction. If that was the case for Leslie, he would recognize it on his own.

Instead, as we approached the village center, I quietly admired the wall on our left, where moss and yellow flowers grew out from between the stones. It was a lovely village, the kind of place you see on TV but never expect you'll get a chance to visit.

"How did it end up being just you and your grandmother living here?" I asked.

Leslie seemed much more comfortable answering this question. "I came back a few years ago, after living in London," he said. "My dad's got a second family up in Robin Hood's Bay, and Mum lives with her sister in Epsom. She wanted to be closer to my brother, Matthew, and his children in the city."

"Your grandfather?"

"We lost him when I was still at school."

"I'm sorry. I never knew mine."

Leslie gave me a short smile. "Nan's been lonely, but I think she's better now she's got me to fuss over."

"Is that why you left London?"

Leslie was distracted temporarily by the pub, where two older men were smoking at a picnic bench with their half-drunk pints. He gave them a nod before returning to our conversation.

"After uni I got the office job I always thought I wanted," he said. "I was away from home just long enough to neutralize my accent before realizing I didn't suit the desk-and-tie stuff. I wanted to get my hands dirty, doing real work. So, I left; headed back up here."

"Your accent changed that quickly?"

"Tends to happen at Oxford. Everyone there wants to sound better than anyone who isn't."

"That seems kind of old-fashioned."

"This is *Britain*. Strand four of us on an island, and we'll have a class system in place before dinner."

I laughed as he gestured for me to turn onto a steep lane. "So how did you learn to build houses?"

"My uncle is a property developer; I used to work for him summers and weekends." He paused, pointing. "Just here."

Leslie's grandmother lived in a terraced house that spilled out onto a cobblestone road. He didn't knock, rather used a spare key to open the door. The foyer was small but clean with floral wallpaper. Savory scents floated out from the kitchen, making my stomach rumble.

"Is that Leslie?"

A woman came through from the kitchen, an apron tied around her waist. She was all bones and papery skin, with a plume of white hair, which she had pushed back with a headband. Her large teeth fought through her lips to be seen, and her dark, deep-set eyes matched her grandson's.

Leslie drew her in and kissed her cheek. "Hiya, Nan. You all right?"

"Oh aye. Apart from me stiff bloody hands."

She couldn't have been more different from Gran—who was always curved and soft, and dyed her thin hair blond until trips to the beauty salon were too difficult. But the sight of Leslie's grandmother pushed the air from my lungs and a tear escaped me before I could stop it. Luckily, Leslie and his nan were locked in a hug, so neither noticed.

When they parted, her openmouthed smile widened. "Who have we here?"

"This is my mate Audrey," Leslie said, keeping one hand on Nan's shoulder. "She's come all the way from America for your roast dinner."

Nan gave Leslie a playful shove. "Stop your faffing, Leslie! I'm old, not daft." She opened her arms for me and I went willingly, surprised by how strong she was. "Good to meet you, petal. Is he treating you reet?"

"Nan!"

She leaned away and cocked her chin at Leslie. "You've lost one lass, love. I won't see you frighten off another."

Leslie's face went sour with embarrassment, but I was tickled. "Thanks so much for having me," I told Nan. "I hope I'm not imposing."

"Course not. There's plenty to go round. Takes a lot of feeding, my grandson." Nan pushed a lock of hair off my shoulder, seemingly pleased with the look of me. "Les—? Be a lad and take Audrey's coat whilst I stick kettle on."

With a surprisingly blithe step for an eighty-six-year-old, Nan spun and floated back into the kitchen.

Leslie turned his back and made a face. "Sorry about her. She's taken my divorce pretty hard."

Removing my jacket, I tried to keep my face neutral. It wasn't something he'd mentioned before. I wondered if his divorce had been the real reason he left the city.

Leslie gestured me through to the kitchen, where light flooded in from a shared courtyard behind the house. The table was already set with tea things, the pot in a hand-knit cozy shaped like a rooster. Leslie went to the large hutch for a third cup and saucer. One had pictures of Princess Diana and Prince Charles on the front, with the date of their Royal Wedding: 29th July 1981. Another had Prince William and Kate Middleton.

"She's got the queen's coronation and wedding as well," Leslie said as he sat beside me. "We're not allowed to use them anymore. *Antiques.*"

I laughed at the face he made, but quickly bit my lip when Nan came to the table with the kettle and filled the pot. "It's lovely to see Leslie's found himself a nice lass. You know, he's been frightfully lonely since the"—the next word was whispered in my direction—"*divorce.*"

His eyes rolled back, and the rest of his head followed.

"All he does is work, now, my grandson," Nan said, replacing the pot lid. "Suppose without a wife, he's got bugger all else to do!"

Leslie, pale as I'd ever seen him, interjected before she could go on: "Nan, you'll never guess what. Audrey's inherited Sparrow Cottage from her gran. We were there yesterday aft."

"Never!" Nan took the chair opposite him. "Not Dottie? When did she pass?"

It was so strange to hear Gran's name on the lips of someone I had only just met. "A little over a month ago. She was going on ninety-eight years old."

"Bless her!" Nan let out a puff of air and shook her head. "We all wondered what happened to the Smiths."

"You don't know why she left?"

"Afraid not, petal. One day, Sparrow were empty, and it seemed they'd gone."

I sat back, wishing it had been as easy as asking her that one question. What could have happened to the family that they had had to abandon their home and all their belongings? And how did Gran end up in the States, when Sparrow was left in her name?

"Audrey doesn't know much of her grandmother's past," Leslie said, resting his hand on the back of my chair. "We were hoping you might tell us what you remember of the family."

"It were a long time ago, now . . ." I thought that would be it, until Nan stood and said, "Pour the tea before it gets cold, Leslie, love. Then we'll have a natter."

Once we all had a steaming brew in front of us, I told her more about Gran and her secrets. I recalled how, growing up, we were never told stories of our great-grandparents or how Gran came to be married or live in New Jersey. Even my sister, who was eleven—five years older than me—at the time of my mother's death, couldn't remember hearing stories from Mom.

"I wish I could tell you more, love," said Nan, stirring sugar into her tea. "But they kept themselves to themselves, the Smiths, easily done from the fringes of the village. Never helped their popularity much . . ."

My curiosity quickened, and I leaned forward. "People didn't like them?"

"People didn't *know* them—and didn't bother trying to," Nan explained. "When Dorothy's mother moved into the cottage with a littlun, there were no husband, no ring. Quite the scandal in those days, and me mum was a frightful gossip. Why I know about it at all—I weren't so much as a babe in arms then."

"Was her mother's name Emilie Smith? I found a ration book at Sparrow with that name on it."

"Aye, Emilie. Mr. Smith came later. He were the quiet sort; never saw much of him. Mum used to say the men of their generation wanted nowt but a good long rest after what they'd come through."

"So Mr. Smith fought in the First World War," I thought aloud. He certainly didn't sound like the lord Gran always talked of, but if Emilie was a VAD, perhaps that's how they had met. "Could he have been my great-grandfather?"

"Suppose that depends on who you're talking to." Nan shrugged her bony shoulders. "It takes all sorts."

I wondered if this could be why Gran never spoke of her parents. In her day, it would have been uncouth for a single woman—a single *mother*, at that—to have a man living in her home. And if nobody was sure who Gran's father was, maybe she'd never met him. Maybe that's why she created a much more interesting origin for herself.

Leslie had been watching me, but I was deliberately keeping my eyes down as I thought everything through. He shifted in his seat, swilling his tea around in his cup.

"They did run the small holding, though, didn't they, Nan?" he asked.

She nodded. "They'd a few cows and chickens, but they did well enough. Course nobody round here would admit to it if you asked them."

"I'm guessing there's no point in talking to anyone else about the Smiths?" I said.

"You'd surely get bags of stories, petal. Not all of 'em nice, mind you." An egg timer began to buzz. "That's the roast done. Les, will you set the table?"

I welcomed the steaming plate of food set in front of me after that: roast beef, steamed peas and carrots, fondant potatoes, and Yorkshire pudding drenched in brown gravy. If I didn't love England already, that meal convinced me. Dessert was parkin, a dense, ginger-spiced cake that made me salivate as I ate two slices.

The conversation was light and didn't return to the topic of Sparrow Cottage. Instead, Nan wanted to talk about Leslie's divorce again, and he moped while she explained that Gemma had been such a patient woman, but the Big Smoke had changed Leslie into a "right wazzock." I guessed the meaning based on the context, and didn't hide my amusement as he broke into a wide grin. They had a lovely relationship, and Nan was clearly glad to have Leslie nearby again. I was heartsick when the meal was over and it was time to go. I missed long afternoons like this one, when Gran and I would chat or watch an old film, nibbling on chocolate bridge mix and peanut butter crackers.

After dinner, we pulled on our coats, Leslie being showered in kisses. He was reminded to take his bins down on Tuesday, and ring his mum, which he didn't do enough. Then Nan gave me another one of her firm hugs and told me to come back as often as I liked.

"How long will you be stopping in Langswick?" she asked.

"No more than a few weeks. Just until I can get the cottage up for sale."

Nan frowned, chafing my arms. "You're going to help her, aren't ya, Les? He knows all there is to know about property matters."

"Course I'm happy to help." Leslie pulled my jacket down from the rack and handed it to me with a sheepish smile. "Should she need it."

As our hands brushed, a flutter of warmth made me step away pointedly.

It was almost full dark by the time we left Nan's. Leslie was quiet, and I wondered if it was because of the conversation over our meal, or whether he was trying to figure out how to tell me he didn't want me in his guest room anymore. It would be three nights now; it was probably time for me to find a more permanent place to stay. As we passed the Cross Keys Inn, I mentioned stopping in to see if Namita had any rooms available, but Leslie suggested I wait until morning. I was too tired to refuse.

At Leslie's house, I sent Beth a quick text that I was okay, and brought my knitting bag downstairs to find Leslie crashed on the couch in the lounge, with Jim lying partially across his lap. When I sat beside him, Jim rolled over onto his back to expose his tummy for rubbing. I obliged, and Leslie chuckled, clearly pleased to see his dog was a hit.

"How are you faring?" he asked.

I resisted the urge to automatically reply. Another lesson from rehab. We were taught to HALT—check in with ourselves when we're hungry, angry, lonely, or tired, the times when one is most likely to drink. Surprisingly, I was none of those things at the moment.

"I'm okay, I think," I said, unpacking my crochet hooks. The last few nights, I'd been working slowly on a scarf to busy my hands. "I just hope I don't mess everything up."

Leslie nodded, in a way that made me think he knew the feeling. "Your grandmother has trusted you with this, hasn't she? Now you have to trust her faith in you to deal with it."

Leslie had no idea that Gran's faith was all I had. I'd forgotten how to believe in myself a long time ago.

Beginning to yarn over on an existing stitch, I pushed the negative thoughts away. "I don't know how to thank you for letting me stay another night."

"Ta," Leslie said.

"Hm?"

"*Ta*—it's how we say thanks in Yorkshire."

"I'm going to sound like an idiot saying that." He chuckled, and I blushed. "But you saved my ass these past couple days. So . . . *ta*."

Leslie was kind enough not to laugh at me, but his smile was kind. "That's okay."

I refocused my attention on forming my first chain, easily falling into the familiar motions that soothed me. "I think I only trusted you because you're handsome—which is such an idiotic thing to do, isn't it? Why has media conditioned us to expect all serial killers to be haggard old men with mustaches and aviator glasses?"

"What about Ted Bundy?" Leslie asked.

I made sure he could see me roll my eyes. "He's not someone I care to understand." When I looked up from my work, Leslie's eyes were soft and glistening. It was only then that I realized what I'd said. "Anyway . . . I'm sorry I called you handsome."

That time he did laugh.

"Are you apologizing for complimenting me?"

"It was unsolicited."

"It was kind."

"I guess it was. Sorry—I'm an overthinker."

"And compulsively apologetic."

"I wasn't always . . . That's new. A symptom of Step Nine, I think." He gestured toward my chain, which I had just begun to turn. "What are you making, then?"

"It's a secret." I was hoping to get at least a scarf done for him before I had to go.

"My nan still mends my socks, if you can believe it," Leslie said, cheeks flushing. "I love her to bits, that woman."

I smiled so hard that I lost concentration, and had to restart my crochet. There was something about Leslie that made me feel safe. He radiated the warm energy I had been craving since Gran's passing and never expected to find again in a stranger. I trusted him—something that wasn't easy for me to do—and I didn't want to lose that again.

"If you're really willing, I'd love your help with Sparrow," I said, setting my yarn in my lap. "Both the dirty work and the official stuff, like getting the planning permissions. I get so nervous around paperwork and authority." I shivered, remembering the stack of documents my attorney had slid in front of me, still warm from the copier.

"I've dealt with a lot of people in your situation," Leslie answered kindly, "and I have a shed load of contacts in the industry. I helped my mum ready my childhood home to sell when she moved south. Her estate agent is local—I'll give him a ring."

"When did your parents split up?" I asked.

"I was only small. Ten, I think?"

"That must have been hard."

"It put an end to the shouting matches." Leslie scratched at his beard thoughtfully. "Didn't save me learning to start my own. Funny thing is, I can't remember what I was so cross about. I had the job, the girl, the flat . . . still managed to be a miserable arsehole."

It was the first time he had spoken about his divorce. I had been surprised, earlier, when Nan had talked about how much Leslie had struggled in London. To see him now, I imagined he had flown through life, knowing exactly which turn to make next.

"How did you get to where you are today?" I asked. "How did you know you were making the right choice when you left London?"

Leslie scratched Jim's ear and his expression drifted far away for a second. He looked tired. He told me he had a team running the business end of his company, so that he could do physical work on the houses he renovated. But it was no doubt a stressful thing to be the boss as well.

When he turned his head, he offered a bashful smile. "I used to drink a hell of a lot." His face reddened and I knew this was hard for him to admit. "It's ingrained in us, you know. Go to work. Go to the pub. Like that pint is a right bestowed upon the working-class Englishman. In London, I was pretty depressed and anxious, self-medicating, and because I didn't understand why I felt like shit, I blamed everyone around me. After Gemma left, Matt convinced me to see a doctor. I didn't want to; I thought I was above all that. But the longer I put it off, the darker my thoughts got. So I booked in, and after a lot of trial and error, we found a medication that works. I stopped drinking, quit my job, and started working with my hands again, and everything fell into place. I've spent every moment since trying to prove to myself that I'm not that idiot getting chucked from bars and spending nights drying out in a police station."

I hardly knew what to say. His admission had come a long way from the casual answer he had given me earlier. Something had shifted in him. Our trust was mutual.

Now it was my turn to admit something equally painful.

"A little over a year ago, I got fired. A coworker suspected I'd been drunk on the job, and filed a report . . ." My chin fell to my chest, feeling the shame wash over me again. "It was just a little something in my coffee to get me past the hangovers, to keep me from—" *Panicking*, I should have said, but swallowed the word. "One day, I ended up giving a patient the wrong medication. I was lucky; it was a mild antibiotic, nothing that could have harmed them. But I was clearly under the influence, and was served with an accusation shortly after."

I was almost too afraid to look up at Leslie, to see the expression on his face, reflecting what he thought of me. It wasn't until he reached across the back of the couch to rub my shoulder that I met his soft eyes.

"My license was suspended, and I had to complete thirty days in rehab," I said. "After that, Gran took me in. I was a mess, mourning the loss of my career, my pride, my friends. Gran kept me steady, reminded me to eat, kept my hands moving. Now I've lost her, I've thrown away a whole year of sobriety that she helped me fight for, and I don't know where I belong anymore."

My voice broke, and I couldn't go on. Leslie was patient, giving me space to breathe through it before speaking.

"Is there any way to get your license back?" he asked.

"I won my hearing, so I can look for jobs again. But I don't even—"

I paused, huffing a shaky breath. "I don't know if I trust myself not to hurt anyone again, or if I even want to go back at all . . ."

"You weren't yourself in that moment," he said gently. "It might feel difficult to make the separation now, cos it's easier to let ourselves believe the pain of our guilt is some kind of penance. But you'll learn, flower, I promise."

His words were wise, and had certainly come from experience. Still, sitting so close to him on the couch with his hand resting below my nape, it was the name I lingered on.

"Why did you call me that? Flower?"

Leslie's face flushed. "Er, it's just a thing we say here? I dunno . . . like, darling or sweetie? I can stop if it bothers you—"

"No, no! I like it." We smiled at each other, and I wanted the moment to last a century. "Can I ask you something?"

He nodded.

"What was with that pint of beer the night we met?"

He rolled his eyes. "I had just found out Gemma is pregnant with her new partner. We never got to talking of children, she and I. I couldn't help but think she didn't believe I was stable enough to be a father."

I sank against the back of the couch, wanting to offer him some physical comfort, but not knowing how. "I'm sorry, Les."

Leslie shrugged, but it was clearly hurting him. "I went into Keys with every intention of necking pints until I was off my head. But once I had the thing in front of me, I got into it with myself and never took the first sip."

"I bet if she could see the way you are now, she'd come running back."

That made him laugh sadly. "Nah . . . I left it too long. But if I'm ever to believe it's possible for me to be a new man, I have to believe it's possible for others, as well. That's why I helped you, if I'm honest. I'm trying to make amends, you know?"

I could empathize. In rehab, there were people who had had it worse than me. They were in no place to judge how far I'd fallen, as they were sitting at the bottom with me. That was the hardest thing about being in the real world, sometimes. Everyone outside thought, as an addict, I was *bad*. A troublemaker, a criminal, a loser, a basket case. It was nice to know someone out here saw past the stigma. I was glad that Leslie's rock bottom had been a little bit higher than mine and he had climbed out. Leslie deserved the sun.

"You'll find where you belong, Auds," he said.

I wasn't so sure, but it was such a sweet thing to say, I didn't argue, only smiled and turned my attention back to my crocheting. For a few minutes, we were both silent, until I heard Leslie take a deep, sharp breath.

"Look," he said, drawing his arm away from me. "I know this will make me sound like a twat, but I thought—if you're off to Keys, anyhow—I may as well take the chance. And if I offend you, feel free to tell me where to go."

I smiled at that. "What, Les?"

"I want you to stay here as long as you need to. You're quiet and tidy and get on with my dog"—he sighed, knuckled his eye before looking at me—"and I like having you around. I like *you*. Christ, I sound like a teenager."

Leslie's blush deepened. This was hard for him, flirting, if that's what he was doing. It was possible I was the first woman he'd tried it with since his ex. I wished I had the courage to tell him it was working.

"Are you sure you won't mind having me?" I asked.

He shook his head, giving me a timid smile. "It would be a pleasure. Honestly."

I couldn't find it in me to refuse.

We turned in a few minutes later, though I found there was too much information swirling in my head for me to get any sleep. I sat on the floor with the uniform I had found at Sparrow, running my fingers over the aged fabric, wondering where it had been and all the horrible things it witnessed. I imagined Emilie must have been looked down upon for being a woman in a war zone, for being a nurse instead of a surgeon, for being a volunteer with no training.

I chuckled to myself. Some things never change.

Then I stood, wanting to lay it out on the bed to see it fully. As the folds opened and the hem fell to my feet, something dropped onto the floor.

My heart was in my throat as I bent to retrieve a worn envelope. It was certainly old—the paper yellowed and soft from overhandling, the ink on the front faded too much for me to read. The envelope was still sealed, and there was definitely a letter inside. The hair stood up on my arms as I sat on the bed, wondering if it would be offensive to the dead if I opened it.

Maybe I couldn't fix up Sparrow Cottage and keep it in the family. Maybe I couldn't return to my job, or make my family proud of me. Maybe I couldn't even stay sober without missteps. But Gran had sent me here, and though I didn't understand why, the one thing I *could* do in this moment was ensure that what was left of her past wouldn't be lost forever.

With that in mind, I carefully tore open the envelope.

Dearest Emilie,

When we parted, I fear I was cold, and for that I apologize. Your words, fair and true as they were, were too bitter for me to swallow in the time they were spoken. You, like my granny, are always telling me that my romantic notions cloud my good judgement. I cannot deny the truth in the accusation, though what I said to you in London was plain. I hope one day you will understand that, for the man who shall return from this war may be unable to dream.

There are only lessons of rigidness and masculinity in the Army, and you know as well as anyone that these do not come naturally to me. In the OTC, I could always keep a firm grasp of who I was, knowing there was an end. But here, under the pressures of an escalating war, I fear pieces of me have been wholly lost. Many nights, I lie awake, thinking of you and wondering: Who shall I be when we meet again? And will you be capable of loving him? Perhaps that is why you refused me. Perhaps I hope it is the reason, for the alternative would sting far worse.

Each and every one of the men here has discarded the revelry of youth in order to take up arms. I only wish there was a part of me that could have known, when I walked bareheaded across Hyde Park with you last summer, that it was to be my final sun-soaked afternoon as a guiltless boy. You go to do a courageous thing, now, a necessary thing, an unselfish thing. When I say I am tearful with pride, you shall no doubt think me patronizing. But I have always adored your determination, little sparrow, and find comfort in the thought that this broken world will only improve now you are free to mend it.

Think of me often, as you know me.

Ever Yours,
Isaac

Five

Emilie

LONDON

JUNE 1914

Rumors spread hastily when all of high society was in London, crowding their schedules with teas and picnics and races and soirees, all ideal places for gossiping. And so it had taken only an hour for the Earl and Countess of Ashwood to learn their daughter had been spotted fleeing the scene of a most scandalous crime: assisting the Women's Social and Political Union to set fire to a gentlemen's club. Mercifully, it had been a friend of the family, so Emilie's involvement was not reported to the authorities. But that did not mean she had averted discipline.

For her crimes, Emilie was given a punishment most women of her age and standing would consider a precious gift. At twenty-one, her parents believed it was high time she turned her focus to becoming a wife, and so she was to step out, at last, with the man they had chosen for her to marry: Lord Rhys Bridgmond, the Duke of Claremont's handsome, and coveted, heir.

And so many hours and layers of silk later, Emilie found herself sat at her dressing table with Mama stood behind her, watching closely as her maid, Grace, used hot tongs to dress waves into her hair. Emilie's brother, Fletcher, was the favored child among their parents, and dressing tended to be the one time of day when Mama gave Emilie her undivided attention. Sons were cherished for many reasons, but generally they could not appreciate such fineries as ribbons and pearls.

Emilie sat quietly and allowed Mama to fuss, if only to elongate the short period of time she was afforded with her mother. The Countess of Ashwood was as beautiful as she was graceful, blessed with perfect eloquence and the confidence to wield it to her advantage. Looking in the mirror now, Emilie saw little resemblance between them besides the clefts in their chins.

Conversation had moved to the ball, and Emilie had gladly gone along. Anything to end the reiteration of Mama's disapproval over how she had spent her morning.

"I expect you to offer Lord Bridgmond your full attention this evening," she said.

"Yes, Mama," Emilie answered, blanching only internally. Rhys was hardly unappealing—she had known him since they were children. It was the idea of marriage that turned her stomach, of being trussed up and handed over to a man like a luxurious gift, to leave her family and her home to be locked away in his, to surrender her dreams of ever doing anything worthwhile.

That time, Lady Ashwood noticed Emilie's dismay, and tilted her head. "Are you looking forward to going to the theatre?"

Emilie reached for the pot of rouge. A matinee of *Madame Tralala* was to be her and Rhys's first outing together—chaperoned, naturally—to show the public they were courting.

"I cannot say what Rhys was thinking," Emilie said. "Everyone knows I don't go in for those silly musical comedies; I live and die for tragedy."

"It would do you good to have a laugh."

Mama snatched the rouge pot from Emilie's hand and set it back down out of her reach. Emilie met Grace's eye in the mirror and she offered a sympathetic glance. They were both easily excited by the beauty products Emilie had purchased inconspicuously at the back of a department store. After years of painting her face with lemon juice to brighten her skin, Emilie felt she was mature enough for a finer toilet. But Mama still found it to be entirely indecent.

"You have no need for these things. You possess true beauty." Mama gave Emilie's cheek a few quick pinches. "This is what we did when I was your age. There—have a look."

Emilie did, and pretended to be satisfied.

"Why is it so impolite to resemble actresses when we spend so much of our time admiring them?" she asked. "There is nary a man in London who does not moon over Lily Elsie's beauty."

"Men may admire actresses when they are at the theatre, but for a wife, they want a natural woman who does not draw attention to herself with paints and powders."

"I shouldn't like to draw attention to myself. I only wish not to resemble a boiled egg."

Mama chuckled. "You have a fine complexion, my dear." She brushed her knuckle down Emilie's cheek, demonstrating the love her daughter often doubted.

Grace carefully tucked a rat of Emilie's own hair combings underneath the strand she had been preparing with pomatum. As she secured it in place with a long pin, Emilie's neck was aching from sitting still. These things took time, particularly during the season, when one perfectly constructed style was torn down, brushed out, and replaced mere hours later. Emilie had begun to dream of one entire day when she could wear her sepia tresses loose to her lower back.

"Peach is certainly your color." Mama selected a pair of pearl earrings from Emilie's jewelry box to place in her open palm. "And will Bridgmond not look handsome in his evening clothes?"

Emilie fastened one earring absently. "Indeed."

Grace finished with Emilie's hair, bringing two glittering bandeaux for her to choose from. Emilie decided on the simpler of the two—a double string of small pearls to match the earrings. Mama had once taught her that embellishment spoke of wealth, but often distracted from one's beauty, if one had it. Emilie wasn't entirely convinced she did, not beside her mother, in any case. But the lesson was one she remembered.

"You would do well not to mention your little venture this morning," Mama said. "Though I am certain the duke has heard of it, he need not be reminded. Not when you will so soon be his daughter-in-law."

The words made the walls close in around her. Emilie had thought she would wait before raising her next point, let her mother forget the fire. But her mouth opened, and in her panic, it all came flooding out.

"I've been thinking perhaps we might delay an engagement? Rhys is so young yet, and in the meantime, I could go to Sussex with Aunty Constance, and have a tutor to help me with the entrance exam to Somerville."

Mama's curved lips flattened, and Emilie knew it would not be good news. Living with a maiden aunt would mean no more WSPU rallies, so Emilie thought the notion might sway her mother. She was very clearly mistaken.

"Your father and I have made it abundantly clear that we do not believe Oxford is the best place for you."

"But Oxford is the best place for Fletcher?" Emilie countered, her voice heightening. "He does not even revise as he should, knowing his diploma makes no difference to how his life shall turn out. He spends most of his time there in his cups!"

"*Emilie . . .*" Her name was often spoken this way, in an exasperated sigh. "I do not need to explain to you there is no use in comparing your life to your brother's."

Emilie fumed. "Because there is no use in comparing a woman to a man, where intelligence is concerned."

"That is not what I said."

"It is what you imply!"

Emilie stood, seeing as Grace was finished with her, and paced to the other end of the room. She knew what her mother was thinking. Education would only lead her daughter to expect more from her life than a marriage to a duke. She would always be vexed that, as a boy, Fletcher had knowledge, had freedom, and even had his father's subsidiary title: Lord Kinsley.

"I am so exhausted of my own ignorance," Emilie told Mama. "Only once, I should like to command a conversation with the boys and not have them snicker at my naivety."

Mama dismissed Grace with a few practiced words, and moved to sit on the edge of Emilie's bed. "You have always been clever, dear girl. I have never said otherwise."

"Cleverness is wasted on an idle mind."

Mama gestured for Emilie to sit beside her. As Mama's hand closed over Emilie's, she found resolve to cease fidgeting. Emilie's senses filled with Lady Ashwood's perfume of violet and vanilla.

"A woman's intellect is not found in lecture halls," Mama said. "You will learn that someday, and then you will understand why we have made this decision for you."

The sentiment was meaningless. Emilie expected she might add a bit about the satisfaction of running a house, of brooding children, of keeping a husband content. Instead, the moment ended, and Lady Ashwood stood, taking Emilie with her for inspection. A smoothing of the square neckline of her gown, and Emilie supposed she was presentable.

Mama touched her chin to lift it. "Come, now. Smile, daughter mine."

It was more difficult than she imagined, raising the corners of her mouth. Emilie became suddenly aware of a clock fixed over her head, and the thunderous *tick, tick, tick* as the seconds floated away, carrying her closer to a wedding.

Emilie was not ready. Not at all.

❧

LATER, IN AN OPULENT salon, Emilie felt the heavy tickle of her mother's gaze on the back of her neck. She reached up to touch the exposed flesh. Mama was nowhere to be seen, but surely watching.

Not to say Emilie was not doing her duty—nodding along with the conversation Lord Rhys Bridgmond was having with Fletcher. But Emilie was also fidgeting with her empty sherry glass, sweeping her eyes across the room in search of anything that might be more interesting than war talk. It was Fletcher's favorite topic of late, and Emilie had learned to let it fade to a distant hum while her mind wandered to a faraway place.

The London ballroom was all too familiar, she found—the crystal chandeliers, the palms, the Paris-made gowns, the elbow-length gloves. There were the debutantes fresh from court, tittering excitedly between dances; the spinsters who gossiped among themselves behind ostrich-feather fans; the packs of ruddy-faced boys not confident enough to speak with girls; and the plump mothers who urgently herded their daughters toward the most eligible bachelors in the room.

Such sights had been a thrill when Emilie had come out at seventeen, with someone else's ideals etched into her mind. This year, whether from her involvement with the suffragettes, or reading too much of the newspaper, the whole thing was now looking rather dull.

"Mark my words," Fletcher said, raising his voice to be heard over the music. "Now the archduke is dead, the fat is in the fire."

Emilie gave the men her attention again. Beside her brother, Lord Bridgmond was nodding politely, a pensive wrinkle in his high forehead. Both of them were fine examples of British gentry, with their straight shoulders and pale cheeks. Fletcher's sepia hair and hazel eyes matched her own. Though only two years older, Bridgmond was far more even tempered than her brother, subdued in a way that made mothers pray he might look in their daughters' direction. Mama liked to say how jealous those daughters would be of Emilie on her wedding day.

"Austria-Hungary will declare war any day," Bridgmond said.

A chill went down Emilie's spine, and she lifted her glass to her lips, forgetting it was drained. "You might speak with a jot more sympathy," she said. "I read that the archduke held his wife as she died. He begged her to live for their children, but she died anyway."

Fletcher tilted his head to one side. "Must you romanticize everything, Emilie?"

"I am not romanticizing! They were *brutally* gunned down; it was a tragedy. Besides, the trouble will simply turn into a third Balkan war."

Emilie had heard an older man say that the day before in the park. Though it had sounded clever to her, it must have been wrong, for both men dipped their chins to chuckle.

"It is not so simple, Em," Fletcher said gently. "Germany shall retaliate, and should they invade Belgium, Britain must protect her allies. Not to worry, though—they are no match for our navy."

How confident men were in their musings! And was that not all it was? Hardly different to how Emilie had imagined what it was like inside of the car when the archduke was shot. Though only *she* was accused of romanticizing.

Her focus returned to the ballroom. There were more couples conversing than dancing, and she had no doubt what they were discussing. The season was nearly over, and they would all return to their quiet country homes to hunch over newspapers and wait for another delicious disaster to entertain them. A war did not worry Fletcher, and it certainly did not worry their peers. So Emilie shook the dread from her shoulders and tried to enjoy herself. This could be the last ball she would attend as a single woman, unattached to Rhys's elbow.

That was when her eye caught on something new. *Someone* new.

And he was staring at her.

The young man stood against the wall, six paces from the nearest conversation. His hands were locked behind his back and he leaned off his shoes by their edges, as if testing whether they were stuck to the herringbone floors. There was something about him that set him apart—his lack of posture, his long face, his hair that disagreed with the pomatum attempting to tame it. Emilie flinched when his eyes finally turned to the band, who were beginning a new song.

She elbowed Fletcher. "Do you know that man, there?"

A few last words dripped out before he could draw a breath and give her his attention. "Forgive me, dear brother, for so *rudely* interrupting you . . ."

Emilie sent her eyes to the coffered ceiling, a gesture Mama had tried and failed to rid her of since she was old enough to be annoyed by her only sibling.

"That man, *there*," she repeated. "Have you met him before?"

Fletcher followed Emilie's nod across the ballroom. "I cannot say I have ever seen him. Why do you ask?"

"He was staring at me— Oh, quick! He's doing it again! How dreadfully crass. Will you go and speak to him?"

Fletcher exchanged a glance with Bridgmond. Silently, they were laughing at her, making Emilie's blood boil. She and her brother were close in age—only fifteen months apart—and ever since they were children she'd wanted to do everything he did. She spent her life struggling to keep pace, reading all she could, following Fletcher and his friends about the house, lingering outside of the smoking room to catch a smattering of male conversation. There was nothing that upset her more than being brushed aside for being a silly, ignorant girl.

"Perhaps he has learned that you were nearly arrested this morning," Fletcher suggested.

Emilie flicked a glance at Bridgmond to see his reaction. But though unsettled on his feet, he either already knew, or was not surprised that she had managed to get herself into such trouble.

"Is it not suspicious?" she said. "None of us know him."

"Leave it, Em."

"But what if he means to follow me down a dark corridor—"

"Don't go down any dark corridors . . ."

"—and press me against a wall to *ravish* me?"

Fletcher erupted with laughter that caught Emilie, but Bridgmond could take no more. "I do not think this is an entirely appropriate discussion for Lady Emilie to take part in—"

"With all due respect, my lord," she cut in, "you do not possess the right to police my conversations."

Fletcher regained some composure and pinched the soft flesh above Emilie's elbow, silently reminding her to watch her tongue. "This is a private ball, duck. No man would have been let in had he not received an invitation."

She huffed, pushing her empty glass into Rhys's unsuspecting gloved hand. There was only one way she was going to get to the bottom of it, and that was on her own.

The stranger remained treading water on the edge of the room. Emilie felt a fire at her temples, already divining how she might take a bite of this boorish young man. But as she approached, his attention turned to his hands. There was something there—something in the slight slump of his shoulders, something in the way he rubbed one palm with the opposite thumb, something in the rounding of his mouth and the flicker of his dark lashes that made Emilie's heart ache.

She felt the completely unfamiliar and perplexing urge to protect him.

He was now concentrated on picking at the edge of his fingernail in a gesture which she might have thought was a sign of bad breeding. Instead, Emilie was moved from being fearful to charmed once more by the simple, inelegant gesture that made him look more boy than man. She saw nothing at all in him that spoke of villainy, though perhaps that was his aim.

"Good evening!" she said, loud enough to startle him.

And she certainly did. The young man brought his face up, eyes out on stalks. Though she was pleased to see his boyhood lessons of posture returning to him as he grew to his full height—which was nearly the same as hers. He was a head shorter than Rhys at least, but wore his evening clothes well.

"Good evening," he said. "Forgive me, I have not had the pleasure—"

"Lady Emilie Dawes." She offered a bow at the neck, which he returned, unoffended that she had introduced herself. "And you are?"

"Isaac."

Odd, that he should offer his forename. How was Emilie to address him properly without his surname? She observed him again. His speech was certainly educated, and the suit he wore was tailored, from a silk she recognized as quality. Why, then, did he choose to ignore the standards of polite conversation?

If he was going to display so much brass, Emilie would have some fun with him.

"I noticed you looking at me from across the ballroom and thought you might be interested in having my next dance. I came to inform you that regretfully, my card is full."

Isaac smiled with his eyes, rather than lips. And what eyes they were—the deepest sort of blue that was only revealed in the night sky during a full moon. He did possess a rather handsome profile, with masculine brow and nose, but a mouth so full and soft it might have been a woman's.

"Consider yourself fortunate, my lady," he said. "I am a terrible dancer."

Emilie was briefly knocked off-center, then found her footing again. "Why have we not met before, sir?"

"It is my first season in London. My grandmother insisted I not miss this particular ball, and wrote quite a few letters to secure my invitation."

His grandmother, whoever she was, was a wise woman indeed. Everyone was here; there would not be another private ball like it until next May. If Isaac wanted to be seen, he had come to the right place.

"If you are here, I must know your people. Why did you not tell me your surname?"

All humor left him. Isaac pressed his lips together, the muscles in his throat working beneath his white tie. The song ended and they paused their conversation to oblige with applause. He noticed her silver dance card holder dangling from her wrist, and a dimple appeared between his brows. "I dare not keep you, my lady . . ."

"Oh, you do not—I haven't anyone down for the next dance."

"You only just said your card was full."

Drat. Emilie was not thinking clearly and forgot her lie. Worse still, Lord Bridgmond was striding in their direction. "Whom are you down for?"

"Er . . . no one." Isaac tugged on his earlobe—frightful habit.

"No one?"

Emilie looked over her shoulder to see Bridgmond hovering outside of their conversation, waiting politely for a moment to step in. He was a fine dancer, Bridgmond, for someone so athletic. It had never been a chore to be his partner. Still, Emilie ignored him.

"Then I insist you dance with me!" she said to Isaac, and took him by the elbow. He did not resist, but moved stiffly beside her, his face gone suddenly pink and miserable. As they found a place and the music began, Emilie was acutely aware of the eyes that had flocked to them—Lady Emilie and the mysterious stranger in a waltz.

Isaac clumsily found the places where his hands were meant to go in their hold. Emilie took up her skirt and waited for him to lead, finding herself staring at the top of his head while he studied his feet. She could feel his thundering pulse in the palm of his right hand.

"You do know the steps?" she asked.

"I suppose I must have learned them."

Emilie laughed, and Isaac's long face broke up and filled with the most joyous smile she had ever seen. It stirred something in her—something she was not yet sure how to identify.

"Search your memory, then," she said. "We cannot remain idling here or we shall be trod on."

Isaac was indeed a terrible dancer. However ungraceful, he recalled the motions, and they pranced inelegantly in their imaginary box. Somehow, in spite of the struggle, the room began to vanish. Emilie found she liked dancing across from a man whose eyes were nearly level with her own, and she caught them each time he looked up from his stumbling feet to share a smile.

He was not so carefree, as if hoping not to reveal something about himself he'd rather keep hidden. But the corner of his oval mouth did twitch each time Emilie pushed into their hold, urging him to loosen. Isaac was no dancer, but he was a lovely partner.

When the song ended, they stepped away from one another to applaud. Emilie felt her mother's eyes again. Mama would surely come and fetch her now, set her back in the right direction—toward Lord Bridgmond.

Isaac seemed to be waiting expectantly for Emilie to suggest what they were meant to do next, or release him from the obligation.

"You look as though you would get on with a breath of air," she said.

Trusting as a lamb, he followed her wordlessly through the crowd to the mansion's walled garden, where the night air was crisp and smelling of the light rain that had passed a time ago. Warm light from within followed at her feet, and she was conscious of the idea that on the dark side of the window, they were made invisible.

If she were someone else, being alone with Isaac might have made her nervous. But all of her fears had evaporated in the waltz, in the anxious way he looked at her sideways as they walked, in the distance he left between them when Emilie stopped to peer through the glass. She spotted Bridgmond speaking to his sister, Lady Harriet. At least he would not notice Emilie's absence for a few moments.

"It seems as if you are avoiding someone, my lady," Isaac said from behind her.

"You are very astute."

"Anyone would have to be desperate to waste a dance on me." It was meant to be a joke, Emilie thought, but was said less than humorously. "You are not in danger?"

"No—oh, no. Not at all." If only he knew what she had been accusing him of earlier in the evening! Still, the idea that he was worried made her like him all the more. "Do you see that man there? He's to be my husband."

Before Isaac could answer, Emilie moved toward a bed of roses, slipping around so she was hidden behind it, and leaned to take a breath of their scent. He followed, hands remaining locked against his back.

"Perhaps we ought to return," he said. "If your fiancé is looking, I would rather him not find you with *me*."

Emilie straightened. Because she had known Bridgmond all her life, he was never anything but another silly boy to her. But as a former prop for Oxford University Rugby Football Club, he must have looked rather intimidating to Isaac.

"Rhys is no threat to you," she said. "But you may go if you wish."

In the darkness, Isaac's pale, round face mirrored the moon. When he stepped away, Emilie thought he would truly leave. Instead, he craned his head to linger on the stars, and she was glad. They were not so bright as they were in Yorkshire, but were brilliant all the same, owing to a rare clear sky. Emilie had thought the ball would be a wash when it started raining before they arrived. Now, it was a most triumphant evening.

"Lovely night for it . . ." Isaac spoke softly, perhaps to himself. "*Oh thou beautiful / And unimaginable ether! and / Ye multiplying masses of increased / And still increasing lights! . . .* "

"Byron!" Emilie was pleased to have recognized it, and pleased it had come from his mouth. Too many of the people in her life did not appreciate poetry. "You are an admirer?"

Isaac's chin came down, expression more open than before. "I hardly trust anyone who is not, my lady."

"You may trust me, then."

She smiled, hoping he might finally admit his surname, though he still looked unsure. He took a few more lazy steps with no direction, skimming the bottom of his shoe over the gravel. It had not been the right thing to mention Bridgmond. That Emilie had rendered Isaac so cautious made her cross. She found an iron bench tucked beneath a rose arch, and sat on its edge. "Are you a poet yourself, sir?"

Isaac spun on his heel, taking a moment to glance around before he spotted her in the dark and came closer. "No, but I am a writer. Not a talented one, mind." This time, a flicker of humor creased his eyes.

"What do you write?"

"Only stories and things. Tripe, really. Nonsense."

"I don't believe it. Not when you look at the stars and see poetry."

Isaac's eyes dropped from Emilie's face, trailing down her gown, and then moved away. Her heart sped, feeling she'd been exposed under his sure gaze. Bridgmond had never looked at her that way—never so unapologetically.

Isaac took another step closer, as if he might come to sit beside her, then whirled again. Emilie had never seen a man move so anxiously. Papa and Fletcher were so sure of themselves, striding about as if the ground was laid there precisely for their feet to step upon. Isaac moved like he did not trust the dirt to remain where it sat.

He was different, somehow. Whatever was behind those eyes—be it a secret sorrow or something else—was churning endlessly.

"Why were you staring at me earlier?" Emilie asked.

Isaac hesitated, but only long enough for his gaze to dart from her lips to her eyes. "Because I found you to be incredibly beautiful."

Emilie's breath hitched, and she swept from her seat, bowing at the neck so he could not see her blush. He was too bold by half, but she could not ignore the flutter his words put in her stomach.

"Only my mother has ever called me beautiful," she said.

"Then I imagine your fiancé to be either witless or gutless."

She sent her eyes to the sky. "One would need to be witless in order to behave so immodestly before a lady who has only just made his acquaintance."

Isaac allowed a small, breathy laugh.

"I yield to you, my lady," he said, sweeping his hand outward in a bow to make her giggle. When he straightened again, his arm fell to his side. "My father was the late Baron Thurston."

Emilie flicked through a mental tome of titles and names it was her duty to remember, but could not seem to recall. She faced Isaac again, surprised to see his sunken expression. "Then I ought to have called you 'my lord.'"

Isaac held her eyes as he slowly shook his head. "The title is extinct. I had no right to it, and so it died with my father."

It quickly became clear why Isaac was hesitant for her to know his name. There were plenty of illegitimate children scattered about the country, some acknowledged and living lavishly, others forgotten and sent away to be someone else's burden, perhaps never knowing of their noble blood. But no matter where they found themselves, they would carry the sins of their mothers, and Isaac knew, as Emilie did, that a highborn lady would marry a titleless bastard only if she cared nothing for her reputation.

A smile spread across Isaac's face, a sheepish and self-deprecating look that wore at something deep within Emilie. What, she could not yet be sure.

"Now I know you are spoken for," he said, "I can see it was terribly imprudent of me to keep it from you. Only in the moment, I suppose—" Isaac paused to wet his lips. "Your fire quite consumed me, Lady Emilie."

For a moment, Emilie could not speak. Saying nothing of how instantly Mr. Thurston had obtained these feelings, he was the first man to ever express such a thing to her. Emilie restrained herself from denying it. Mama's scorn rang out in her memory, and she was reminded of how her life did not belong to her. What would it take to escape her binds? What reckless, riotous move could she make to find freedom?

Isaac was waiting patiently for her to speak.

"Why have you come to London this season when you have not come before?" she asked.

"Lady Thurston hopes I might find my place in society, though I daresay society does not have a place for me to fill."

"You don't sound as if you should like one."

"I feel no want of popularity or distinction. I would just as soon remain an outcast. But Granny saved my life. If she wishes for me to be here, I shall not refuse her."

Before Emilie could ask him to elaborate, something caught his attention and he leaned around the rosebush to look. Whatever he saw made him stiffen.

"Your fiancé . . ." he said.

Emilie stood, hunching beside Isaac. Fletcher stood behind the door, peering through the glass with squinted eyes. Sure enough, Bridgmond was behind him, speaking to Mama. The feathers on her shoulder floated weightlessly as she searched for Emilie among the crowd.

Isaac was so close, their shoulders nearly brushed. Emilie shrank away, hearing her heart thumping in her ears. She forced a drastic smile, not wishing to show her disappointment in needing to part from him.

He hid it well, and no doubt for the benefit of their set, but Emilie knew there was within Isaac a peculiarity that matched the one in her. It was the ease between them—the notion that she could speak and carry on with him without her second skin of Lady Emilie Dawes. Isaac was reluctant to enter society—his birth alone sullied his character, no matter his education, his fine clothes, and his clipped words. But she was fond of him, and plenty of people were fond of her. There was a way she could see him again, *and* help his grandmother's efforts.

"Monday in Hyde Park, some of the men are having a cricket

match," Emilie said. "Would you be disposed to join us? You do play, do you not?"

Isaac's hands twitched at his sides—little wonder why he normally kept them firmly tucked behind his back. "I'm uncertain I will be welcome . . ."

"Of course you shall; I'm inviting you! Bring Lady Thurston—she can occupy a chair in the shade and eat cake all afternoon. Oh, please do! I should like to meet her, and we are for our country seat in a fortnight."

Isaac wet his mouth, hesitating. Then he nodded.

"Good." Emilie smiled. "Play begins at eleven o'clock."

With one final look at him, she lifted her skirts and dashed up the stairs.

Six

Emilie

It was a glorious afternoon. Emilie could not deny herself the enjoyment of a rare cloudless sky and a soft breeze that made the heat bearable. The park was crowded with parasols and prams, families and couples walking arm in arm. There was a feeling of desperation that heightened every June and July, when the ending came to high society's summer holiday. All would begin to part in the coming weeks, and, grumbling that the trouble in the Balkans would ruin their travels to the continent, return to their country houses for winter.

Emilie's family marched on ahead of her, anxious to see and be seen. Before Fletcher could slip away, she grabbed him by the hem of his jacket with more force than necessary.

"My tailor would have your head," he said, wrenching away.

Emilie scoffed and helped him to smooth his white lapel. She had wanted to speak to him earlier, but owing to the tragic state of her hair, they had not had the time.

"I've invited my new friend from the ball," she said.

Fletcher's face fell. He had come into her room the night before, when they had arrived home in the pale grey of dawn. Emilie had explained who Isaac was, how she was mistaken about his motives, and Fletcher, too drunk to do much else, simply teased her for what he called an adorable infatuation.

"Why should he not be included?" Emilie asked.

"The chap is not your concern, and you are certainly not his."

"Please, will you be kind to him? Introduce him to your chums?"

Fletcher moved his gaze with disinterest. "No, Em."

"Oh, please? Please, duck!" Emilie was whining now. "He has been ignored all season, and if he is treated badly after I convinced him to attend, I'll blame you. Fletch?"

He looked at her again. "You must know you are leading that man each time you give him your attention, and when he discovers there is no future with you, it is his heart which will bear the wounds."

"I don't care a jot about how he was born."

"It is more than that, Em. There are things you don't know."

"What things?"

With a great breath, Fletcher looked about them, but there was nobody close enough to overhear. Emilie braced for the worst. Had she made a mistake?

Fletcher removed his cap with a sigh. "Since your waltz, I've inquired around about the Thurstons," he said. "They have *nothing*. The late baron gambled it all away and has left them completely house poor. Thurston Hall is sold—that is why they are in London, living in the baron's old flat. I shouldn't wonder if the fellow is out hunting for a dowry. What respectable woman in her right mind would have him, I cannot say."

Emilie rubbed her fingers together, sticky and hot in her lace gloves. Isaac had mentioned nothing of his wealth. What if what Fletcher had learned was only rumors? There were plenty of those in London, not all of them true. If Thurston was a bad name once, people were cruel enough to ensure it remained that way.

"If they have fallen on hard times, then all the more reason for us to show them kindness," she said.

"He is not one of your charity cases."

"I fancy the pair of you will get on."

Fletcher lowered his chin. "We shall see about that."

"So you will take him under your wing?"

"I will *tolerate* him." He moved her forward with a hand on her back. "But if I do this thing, you will forget him, is that clear? You have no use for Isaac Thurston, and he has everything to gain from you."

Swallowing her pride, Emilie nodded, and took Fletcher's arm to continue into the park. She had no reason to believe Isaac was after her money. After all, he had remained with her in the garden, even after he knew she was promised to Bridgmond.

Rhys's family had set up within perfect viewing distance of the pitch. Rugs were laid across the grass with lawn chairs and a hamper overflowing with a carefully packed luncheon. His parents, the Duke and Duchess of Claremont, stood in a circle of conversation with Mama and Papa, while Lady Harriet helped the neatly dressed governess look after the youngest siblings—twin eleven-year-old boys and a girl of seven.

Fletcher broke away to join the other men, and Emilie took a deep breath, entering the fray. Sometimes it was difficult to imagine herself at home with Rhys's family—all seven of them. She had once heard Mama tell his mother late one evening that her large brood spoke of the love between her and her husband. The two older women had giggled like little girls, bowing their heads close. At the time, Emilie had not understood what that meant. Having acquired a more worldly understanding as of late, she often hoped Rhys did not wish for so many children.

Clara, the littlest, came running to Emilie's knees to hug them. It was a rare occasion that the children shared an outing with the whole family, making them more excitable than usual.

"Hello, there," Emilie said, and righted her hat. "How do you do, Lady Clara?"

"Quite well, thank you very much indeed." Clara was terribly proud of her manners and used them whenever possible.

Emilie gave her a smile and looked to Harriet, who was wrangling a jagged stick from one of the twins' hands. Was it Peter, or John? Emilie could never tell them apart.

"Will you please take them away?" Harriet said to the governess, holding the stick out of her brother's reach. "Down to the pond—they may feed the ducks to their hearts' content, so long as they are quiet."

The woman bowed and took a boy's hand in each of hers, leading them from the picnic. Clara remained, finding a spot to sit on the rug, and returning to her custard tart.

"Forgive me, Emilie," Harriet said, kicking over a folded corner of the rug. "Have you been standing there long? Has someone offered you refreshment? Oh, now, look! Off they go."

All around them, fellow picnickers cheered and waved boater hats as the first bowl sailed across the lawn. Emilie sat on the rug beside Clara, scanning the pitch for a familiar face. And there he was— fielding beside her brother, no less. Fletcher gave him a slap on the shoulder, and Isaac Thurston laughed at something he'd said. Fast friends; she knew it! Even Bridgmond was indulging the new addition, with that stiff grin of his. Between the two taller men, Isaac almost looked like their little brother.

The sun was high, and most of the lads had already rolled their sleeves to their elbows. Isaac's hair was tousled loose, and he scrubbed at it, momentarily drifting off in visible thought. As the first batsman approached the wicket, Isaac widened his stance, bending his knees. His eyes were locked on the bat like a leopard on its prey. When the ball took to the air and Isaac dashed toward it, Emilie gave an inelegant *whoop*. The ball came down from the sky into his hands and his teammates cheered.

Isaac was fast and agile. Emilie was mystified by the way his flannels gripped to damp patches on his torso; the way his forearms caught the light, pinkening in the sun. Emilie opened her parasol and was glad it hid her blushing cheeks.

Apart from Rhys, Fletcher's team were certainly the clowns of the group, and their antics did nothing for their progress. Like puppies, they darted about the lawn, tumbling over one another for the ball and laughing, their faces red and their knees green with grass stains. For once, Emilie was glad not to be a part of it. There were plenty of things reserved for men that she wanted access to, but she never did feel a call to sport.

When the game paused for a tea interval, the men descended on the party in a swarm of white. Emilie's heart began to thump again. She silently prayed Isaac would somehow make it through his introduction without being completely humiliated.

As they arrived, the three young men removed their caps. Emilie closed her parasol, waiting for Isaac to notice her, but he was eager to smile politely for the higher ranks.

"Good show, gentlemen," Lady Harriet said. "You nearly had them in the last inning."

Fletcher put on the grin he was famous for and mopped his brow with his sleeve. "Hardly. Bridgmond is wasted on our team, though our new friend has brought some much-needed muscle."

Isaac simpered. "I'm pleased I could be of use."

Fletcher slapped a hand on his shoulder, letting it rest there. "Everyone—may I introduce Mr. Isaac Thurston . . ."

He went on to put names to all the faces, and Emilie watched Isaac's cheeks fill with color as he realized what he had walked into.

"And you have been acquainted with my sister, I believe?" Fletcher said.

When he saw Emilie, he eased at last, bowing at the neck with a smile. "It is good to see you again, Lady Emilie."

Emilie returned it warily, knowing Mama was watching. "I'm pleased you could make it, Mr. Thurston. Won't you all sit down?"

Clara stood and plopped down on Emilie's lap in order to make more space. After the boys were offered potted cheese, pâté, sandwiches, and lemon cake, Fletcher settled in a lawn chair, and Bridgmond sat beside his sister. Isaac, without an ounce of hesitancy, dropped down beside Emilie, so close she could smell the juniper of his aftershave.

Suddenly, she could not look at him. Emilie could not even breathe for fear she might somehow reveal how vigorously her heart was thumping.

Instead, Clara spoke to him from her lap. "How do you do, sir?"

Emilie heard the smile in Isaac's reply. "I am well, my lady."

"We have got some cake, if you like. You need only ask."

"You are very kind."

It was then that Emilie finally flicked her eyes in his direction. Isaac sat with his legs bent, his wrists resting on his knees. His face was rosy from the sun and the exercise, and she noticed for the first time the elegant slope of his nose as a bead of perspiration fell from the tip. When he met her gaze, Emilie inhaled sharply. He opened his mouth to speak, but was interrupted by Rhys, who sat opposite them.

"You have quite the arm, Thurston," he said. "You don't play for Oxford?"

"I have never played formally," Isaac answered.

Fletcher leaned in to say, "Thurston is a cadet in the Officers' Training Corps, are you not, old boy?"

"Good man," said the duke.

Isaac had the chance only to nod before Rhys went on, "You ought to consider it, you know, if your schedule allows. You might do well."

Fletcher took over the conversation, something about the OTC and the war, and Emilie could see Isaac's accomplishments being buried by the louder men. There was something in her so desperate to claim him, to sing of what set him apart from the others.

"Mr. Thurston is a talented *writer*," she announced.

By the way Isaac cut his eyes at Emilie, she knew she had done wrong. Was it not something he wished to be known? Then why had he so easily told her?

Harriet, who was well-read, leaned forward from her chair. "And what is it that you write?"

Isaac took a moment to answer, perhaps contemplating if it would be ruinous to deny the question altogether. "I am working on a novel."

From the group, a resounding noise that proved their interest. He may have thought he could sit quietly beside Emilie and be forgotten, but there was no chance among this lot. Now he had their attention as much as he had hers.

"How clever are you?" Harriet said, then prodded: "You must tell us what it is about! Who is the main character?"

"It is an adventure story," he said. "Following a pirate called Captain Ridley."

The group continued to make all the right noises. Emilie felt the same rush of pride in him that she had during the game. What did it matter what his father had done? Isaac was thoroughly charming.

"So it is a book for children," Papa put in.

Of everyone, Emilie did not expect her father to contribute, but she could tell by his manner that he was skeptical of their visitor and could not go another moment without voicing it.

Isaac breathed a laugh, but answered politely. "No, my lord—I should think it too violent for children."

"Heavens!" The duchess clutched her chest in good humor. "What is it that draws young men to such grisly stories? My boys haven't a moment to spare for anything lacking murder and gunpowder."

That got a chuckle from everyone, and knowing nods from Lady Ashwood.

Harriet was all the more interested. "Then Captain Ridley must be fierce and terrible. Is he?"

"She is fierce, yes," Isaac replied. "And terrible, only when she must be."

Emilie looked at Isaac as if she might devise more information from his expression. Had she misheard, or had he said *she*?

"And what happens to her?" Emilie asked.

"Well, she takes a navy ship, and there is a young lieutenant aboard, James, who gives her trouble"—Isaac was suddenly unable to hide the enthusiasm in his tone, and addressed the group more fully—"and so they duel for the freedom of his men. He wins, and Captain releases the prisoners. But James is the finest swordsman she has ever seen, so she tricks him into service in her crew, just in time to be thrown into a war of their own on the high seas."

Harriet clapped her hands together. "How thrilling! Wouldn't the twins devour it, Mama?"

Nobody else seemed to have noticed the changing pronoun, instead beginning to talk among themselves about this novel, or that play, forgetting they were speaking of Isaac's work in particular. He was clearly glad to relinquish the focus, shoulders shrinking down from his ears.

The only person other than Emilie who was still paying him any mind was Clara. She reached out to tap him on the arm and asked, "Will your novel be like *Treasure Island*?"

"A bit like that, yes," he said.

"Then I should like to read it, sir—when I'm older."

Isaac smiled again, revealing the smallest dimple in his left cheek. Over Clara's shoulder, Emilie spotted Rhys laughing with Fletcher and again heard the *tick, tick, tick*ing of an unseen clock. She imagined him sitting beside her, close as Isaac was now, and shivered. What was it about dear old Rhys Bridgmond that set her teeth on edge?

Emilie gently removed Clara from her lap, and Isaac stood with her, brushing his hand on his trousers before offering it. She blinked, staring dumbly as though it might burn her, then gave in, noticing his warmth through her glove as he pulled her gently to her feet.

They were facing each other properly for the first time all day, and now she could see the gooseflesh raising on his throat.

"Leaving us, Thurston?" Fletcher asked.

Isaac swiftly dropped Emilie's hand. "You have all been very generous, but if you will excuse me, I must see to Lady Thurston before play begins."

Emilie caught her father thinning his eyes at Isaac curiously. Beside Papa, Mama's expression was neutral, though she was finally taking notice of how close Emilie was standing to the newcomer. Emilie instinctively took a step to her left.

"I had hoped I might introduce you," Isaac said to her, but loud enough for anyone to hear. "If you would allow me."

Emilie was stuck—a West End actress who had forgotten her blessed lines, and stood frozen stiff before an exacting audience. Of course she wished to go with him, but how would it look?

It was Harriet who spoke first: "Go on, Emilie. But be quick about it—our team needs Mr. Thurston in the game!"

Their peers showed their agreement, Rhys among them. It was clear he did not see Isaac as a threat to his territory, and the very thought was enough to propel Emilie forward. Not bothering to look for her parents' disapproval, she led Isaac away from the picnic.

Isaac kept a sensible distance, shoulders bent, hands in his pockets. He had the habit of walking like a disgruntled schoolboy. Things were quieter away from the pitch—families and couples lounged on the lawn or fed the ducks at the water's edge. A few boys dribbled a football between them. Farther down, a woman sat painting at an easel, resting an umbrella on one shoulder to soften the light. It was all that was special about London in summer—the trees, the birds, the lush flowers and laughing children.

Neither of them spoke until they were well out of earshot, at which point Emilie removed her hat to feel the breeze across her neck, slipping the pin back in it for safekeeping. Mama would be aghast, but she would replace it before she saw her again. Isaac's eyes burned into Emilie, but when she turned, he quickly averted them.

"I was surprised to hear you are in the OTC," she said. "I did not have you as a military man."

"Did you not?" Isaac's chin went down to inspect himself. He came up with a wink that stole Emilie's breath. "The old boys from Harrow would agree. No, one must make friends, and an open-air club seemed the least dreadful option. That, and the annual camp is a nice holiday."

"What do you say to talk of war?"

"I try to say nothing. I do not want a war, but my opinion will hardly prevent one."

"That alone sets you apart from most men I know."

"Then pray, keep it quite between us." Another wink.

Emilie grew hot and used her hat to fan her chest. Perhaps she ought to have brought her parasol along; her skin would be frightfully pink tomorrow.

That reminded her of something. "Whatever led you to make your Captain Ridley a woman?"

Isaac smiled impishly. "I know it isn't terribly usual, and the publishers will probably tell me to change it if there's any hope of selling. But I was inspired by the two most courageous people in my life, and they were both women."

"You speak of Lady Thurston?"

"And my mother, yes."

Emilie was more astonished by him than she had ever been. From what little she assumed of his mother, *courageous* may not have been a word she would have expected.

"What is she like, your mother?"

"I haven't much of a memory of her; she died when I was small." When Emilie looked at him aghast, his smile deepened. "She was lovely, though. She was a barmaid in the market town nearest Thurston Hall, but she brought me to live in Halifax, where there was more work. Most people assume I must be ashamed of her, given her background, but the opposite is true. She might have given me up as easily as my father sent her away. But she had the courage to oppose her situation and bring me up on her own. I will always seize an opportunity to speak well of her."

Emilie was charmed as much as she was jealous. Odd, when he had lost his mother so young and hers was still alive. But she and Mama lacked unconditional affection. "How, then, did you come to live with Lady Thurston?"

"By the time my mother was gone, the baron had been dead two years, and so Granny sent someone to bring me home."

"Now you write of her to keep her memory alive," Emilie said, and he nodded. "I should like to read your work someday."

Just then, a football rolled up onto the gravel, hitting Isaac's toe. He lifted his chin to find where it had come from, as two little boys ran in their direction from the lawn. Isaac pivoted, and with hands still in pockets, gave the football a gentle kick. The boys waved their thanks and were off again, bickering about who was to blame.

"Quite the family you are marrying into," Isaac said. "You certainly shall not have a dull life."

"You clearly have never held a full conversation with Lord Bridgmond . . ."

His face tipped up to the sky. "He is a keen sportsman."

"Oh yes."

"But not a wordsmith?"

"I should think not. He is Fletcher's dearest friend, clever and kind, but he does not understand me, and has never attempted to. And frankly, even if I fancied him, I would still reject the idea that I have been promised to him like a prized animal."

"I cannot fault your reasoning. Though, I do suppose there are advantages to marrying the heir to a dukedom."

"Certainly. I shall be wonderfully rich and outrank my mother."

Isaac's face broke into that full smile, and Emilie noticed the flex of his neck. It made her dizzy. She decided she must learn how to make him laugh again and again.

"Before I was so much as baptized, my parents had decided on a man for me to marry," Emilie told him. "Can you imagine how it feels to have parents who care more about their status than their child's happiness?"

"Yes."

She had not been expecting the clean reply. Emilie did admire Isaac for his reckless honesty. His depth of emotion was almost *defiant*, and that excited her.

"It is your life he asks for," Isaac added. "Only you have the power to give that away."

"My refusal would cause a rift between our families."

"So you must act as a lamb for sacrifice?" He shook his head, amused, but Emilie was pained by the harsh comparison. "I myself am unburdened by propriety," he went on. "I have no interest in this veneer of grace and perfection good society is obsessed by."

Emilie became defensive. "I tire of this as much as you. I have become frightfully bored of the things that, by design, are meant to take my breath. But without them, what have I? I've no money of my own, no practical skills to make my way. I am the useless, pretty doll they have made me."

It was only as she'd said it that she came to the realization herself. The truth was, she was afraid. She knew nothing at all of the world, and was aware of her ignorance. That was why she had wanted Somerville.

Isaac's face softened into a look of tenderness. "You may do all of the things you dream of, Lady Emilie. What a pity it would be to allow such a sharp mind to go to waste."

A warmth crept from her chest to her toes, and she had to look away.

"May I ask you something?" Emilie asked.

Isaac stopped on the pathway and she did, too, ruining the brim of her hat with how she was worrying at it. He nodded.

"My brother says that Thurston Hall has sold. Is that true?"

"I'm afraid so. Granny is anticipating her own death duty, I should imagine, and I hardly have the authority to oppose her."

"What will you do?"

"I hope to someday make a living from my writing, but until then, I shall find a position here in London. I don't wish for my grandmother to worry over expenses at her age."

Emilie opened her mouth to ask another question, but was interrupted by the excitable shouting of twin boys. Peter and John, herded by their governess, were coming up from the duck pond, throwing crumbs at one another rather than the birds. They didn't notice Emilie—thank heaven—but the sight brought her back to the present.

They were far from the cricket pitch, now. Too far. A worldlier woman might have been fearful at the realization, but Emilie was young and trusting of her new friend.

"Where *is* your grandmother? She cannot possibly be any farther."

"Yes, there's a spot of bother with that . . ." A smirk tugged at Isaac's mouth. "She is not here—but she hopes you will call on her Wednesday."

While Emilie stood dumbfounded, Isaac put Lady Thurston's calling card in her hand. "You've led me all the way here only to say she has not come?"

"No," Isaac answered plainly. "I just wanted to speak with you again."

He made her blush again, the cheeky thing.

"Wednesday?" she asked. He nodded. "All right, then. Now, would you be so kind as to escort me back to where I belong?"

Smoothing away his smile, he pivoted and swept a hand between them.

"After you, my lady."

WEDNESDAY, OF COURSE, HAD already been promised to Lord Bridgmond. And so, instead of seeing Isaac Thurston, Emilie sent her regrets to the dowager and sulked into a seat at the sweltering Lyric Theatre. She sat impatiently between Rhys and her maiden aunt, who spent the duration of *Madame Tralala* checking to ensure the young man's hands remained in his lap, and his shoes on the floor. Emilie could not decide what was more insufferable—her chaperone's looming presence, or the ridiculous musical.

In the lobby during the interval, Emilie was forced to say hello to three different acquaintances, and with every smile she faked, she saw another minute of her precious time ticking away. Now that she and Rhys had stepped out together, everyone would be expecting a proposal. If Emilie was seen alone with another man, she would be finished.

Lady Thurston's calling card indicated only Wednesday as an "at home" day, and so Emilie had run out of time. Next Wednesday there was a garden party she could simply not miss, and they were to return to Hallesham Park at the end of that week.

Once home, Emilie went upstairs to remove her hat, ringing for Grace. She was planning on a long, cold bath when she noticed a large unmarked envelope that had been waiting on her writing table beside a bouquet of roses and freesias in brown paper.

"They arrived whilst you were out, my lady," Grace said, coming in the door Emilie had left ajar. "Pretty, aren't they?"

"Who brought them?"

"A messenger boy. Is there a card?"

Emilie shook her head. But there was a note tucked within the envelope, along with a short stack of typed pages. All at once, she forgot her woes.

E—

It may be presumptuous of me to assume you were speaking truthfully when you said you would like to read my work, but I would value your opinion. I have made copies so there is no need to post the pages back. Though if you hate it, please dispose of the manuscript however you see fit.

I regret that we did not meet today to say farewell, but I do hope you will write to me from Hallesham Park.

—I

Seven

Returning to Hallesham Park was always as much of a disappointment as it was a relief. Emilie would never admit to it, but she often silently agreed with Papa's line: It was good to be home.

This was the one time of year when Emilie truly appreciated the amplitude of her father's ancestral seat. After months in the town house, cluttered by the mismatched buildings and grey rush of London, Yorkshire appeared clean and endless. Emilie stepped out of the train, drew a breath of damp, misty air, and thanked her stars that this was where she'd been born. There was magic in the very soil of Yorkshire. In its foggy, green embrace, London was easily forgot.

Once home, Emilie dashed to her bedroom, which she had dearly missed, with its hand-painted wallpaper depicting a classic Regency park scene, trees and horses and ladies and dancing. She smiled at the characters she'd named and dreamt up stories for, tiptoeing her fingers along the roads they drove their barouches endlessly down. She crossed the room to drop onto the cream silk bedspread, dotted with roses—the same pattern that adorned the curtains, cushions, and crown.

A few of her books had been unpacked and left on her bedside.

Along with them, Isaac Thurston's manuscript. Emilie sat up to reach for the pages, falling back down against the pillows with a smile, touching the worn edges where his fingers had been.

Though she had read them many times by then, seeing Isaac's words in his handwriting still gave her a flurry of excitement. He had bestowed upon Emilie the privilege of entering a world that had existed only within his own mind. And what a world it was.

He'd called the novel *On Seas of Iron*. Emilie liked the way those words felt on her tongue. The story was penned so consciously with surprising depth, and prose that spoke of all the poetry its author had read. Captain Ridley breathed, reached out, and took hold of Emilie from the page. She sensed a romance brewing between Ridley and James, and the idea made her sigh.

It had been mere weeks since Emilie last saw Isaac, but in her young mind, it felt an eternity. In the time away, she had read his pages countless times, tried and failed to formulate her thoughts into a letter that both spoke of his talents and concealed her growing affections. She wondered how long he would await her response before he forgot her altogether.

Emilie rolled onto her side, clutching her pillow like a buoy. Breathless thoughts of Isaac often turned to something gnawing, something painful—the remembrance that Lord Bridgmond still stood in her path. To refuse him would devastate their families' friendship, but to marry Isaac Thurston instead would be ruinous. He was not, she feared, an alternative. Merely a distraction for the moment.

Across the room, Emilie's eye caught on the wallpaper people once more, smiling in the knowledge that their perfect day would go undisturbed for an eternity. The women would always gaze so lovingly at their suitors, the men would never grow old and ugly, the horses would trot on with the same strength until Hallesham Park was no longer standing. They might have been made of paper, but it rendered them invincible, like the fair pipers in Keats's urn.

Emilie did not wish to be trapped for life in the faults of her youth.

She sat up, beginning to formulate a scheme. Isaac Thurston had charmed everyone at the picnic, had he not? If he could do that within a few moments of conversation, think of how much more he could do in an entire weekend.

If she could convince her parents that Isaac was a worthy suitor, she might save them both from an uncertain future. Her dowry would keep Isaac from financial ruin, and their marriage would ensure she would never lose herself.

Emilie penned the letter quickly, leaving out any mention of the manuscript. There was no time for such careful consideration now. The shooting party was mere weeks away.

SUMMER ENDED WITH BOLD headlines, and the acceptance among the British that the anxious fears they'd been nursing for years would soon be actualized. When the day finally came, Fletcher declared he would be among the first men to volunteer. Their parents did not fight him, though there was tension. Of course Fletcher ought to go and defend King and Country, but he was also the singular male heir. If anything happened to him, the earldom would be extinct when Papa was gone.

Then Rhys sent news that he, too, had applied, and like that, two of the most important men in Emilie's life were set to abandon her.

In the following days, there was a general intensity in the air that Emilie tried desperately to ignore. Disregarding the calls from *Country Life* for the wealthy to live sparingly and urge staff to join up, Papa declared that the shooting party would go on. They would toast the boys who were answering the call, and celebrate their great country and her impending victory. The war would be over by Christmas, everyone said. Emilie could not be sure if it was blind ignorance, patriotism, or a desperate need to cling to a thread of hope, but she joined them.

Each morning, Fletcher ignored his food until the post was brought on a silver salver, his feet tap-dancing under the table. He was waiting to be gazetted, and could think of nothing else. Papa sorted and distributed. Nothing, today, from the War Office.

Though something had come for Emilie.

She immediately recognized the hand. In all the excitement, she had given up waiting on Isaac's reply.

15 August 1914

Dear Lady Emilie,

Please forgive me for not writing sooner; your letter arrived whilst I was away at Salisbury Plain. The declaration of war has ended our camp prematurely.

Lady Thurston and I would be delighted to attend the party on Friday next. I hope this has not come late, though if the notice is too short, Lady Ashwood ought not to feel obliged to accommodate us. In any event, please express our sincerest gratitude to her ladyship for the invitation.

I await your reply.

Yours respectfully,
I. Thurston

Emilie stared down at the letter, the dining room quiet except for the scraping of forks and sipping of coffee. Here were Isaac Thurston's words in her hands. He had touched the paper, he had licked the envelope. He had thought of her while writing this note in the ink he used for his precious stories. This simple note was a monsoon after so many weeks parched of Isaac.

The time had come for her to face the consequences of her whim.

It would cause a stir with Mama and the housekeeper who would need to compensate for two extra plates at each meal, rearrange the seating, open two more guest rooms, and shuffle about the assignments . . .

But Isaac Thurston could be *here*, at Hallesham Park, for an entire weekend. Being a cadet in the OTC, he was sure to follow the rest of them to war, and then when might she see him again? What if he did not come home at all?

Finding herself at a loss, Emilie slid Isaac's letter across the table for Fletcher, who could muster a solution for any situation. He regarded her curiously, opening the fold. She watched his face as he read through it, and when his eyes came up, they gave nothing away.

"I have invited Isaac Thurston to the shooting party," Fletcher announced with his usual confidence. "I hope it isn't too much of an inconvenience, Mama."

Emilie hid her face in her teacup. Opposite her, Fletcher folded Isaac's letter and concealed it on his lap. Emilie would be doing him odd favors for the remainder of her life to repay such a debt, but it would be worth it. He could do no wrong in their parents' eyes.

"That boy seems to have appeared from thin air," Mama said. "I did not expect we would be seeing so much of him."

Fletcher took a bite of bacon, swallowing it down quickly. "When we went motoring in London, we got to talking about shooting. He has never been."

Mama made a noise of uncertainty. "A novice? In this set? He will not be popular."

"He knows his way around a firearm," Fletcher assured her. Emilie was impressed by how easily he could expound upon the lie.

"Still, you ought to have told me sooner. Another man will throw the numbers."

It was, perhaps, the most polite way to say she did not want him here.

"The dowager will accompany him."

Papa set down the newspaper. "Lady Thurston is not highly thought of, and I found the grandson to be a bit"—he sputtered, searching for a word—"*awkward*, and unrefined."

Emilie did not appreciate the slight. But she dared not draw attention to herself with an outburst.

"He is a writer; they are all odd," said Fletcher, "but the Claremonts found him amusing enough."

"People will talk," Mama said.

"All talk will be of war, I assure you."

Mama watched their father's face, waiting for his decision. It did not matter that his wife was the one who did all of the planning, the inviting, the orchestrating of events—Papa would have the final say.

"I don't suppose any harm will come of it," he said, and Emilie let out the breath she'd been holding. "I would urge you, however, to choose your friends more carefully in future. And do keep an eye on him whilst he is here." That was spoken with a pointed glance at his daughter.

Fletcher nodded and that was that.

Later, Emilie was sealing the envelope for her reply to Isaac when her bedroom door shook on its hinges and Fletcher stormed in. He tossed Isaac's letter down in front of her on the writing table and placed both hands on the surface, filling her vision with his scorn. Emilie was shocked by his anger, seeing how aloof he had been at table.

"It ends after the party," he said. "I will not be an accessory to this any longer."

"But they may come to respect him," she replied, "if only they are given time."

Fletcher shook his head. "This is not one of your romantic novels."

"Why shouldn't it be? I am sorry, duck, but I can't marry—"

"You so often forget that Bridgmond was *my* friend first, and so any shot you take at him wounds me also." In a huff, he removed his hands, standing to his full height. "We all of us must make sacrifices, Em. It is time you stop playing these childish games and take on some responsibility."

His words shook Emilie, but she did not have the chance to reply, for he quit the room nearly as swiftly as he had entered it.

Eight

Emilie

On the day of the shooting party, Emilie sat under the window in the blue drawing room, where she could watch the guests arrive. There were five parties in all—three couples, Lord Bridgmond, Lady Harriet, the duke and duchess, and the Thurstons. The horseshoe drive hosted a parade of motors, arriving one at a time, piled high with luggage that was driven round to the back to be unpacked. The butler would show the guests to the rooms they were assigned, ensure they were given refreshment, and allocate help if they had not chosen to travel with staff.

When Lady Thurston's motor arrived, Emilie had been clouding the window with her hot breath, bored of the cavalcade. It was her intention to catch a long-awaited peek at Isaac before retreating. After how she had left things with Fletcher, she did not wish to upset him further.

But as soon as Isaac climbed out of the motor, she forgot all else. In the long weeks they had been separated, his face faded enough that she began to repaint it in her own memory. Part of her worried all the exquisite lust might be ruined after so much time.

There was no need. As Isaac handed Lady Thurston down from the car, he looked over his shoulder and Emilie was given a brief display of his ethereal, Greek profile, even more handsome than she re-called. His charcoal greatcoat made him look taller and elegant, a wave of dark hair blown loose to tickle his forehead.

All of Emilie's resistance fell away and she sprang to her feet and checked her face in a mirror before heading through.

When Isaac looked at her across the main hall, they were caught standing on opposite ends of the room, eyes locked, neither making a move to close the gap. Lady Thurston rescued them, smiling broadly to reveal wine-stained teeth.

"You must be the gracious young woman who rescued Isaac from drowning at his first ball," she said.

"You are far too kind, my lady," Emilie replied, approaching them to see a flush cross Isaac's cheeks. "I merely needed a dance partner."

"That you got him to dance at all proves you are a heroine indeed."

Lady Thurston was still bundled in coat and hat, leaning on an ivory cane. Her white hair was arranged high, her lace collar dusting the bottom of her chin. She was a tiny thing, frail with age, but her presence was enormous. Perhaps it was only that Emilie was so in-trigued by her—this woman who Isaac claimed saved his life.

"Hallesham is as fine as I remembered," the dowager said, grin-ning. "A prominent family, yours. Oh yes." She grumbled a bit, neck unsteady. "Though I daresay travel is not designed for old bones."

She did look exhausted. Isaac had one hand on her ladyship's arm, the other on the small of her back. He might have been holding her upright, or at least splitting the weight with her cane.

"There is time to rest," Emilie said. "The first tea is informal, and no one will complain if you take it in your room."

"Perhaps I shall do just that. Isaac?" He stooped to her ear. "Do remember your manners when you greet Lord and Lady Ashwood; they have been very generous to you."

His ears turned pink as he straightened, avoiding Emilie's eyes. "Yes, Granny."

A footman came to take their coats, and Emilie was stuck idling, not wishing to leave Isaac's side. As his coat slid off his shoulders, his eyes went to the painted ceiling, carved from the same limestone as the exterior.

"Remarkable," he said. "You must find something new to marvel at every day living in a house like this."

Emilie could only smile. She couldn't remember the last time she noticed the ceiling.

"Is Thurston Hall not grand itself?" she asked.

"It was—some three hundred years ago. Now it is dark and damp and grim . . ."

As he straightened his tie, Emilie lingered on his elegant long hands, and the fine cut of the Shetland tweeds hugging his figure. She detected a hint of regret in his tone. However grim, Thurston Hall had been his home since he was a boy of six. He would surely have been sad to leave it.

Emilie escorted the Thurstons upstairs. It was like a dream, seeing Isaac at Hallesham, a place where he surely did not belong, and might never have been if she hadn't thrown herself into his path. Once Lady Thurston had approved her view of the garden, Emilie went the short distance with Isaac to the next door. He marveled at the little card on the wall that read *Mr. Thurston* in her mother's careful script.

"I never," he said. "Did Lady Ashwood imagine I would get lost?"

"Have you never been to a house party before?" Emilie asked.

He shook his head, a glimmer remaining in his eye. This was something special for him, and despite it all, she was glad she had been the one to bring him here.

"I've read your pages," she said.

Isaac's expression sobered. "Have you? And how did you find them?"

Emilie noticed his jaw tightened in anticipation. It meant everything to him, this novel. She would have lied if she had not enjoyed the chapters, if only to prevent his heart from breaking. Thankfully, she did not need to.

"I rather enjoyed them. They knock the spots off of plenty I've read."

Isaac sighed happily and smoothed a hand down the front of his jacket, as if calming the nerves in his stomach. "Thank you. God, I am relieved. I would have thought a fine lady such as yourself might find it frivolous and crude."

Emilie was delighted to hear he was anxious for her approval. "On the contrary, I found there's rather a sensitive depth to it. I would be pleased to read more, if you'll allow me."

Isaac hesitated, looking again at his name beside the door. "Where is your room?"

"Oh . . ." Emilie's face burned. The cheek of him!

"Please don't mistake my meaning!" Isaac added breathlessly. "I have brought more pages, but they are in my case. I thought I might slip them under your door . . ."

Emilie's shoulders eased, but only briefly, as someone was coming up the stairs. It was the butler who turned the corner, leading Rhys and his parents to their rooms. In the corner of her eye, she saw Isaac step back and push his door silently into the jamb. She breathed a bit easier, placing a smile on her face for the Claremonts, who each greeted her in turn, exchanging pleasant words of excitement about the shoot to come.

Rhys lingered as the duke and duchess marched ahead, retrieving something from the pocket of his fine tweed trousers. He held his hand toward Emilie, and she opened hers to accept whatever it was he'd brought her. It was the brass cap of a shotgun shell, warm from where it had been pocketed against Rhys's leg. He smiled wider as she craned her neck to look at him curiously.

"From last year's party," he said timidly. "It was your winning shot against Fletcher. I meant to give it to you then, but forgot."

As a party rule, nobody was to keep score, as Papa found it unsporting, but Fletcher and Emilie always competed among themselves. The gesture was certainly sentimental—something Emilie might have even found romantic coming from a different man.

"You've kept it all this time?" she asked, noticing the tips of Rhys's ears go pink as he nodded. "Why?"

"I thought you might like it for luck—though I've no doubt you will thrash us all again."

Rhys smiled and bowed at the neck, leaving Emilie standing in the corridor. It wasn't until he had turned the corner that Isaac's door cracked open. His smile was humorous, making her stomach flutter as she turned and put the shell behind her back.

"I have the corner room," she told him finally. "I'll tie a pink ribbon round the doorknob so you don't miss it."

A flash of mischief crossed Isaac's dark eyes. "May I escort you down to tea?"

Oh, how Emilie would have relished it. But it was not the right time. "Thank you, but we had better not be seen arm in arm."

Isaac's chin dropped to his chest. He bent his ankle, lifted one of his shoes partly off the floor, an anxious tic that was now familiar to her.

"My parents believe it was Fletcher who invited you here," she explained. "He cut in to protect me, I suppose. In any case, you ought to spend tea talking to him."

Isaac nodded, as if he knew already. When his eyes came up, he was smiling sadly, but he gave her one of his winks. "Understood. Rest assured, I shall not interfere."

❧

FOR DINNER, EMILIE WORE a gown of cobalt blue velvet and pearl beading, sleeves and belt in black silk gauze. It was a dark, brooding frock for her usual taste, but that was what enticed her about her dressmaker's design. In it, Emilie stepped out of a girlish, naive body and into one of a strange new woman she was unsure of, but trusted. This new woman was courageous enough to defy her family.

Emilie entered the yellow drawing room alone, her gown feeling pleasantly heavy on her shoulders. She was glad to see Isaac standing at the window with Fletcher and Lord Harrington, no doubt discussing the war, if his expression was any indication. Something about the hard lines and stark colors of Isaac's dinner clothes, and his shiny, scraped-back hair, emphasized the softness of his features—the boyish roundness of his jaw and mouth, dense brows set in their usual somber glower. She longed to approach him, to see his face brighten at the sight of her. For a moment, Emilie felt adrift, alone in a crowded space, unwelcome in her own home. Would she ever be free to make her own decisions? Even small ones, like engaging with those she'd like to be speaking to rather than the ones to whom she was obliged?

Rhys appeared at her shoulder, as if summoned by her thoughts. Emilie turned to find him carrying two glasses of sherry, looking fine in evening clothes. Though her notice of the handsome symmetry of his face remained objective: a bloom in a garden that anyone might admire in passing.

"Is that a new gown?" he asked, without allowing his eyes to sweep boldly downward. "The color is lovely."

"It is, thank you," she answered, accepting a glass. "I didn't ask earlier if your journey was pleasant."

"Yes, it quite was." Rhys tipped the sherry against his lips. "If the weather holds, we shall have perfect conditions for the shoot tomorrow."

Emilie nodded, catching herself glancing at Isaac again. "We are fortunate to enjoy such indulgences whilst our boys are fighting bravely across the channel."

Rhys concurred, "It shall be a fine reminder of what we'll be fighting for."

Emilie finished her sherry too quickly and shivered as it burned her throat. Though Rhys had never won her romantic favor, the thought of losing him to uniform clenched her heart. Who would be left when they all went abroad? How would they get on without the men?

"I did not expect to see Thurston here," Rhys put in. "He must have made quite the impression on you in London."

Emilie kept her tone neutral, worried Rhys had followed her eyes across the room to Isaac. "We all found him rather charming."

"My sister certainly did. Though I cannot say I have much time for literary sorts; I prefer men who speak plainly. I do wonder what the fellow wishes to accomplish here. It's clear he hopes to rise above his illegitimacy—but among this set?" Rhys paused to drink, and shook his head. "They are too polite to turn up their noses, but they see only one thing when they look at him. Ah, we're going in."

Emilie was relieved the conversation had been cut short.

It was not a large party, but a traditional one, and so each woman was escorted into the dining room. Mama had cleverly sat Isaac beside Harriet, knowing the two had books in common, and put Rhys beside Lady Thurston, with Emilie on his right. All of the other couples were split and scattered carefully to encourage conversation.

Across the table, Isaac's face was in its natural state of gloom, even as the candlelight flickered warmly across his eyes. Emilie wondered if something—or someone—had upset him, or if he was already fatigued by the *veneer*, as he called it. When he noticed her staring, she shifted her attention to her gloves, which she removed and folded beneath her napkin.

Dinner was served *à la russe*, and like so many meals Emilie had endured, it began quietly. Conversation had dwindled in the drawing room, and everyone was eager to fill their stomachs and sample vintages from her father's vast cellar. The wine would loosen them again, in time. For now, it was the din of silver on china, and the humming of satisfaction over the salt cod with cream sauce, chicken *à la Barbarie* with truffles, red currant ham, and calf's-foot jelly. Around the time Emilie's corset felt tighter, bites grew further apart, and faces came up, looking for respite in tête-à-tête with their neighbors. Unwilling to endure Rhys, she instead stretched her ear to hear Mama speaking to Lord Harrington.

"I have been thinking often of your son," Lady Ashwood said, and then to Papa on her right: "His lordship's youngest is a cavalry officer. Have you any news from the front?"

Harrington cleared his throat and patted his mustache with his napkin. "In fact, we have just had a letter from him. I fear the cavalry is no match for modern artillery. Benjamin writes he is hopeful they can be effective dismounted, though it is a great shame to see so many horses slain."

On Rhys's other side, Lady Thurston *tsk*ed audibly at the remark.

It was clearly not the answer Mama was looking for, and she went flush, disappointed by her error. Would war be considered as criminal a topic as politics? She treaded water for a moment before Papa rescued her.

"Kinsley and Bridgmond are to be infantrymen," he said. "I daresay if the war remains static, they will need as many men as they can get."

"Quite right," Lord Harrington said.

Fletcher overheard, and lifted his wine. "Do not forget our new friend, Papa. Thurston will be leaving with the rest of us in a few days' time."

From the way Isaac's face drained, Emilie guessed Fletcher spoke a truth he had not wanted revealed. Though Emilie had been expecting to hear it, the news still made her tongue go sour. All three of her boys were off, then, and soon enough she would be on her own. For the first time she thought nothing of marriage—only of funerals.

"Yes, well done, son," Papa said. "What regiment?"

"The King's Own Yorkshire Light Infantry," Isaac answered warily, then added, "my lord."

"Where do they train?"

"I am to report to Berkhamsted Common."

From the men, a general hum of acknowledgment. Harriet beamed at Isaac, offering him a string of patriotic congratulations until he could not help but allow a full smile. They were terribly proud, all three of her boys, lighting up the room with eyes brightened by the promise of what greatness lay ahead of them.

"A toast to you, then, gentleman," Sir Andrew put in from the other end of the table. "I only wish I were still young enough to wear the uniform."

The duke raised his glass. "Hear, hear."

When the excitement dimmed, Isaac stared pointedly across the table at his grandmother. Lady Thurston, who had already shrunk from the war talk, had turned a diseased shade of green. The news must have been as much of a shock to her as it was to Emilie, and what a dreadful time to be given it as the *oeufs à la neige* were brought from the sideboard.

When the women stood to go through to the drawing room, Emilie went to Lady Thurston's side, helping steady her as she took up her cane. The dowager laughed at herself, allowing Emilie to escort her into the next room. She tried to lead Lady Thurston to the sofa nearest the fire, but the old woman hesitated, leaning close to Emilie's ear.

"I might take my leave," she said. "My head is splitting . . ."

"Shall I go with you?" Emilie asked. "It is easy to get turned around in this big old house."

And so they went, slowly and silently, until they arrived at Lady Thurston's bedroom door. The dowager paused to thank Emilie, but there was more behind her eyes.

"You weren't aware Isaac joined up, were you?" Emilie asked.

Her ladyship shook her head. "We have argued many times over it, but I never thought he would go against me."

"My brother is entirely thoughtless. He must have got it out of Isaac before dinner."

Emilie opened the door, helping Lady Thurston to the dressing table before pulling the cord to ring for her maid. She sat on the settee at the end of the bed, not wanting to leave the old woman alone. Watching her tired neck jerk as she removed her gloves, a piece of Emilie's heart broke. With Isaac away, would she be all on her own in London?

"He is acting on my instruction, I suppose," Lady Thurston mused, as if thinking aloud. "I was so desperate for him to make a gentleman of himself. I failed my own son—brought him up to be arrogant and gluttonous and foolhardy as his father was."

"Your husband died some time ago, did he not?"

"Oh yes, donkey's years." She removed her other glove and tossed it on the dressing table. "His death gave me the independence I had always longed for, but my son suffered for my negligence. I have much to atone for."

It seemed Isaac had inherited his affinity for honest conversation.

"You have done a fine job with Isaac," Emilie said, "and you mean the world to him. There is no reason to carry such guilt any longer."

Lady Thurston offered a sad smile. "Perhaps I am overprotective. But he is all and everything I have got left."

"May I say, it is a truly selfless thing you've done, giving Isaac a home. Did you not fear what people would think?"

"I have no wish to associate with people who would turn their backs on their own blood for a clean reputation. I would not trade my grandson for all the wealth and power in the world. You look at me, and you see an old, withered thing, no doubt. But under all this dust remains the debutante—exhausted as you must be of all the pageantry."

Lady Thurston had a talent for seeing straight through Emilie.

"Is it crass to long for more than elegant gowns and gilded drawing rooms?" she asked. "My mother says I ought to learn to be satisfied if I'm to ever find happiness."

"Satisfaction is a kinder word for complacency. And complacency is for the ignorant."

The door opened, and Emilie stood, expecting the maid. But it was Isaac who came through, breathless and smelling of cigars. Without acknowledging her, he flew to his grandmother's side and dropped to one knee. Lady Thurston hardened at the sight of him, unwilling to allow her affection to stifle the anger.

"When did you intend to tell me you had signed your life away?" she asked. "From the motor as you were driving off?"

"I had only just heard when we left, and hadn't found the right time."

"If I knew you were so reckless I would have locked you in your room."

Isaac's face soured. "I have a responsibility to my king. As an able-bodied—as an educated man—"

"His Majesty has enough soldiers."

"Soldiers he has lost already."

"And you wish to be one of them, do you? A body in a mass grave?"

"I should be glad to die for my country!"

Lady Thurston let out a condescending puff of air. "You are a *child*, Isaac. You speak of what you do not know. Lord, sometimes you are so incredibly arrogant. So like *him* . . ."

Isaac's brow knitted in pain as he bowed his head. "They say the war will not last the year. You'll hardly have the chance to miss me."

"And who are *they*? Hm?" Lady Thurston said. "War is a wild animal. Any man who believes himself capable of predicting its outcome is a fool indeed."

This was no longer a conversation that Emilie felt comfortable witnessing. She took up her candle and slipped through the open door, flooding the corridor with light. When she turned to close it, her curiosity got the best of her and she watched through the crack.

"Then I am a fool?" Isaac raised his voice, the sound sending prickles down the back of Emilie's neck. "I am not honorable for defending my country—for defending you?"

"You are nothing but honor and courage and spirit, my boy. But I fear your good nature cannot protect you. Not here, nor in France . . ."

Isaac kneaded his eyes with the pads of finger and thumb until Lady Thurston reached out. When they clasped hands, the small touch extinguished the tension in the room. Isaac placed a kiss on her ladyship's swollen knuckles. She touched his hair so lovingly it nearly brought a tear to Emilie's eye.

She gently pushed the door into the jamb. Lady Thurston's maid was approaching with a pitcher of water for washing. Emilie nearly told her that the dowager would need another moment with her grandson when the knob jostled and Isaac came through. He gestured for the maid to enter and shut the door behind her. As he stepped into the light of Emilie's candle, the flame danced between their breaths.

Emilie could not think of what to say. An apology for eavesdropping? A word of assurance that he had made the right choice to go to war? His face was so beautiful, she felt no need to fill the silence at all.

"When I didn't see you, I thought you must have come up with her," he said.

"I wanted to be sure she was all right."

"Thank you. She needs more looking after than she lets on . . ." Isaac pressed his lips together, his nervousness returning in the restlessness of his hands. "Shall we go down?"

"I was thinking of turning in."

He looked to his door, as if contemplating the same. It was much too early to be retiring—the drinks and cards and music would go on until light began to peek over the moor. By his eyes, Emilie could see Isaac was tired, though she understood his hesitation. Of all the guests, he had the most to prove, and parting from the men now could mark him a milksop.

"Here," Emilie said, "take my candle with you—I know my way."

His face returned to the orange glow, anguished. Would a gentle hand on his cheek bring his smile back? A soft kiss on his brow?

There was so much more within Isaac, more than sword fights and pirate stories, more than poetry and an arm for cricket. He was an honest man, but the indifference was a shield he had forged to hide behind, to protect a tender, jaded heart. His past brought him no shame, but it was an unhealed wound that ached in these moments when his grandmother reminded him of all they had lost.

Emilie wanted so badly to strip away his armor, to be a salve that might one day heal him.

His lips parted as he watched the candle dance. "I'm sorry you heard that. I don't normally—I'm not—" He sighed. "She believes me to be faultless, but it has become increasingly difficult to meet that expectation, and each time I fail, it breaks her heart again."

Emilie gently took up his wrist to set the candle in his hand, overlapping it with hers long enough to feel the warmth of his skin through her gloves.

"You are not faultless," she said. "But you are lovely, Isaac Thurston."

They were close enough that Emilie felt the warmth of his breath on the fine hairs of her cheek. She knew that she wanted to kiss him, and that he wanted to return it. She leaned toward him, noticing the peppering of whiskers emerging across his chin, and then all at once came to her senses.

Emilie lifted her skirt and whirled, feeling his gaze scorching the back of her neck.

Nine

Emilie

There was something satisfying in donning her tweeds. They had the effect of a uniform—uniting all of those who together would tramp across the moors for grouse and partridge. On this rare occasion, Emilie could be one of the men, be a part of their conversation, take hold of the challenging weight of a shotgun, even impress some of them with her skill.

Mama did not shoot, and neither did the other ladies in the party, so Emilie was the only one in a skirt. The women would play bridge in the hunting tower, then join them outdoors later in the afternoon, where a picnic lunch was served in a marquee outside the keeper's lodge.

It was a fine day for shooting—crisp and cool, with an overcast sky. In the brake, they were driven out past the parkland to the moor, where they continued on foot to the location of the first drive. The ground rolled along like waves on the sea, burnt orange and gold, swaying in the autumn breeze. Between the bracken, the heather was blooming again, pockets of purple that never failed to take Emilie's breath away.

She bent for one of the stalks, finding Rhys smiling at her when she straightened. He had found her early on in the trek, and she thought it best to stay near to his side for a time. Her mother would be pleased to see it, as would Fletcher.

"Here you are." Emilie slipped the stalk through Rhys's buttonhole. "Heather is good luck, and you'll need it now you've given me your charm."

He removed his rabbit hair trilby so she could better see his eyes. "Will I not be needing a fair bit more than that?"

He would, bless him. Though Rhys delighted at rugby, he was not one for this particular sport. He had been sore the first time he shot beside Emilie, not expecting the woman he intended to marry to best him at something so masculine as gunmanship. How far he had come since then, she thought. How accepting he was. With that in mind, she bent to pluck another sprig of heather to add to his buttonhole.

"You're too kind," he said with a chuckle. "Perhaps I shall return from war a better shot, and best you yet."

Emilie smiled, but wanted to say no more on the subject. She was still of the mind that if she gave no particular attention to the war, it would end before it could hurt her.

Instead, she continued moving. There was lightness in her step, in her chest. This was her favorite place in the world, and she felt nourished by the misty air, the musk of wet dogs, and the mud sucking at her boots. She spotted Isaac ahead, recognizable among the other men only by his stunted height. Though he held himself with such assurance, Emilie doubted he noticed the difference. When she looked at Rhys again, he had grown in both height and width, stalking through the bracken like a stag. She was not sure she had ever found him so imposing.

Another quarter mile, and they came to the edge of the wood. The picker-up dogs were whining and grumbling at their heels, pink tongues swinging as they were stirred to excitement to do their job. Each gun—there were nine of them in all—was assigned their own loader, who carried the equipment and ensured a quick exchange.

Emilie put herself between Fletcher and Papa, and was handed one of her two over-and-under shotguns. Savoring the comfortable weight of it, she held it broken over her arm, glimpsing down the line as they waited for the beaters to get into position.

Isaac was on the other side of Fletcher to her right, the bill of his tweed cap pulled low over his eyes. He was using a rather old Holland & Holland—perhaps something his father left behind. His eyes crinkled when he noticed Emilie staring. Her heart fluttered, wondering what he must have thought of her parting words the night before. Wondering if he had spent the moments before sleep thinking of her lips, as she had of his. She'd been so aware of his nearness last night.

"I did not expect you would shoot, my lady," he said to her now.

Emilie beamed. "It is one of the few thrilling activities my sex is allowed."

Fletcher stepped forward, resting the barrel of his gun across his thigh. "My sister is a crack shot. Always been the better of the two of us, haven't you, Em? Bridgmond has seen her, he can keep me honest."

Rhys had joined the line between Isaac and the duke. The former slowly turned to acknowledge him with a nod, then looked to Emilie again.

"If only they let women join the army," she remarked, "then I would be off with the rest of you."

It would have brought her some comfort to go, rather than be left behind. Mrs. Pankhurst had suspended the suffragette cause in favor of the war effort, hoping the women would do their bit in whatever ways they could. Emilie had not yet found where she would be of use.

Rhys scoffed, tossing his knuckles so they brushed Isaac's upper arm. "First they come for the vote, and now they want the military?" Fletcher added an agreeing laugh.

Isaac was clearly unamused by the comment, directing his gaze down to his gun. "I am for the vote, my lord," he said. "And if a woman should possess the courage, I see not why she should be barred from giving her life for her country, same as a man."

Emilie bit her lip as the two other men were knocked by the statement, and checked to see if Papa had heard. Isaac's opinion would certainly not help his reputation, but she was proud of him for voicing it, and glad he agreed in her cause.

"Women have their own duties on the home front," Rhys said. "Someone must keep house, send letters of support. And what of the children?"

"Not all women are mothers," Isaac offered.

"Women are not capable of the fortitude required of combat."

"I am uncertain how your lordship could know this, seeing as you have never been one."

Rhys adjusted his stance to face Isaac, using his height. "Don't let's go on about this here, old boy. I think you will find this is not the setting for Bloomsbury philosophers."

Isaac's lips twisted into a wry grin, but he digressed, moving his eyes out toward the trees. Fletcher tilted his head in Emilie's direction, but spoke loud enough for them all to hear: "Aren't I fortunate to be so jolly simpleminded?"

His humor touched each of them, even Isaac. Rhys appeared to be at ease with the last word, and Emilie wondered if he was not so confident as she gave him credit for.

By then, there was no time to talk. The gamekeeper shouted down the line to ready the guns, and they spread out, their loaders staying in their shadows. There was visible movement in the trees as the beaters and dogs began to drive forward. Emilie closed her gun and raised it, keeping her eyes on the sky.

With a great burst, the first of the partridges broke up from the brush, taking to the air in a hurried panic. Then came the rhythmic *pop, pop* of the first shots and the scent of gunpowder that followed. Smoke swirled in the space between the guns and Emilie's heart was pounding—not from excitement this time, but something else, an irrational fear she could not understand. Her mind was telling her to aim, to pull the trigger, but she found she could not move. What was the matter with her?

More birds went up, thick and fast. The guns continued, and partridges fell and fell, lifeless as stones, the wind catching them and turning their bodies. They found the earth with a sickeningly hollow sound, and bounced before lying at rest, some of them still twitching with life until a dog snatched them by the neck.

Emilie swallowed, the back of her throat sour. Even on her first shoot, she had never been so unsettled by gunfire, never so horrified by a clipped wing. Now she felt she might be sick.

Her barrel came down, and Emilie stumbled out of the line, her vision blurring. She was distantly aware of the loader beside her, calling out her name over the firing. He took the shotgun from her hands as she bent double and tried to remember how to breathe. But her lungs would not fill or empty. Could it be that she had been shot by mistake? Was this how it felt to die?

Two firm hands pulled Emilie back to reality, and the ringing in her ears began to fade. Blinking, she could just make out the shape of a man, and then his voice. The guns had all stopped but there was a great bit of commotion, growing closer, closer . . .

"I have got her. Give us some room."

The voice belonged to her brother, and so did the hands still holding her on her feet. Emilie moved toward them, finding his chest, curling into him as hot tears ran down her cheeks.

"Shall I send someone for a doctor?" This was Isaac, perhaps an arm's length away.

Then Rhys, with a slosh of his flask: "Give her this; she may swoon."

Finally, Papa with a sudden severity she hardly recognized: "Thurston, fetch a brake here—make haste. Why is she not speaking? Sit her down . . ."

"Em?" Fletcher pulled off her hat, exposing her head and ears to the cold. "Look here, what's this? Listen to me, are you hurt?"

Emilie shook her head, but could not yet find words.

"There, there, dear girl." He placed his warm hand on her nape, and spoke to the men: "I have got her—you may all walk on. No—no, go on."

It was only Fletcher and Emilie for a time. She focused on the beats of his heart against her ear, and eventually, the darkness clouding her periphery dissolved and Yorkshire took shape about them—the grey light, the swaying moors, the trees in the distance hidden by fog.

Emilie pulled away, rubbing her eyes, suddenly shy with her brother, who had surely never seen her lose her footing so inexplicably. He returned her hat, and she made a useless attempt to scrape her hair back before replacing it.

"That was some turn," Fletcher said. "It cannot be the shooting that has bothered you . . ."

Not far, a footman with partridge carcasses strung up over his shoulder approached. Emilie knew then what had turned her stomach and caused a crippling fear to clutch her throat.

"Not the shooting here," she said. "But it is a frightful reminder of the shooting going on *there*."

"Oh, duck . . ." Fletcher removed his handkerchief from his chest pocket and handed it to Emilie.

"What must it be like to hear that banging all day long, knowing it is aimed at you?" she asked. "And the three of you are so *eager* to be in harm's way."

"It is our duty."

"But don't you think it shall be terrible?"

"War is war. We do what we must in order to survive."

"That sounds archaic."

"War is hardly a recent invention."

Emilie sighed, watching the cart again. It was no wonder the men were so excited, why the boys all joined up as soon as Lord Kitchener gave his call. There was something ingrained in them, some primal need to maim, to draw blood, to prove dominance over weaker creatures.

Perhaps these were only birds, but their deaths were senseless and unnecessary. The poor things were bred and fostered on the estate only to die for sport. How had she not considered it before?

Fletcher had removed his hat, allowing the wind to tear through his hair and ruddy his cheeks. How young he was, speaking of war and duty. What did he possibly know of it? He was only a boy.

"I don't want you to go," Emilie said, tears bubbling once more.

Fletcher chuckled as somewhere near, the pops of rifles began again. "I am not going anywhere just yet. Well, the midlands, but it's hardly dangerous."

The brake stopped and Isaac leapt from the back, carrying a tartan knee blanket over one arm. He hesitated until Fletcher raised a hand to wave him over. Emilie wiped at her eyes again, hoping all evidence of her turmoil had gone.

Isaac's cheeks were pale with worry, his cap folded and sticking out from his pocket. His breeches and socks were splashed with mud from running at her father's instruction.

"Is everything all right?" he asked.

Emilie's brother looked to her to answer, and she nodded sheepishly.

"Let us be off, then." Fletcher pressed a hand to the small of Emilie's back. "Go and catch them up, Thurston. There'll be another drive before luncheon."

Isaac nodded, but neither of them moved. Emilie saw what was perhaps her only opportunity to speak to Isaac properly before he left her again. She reached out for the blanket, which Isaac then unfolded and laid over her shoulders.

"Allow me to escort Lady Emilie," Isaac said. "It would seem I'm no good with moving targets, in any case."

This was a lie. Before Emilie had lost her bearings, she saw Isaac hit three of his four marks.

"Go on, Fletch," she put in. "You'll not want to miss the drive."

Fletcher's eyes darted between the pair of them. Emilie could not be sure if he had a change of heart, or was too exhausted to argue, but he let his head fall in a nod, and replaced his cap.

"Very well. Rejoin us at the marquee when you're through, Thurston. You look as though you could do with a drink."

Isaac handed Emilie up into the brake, then fell down on the leather bench across from her. As the motor rumbled to life, Isaac removed the cap from his pocket to wring in his lap, and leaned forward on his elbows, hands only inches from touching her knee.

"He is kind, your brother," he said. "Underneath it all."

Emilie felt an unexpected chill of defense in her chest. "Underneath?"

Isaac held her eyes boldly, but there was nothing but sympathy in his own. "I believe Fletcher wears a mask, pretending to be the confident heir. But beneath it, he is just as unsure as anyone. As *me*, even . . ." Isaac chuckled at himself, but there was little humor in it. "What is it you were thinking of when the guns went off? I saw terror in your eyes."

Emilie lifted a shoulder, allowing him to move beyond the topic of her brother. "It was nothing. I didn't eat enough breakfast."

Isaac tapped her leg with his folded cap, and the spark of it traveled through the whole of her body as if he had touched her for real. Of course Isaac, of all people, would not take an empty answer. Pulling the blanket closer over her shoulders, Emilie leaned into the depths of his ocean eyes and found a place of comfort.

"I was thinking of how much more familiar we will all be with death soon enough."

Isaac considered this, and then he touched Emilie for real, using a finger to brush the knuckle of her thumb. She took a chance, uncurling her hand from gripping the blanket, and laid her palm over his. He checked the driver could not see them from the other side of the partition, and grasped her hand with a tender desperation.

Emilie's laugh was nervous, and she wasn't sure where it came from. "You must think I am such a frivolous little girl . . ."

"No," Isaac said, perfectly staid. "No."

Emilie pored over his features for the thousandth time, the handsome curve of his nose, the swell of his lips, where, when he was guarding himself, a half smile always crouched in the corner of his mouth. "I wish they could see you the way that I do," she said.

Again, she saw the flame that existed within him. It wasn't just melancholy, not always. There was enmity, as well. And why shouldn't there be? He had been torn from one life that didn't want him and tossed into another just the same. Caught between two worlds, he must have been terribly lonely.

"I—" Isaac hesitated, dropping her hand to rub his mouth.

"Go on," she said. "Please."

"You will think me too compassionate . . ."

"There is no such thing."

Isaac started again. "I did not come here to prove myself to them, but the moment I saw you appear in the hall, I knew I would do anything—*anything* . . ." He sighed, then shook his head. "There is nothing for it, Emilie. They will not see me; they only see from where I've come."

She could not bear the hurt on his face. Emilie reached out, took his cold hand in hers once more.

"If I was a better man," he said, "I would be pleased to see you married to someone who can give you the life you deserve."

The sun was coming through the clouds, warming the car, burning off the mist. Emilie removed her gaze from Isaac in order to think properly. Had she ever thought she would find a man who felt so much for her? A man who might have been sculpted to match the soul inside of her body?

"You are worth twenty of any man who believes a woman needs fine things more than she needs to be understood."

Isaac brushed his thumb against hers again. It was such a small gesture, barely noticeable, but it spoke volumes.

Emilie allowed herself to lean closer, desperate for something to cling to, to anchor her in the moment when her head and heart were moving more rapidly than she thought possible. In that moment, Isaac was more beautiful to her than he had ever been, and sitting near enough she could see the flush crawling down his neck. Emilie felt a boiling within her, the steam pushing her forward slowly and then with steady determination like a train engine. She was close enough under Isaac's nose that a mere stretch would touch hers to his. So close she felt his careful exhale, hot on her lips.

Emilie had never been kissed before, hardly knew what was required of one. Now she felt a yearning, a gripping so painful in her gut that if she denied herself the chance now, she would break into two pieces and crumble to the ground. She leaned forward until Isaac's nose touched her cheek. Emilie smiled, crawling all over with nerves, and pressed her lips to his.

It was so quick that their mouths popped as they came apart. Emilie sat straight up, running her tongue over her bottom lip. Before she could speak again, Isaac dipped his face to find hers, kissing her fully this time, and with such conviction that Emilie's spine went to jelly. Somehow, lost in the warm surrender of his mouth, she found she knew precisely what to do.

When they broke, Emilie could hardly breathe. She was humming from head to toe.

He whispered in her ear, making her shiver: "Your fire will be wasted on him."

Isaac studied their clasped hands, giving Emilie a moment to peer at him unapologetically, to drink him in and stow him in a safe place she could revisit while he was gone.

When Hallesham came into view, they leaned back into their seats, adjusting their clothes. Emilie checked the driver, who remained oblivious, not hearing their conversation over the sound of the motor. He would be off with the rest of them, she thought. The footmen, too.

"Are you frightened to go?" Emilie asked Isaac.

He shook his head, straightening his cuffs. "It will be no different to Salisbury. It's likely the war will end before I see combat."

"Do you really believe that?"

"Perhaps I only choose to believe it because I'm frightened."

In his truth, Emilie found unexpected relief, and wondered how different the world might be if every man was brave enough to admit when he was afraid.

"Promise you will return to me," she said. He nodded without second thoughts, but that was not enough. "Say it."

"I promise."

As all exciting news seemed to do at Hallesham, word of Emilie's turn had reached the house as if by magic. Mama was coming down the stairs as the brake stopped in front of the house. Isaac got out first and raised his arms to help Emilie down. Mama rushed toward them, and Isaac stepped away.

"What has happened? Are you unwell?" Mama looked Emilie all over, brow tight, and removed the blanket from her shoulders, handing it to Isaac without looking at him, as if he were a member of her staff. "Come indoors—Grace is drawing you a bath."

While she was herded toward the house, Emilie looked behind her at Isaac, standing near the brake. Surely if Rhys had been the one to deliver her, he would have been received with thanks and praise, offered a hot drink and a seat before the blazing hearth.

Looking at Isaac, Emilie became aware of a great depth within her gut that throbbed like a sea cave, waiting to be filled by high tide. It was identical to what she had felt when she returned to Yorkshire after season. The strange, inexplicable comfort of nostalgia. Of home.

Once they were indoors, Mama led Emilie up the stairs to her room. Emilie went to the window, watching as the motor rumbled down the drive, carrying Isaac back to the shoot. Her lips still burned from where his had met hers so fiercely.

Mama sighed and threw the curtains closed, causing Emilie to flinch away. "I do not want you to be alone with that boy again, have I made myself clear?"

"Do you mean Mr. Thurston?" she asked dumbly. "He was very kind—"

"His father was not." Mama placed a hand over her heart, as if to silence it. She was all at once more flustered than even Emilie. "In these cases, you must understand, dear girl, that the apple falls not far from the tree."

Ten

Emilie

Before boarding the train for Grantham, Fletcher assured Emilie there would be no society weddings until the war was over. Still, she worried the romantic nature of their separation might still move Rhys to propose. Men could become so sentimental when going off to war, suddenly desperate to have someone back at home longing for their return. Even Fletcher, who paid so little attention to women, had acquired a sweetheart out of thin air.

And then, just as Emilie feared, Rhys came to tea and proposed to her in Hallesham's sculpture gallery.

As he formed the words, he did not look at her, but at a great marble lion lying before them on a pedestal, mouth open wide to bare enormous, deadly teeth. Emilie had stared into the back of its throat, wishing it would come alive and gobble her up.

"Your friendship—and your brother's—have always meant a great deal to me," he had added, as if the sentiment might convince her to speak.

Instead, it only made Emilie wonder if Rhys's pal Fletcher was the only reason he had considered the marriage at all.

But in that moment, as a nervous bead of sweat escaped his hairline, Emilie saw the introverted boy whom she spent summers with, playing tennis in the garden, watching the Boat Race, explaining polo to her while she cheered inelegantly. Despite her efforts, she could not find reason to hate him.

"Must I give you my answer now?" she had asked, timid as she'd ever been.

Rhys had swallowed, the stone in his throat twitching, and shook his head. "Think on it. Take as long as you need."

And so Emilie took her time. Rhys did not object, and when he left that afternoon, she had set her winning shotgun shell in his palm.

"For luck," she had said, closing his fingers over the metal. "It will last far longer than a sprig of heather."

In the meantime, Emilie took Home First Aid with Harriet, whom Rhys was eager for her to be closer friends with. It was a satisfyingly uncomplicated distraction. In a room of women from a certain background, Emilie learned from a doctor about the importance of cleanliness, how to treat various wounds and illnesses, how to make beds and wrap bandages. Many of the girls thought it was a laugh, this, but Emilie could not find the humor in it. The newspapers had printed horrifying images of war-torn West Flanders, proving that somewhere not far from where they played nurse like children, men were bleeding and broken.

She took a pamphlet about the Voluntary Aid Detachments, envying the smiling women in their blue-and-white uniforms. These were the women, she thought, who were fighting the war alongside the men.

Without Fletcher, all the lights at Hallesham Park dimmed. Emilie thought she would not miss him any more than she did when he was at Oxford, but his absence weighed more heavily now, knowing what he was doing, where he was bound. Being neglectful about correspondence, Fletcher sent one letter a week, addressed to his *Dear Family*.

It all made Emilie's humble first aid courses laughable. What had been the point of learning how to clean and bandage a flesh wound when she barely moved beyond Hallesham's gardens? Had it only been a way for elite ladies to feel they had contributed something to the war effort, and had Emilie fallen into the trap as easily? She wrote this to Isaac, and the response was written with all the care he would give his novel.

You have learned a skill, and so the time was not wasted, he'd said. *Ponder on how you might use your new knowledge. I have no doubt you shall do something brilliant.*

She had become obsessed by Isaac's words as much as she was by his laugh and navy eyes, and her affections would not exist without them both. The word *love* had not occurred to her yet, but she had written to him saying, *My life shall never be the same if you do not return to me*, to which he had replied, *I shall return to you, Emilie, or not at all.* And if ever they wished to remind each other of the small intimacy they had shared, they simply wrote of *that splendid morning I last saw you.*

Christmas arrived, and still the war raged on. All of the spirit Mama had once used to plan a shooting party in wartime had long dwindled, and so the holiday was a muted affair. The ball normally thrown upstairs for the staff was canceled, and the usual decorations forgone—no tree in the main hall, no garland on the banisters and mantels. Instead, there was a single wee spruce in the yellow drawing room, humbly adorned with bells, glass balls, dried oranges, and silver stars. Papa proclaimed a strict ban of presents. Instead, they would send a bounty to the boys at the front. After all, they had been promised to be home by now.

To their surprise and delight, Fletcher was granted coveted Christmas leave, and arrived on the twenty-fourth to more hugs and kisses than he'd had in all his life. Emilie hardly recognized him in uniform, impossibly tall and brawny. There was a more chiseled nature to his face, and his hair was shorter than it had ever been. He smelled oddly to her—like harsh soap and leather and horses.

Dinner was no glorious feast, but none of them took note of the food. They were too glad to have Fletcher, too aware that it may be the last time before he truly entered the fray. Even after plates were emptied, they remained at table, guzzling wine and talking of anything. Once their parents had both said good night and gone up, Fletcher and Emilie sat on the rug beneath the tree and shared a decanter of whisky—a rare treat for her. There were so many things she wanted to say to him before he was gone again. But for a long time all they could do was sip and watch the candles flicker.

"I shan't survive if you are killed," Emilie finally said.

Fletcher hummed a snicker into his whisky. "I shall not be killed. Though it would be humiliating to return without a wound."

"What sort of wound should you wish to have?"

"Nothing too painful, but I fancy returning with a scar." He sat up with a wobble. "Oh! Perhaps a bullet in the shoulder? Or the arse?"

"No one would see a scar on your arse."

"No, but I'd know it was there."

His face softened, eyes drifting to the Christmas tree that suddenly looked garish in the light of war talk. Emilie knew Fletcher was thinking it, too—that while they sat in the almost obscene comfort of a Hallesham drawing room, men endured gunfire in the trenches, hungry, shivering. Missing home. Missing their mothers.

"Are you frightened?" Emilie asked.

Fletcher shook his head.

"Isaac said he is frightened."

A tear fell from Emilie's eye before she could close it, and she quickly thumbed it away. But Fletcher had seen, and after throwing back the last of his whisky, he reached out for her hand. Emilie could not recall the last time they'd held hands. They must have been only children.

"Be good while I'm away, Em. It will all come right in the end."

FLETCHER LEFT SHORTLY AFTER New Year, and come February, all merriment was behind them. Life turned grey and cold. Emilie had completed her first aid courses and passed her examination, returning home to little fanfare, though she was rather proud. It was the first thing she had ever accomplished on her own, and she felt it proved her potential. Harriet thought she might volunteer locally, but backed down when Emilie suggested they find positions in London, where patients were fresh from France. Military hospitals, desperate for more hands, had lately allowed volunteers—trained or not. But Harriet was sure she could not tolerate the illness and anguish, writing, *When the tea is made and the brows are dried, there is unseemly work to be done.*

Unseemly work was what Emilie longed for. She woke each morning in the comfort of her bed, sipped tea made and brought to her at perfect temperature, and became disgusted with the luxury of her own life. She saw no reason for her to lounge, to eat, to read, to have hundreds of idle minutes when men—her own men, now—were setting their muscles to work at all hours to ensure the country's safety. She wanted to push her own hands into the dirt and grime of it—she wanted to be a cog in the great, churning machine of war.

She wanted to avoid the conversation she'd been having each morning at breakfast, the one she was having now with Mama.

"Will you write to Rhys today?" Lady Ashwood asked.

"Perhaps," answered Emilie, indifferent.

"The duchess says it would not be difficult for him to beg an afternoon's leave and meet you in London."

Emilie lifted her cup and saucer. "Mhmm."

She eyed Papa, who was reading the paper. She knew that he had given Rhys his blessing before the proposal, but it appeared that he had granted his wife the task of pushing Emilie to accept it. Weddings were not exciting enough to draw his mind away from the war.

Papa was interrupted by the post. He looked at Mama, who in turn looked at Emilie. Something was not right.

Emilie put down her fork, hoping it was not more bad news. They had lately heard that Lord Harrington's son, the cavalry officer, had been killed in action, only one of many losses that had already touched their circle of friends. So many of the bright young men Emilie had danced with in great salons were gone.

Papa drew back in his chair, and Mama followed. Such ceremony was not typical at a family breakfast, but Emilie stood as well, tensing for someone to explain.

"Emilie, will you come to my study?" Papa asked.

She swallowed. He hardly ever wanted her in there.

It would have, under any other circumstances, been a thrill to be in Papa's study. It smelled of him—peppermint and leather and woodsmoke, and the strong coffee he preferred to tea. This was certainly a man's space, the furnishings heavy, the cushions spare, and the books locked in cages that made Emilie feel a bit sad.

She sat across from her father's mahogany desk in a carved chair, and Mama stood behind Papa. He had something in his hand—an envelope.

Oh dear.

"This arrived for you this morning." He pushed it across the desk. "Go on."

She obeyed. As expected, it was from Isaac, addressed formally to her. Already her blood was boiling, knowing her parents must have been discussing her correspondence behind her back. But she would play demure.

"Oh yes—it is mine," Emilie said lightly. "Had it got stuck to one of yours? I suppose it did rain earlier. Nelson ought to have dried them before he brought them up."

Mama's mouth tightened, and she allowed Papa to take the lead on the conversation, which was worse.

Her father steepled his hands and propped them on his rounded belly. The grey wisps at his temples were beginning to fall out, and Emilie was distracted, momentarily, by envisaging Fletcher as a bald old man. So much of his vanity was in the coif of his chestnut hair.

When Papa took a sharp inhale, Emilie returned her thoughts to the room. "It is from the Thurston boy, I presume?"

There was no denying it, and so she would instead need to convince her parents she had no feelings about Isaac Thurston, one way or another.

"Yes, it is," Emilie answered. "We discuss novels and things. I don't suppose he has anybody else at home to write to, as Lady Thurston can hardly hold a pen for the rheumatism in her hands."

Emilie could see Papa was preparing to call it a misunderstanding and dismiss her. Men don't enjoy such confrontations. But they gave Lady Ashwood much-needed stimulation, and her color was rising.

Papa tapped his fingers together. "Do you believe it is entirely appropriate to be writing to this boy so frequently?"

"Man," Emilie said.

"Hm?"

"Mr. Thurston is twenty-one. He is a boy no longer."

Papa grumbled, drifting off, so Mama took the reins. "What your father means to say is that *we* do not find it appropriate for you to be corresponding so frequently with a boy of whom we know nothing. We cannot intuit whether he is a respectable sort of person—"

"You spent several days with him here."

"—*and* you forget that you are promised to another man."

"Why do you consider *Rhys* a man? He is only two years Isaac's senior."

"Emilie Rose."

She sat back in her chair, rubbing her thumbs against the envelope, desperate to know what was inside. Wishing that there was somehow a way to feel Isaac's hands through the paper he had touched so recently.

Papa leaned forward, reaching for his pipe, which he turned over and over in his hands. "You wish to bring Isaac Thurston comfort in a tumultuous time, and that is admirable, dear girl. But the man has no title, no property, no great fortune, and so when he writes to you, his motivations may not be so modest as they appear."

Emilie didn't know whether to rage, cry, or laugh. They had not suspected a romance at all, only a desperate attempt by Baron Thurston's bastard son to elevate his social and financial position by wooing a naive young woman. Worse still was the truth that they thought marrying for gain was virtuous when it was the pair of *them* who wanted to use Emilie.

"We are merely pen friends," she said. "Am I not permitted even to have friends of my own choosing?"

"We have always permitted you to spend your time with whomever you choose," Mama said, "even when we hoped you would find a solid friendship with a dignified group of women."

"I thought I might call on Lady Thurston later this week."

Mama sighed. "We ought never to have invited them here . . ."

Now Emilie's breaths were coming too quickly. She pressed her hand against her stomach, feeling the boning of her corset creak. If she could not go to London to see Lady Thurston, nor write to Isaac, she would have nothing left.

"Daughter?" Papa was closer now, and when she opened her eyes, Emilie found him bending over her, offering his handkerchief. "There is no need for all this—this"—he waved his hands about—"*excitement.*"

She blotted her eyes, sniffing like a child. "I know you do not know him, Papa, but I promise that Isaac Thurston respects me. He is *good*, and he would never— He doesn't want anything from me but good conversation, and you know how difficult that is to find."

Mama did not soften. "Any young man who wishes to converse with you does so because you are beautiful, and you are your father's daughter."

"Then I have no other remarkable qualities? You believe I am naught but a—a handsome coin purse with a *Lady* before her name?"

"No, no, no—" This was Papa. "You have many attractive qualities, but you cannot expect Lord Bridgmond to sit idly by as you give your attention to another man."

Emilie's head spun, so she shut her eyes. She missed Fletcher—longed for him to be there to offer his support. He never condoned her flirtation with Isaac, but he would not allow his sister's life to be stripped of every ounce of joy.

Emilie would not do it. She could not hand her life completely over to her parents' control—to Rhys's control. She had to find a way to hide it all, or lie, or escape entirely.

She wobbled to a stand. "Lord Bridgmond is not my fiancé until I accept his proposal. I will cease writing to Isaac Thurston, but I will no longer profess that I intend to marry anyone at all. I—I'm going to apply for a Voluntary Aid Detachment, to work in London."

"There is no need to go to London," Mama said. "You shall find a place to volunteer locally, as Harriet has, and live at home."

"I want to help the men who come right across. I want to be there in the case that—" Emilie pressed Isaac's letter to her tightening core. "In the case that Fletcher is wounded."

Papa rubbed his chin, studying the objects on his desk as if they might give him an answer to his unspoken question. Emilie looked again at Mama, who was paling at the idea of letting her only daughter go it alone in the city, surrounded by strange men.

"No," Mama said. "I have had enough of this, Emilie—you will not be leaving this house until you learn to do as you are told."

Emilie balked, shocked by her mother's assertiveness. Papa, too, had not expected it, but did not cut in.

"You will accept Rhys's proposal," she said, gently prying Isaac's letter out of Emilie's hands, "and we will be finished with these silly games once and for all."

With that, she tossed the letter in the fire, and all three of them watched it curl into the flames and crumple to black nothing.

The walls began to close around Emilie, but she bit her tongue. Mama wanted her to be pretty, to be silent, to be obedient, and so she would be. She would meet Rhys in London as she was told. She would accept his proposal and his ring. She would say goodbye to the life she knew at Hallesham Park, to her parents, to her brother. For she knew, if she did the terrible thing she was planning as she stared into the fire, she would never see any of them again.

Eleven

Audrey

APRIL 2014

I woke to an empty house, still thinking of Isaac's letter. Sitting up, I spotted the VAD uniform where I'd laid it carefully over the footboard. I leaned forward to touch the worn hem, again feeling a connection to the woman who had owned it. I was desperate to learn more about her.

Leslie had already left for work with Jim, so the kitchen was empty. The night before, I'd shown him the letter, and asked if I could borrow his laptop. Since Sparrow Cottage was Grade II listed, and local authorities sometimes took a year or more to grant consent for a proposal, there was no chance of doing any work on the house. I was going to have to sell it as is. But I wanted to find out as much about Gran's family as I could before doing so.

Leslie had left the laptop on the kitchen table, along with his phone number—we'd forgotten to exchange them. Across the rest of the kitchen, he'd left notes labeling everything. On one cabinet: MUGS, and another: BOWLS. A drawer was labeled: FLATWARE, and a ceramic jar: TEA. Giggling, I poured myself a bowl of Coco Pops, amused by the idea that Leslie ate children's cereal before going to his job of hammering and sawing and lifting heavy things. With my breakfast and a hot cup of tea, I sat down and opened Google.

The first name I typed was *Emilie Smith*. To no great surprise, the common name led me to thousands of entries, most of them social media accounts of strangers who were still alive. I tried *Emilie Smith Langswick*, *Emilie Smith VAD*, and *Emilie Smith Sparrow Cottage* to no avail. I tried Gran's name in the same combinations, and groaned. I was getting nowhere.

Having another sip of tea, I clicked onto a popular ancestry site, wincing at the price, and wondered if there would be anything to find in the first place. Clearly, the Smiths did not wish to be known, not even by their neighbors. If I was the last person to know who they were and where they lived, there wouldn't be much of a family tree to discover. The thought set a heavy weight on my shoulders. I wondered how often entire lives' worth of memories were forgotten, either tossed away on purpose or simply lost.

The letter I'd found in the VAD uniform was sitting beside the laptop. I picked it up carefully, reading over the words for the dozenth time. It was a beautiful letter, the kind that made one mourn the lost art. This man named Isaac clearly loved Emilie once, there was no denying that. If he had any link to my great-grandmother beyond this sweet romance, it didn't make sense to me why Gran would never mention him. Maybe he was killed like so many others, eventually forgotten by their first loves.

Groaning, I shut the laptop and let my head fall to the table.

"Steady on—that cost me nine hundred quid."

I bolted upright to see Leslie coming through the door from the utility room. He bent to let Jim off his leash, and straightened, pushing a hand through slightly damp hair. I was completely aware that I was staring, but couldn't remove my eyes from the slim, bare torso, the tufts of hair from belly button to the elastic band of his sweatpants, the flower tattoo over his heart.

I didn't look away until Jim's nose bumped my knee, and I leaned over to pet his ears.

"I'm sorry," I said, feeling my cheeks burn. "The computer is fine, I promise."

Leslie smiled, retrieving a glass from the shelf, and filled it with water at the sink. "I'm winding you up. Find everything all right?"

I nodded slowly. "Your notes were helpful."

Leslie swallowed a gulp of water. "Yeah, sorry. I'm a bit neurotic."

I sat tongue-tied, waiting for Leslie to apologize for being half-naked. Weren't English people supposed to be reserved? But he was perfectly relaxed, leaning against the counter with one Nike sneaker crossed over the other.

Picking my jaw up off the floor, I decided to be the one to point it out before my hormones completely shut down my motor functions. "I like your tattoo."

He looked down at himself, then up at me, the only evidence of shame crawling across his chest in the form of a blush. "Shit—sorry. I'm just back from a run with Jim—I normally throw my shirt in the wash on the way in."

I smiled and wrapped my hands around my empty mug. Clearly he wasn't going to take action, so I forced myself to hold his eyes. "What kind of flower is it?"

"The White Rose of York, actually." He rubbed the ink with a flat palm. "It's a symbol of Yorkshire. Got it when I was sixteen."

"You must be really proud of where you're from."

"It sort of comes with the territory. My nan will tell you anywhere south of Sheffield may as well be France."

"It's a lovely place."

"God's own country, as they say." Leslie set his glass down on the counter and slipped one palm behind his neck, inadvertently showing me the strength in his biceps. "You're finding you like it here, then?"

"I am," I answered honestly. "This is going to make you roll your eyes, but I sort of feel like my gran is here. I feel her more strongly here than I have anywhere else."

"I work in a lot of historical buildings in an old country with a grim past. I'll be the last person to tell you there's no such things as spirits."

"Have you seen any ghosts?"

"Not as such. But I'll never deny a presence. That's why I try to be respectful to the original structures of the homes I restore. Just because there are new residents doesn't mean the previous owners have moved house." He laughed nervously. "Probably sounds a bit airy-fairy to you."

A week ago, it might have. Now, though? "No, it doesn't, actually."

Leslie and I were fixed there for a moment, smiling at each other, until he drew in his lips and ran a hand down his beard, then turned to the sink.

Thankfully, I was let go from the spell of his abs. Though I couldn't help but be charmed by him. When I'd first seen Leslie at the pub, I certainly hadn't imagined him to be so open and intelligent, and that little bit weird that made him special. I had never clicked so well with someone, even in a simple friendship.

Leslie turned the kettle on and came to take my mug, setting it beside his. He put a tea bag in each, and then let out a heavy breath. "On my run, I stopped at the cemetery. I didn't see a gravestone for Emilie."

I nodded, feeling a twinge of regret. Knowing when Emilie had died would have taken care of one mystery. She might have lived several more years after Gran left. If so, had they been in contact? Or was their relationship completely severed?

I was familiar with the pain of losing my own mother—it hit me hard and sharp like a rogue wave when I least expected it, even in my adulthood. I thought back to my time with Gran, searching my memory for a moment where she might have looked mournful over what she had lost. But all I could recall was her smiling face, her kindness, her warmth. It was only in her final days that she allowed me to see her weakness as that golden facade began to melt away.

I forced myself to remember further back, to the week of Mom's funeral and the months afterward. If Gran had been reminded of losing her own mother, she didn't show it. Though maybe there was something more to her presence in our lives after that. Maybe she was trying to mend old hurts by ensuring my sister and I never suffered the same.

LESLIE OFFERED TO COVER the leaking windows before heading off to work. It was a perfect day—the first real sun I had seen since arriving. The air was still as we approached Sparrow Cottage, thick with the sweet scent of wisteria that clung to life on the exterior. An orange cat stretched out in a patch of sun beside an iron bench, swatting at a butterfly that tickled its ear. Birds chirped overhead as I put the key in the door, and I gazed up at a cloudless sky, thinking of Gran.

Leslie suggested we open some of the windows to air out the house. We went from room to room, making note of any that wouldn't open easily. Only a few of them were stuck, and when we reconvened in the kitchen, I caught Leslie jotting notes on a pad of paper before replacing it in the back pocket of his jeans.

"Your phone does that, you know," I said, pushing up my sleeves. I'd pulled my hair back and worn a bandanna over it, ready to get dirty.

Leslie wagged his stubby pencil at me like a schoolteacher. "Paper doesn't run out of battery. I prefer analog methods."

"That explains the fancy watch."

He shook it around his wrist self-consciously, the silver links jingling. "One of the few remnants left over from my London life."

"Doesn't it get dirty while you're doing construction work?"

"James Bond wears a Rolex. I'm pretty sure it can stand up to sawdust."

"Except James Bond isn't *real* . . ."

"I will not hear your lies and slander."

I allowed myself to giggle. I was going to be in trouble if he continued to be so damn cute.

When he headed back to his truck for the tarp, I idled near the sink, using my finger to draw a streak on the dusty porcelain. The cottage had electricity, but no plumbing at all. It was difficult for me to imagine people living this way as recently as the 1940s. How easy it was for me to take everyday conveniences for granted.

I spotted Leslie through the kitchen window over the sink, carrying a ladder under his arm like it weighed nothing at all. Passing through the boot room, I joined him outside, and lifted a hand to my brow to shield the sunlight. In a few effortless motions, he slid the ladder to its full height and set it against the stone facade of the house. Then he lifted a square of folded tarp and nodded for me to join him at the base of the ladder.

"Could you hold this steady, please?" he asked. "Won't take a minute."

I stepped in line with him, craning my neck. "Is it safe?"

"Safe as houses." He grinned at his cleverness and gave me a wink. "Water damage destroys old buildings, and if you've not noticed, it rains rather a lot round here." Seeing the look on my face, he lightly punched my arm. "It ain't my first time on a ladder, love."

There was the accent again.

I was instructed to straddle the ladder and then he began to climb, using only one hand, tarp in the other. The rungs creaked as he ascended. I hadn't considered myself afraid of heights, but suddenly felt sick imagining Leslie falling backward into the overgrown rosebushes.

"Oi," Leslie called from where he'd settled in front of the window. "Anything happens, the number to ring is 999."

"If you survive a fall, I'll be killing you myself."

"Good to know you care, flower."

Once he was up, Leslie hammered nails in to keep the tarp in place, the sound echoing across the garden. The task took all of a few minutes, and then he was coming down again, hammer swinging from his tool belt.

"Right, we're making progress," he said, dusting his hands. "We won't be able to make the repair unless we've got planning consent, so we ought to clean up in the meantime, if that sounds okay?"

I nodded. "You go off to work. I wouldn't mind a few hours here alone to start looking through everything."

Giving me a sympathetic smile, he agreed, and told me to call him if I happened upon any issues that needed addressing immediately.

With a deep breath, I set my fists on my hips and took in the overgrown garden, the dilapidated cattle barn, the rusting hinges on the door, and the family of sparrows nesting in the eaves. My head went light for a moment as I considered everything that needed to be done. Part of me wondered if I was doing everything the *right* way. It was a historic house with historic items inside. How would I know what was worth keeping?

I shook myself out of it and went inside. This was Gran's house—*my* house now—and she wanted me here. If she was concerned about her valuables being mishandled, she might not have abandoned them all in another country with only a grumpy old man to keep watch.

Walking slowly through the house, I skimmed over each room to see if anything in particular caught my eye. The mantel in the dining room had a few framed photos, all of them sepia. My eyes filled with tears as I recognized the wide eyes and gap-toothed grin of my grandmother. I had never seen a photo of her from youth; in my mind, she had always been old, with a perm and soft wrinkles around her eyes. But she had been a chubby baby with a full head of dark hair—what color, I couldn't be sure. Then she had been a little girl in a shapeless dress, with a curly bob haircut, arms and legs like twigs. Finally, she had been a young woman, beautiful as a movie star, her lips painted, her wild curls pushed back from her face with a ribbon.

I looked over the mantel again, but there were no photographs of a wedding. There was, however, one of a young man. He was sitting on well-kept grass, wearing what might have been either a tennis or cricket uniform—light pants, shirt, and sweater. He smiled with only his eyes at whoever was holding the camera, his face slightly blurry as if he'd been moving. The hair and eyes were dark, but there was no way to tell what color. Could this be Mr. Smith?

I carefully removed the back of the frame, hoping to find a name or date scrawled on the back, but it was blank.

A new fire was lit under me to learn more. I went upstairs to the smallest bedroom, with a mind to go through the writing desk. Bernard had boxed some things here. I tried picking one up to find it was not overly heavy. Underneath, the protected section of the rug was revealed in vibrant shades of crimson and blue. I set down the box and carefully stepped around the others. There were three drawers on either side of the desk, and one long, shallow one in the center. I tried one. Locked. Another—locked, too. Bernard's ring of keys was dangling from my belt loop. I sorted through each of them, but none were small enough to fit into the brass holes. I'd have to ask him if he knew where one might be, or have Leslie dismantle the desk. Surely, there was something important in here, maybe even something that Emilie wanted to keep secret from Dorothy . . .

In an attempt to ease the tension in my shoulders, I went downstairs and turned my eyes to the books in the living room. The shelves were built into the wall, with volumes leaned and stacked in any empty space. Some looked much older than even Emilie would have been. After blowing off dust, I pulled one down, a collection of poetry by Lord Byron. The tattered cover cracked as I opened to the first page and paused.

Inside, under the title and the author's name, was something handwritten in fountain ink.

From the library of Lady Emilie Dawes

I read it again to be sure, then flipped through the other pages, but there was no other evidence of the owner. I gently wedged the book under my arm and went for another, a novel I hadn't heard of, but there was no such inscription. I pulled three more before I stumbled upon the familiar handwriting a second time. Then a third.

A smile spread across my face. Gran hadn't been joking; she hadn't been confused in her old age. Her father may not have been a lord, but her mother was most definitely a lady.

With the books nestled against my chest, I headed for the door.

THERE WASN'T MUCH TO be found about Lady Emilie Dawes on the internet, but after scouring every inch of Wikipedia while drinking three cups of tea and polishing off every Digestive in Leslie's biscuit jar, I found her marriage.

Lady Emilie was married to a Lord Rhys Bridgmond in the spring of 1917. There were no children listed, though given Gran's birthdate, she certainly could have been the man's daughter. Neither was there mention of a divorce. Their marriage apparently ended officially when Lord Bridgmond died in the 1930s after suffering years of debilitating shell shock. There was a small note about his sister, Lady Harriet, who worked with charities to help veterans of the Great War, and was an advocate for better psychiatric care in England.

I sat back in my chair, sweeping biscuit crumbs from the keyboard. If there had been no divorce, that meant Emilie left Lord Bridgmond a few years after their marriage, just when his shell shock began to take over his life. It struck me as cruel, to leave a man when he most needed support, for something that was out of his control. I would have expected Emilie to have more empathy, considering her time spent as a nurse. Though, it explained why the locals here didn't think highly of her.

That was where the bulk of the information ended. Bridgmond's younger brothers both died in the Second World War, ending the dukedom. Their country home was lost to the expense of postwar life, and increasing death duties, and demolished in the '70s. No other family was listed, apparently no longer important enough to warrant a mention.

I stood to take my mug to the sink. It was not the story I wanted, but at least it was something. And it seemed that though the Smiths lived a quiet life in the end, there was plenty of drama in their past that may have given Gran reason to break away from her parents and leave behind the secrets she mentioned in her letter. But what exactly had caused the rift between them?

There *had* to be someone in this village who knew more—and I was willing to bet he was at home.

This time, I was confident approaching Bernard's house. Like the previous visit, his curtains were drawn, clearly hoping to keep out nosy neighbors. And nosy foreigners. Grasping Emilie's book of poetry, I lifted my hand and knocked briskly.

He took a moment to get moving, and I noticed him peek through the curtains, then hesitate before finally opening the door to poke his head out.

"Hi, Bernard!" I said, too cheerfully. "I hope I'm not disturbing you?"

If his expression was any indication, I clearly was. But he shook his head, worrying his thumb over the top of his cane. "Something wrong up at Sparrow?"

"No, nothing's wrong. I just wanted to ask you a quick question, if that's okay? I could come in for a minute . . . put the kettle on?"

"If it's quick, you can ask it from there."

That was fair. I was probably being pushy, seeing as we were strangers.

"I was wondering if you could tell me anything about Emilie, Dorothy's mother," I said. "Because I found this at the cottage, but there isn't much information about her on the internet . . ." I lifted the book. "It says Lady Emilie Dawes."

Without reaching out for it, he leaned down to see and then flicked his glassy eyes up to me. "I know how to read."

I forced an apologetic smile. Of course—if he'd been looking after a small holding, his eyesight hadn't left him.

"I know nowt about Dorothy's mum," he said.

"What about Mr. Smith?"

Bernard coughed wetly, making me cringe. It was so easy for someone of his age to come down with pneumonia. "Mr. Smith, he er . . . didn't talk much. Had an odd sort of stutter. Used to forget the names of regular things—like scissors, or the toaster."

"So you must have met. Did Dorothy ever speak of him? Or her father?"

Bernard put one foot behind him, already prepared to shut me out. It was too much at once, I could see that now. I took a step back, giving him some space.

"I were just a farmhand," he said timidly.

"Right, sorry. Just one more thing, if you don't mind?" He waited, so I went ahead: "Do you know where I might find a key to the desk drawers?"

Bernard shook his head so that his cheeks wobbled. "You have all the keys I were given." It was then that his patience ran out, and he shut the door.

I headed back toward the road, hot with frustration. Outside of the pub, there were two inviting picnic benches. A young couple sat at one, their bikes resting against the stone wall. They sipped from golden pints that I gazed at longingly until I remembered Namita. Being the barmaid at the local, she spoke to everyone—and after a couple of drinks, they might have told her a thing or two.

Steeling myself, I went inside, finding the place was mostly empty apart from a few older couples eating lunch. Namita smiled as I approached the bar, and threw down a paper coaster.

"All right, hon?" she asked. "Can I get you an orange juice?"

I was flattered that she remembered. She filled a half-pint glass and set it in front of me, and I took a sip, grateful for something cold to distract me from the line of bottles behind her.

"Are you after summat to eat?" she asked. "We've got a lovely steak and ale pie today, with chips or mash."

I shook my head and checked the bar for spills before setting the book down. "I've come for your expertise."

I gave her a quick recap, including the failed research, the VAD uniform, and the letter from a man named Isaac. She listened closely, moving away only once to refill a wineglass. She was good at her job. By the end, I could tell something I'd said had rung a bell.

"Dawes . . ." she said, playing with her earring. "I do know that name. Wouldn't have thought of it without the 'lady.' Dawes was the Earl of Ashwood—his stately home is not too far from here. One of our guests had visited and talked my ear off about the damn place. They ended up leaving behind a pamphlet on the bar, and I read it through. Slow night."

I could barely formulate words to reply, my mind was racing so fast. "You said it's nearby? What's it called?"

"Hallesham Park. There's a bus that'll take you right there from the next village. It's a National Trust property—big with day-trippers. They were up there filming *Antiques Roadshow* about this time last year. The locals went mad, packing their boots with old rubbish hoping to learn they're sitting on a fortune."

I jumped out of my seat, only half listening. Hallesham Park was another treasure trove of answers, and it sat near enough that I could be there tomorrow.

But something still didn't make sense. Emilie's home was not only standing, but open for visitors; why didn't more about her come up in my research? Why had history decidedly forgotten her?

I dug in my pocket and put three pounds on the bar—the orange juice couldn't have cost more—and gave Namita a smile. "Thank you so much. You just made this whole trip worthwhile." I began to leave, then spun again. "Oh, and have you seen Bernard in here lately?"

"I haven't, now you mention," Namita said. "He normally comes round for a ploughman's lunch and an Old Peculier."

I frowned. It was as I suspected. Something was wrong with Bernard, more than he was willing to admit. Someone was going to have to step in and help.

Twelve

Audrey

After I told him of my discovery, Leslie took the morning off work to drive us to Hallesham Park. I argued that I could get there easily by bus, but he wouldn't take no. I suggested we invite his nan, and she agreed eagerly, walking down from the house to the car with a packed lunch. We were only ten minutes out of the village when she opened a plastic container and pushed her pickle sandwiches until Leslie and I ate one each.

"We've a good bit of walking ahead of us," she said from the passenger seat. "I won't have the pair of you slowing me down with empty stomachs."

"We've both eaten breakfast, Nan," Leslie said.

She twisted in her seat to look over her shoulder at me in the back. "It were that sugary cereal, weren't it? Just because you starve yourself, doesn't mean you've got to starve the poor lass as well!"

It was not a long car journey, but I enjoyed listening to them bicker back and forth as I watched the North York Moors National Park roll by outside of the window. Leslie was as patient as he was stubborn, and it made me happy to know that, despite losing his wife and being far from his other family, he still had someone looking after him. Once in a while there was a break in the chatter as we all paused to marvel at a valley of blooming bright yellow gorse, a particularly quaint village, or a towering church ruin. I tried to imagine what it would have been like to be a young woman in 1914, to grow up here in one of the finest houses in England, to not know that perfect spring days like this would be stolen by a terrible war.

Once we turned off the road at what promised to be the entrance to Hallesham Park, I expected to see the expansive manor house come into view. Instead, there was a long stretch of dirt road through well-maintained parkland, dotted with mature trees. Leslie slowed the car as we drove over a bridge that cut across a meander of the River Rye, and I spotted the Elizabethan hunting tower on a distant hill.

I was struck by the idea that my great-grandmother's family had owned this land and everything on it. I was a tourist here, but I was also rooted to the place by blood. It was thrilling, and intimidating all at once. A hundred years seemed such a long time ago, yet these people were not far gone from this world.

The Gothic gate at the front of the manor came into view, flanked by two stone horses. A glass door was sheltered by a Palladian portico with four columns. Precise bricks of limestone glittered in the diffuse sunlight of an English morning. Cornices and balusters were blackened by lichen, almost as if the manor sat beneath a layer of dust and grime, a moody contrast to the effervescent green of the pristine lawn.

Pictures on a laptop screen could not do Hallesham Park justice. It was proud and imposing, grand and ostentatious, but it was also melancholy. What a strange contradiction, that a place that was so meticulously kept could look so completely lonely.

Leslie pulled into the small gravel car park, and a little of the magic faded as I saw the stream of other visitors with tickets in hand moving toward the house.

"Have they got a café, Les?" Nan asked as he helped her down from the Land Rover. "I could do with a brew, you know."

"We haven't even got in yet." He locked the car, offering his elbow for her to walk with, but she waved him off. "Wouldn't you like to wait until after the tour? Then we can show Audrey a proper cream tea."

"Oh, all reet."

As we neared the ticket booth, Nan shouldered both of us out of the way with her purse, insisting on paying the entrance fees. When Leslie didn't argue, I decided not to try either, and we waited to one side while she collected our tickets. I rocked up and down on my heels, eager to get inside.

"You must be buzzing," Leslie said, squinting in the sun.

"I think it's nerves, to be honest," I answered. "It's like the first time we went inside Sparrow. There's so much possibility."

Nan approached, waving our tickets, bracelets jingling on her wrist. "I've convinced the man at the till to squeeze us in the first group. Jump to it now, or they'll leave without us!"

Leslie gestured for Nan and me to lead the way, and we joined the small parade of patrons heading toward the house. We followed signs to the left where the entrance was tucked away in a cobblestone court-yard. Outbuildings that were once stables and carriage houses now housed a gift shop and café. Nan handed me a pamphlet that she had collected from the ticket booth, and I flicked through it as we waited to be let in.

Hallesham Park, as I already knew, had been the seat of the Earl of Ashwood. The title went extinct in 1919 when the twelfth earl died without an heir, and Hallesham was purchased by a wealthy business-man, whose family owned it until 1967, when it became too expensive to keep and was given over to the National Trust. This particular point worried me. If it hadn't belonged to the Daweses in the end, would there be anything left of Emilie inside?

I looked up from the pamphlet when I heard the doors opening. Though guests were let inside the house in timed groups, it wasn't a formal tour, so we were told to stay within the velvet ropes and raise any questions we had to the stewards in each room. As the crowd

funneled in, I felt a gentle hand press against the small of my back and
looked up to see Leslie beside me with his eyes on Nan, ensuring he
didn't lose either of us. I folded the pamphlet, not wanting to miss out
on any of the sites by being too focused on reading.

Nan, however, kept hers out, referencing it as we went along. "This
is one of two halls. The humbler of the pair, this would have been used
only by the family coming and going."

As my eyes adjusted to the dim interior, the scent of the outdoors
shifted to the thick, dusty air of a museum. It was difficult to imagine
the place alive with the warmth of a family, of excited chatter, of
children laughing, of heels on the stairwell. Centuries of lives had
come into the world in this place, had grown and lived and died here,
but now it was cold and impersonal.

If this hall was humble, I couldn't imagine what the other looked
like. A wide, dark wooden staircase led us up into the house, where
light poured down from a window overhead. White walls were lined
with massive oil portraits in elegant gilt frames, all of people from
bygone eras. I hurried over to a plaque that explained some things
about the room, and skimmed through the text. Not all of the paintings were original to the house, but a few had been found and returned when the Trust took over. Directly overhead was a portrait of
the first Countess of Ashwood.

I found Leslie and Nan waiting near the door to the next area,
and we all went through a string of elegantly furnished rooms—a
study, a smoking room, a billiards room, and the countess's personal
parlor. I tried to imagine why a young Lady Emilie would have left
this stately manor, with its floor-to-ceiling windows, its elegant frilled
draperies, its bronze cherubs, marble busts, and brass candelabras, for
a humble small holding. Had she felt, as I did, that she didn't fit in a
place like this?

In the library, I gazed over a mahogany desk, displayed to look
like someone had just stood up from writing a letter. This, the plaque

said, was one of a few pieces of furniture original to the house. I longed to sit in the cushioned chair, to grasp one of the brass drawer pulls and feel a connection to the people I could have called my family.

"That's her, there, aye," I heard Nan say behind me. "Audrey's the great-granddaughter of your Lady Emilie!"

She was talking to a slim older gentleman in a tie and a National Trust badge. Seeing I wasn't going to escape this without introducing myself, I pushed a piece of hair behind my ear as I crossed the room to where they stood under a window.

Nan put an arm around my back, holding me close. "I were just telling him your connection to the house, petal. He says they haven't got any portraits of our girl, I'm afraid."

"Were they sold when the earl died?" I asked the steward.

"It's difficult to say if there ever *was* a portrait of Lady Emilie," he answered, in the singsong voice of a tour guide. "We don't know a great deal about the last earl's family, but we think part of that is because his heir seemingly vanished from history, and his daughter became estranged around about the same period. The Countess of Ashwood, being widowed, went away to live with her sister, who was a spinster, so had no children of her own to pass any history to."

I found myself staring at the little poppy pin on the man's lapel, rather than into his eyes. It was a lot to process. Emilie had been estranged—that much I might have guessed, considering where she ended up. Did running away from her ailing husband have anything to do with it?

"We do get quite a few guests who claim a connection to the family," the steward added. "But if you are truly Lady Emilie's great-granddaughter, I suppose you may be the closest surviving relation to the Daweses!"

There was something about the little chuckle he shared with Nan that made it all seem so insignificant. And it was, truly. England was not a large country, and there were plenty of other ordinary people who could say they descended from noble lines.

"What do you mean his heir vanished?" I asked.

"Emilie had a brother called Fletcher. We know because his birth is written in the parish records, but no other life events were recorded for him. Lady Emilie was married to—"

"Lord Bridgmond," I finished for him.

"Quite right. The heir to the Duke of Claremont. His seat was in Northamptonshire. The Claremonts were another aristocratic family devastated by the world wars."

"Why wouldn't her brother's death have been recorded?" I asked. "Did he die in the war?"

He sighed and folded his arms over his badge. "It's likely, given what his age would have been, but his name isn't on the memorial in the village center. I'm certain there is more of the story to find, if one is willing to do a bit of digging. Ah, hello. Have you got a question, sir?"

Another guest had approached, so Nan and I stepped aside. After seeing several drawing rooms and the main dining room, we proceeded through the grand hall with its marble floors and carved stone ceiling. Then it was upstairs and through the bedrooms, each more elaborately decorated than the next. We stayed long enough for Nan to start complaining about her knees, and then we all finished the tour and went outside to find the café.

We chatted lightly over a pot of tea, while eating plump scones with a healthy dollop of clotted cream and raspberry jam. The sun was bright and warm, coloring my arms. When we were finished, Leslie suggested we take a walk through the gardens, and Nan decided she'd rather stay at the picnic table and work on a second pot of tea. Leslie brought her one, and then he and I set off.

At first, we walked in companionable silence. I knew Leslie well enough by then that I expected he wanted to talk about how I was dealing with everything. But he was patient, offering only a few anecdotes about the beauty of the roses, and the engineering used in the eighteenth century to get a fountain spewing water so high into the air. We wandered along the nature trail, dodging running children and dog walkers, and eventually found a quiet spot on the edge of one of many follies that overlooked the parkland below. It was breathtaking, and for a few minutes, all we did was sit and let the view wash over us, listening to birdsong.

Leslie pushed his hair behind his ears as the breeze brushed over us, and I smelled a hint of his cologne. We were far enough away from anyone else that I started to feel self-conscious. Being so suddenly alone with him in a place so romantic made me flustered. Maybe it was only the emotion of the day playing tricks on me, but the tightness of his shoulders made me think he was feeling the same way.

"Do you think Emilie ever came all the way up here?" I asked him.

The sound of my voice made him lean back on his hands. "I hope so. Shame to think such a lovely place might have been taken for granted."

I drew my knees up to hug against my chest. In the shade, there was still a chill in the air, but the bright afternoon promised the approach of summer. I wondered if a new family would be living at Gran's cottage by then.

"It's strange," I said. "This is probably the most incredible place I've ever been in my entire life. I expected to feel special, having a connection to it. But now that I'm here, I just miss Sparrow."

A smile crept slowly over Leslie's face. "I think I understand how you feel."

Of course. He'd gone off to the city after years of wishing he could escape the little village he was born in. London had been as thrilling as promised, but it wasn't home. It wasn't where his soul was rooted into the soil.

I moved my eyes back to the hills, like swatches of silk, the river a glossy ribbon, the copses knots of thread. Hallesham Park was not a home, but Yorkshire certainly was, and perhaps that was why Emilie had returned to it in the end. Like Leslie's tattoo, the county was inked on her heart. I couldn't imagine leaving it now that I was there. So why had Gran?

"The answers aren't here," I said. "If they exist, they're back at the cottage."

"Are you glad you saw it anyway?"

I nodded. "It's made me realize that what's important isn't how remarkable my family's history is, but that I have a history at all. Look at how much of Emilie's life was so easily forgotten once this big house was sold."

"You don't have to sell Sparrow, Auds."

I let out a long sigh. "My family and I spent a fortune on an attorney to fight for me to keep my career," I said. "I can't throw it away for an old house filled with junk."

When I looked at Leslie, he was smirking. "I reckon someone put those words in your mouth."

Rolling my eyes, I drew one leg under me to face him. "My sister," I admitted, and his smirk deepened. "But she's right. Beth and I have never gotten along, but I think—I don't know. Losing my job the way I did, I think it rattled her—and my dad. They want me to see this through, to do the responsible thing for once in my life."

"And what do *you* want?" Leslie asked.

I shook my head, unsure, and turned my eyes back to the view. A trio of deer dashed out from the trees to cross the immaculate parkland, stopping only briefly to observe a little dog from a few yards away.

There was no easy answer to Leslie's question. I knew that I once had an enormous passion for nursing. I also knew that despite that passion, my job had been so increasingly stressful that I'd self-medicated with alcohol just to find some peace at the end of the day. The very thing that once gave me a reason to be alive was killing me. It terrified me to think of returning to it, but what else could I do? My career had been my entire life. Losing it was like losing myself. Choosing not to return to it meant becoming a whole new person—

the person I was without it. If that person even existed. I wished desperately that Gran had been present enough to give me some direction in her letter. What I wouldn't have given to know what she wanted me to find here.

With that thought, I jumped to my feet, not wishing to linger any further on my feelings. We headed back down the hill and found Nan happily chatting to the same steward as before. Apparently she'd shared her pot of tea.

On the drive back to Langswick, I couldn't stop thinking about how Sparrow Cottage, the very essence of it, had wrapped itself around my heart. Seeing Hallesham in such contrast had made me love Sparrow even more. I couldn't stand the thought of its history being forgotten the way Hallesham's was, even if the people living inside were ordinary. Gran hadn't kept it all those years for nothing— I may not have known anything else, but that truth I felt in my gut.

After we dropped off Nan, I leaned forward to ask Leslie to take me to Bernard's house.

"What do you reckon you're going to accomplish there?" he asked.

"I don't have time to go scouring through each and every room of the house before I sell it—there's just too much stuff. If I want real answers, I'm going to need his help to whittle it down."

Leslie tapped his thumbs on the steering wheel. "How are you going to convince him?"

"Kindness. And bribery."

We stopped off for a few bottles of Theakston Old Peculier, and then for a massive helping of fish and chips, and a battered sausage for good measure. It was still warm in my lap when we arrived at Bernard's little house, making Leslie's car smell like a deep-fat fryer.

"Best of British to you, flower," Leslie said. "If he doesn't answer, leave the beer on the doorstep and bring the chips back to the house, reet?"

I gave him a wry look and climbed down from the car. "Don't linger—he really doesn't like you."

Leslie lovingly raised his middle finger to me and put the car in reverse.

As I approached, I could see a light on in the cracks between the curtains, and, cradling the beers in one arm, gave a knock. Like the last time, Bernard took a moment to appear at the window, where he had a peek at me before coming to unlock the door. A laugh track from the TV leaked out into the evening, and he scowled, still leaning on his cane.

"I told you, I've no key," he said.

I raised the bag of food. "I remembered you said you had a fall, so I thought I would bring you dinner. It probably isn't easy to get around the kitchen, is it?"

Bernard tightened his mouth and looked down at his cane. He was definitely favoring one leg. "I've already had my tea."

I raised the beers, thinking for a moment how ridiculous it was to be holding them. Earlier in the day, I might have left Leslie, walked around the corner, and cracked one open. Now, though, I was back in control. Tempting as the beers were, I knew this would all be worth it if I could convince Bernard to open up.

"Namita told me this is your favorite," I said. "Would you like one?"

I waited anxiously, watching Bernard check behind him, as if to decide whether or not the interiors of his house were worthy of guests. Then, after a sigh, he opened the door wide.

"Come through, then. Take off those mucky shoes."

I obliged, padding through the foyer in my socks.

"Mind the step as you come," he said, and grunted as he went down into a small kitchen.

There was something wrong with his gait, and when we sat down together at his kitchen table, I realized what it was. Even the smell of the greasy fish and chips could not mask the odor of infection.

Bernard opened one of the beers and offered it to me, but I politely declined, too focused on his injury to explain. While he poured the beer into a pint glass, I wondered how to ask him about it without insulting him. If he had an open, infected wound, he could already be ill, and at his age, a fever could be his end.

"You favor her," he said.

My head shot up. "Sorry?"

"Your grandmother. I didn't notice the first time you came round."

Even after seeing Gran's photographs at Sparrow, I hadn't thought we looked alike, but it was a compliment, and it made me feel close to her.

"What is it you've come for, then?" Bernard poked at the bag of food. "I know you ain't really here to feed me—not when that pillock Whiting's involved."

"Leslie has nothing to do with this."

"Aye, but his big, noisy car were outside." Clearly, ninety-one years had not affected the man's hearing. "Ruddy nuisance, that lad is."

"I came to ask you about what you put into the boxes at Sparrow," I said. "I wondered if there's anything inside of them that could help me understand why my grandmother left so suddenly. Maybe some photo albums? Or journals? Something like that?"

Another wordless grumble as he went digging in the bag and fished out a chip. He inspected it before taking a bite, then popped the whole thing in his mouth to chew and wash down with a glug of Theakston's.

"I can't remember what I put in there," he answered.

I watched Bernard investigate the battered sausage and tried to think of a way to get through to him. There had to be something remaining of his time at Sparrow as a boy, especially if he saw Gran's face in mine. He had to know something; he just wasn't saying.

Bernard scraped his chair back, and he reached for his cane.

"Can I get something for you?" I asked, standing before he was out of his chair. "Do you need a plate? Or a napkin?"

"Bah!" Bernard waved his hand at me, but when he tried to get up, he winced, and with a little whimper, fell back into his chair heavily.

I wasn't going to sit by and watch a man live in pain when something could be done about it. There was a reason he hadn't been to

Sparrow or the pub; he couldn't get around outside the house if he tried, and I was glad he hadn't.

I knelt on the floor and tentatively reached for the leg of Bernard's slacks before withdrawing. I wasn't in a hospital now. He didn't know me, so I would have to gain his trust.

"I'm a nurse," I told him. "I smell infection, and that's not good. Did you cut yourself, Bernard?"

He let his hand fall into his lap, fingers curling into a tight fist that spoke of the pain he was feeling. "I were just puttering about in the back garden, like I do every morning. But I lost me balance and caught my ankle on summat. It didn't bother me much at the start. Now, though . . ." He shrugged.

"Do you mind if I take a look? I can get it cleaned up and tell you whether or not you'll need to see a doctor"—I could see him beginning to complain—"and you *will* need to see a doctor for antibiotics if it's too far gone."

Bernard looked hard at me, and after a moment, the wrinkles around his eyes smoothed as if he was about to smile. Instead, he reached for his beer and gave me a nod. "There's a first aid kit beneath the sink."

I fetched the kit and brought him a plate, napkin, and the bottle of malt vinegar from a cupboard he pointed out to me. Then I washed my hands, knelt again at his knee, and carefully rolled up the leg of his trousers. I pulled on rubber gloves before drawing down Bernard's sock and finding the root of the problem.

He had covered the wound haphazardly with three large adhesive bandages, but it didn't look to have been changed within the last few days. I didn't have to wonder why he'd been neglecting it—the ankle was not exactly the easiest place for a man of his age to bend and reach, and given he was wearing slip-on shoes, it was a problem for him. Peeling away the soiled bandages, I braced against the familiar, mousy odor and examined the wound.

Whatever caught on his ankle hadn't been sharp. The skin tear was surrounded by bruising, and though inflamed and warm to the touch, it didn't have any dirt or debris stuck to it. Elderly people tended toward poor circulation, and with a weaker immune system, Bernard wasn't going to see such a wound healed this way.

"Will it need to be stitched?" he asked.

"Sutures would only cause more damage," I said. "We need to get this cleaned up and dressed properly—then the skin will adhere itself into place."

Bernard wrinkled his nose and pushed away his plate of fish. I couldn't blame him. The wound wasn't the most pleasant thing to look at. But the sight of it was filling me with adrenaline. There was great satisfaction in looking at a patient, identifying the problem, and knowing precisely how to fix it. I felt a tug of regret as I stood to get a bowl of warm water.

Bernard watched as I worked to gently clean the wound.

"Do you have any children of your own?" I asked. Good bedside manner could earn the trust of the fussiest patient and distract from uncomfortable treatments.

Bernard took a sip of beer and shook his head. "I never married."

"How long have you lived here?"

"Me whole life."

"That long?" I began using a cotton swab to clean the wound. "When did you start working at Sparrow?"

"When the war began, the Ministry encouraged people to grow their own produce to supplement rations. I were only sixteen, too young to be called up, so Mrs. Smith asked me on to help with their crop. All the other men in the village had gone."

The story was simple, but gave me vivid images of wartime Britain. Sparrow was beginning to come to life in my mind, to breathe deeply and bat its eyelashes.

"Mrs. Smith were a nurse in the Great War," Bernard added.

Keeping my eyes on the film dressing I was opening, I nodded. "That's right. I found her VAD uniform."

"Dorothy wanted to go across and do the same. But her mum wouldn't allow her."

"Why?"

"Said it were too dangerous."

"I wouldn't have thought they'd let women anywhere they could get hurt. Then again, I don't know much about VADs . . ."

I returned to my task, hoping he might elaborate, and carefully dried the skin with clean gauze. I held the flap against the wound and applied the film bandage to hold it in place. Since the dressing was transparent, Bernard could easily check if things were looking all right, and if we were lucky, the body would do the rest of the job. I sat back on my haunches as he leaned over to inspect my work.

"Does that feel okay?" I asked. "Not too tight?"

"Aye. Ta, lovey."

I smiled and slowly got to my feet, stepping backward from a whiff of beer coming from Bernard's glass. "Try not to scratch it or get the bandage wet. If you want, I can come back tomorrow and check on it. We'll probably need to change it again."

Bernard nodded silently, not agreeing or disagreeing. I knew better than to push.

"Will you have a cuppa?" he asked.

Glad as I was for the offer, I declined. I needed to get back to Leslie's house and start making plans for Sparrow. Bernard wanted to walk me to the door, so I helped him to his feet and walked beside him as he hobbled on his cane, silently wishing he had someone else living with him. Another fall could do a lot worse than a skin tear.

At the door, Bernard tapped his cane against the ground and formed what was his idea of a smile. It made me sad to think he may have forgotten how to do it properly—to allow himself to show joy. I would come back tomorrow, whether he wanted me to or not. He had been important to Gran, and now he was just as important to me.

"I'll see you around, Bernard," I said, and started down the path to the road.

"Er, hang on a minute—"

I took a hopeful breath. Bernard reached out one liver-spotted hand, his crooked first finger pointing at something that wasn't there.

"There are plastic file boxes in the old larder," he said. "I put all the papers in there—anything might get ruined." He paused, moving the finger to his brow, which he scratched thoughtfully. "Perhaps you might find what you're looking for in those."

I let out a long breath of relief. "Thank you, Bernard. You've been really helpful."

Thirteen

Audrey

With my jacket draped over my head, I dashed from Leslie's Land Rover under rainfall, splashing through muddy puddles in my new Wellington boots. At the cottage's front door, I fumbled with the keys as my jeans soaked through. When the door was unlocked, I let my jacket fall to the floor in time to see Leslie coming up the path.

I huffed, adjusting my damp clothing. Patrick, my estate agent, was on his way, and I had wanted to look presentable. Now I was splotched with wet spots, my hair sagging, mascara dribbling down my cheeks. So much for first impressions.

Leslie came bounding through the door, shutting it behind him. Though he was smart enough to use an umbrella, he looked as disheveled as me. It somehow worked in his favor, making his T-shirt cling.

"Welcome to Yorkshire." He laughed. "We had you spoiled with those first few days of sun, didn't we?"

I pushed my wet hair behind my ears. "I'm glad we got that window covered."

"Aye. I just hope it holds."

In the kitchen, Leslie began to unpack the tote he was carrying, with electric kettle, bottled water, milk, and sleeve of biscuits. "Cup of tea? No doubt Patrick will want one when he arrives."

"Sure, thanks," I said, looking around for the pantry. "I want to find those boxes Bernard mentioned. I know there isn't time to get into them right now, but I'm dying to see what's inside. I'm hoping there might be a bill or something with Smith's first name on it."

Leslie opened the biscuits, spilling crumbs down his front. "That reminds me. I hope it's okay, but I gave Emilie's brother's name to Matt. He'll go down to the National Archives and have a look."

"You didn't have to do that. I'm sure I could have found something on the internet."

Leslie waved me off. "He likes that sort of stuff. Last year, he was laid up after a knee surgery and ended up using his leave to trace our lineage."

"Let me guess—you're Guy Fawkes's great-great-grandson?"

"Nothing of the sort, I'm afraid. And I'm not sure that's enough *great*s."

"Well, I was never very good at math."

We smiled at each other, and I felt a larger-than-normal flutter in my stomach, so turned pointedly to return to my search. There were two large double doors in the cabinetry that had to be the pantry. Inside were a breadbox, a half dozen ceramic jugs and jars, and more pickled onions and beets. Beneath the higher shelves was a stack of pots and mixing bowls, and beside them, the file boxes Bernard had mentioned. There were three total. I brought them out of the pantry to set on the kitchen table.

Bernard hadn't bothered with hanging folders, instead stacking papers up from the bottom, with no apparent organization. I took a deep breath, reminding myself not to get too overwhelmed. I was closer now than I had ever been—I just needed a few hours to dig in.

There was a knock at the door before I could open the second box. Leslie went to the door to let Patrick in, and I set the boxes under the table for later.

Despite the weather, Patrick wore a full suit and tie, and shook each of his dress shoes out on the rug before handing Leslie his umbrella. He had the typical close haircut and shiny, clean-shaven jaw of a real estate agent. As I waited to be introduced, he commented on how lucky Leslie was to be able to go to work in jeans.

"A perk of the trade, I suppose," Leslie answered. He was clipping his words more than usual, and I wondered how much his demeanor changed around colleagues and clients. Was this the man he had been in London? "Patrick, this is Audrey, the owner."

Patrick shook my hand firmly. "Pleased to meet you at last. Leslie talks so enthusiastically about this old place, I've been so looking forward to seeing it myself." His eyes trailed from me up the hallway. "Good God, it hasn't changed at all, has it?"

Leslie and I exchanged a smile, proud as ever of Sparrow, but Patrick was skeptical. He studied the worn stone floors, the dusty drapes, and probably smelled the damp in the air.

"Right, shall we give you the tour?" Leslie said, pressing a comforting hand to my back. "Straight through is the kitchen, Pat; mind your head."

The tea was distributed, and I was happy to allow Leslie to do the talking. He fell easily into his role and was good at his job—pointing out fine details that I wouldn't notice, and things that would attract new buyers, like the access to the walking trail from the back garden, and the potential to expand the kitchen into a conservatory like his own.

Next, we went into the living room, where Leslie suggested installing a modern wood-burning stove in the fireplace, while maintaining the charm of the stonework surround.

"It's characterful, I'll give it that," Patrick said, facing the interior wall. "Can this come down? There has got to be a natural flow between kitchen and reception rooms."

I lifted a hand to smooth over the striped wallpaper, trying to imagine it gone, and found it too difficult.

"It isn't the right sort of house for open-plan living," Leslie said, to my relief. "I find that isn't as popular as it once was—plenty of new buyers are looking to keep their rooms separate, everything with its own purpose."

Patrick was shaking his head. "It's too broken up, and the kitchen will be a tough sell at that size unless I can promise the buyer there is a way to make space for a dining table."

"You saw there's a lovely farm table in the kitchen—"

"Which makes it impossible to move about, and if you're looking to install an island, you'll lose the seating. Parents want to be able to see their children playing in the next room whilst stirring the bread sauce . . ."

I worried Leslie might back down from Patrick's insistence, but though he remained calm and polite, he had a rebuttal for every argument. As we moved into the dining room, Leslie explained how it could be used as the lounge, as it was larger, while the current snug could house a small table. He had me sold, obviously, but there were still problems in Patrick's eyes—the low beams, which would eliminate any tall buyers who didn't wish to duck through their doorways; the lack of space for a ground-floor loo; and the arrangement of the bedrooms.

"I don't see how one could manage to add a family bath without losing a bedroom," Patrick said in the largest of them.

"That's why I'm the builder and you're the salesman." Leslie was standing beside the French windows, clearly hoping Patrick would take note of the view.

Patrick set his hands on his hips and moved across the creaking floors to duck for a glance at the meadow beyond. Then he straightened and sighed as he took one final look at the room. I stood in one corner, holding an old clock that had sat on the bedside, wondering how many mornings it rang to wake whoever had slept here to get on with their chores. Lady Emilie had given up her four-poster bed and damask curtains for this iron frame and humble quilt. Had she let baby Dorothy slumber beside her in the late mornings?

Patrick stepped away from the window to look at his phone. In the meantime, Leslie caught my eye, his expression hopeful.

"Best view in the county," he said.

Patrick did a little laugh. "Right view, wrong location."

"What do you mean?" I asked. "It's a beautiful village, and the pub is only a fifteen-minute walk . . ."

"Don't get me wrong," Patrick replied. "The village is idyllic—and the cottage is a chocolate box. But there's no primary school, no bus that comes to the high street, and the nearest rail is nearly an hour away."

"We're within the Howardian Hills Area of Outstanding Natural Beauty," Leslie put in. "The next market town is only six miles and has loads of places to eat in . . ."

Patrick shook his head. "Langswick isn't convenient enough to draw young families, but pensioners won't want so much house and land to look after. You're seeking a very specific buyer, even if you added all the mod cons. I've seen similar properties sit on the market for eighteen months to two years. It won't even be livable until the plumbing is run through."

My gut clenched, and with it, the light began to close around me. As my heart sped, I excused myself downstairs to the kitchen. Trying to draw even breaths, I began to ground myself, noticing things: the creak in the floor under my boots, the sound of the sparrows nested in the eve, a dust bunny tucked under the oven.

To busy my hands, I filled the kettle again and set it to boiling. The men's voices began to fill the foyer, and then the front door opened. Leslie was seeing Patrick out, and with that, I breathed easier. He came into the kitchen by the time the water was done, and I poured us both a cup without asking him if he wanted another. Warmth radiated from my mug to the palms of my hands and spread up to my elbows. My vision widened, and finally, the panic subsided.

"Patrick's heading back to the office to look at some comparative properties," Leslie said, "and he'll let us know what he thinks the house is worth. Not the first time I've been glad to see the back of that man. But he's a bloody good salesman."

I stared down into my tea, picking at one of the knife marks in the wood countertop. "Is he right?"

Leslie rubbed his jaw, creating a shushing sound with his whiskers. "I wish I could tell you there's a perfect buyer out there just waiting to get their hands on a place like this. But we're up against it. If you decide to do the updates, you'll make more money, but it would delay the sale."

There was no easy way out of this, and now it seemed silly that I ever imagined there could be. I didn't have the time for renovations, but I also shuddered at the thought of tearing up the remains of Gran's past. It was getting more difficult every day to imagine letting it go.

As I cleared the mugs and wiped up a spill of milk, I could feel Leslie's eyes on me. He took the mugs to the sink and bumped my shoulder with the back of his hand. "I know this has been difficult for you, but you're not alone, mate."

I tilted my head in his direction. His arms were folded across his chest, accentuating the lean muscle. I wondered, momentarily, what he would do if I reached out, leaned into him. Would he wrap himself around me? Would he press a kiss against my hair?

There was no use letting myself fall into Leslie Whiting.

"Have you considered keeping the house?" he asked.

I nodded. "I imagine I would, if I was on firm ground, but the timing is all wrong. My waiting period is up in a few weeks, which means I can renew my license and finally get back to work."

His face looked earnest and serene. I knew he wanted me to keep Sparrow because he wanted to continue working on it. But he didn't understand the weight on my shoulders.

"I understand you've got a life to return to," he said, though there was something in his tone that read *skeptical*.

"My old life," I replied, and the corner of Leslie's mouth turned up.

Either I was terrible at hiding my emotions, or Leslie was a mind reader. In any case, I knew then that he understood my situation better than anyone else had, or could. He understood, because he had already been faced with the same conflict I'd been struggling with for months: Would I continue to pursue the life I *should* want, or the one I *actually* wanted?

I thought of the hearing again, the ill-fitting blazer, the bad perfume. I'd fidgeted in my hard plastic chair, trying to ignore the part of me that was hoping the board would end my career so that I didn't have to decide myself that it no longer suited me.

I turned from the sink, throwing the dish towel over my shoulder. "Do you think, realistically, there's some way for me to keep it? To stay here?"

"Well, the cottage is yours, ain't it?"

"Yeah, but it's way too big for one person to live in—and you know how costly maintenance can be."

"You wouldn't have to live in it alone. Houses like Sparrow are often made into bed-and-breakfasts or holiday lets. You could convert the outbuildings, add more rooms. Set up caravans, or glamping tents . . ."

The idea was overwhelming. The last thing I needed was to think about running a business on top of everything else. Leslie wasn't the one who had to deal with the stress of it all—he just wanted to see Sparrow thriving again.

I had a lot to think about, but right now my heart was thundering, and I had to move my mind away from it before I panicked again.

"Anyway"—I threw my towel down on the counter—"for now I have to go and check on Bernard's leg."

Leslie uncrossed his arms, slipping his hands into his pockets. "It's very sweet what you're doing for him."

"I'm just doing my job."

He looked at me, and I could tell there was something more he wanted to say, but he decided to keep it to himself.

Instead, he reached out, almost as if he was going to give me a friendly pat on the back. He smoothed his palm gently across my shoulders, and up to briefly pinch at the nape of my neck, giving me shivers I hoped he couldn't feel. He lingered there, even as I trailed his arm with my eyes, all the way up to his, offering a silent invitation.

I knew it would only make leaving England all the more difficult.

But if I couldn't get lost in the oblivion of a bottle, I wanted to allow myself the pleasure of sinking into Leslie. To be swept up in a kiss, a touch, a whisper . . .

But after another breath, his hand fell away, following my spine until he let it drop altogether. He adjusted the hem of his shirt and grabbed his car keys. I understood his hesitancy; there was every chance that sex would make it awkward to share his home for the duration of my stay. He might have even been reluctant to get involved with someone so unstable when he had just gotten his own life on track.

It was the right choice, though it didn't prevent me from being disappointed.

As we headed out the front door, I remembered the file boxes under the table and ran back to get them, feeling a ghostly tickle on the back of my neck as I removed the precious articles from their mausoleum.

Fourteen

Emilie
LONDON
SPRING 1915

It had all happened rather swiftly. One moment, Emilie was sneaking away from home with a single case bound for London, the next she was sitting in a fine restaurant, being handed a glimmering diamond ring.

"Yes," she had told Rhys, and he had smiled.

Yes, she would have his ring. But no, she would not be marrying him.

Lord Bridgmond had been reluctant to part ways with her in front of the Savoy, wishing to escort her back to her lodgings. He did not know that she'd been staying at the Thurstons' own flat, where the dowager had welcomed her warmly and offered her Isaac's empty bedroom before she could ask to spend the night. Emilie had explained little of her intentions, but somehow Lady Thurston had understood. They had once talked of independence, and the dowager knew how important it was to Emilie.

From the Savoy, Emilie had gone directly to the pawnshop. She had never been inside of one before, but adrenaline pumped through her veins as she set the diamond ring on the counter and waited to be handed a stack of banknotes in return. She wanted it out of her hands quickly, before she had too much time to think on the significance of what she was doing.

The War Office had declared that VADs would now be permitted to work overseas in military hospitals, and Emilie happened to be fluent in French. She saw this as her one chance to break completely away from her restrictive old life, and would take hold of it firmly.

She wrote to Isaac, with a smile on her face, *I have done it! I am an uncaged bird prepared to spread her wings for the very first time. I cannot yet devise whether the racing in my chest is fear or excitement, but the sensation is indeed a refreshment.*

All had gone well, and she was sure she'd gotten away with it until one afternoon, after purchasing her VAD uniform from Garrould's in Edgware Road, she returned to the flat to find Lady Thurston had a caller. Another man in khaki, but to her upset, he was not Isaac.

He was Fletcher.

As pleased as she was to see him after so many months, Emilie could not be glad. For as he stood and turned to face her, his lips pressed into a thin line and she knew what he had come to speak to her about. He wanted to convince her to go home—to stop playing her silly little games and obey their parents' wishes. But she had never felt this in her life, to be on her own, to be independent, to make her own choices. *Finally.* Her brother could not ruin that now.

"Emilie," he said. "Lady Thurston has been kind enough to offer her parlor to us for a few moments. I believe we have some things to discuss?"

Emilie backed out of the room, pulling her coat back on. "Actually, I was just on my way out—"

She had made it as far as the lift before Fletcher caught her elbow. Emilie whined and wrenched like she had when they bickered as children. "I've already accepted a post in France. There is nothing you can say to convince me to go back home."

Fletcher huffed through his nose, squeezing her elbow tighter.

"Why did you not do this properly? I am more than sure Mama would be happy to send you off to do your bit."

"She would *not*," Emilie spat. "You weren't there. You cannot imagine the things they said to me, how little they think of their own daughter."

"We all argue with our parents, Emilie."

"They never argue with you—their precious heir. You may do precisely as you like."

The lift doors opened, and as the operator smiled at them, Fletcher let Emilie's elbow slip from his grip. Fletcher lifted his hand to the small of her back, gently pushing her into the lift before she had a chance to slip away. They rode in silence to the ground floor, where Fletcher continued to usher Emilie through the lobby and out the door.

It was bitingly cold, and Emilie had not had the chance to grab her hat. She lifted her shoulders in a sad attempt to warm her ears, until Fletcher removed his greatcoat and draped it over her shoulders. The wool was still warm from his body—he had not taken it off inside the flat, perhaps not expecting he would be staying long.

Emilie watched as he donned his peaked cap, looking every bit the officer. His breaths puffed in heavy clouds as he checked that the pavement was clear of onlookers.

"I sincerely hope you are not here to see Thurston," he said.

"Isaac is training, as you should be. I doubt I shall see him before I embark."

The sound of that did not please Fletcher as she expected. Instead, his brows tilted downward. "You are truly going to France?"

"Please say you are proud of me, duck."

Fletcher's mouth opened as though he was going to release a snide remark. Instead, his cheeks raised into a smile. "Of course I am. Only I wish you were not so dangerously impulsive. What will you do after the war? Do you expect our parents will so easily allow you to return home after what you've done?"

He did not know the half of it. Emilie had convinced Rhys not to announce their engagement. Fletcher had no idea of her true intentions, had no notion she had accepted a proposal from his best friend and pawned the ring in order to buy aprons and oversleeves.

"I told you I shall not be returning home," Emilie said.

"And where will you go instead, here?" He nodded his head up toward the Thurstons' flat as though it were the most absurd idea one might have.

"I cannot marry Rhys. Forgive me, I know he is your friend, but I will not be trapped in this life against my will."

"You would prefer to be trapped in a life of poverty?"

Emilie scoffed. "What do you know of poverty?"

"I know that Thurston is penniless. Does he know if he marries you, you will not come with a dowry?"

His words hurt Emilie as much as they made her angry. Fletcher sounded just as their parents had. Why could they not believe she was worthy of being loved?

"Isaac will have money enough to look after us," she said, but her resolve was thinning by the second.

"What will he do?" Fletcher asked.

"Work, I suppose."

"And what will *you* do?"

Emilie was unsure, but answered as confidently as she could, "I shall work as well."

Fletcher laughed at her. "You wish to marry him for freedom, do you not? But what you do not understand is that marriage, no matter to whom, will make you a *wife*. Isaac will expect you to be his wife as much as any man does—to be a mother to his children, to keep his house. I don't care how modern he believes himself to be, you will be bound just the same. So pray, bind yourself to someone who has something to offer you in return."

Emilie wrinkled her chin, watching a motor pass on the road. She could not think why everyone was so concerned with the matters of her heart when there was a war on. Would it be so simple to appease them? If she left for home tomorrow, wrote to Rhys that she was his forever, forgot the Thurstons, and shifted her ambitions to being a duchess, would there be a great and sudden peace in the world? Emilie was so insignificant. She was reminded each day when she read the names of the dead in the newspaper of how little a single human life meant to the universe, how time would continue to trudge on, how easily a soul was forgotten.

She thought of meeting Isaac for the first time, of dancing shyly in a London ballroom. If only she had known then that one day she would end up here, arguing over him on the pavement in front of his own flat while he trained for battle. She had liked him then, so very much. As she did now. But would she have followed his path? Or forged her own?

Fletcher was waiting for an answer. His nose was pink from the cold, and his leather gloves were wrapped tightly in fists at his sides.

"I shall not deny Isaac for status and fortune," Emilie said at last. "And I shall not lose myself in order to please my family."

She expected Fletcher might groan, roll his eyes, or throw up his arms. As stoic as he was in his role as heir to an earldom, he had a temper, and she had seen him lose it more than once.

Instead, he let out a long, exasperated breath. "Then you shall lose your brother."

Emilie blinked, not believing his words. "You would turn your back on me so easily? For seeking happiness?"

"I would turn my back on you, Emilie, because you are thinking only of yourself."

Hot tears blurred her eyes, and she pinched them with her lids, letting them run down her icy cheeks. Of all the blows she had been dealt, this was the hardest. She tried to conjure the courage she had used to leave Hallesham Park, but found herself wanting. Her brother had always been the most important person in her life. Without him, would she be able to go on?

Then Emilie thought of the VAD uniform she had purchased earlier that day, thought of the lessons she had learned in her courses, and all the brilliant things she knew now that she wouldn't if she had not believed in herself. Perhaps she could learn to survive without her brother.

"So be it, then," she said, and threw Fletcher's coat off her shoulder. He called her name, but she refused to look back.

WHEN EMILIE HEARD ISAAC'S voice in the foyer, she threw the sock she'd been knitting and ran straight into him, knocking her cheek on the cold buckle of his Sam Browne belt. Isaac startled at first, then eased into the embrace, holding her fiercely with desperate strength that made her bones go to jelly. She buried her face in his shoulder, breathing the new scents and the familiar.

Behind them, Emilie heard the thump of Lady Thurston's cane. "A notice would have been welcome," the dowager said. "We haven't got a bed for you, dear boy."

Isaac chuckled, his chest shaking against Emilie's. "Don't worry yourself. I am well accustomed to sleeping without one these days."

Emilie released him, stepping back to have a look. Had Isaac always been so frightfully striking? He wasn't the scrawny boy she had met, but a man, rigid and stout, his hair shorn so that it no longer curled. She felt his presence all over her body—crawling up her arms, slithering down her spine, twisting in her gut. It was all she could do not to take his chin in her hand and kiss him thoroughly.

"Damn, is it good to see your face," Isaac said, his voice a sonata.

Emilie found she was strangely shy to reply, standing before the man she had longed for, but had only exchanged letters with over six long months. "Why did you not tell us you were coming?"

"I thought I would surprise you." He addressed the dowager next. "Both of you."

Lady Thurston huffed, shaking her head at him. "At my age, too great of a surprise could be the death of me."

"You are right, of course. All the same, might I trouble you for a cup of tea? I'm utterly gasping."

He hurried to plant a loving kiss on his granny's cheek, and then the maid brought tea. Emilie smiled her way through it, staring at Isaac as though he might vanish at any moment. Saying goodbye to Fletcher—to *anyone*—was worthwhile if she could keep this man beside her always. He was so clever and handsome, and best of all, kind. Isaac Thurston was wonderful, and he looked at Emilie as if she was wonderful, too.

Once they were finished, Lady Thurston excused herself to lie down in her room, trusting the two of them to remain alone together as Emilie's own mother never would. Isaac suggested a walk in Kensington Gardens, and though the weather was brisk, the sun was shining, so Emilie agreed. She savored the chance to let Isaac tuck her hand under his arm. For once, she did not worry if someone she knew might see her, a woman promised to Lord Bridgmond, on the elbow of another man. This might be the last time she saw Isaac. It was worth the risk.

At first, they had little to say. Lady Thurston had led the conversation over tea, and Isaac, ever the storyteller, went on and on about training. Now that they finally had a moment to speak privately, Emilie was finding it difficult to put two words together. She knew she ought to tell him about Rhys, about how she had jilted him, but wondered if it would change his opinion of her. Instead, she chose a much safer topic.

"Have you brought me any more of your novel to read? I'm desperate to spend time with Captain Ridley."

His deep blue eyes moved glumly across the park. "I'm afraid there isn't much new to share." Emilie gave his arm a rub. When he looked over at her with such sincerity, she stopped breathing. "I've missed you."

All at once, they had the same idea. Isaac slipped his arm out of their hold and took Emilie's hand, leading her off the gravel path and away from the pond to where the trees grew closer together. Another few paces and they might have been completely alone. Isaac rounded on her until her back was against the rough bark of a sweet chestnut, and she laughed, giddy from the run and their closeness. Tilting her head, she removed his leather gloves one by one, letting them fall to their feet, and brought his newly rough knuckles to her lips, smelling his last cigarette.

They were both greedy for air, and before long, Emilie could not tell which warm breaths were his and which were hers, but what filled her lungs was sweet and intoxicating. Isaac tipped forward, and his lips brushed the space beneath Emilie's ear, whispering her name against the prickling flesh. She let out a stuttering sigh.

Then she was kissing him.

The heat of his mouth was a pleasant shock as it fell open to hers. The sensation was so enormous, so fulfilling, Emilie could hardly breathe. There was no shame with Isaac, no fear. She fell into him like a soft bed already warmed by another body, slipping ever further under . . .

Then all at once, his hands fell away, his face drew back, and Emilie was left cold and frustrated, her heart thundering in her ears.

"What's the matter?" she asked.

Isaac wiped his mouth with finger and thumb. "If any more of that continues I may forget myself."

The notion flooded Emilie's sensibility and she released her grip on his lapel. A quick glance revealed no passersby had seen them. But what if they had? Emilie giggled again, drunk on danger. What was the matter with her? In the last few months she had completely lost herself to the intense thrill of misbehaving.

"Is it not strange to think how little time we've spent with one another?" she asked breathlessly. "I feel as though I've known you all my life."

"We have exchanged enough letters for a lifetime," he said.

"But don't stop!"

"Never." Isaac smirked, and dropped a kiss on her brow that was somehow more intimate than what they had been doing moments ago. Then he went quiet, resting his head on Emilie's as they allowed their pulses to find a gentle rhythm.

"Em—? I must ask you something," he said.

Emilie's stomach clenched as all the warmth drained from her body. There was no doubt what he would say next, and that he would be unhappy with her response.

Isaac took her hands in his and gripped them tight. "I hoped for better circumstances. I wanted to do things properly—call on your father to ask for his permission—but I daresay he will not give it. Not now."

The claw of dread bored into Emilie's stomach. "Isaac—"

"May I finish? I cannot offer you a title, and I understand that my—my background may mark you and our children. But I *can* promise never to own you, never to put you in a cage—only to cherish and adore you. Emilie—" He drew a sharp breath. She had never seen him so ruffled and unsure; it only made her feel worse. "Emilie, will you be my wife?"

Even having anticipated the words, she felt the sharp blow of them, and remembered her conversation with Fletcher. She had been so sure then, as she had been sure only this morning that Isaac could have her life. Now, faced with this question yet again, she could feel only anxiety and fear.

"Oh, Isaac, no . . ." she said, "please don't ask it of me . . ." Emilie swallowed fast before any tears could get the better of her and kissed Isaac quick on the tense line of his mouth. "I have only just won my independence. I could not be a wife and a nurse."

"You may do as you please; I will not stop you. I am in love with you, Emilie."

"And I love *you*, my boy!"

"Then is it something else? My reputation? Money?"

"No! No, darling." She cupped his cheek in her hand. "Your intentions are noble, but you do not truly want this. You would never have asked if your life was not in danger."

Isaac's face pinched into a sickly grimace. She waited for him to deny it, but he held her eyes fiercely. "It is true I have every chance of being killed in this war and there is no nobler death. So why chastise me for preferring to be buried with your ring on my finger?"

"Bless you—you are a romantic, and I swear to you that I am entirely yours. But I do not wish to be a widow already at twenty-two."

Isaac was stiff and blank-faced, his heart lying broken at his feet. Emilie's doing. She put her arms around him again and he allowed himself to be held. She could have easily wept, but some instinct was keeping her pain buried deep. It was Isaac who was grieving now, Isaac who needed comforting.

"Forgive me," Emilie whispered. "Please, please forgive me."

His arms tightened around her with reckless strength. "I'm afraid I'll lose you to him."

Emilie knew now that Isaac must learn of what she had done to Rhys, must be assured she had no intentions of marrying another man. So she rehashed the scene, the fine restaurant, the velvet box with a diamond inside. He listened quietly, that dent between his brows darkening. Of course he was now wondering if Emilie cared so little about him. If she was capable of real love—or as Fletcher had said, only thinking of herself.

"So you see," Emilie said, "I have lately fought my way out of one marriage. It would be unfair to myself to leap straight into another— even if I do love the man with all my heart."

Isaac was clever and full of empathy—if anyone could understand her reasoning, it was him. He softly kissed his way over her cheek to her lips, lingering there long enough as to nearly convince Emilie she had made the wrong choice.

Their mouths separated with an exhale.

"Let us wait until this dreadful war is over," Emilie said. "Let us wait until we are older and are absolutely sure that both of our lives will be improved by a wedding."

"Are you so certain it's the right thing?"

"I am certain of nothing any longer."

In Isaac's silence, he agreed.

The next morning, when they said their goodbyes at Charing Cross, Emilie stood outside of his carriage, and they held hands through the open window as she tried to draw his features in her mind. When the train began to move, Emilie walked beside it, suddenly desperate.

"We shall see one another again," she said.

"Perhaps I shall end up under your care, Nurse Dawes. What heaven that would be."

Emilie dared not even acknowledge how frightened the idea made her.

It became more difficult to keep up with the train, and they were running out of platform. Emilie gave Isaac a chaste peck and smiled. But he leaned out to kiss her properly for anyone to see, ending with a primal groan that made them both laugh.

Their hands slipped apart and all they could do was wave.

"Now, spread your wings," Isaac shouted, with a grin. "Fly, little sparrow!"

And then he was gone.

AT DINNER, THERE WAS tension from Lady Thurston's side of the table. Emilie knew Isaac must have told his granny about the proposal, and perhaps the woman was bitter at her for turning him down. The dowager loved her as a granddaughter, she had no doubt. But Isaac was the sun in her eyes, and any woman who would dare break his precious heart would know her contempt.

There were new fears Emilie had not expressed to anyone, fears that emerged when Isaac asked for her hand and had only worsened since she'd said goodbye to him. Fears that held her awake at night, that made her question every beat of her own heart.

What if Fletcher was right? What if *any* marriage would be an end to her ambition?

Isaac was a romantic—he wanted a wedding and a wife, and a half dozen children running about. Emilie could not say she longed for any of those things; she had fought against them for so many years that it no longer mattered to her whether she would have them some-day when she was ready. She loved Isaac, and he deserved the life he dreamt of.

Emilie had to make a choice. She had to let him go.

She left the flat early on the morning of her departure, with her steamer strapped to the back of the taxi car, bound for Charing Cross. It was goodbye to Lady Thurston, to Isaac, to Fletcher, to her old life. What lay ahead, she could hardly guess. But now, she would make her own way.

And that was very good indeed.

Fifteen

Emilie

Somewhere along the train journey, Emilie forgot that nearby, a war was churning up this fine landscape into burnt ruin. Everywhere else was countryside and orchards, enchanted woodlands of thin trees, and seas of wildflowers—hyacinth, bluebells, daffodils, pink Carthusian, and poppies. She could not even be bothered by the heat, for the sky was so endlessly blue and bright, it lifted her spirits considerably.

It was not until they had left the train station that Emilie was struck with the harsh realization that this was no holiday, but active service. A motor ambulance had been sent to collect them. As she climbed into the total darkness of the vehicle, reality well and truly set in. The stink of petrol was thick, and the only light peeked in here and there as the canvas flap bumped open. Emilie's bones vibrated painfully as the motor took to an uneven road, and her mind drifted to the wounded soldiers who were transported in these same vehicles, shaken about as they lay broken and bleeding.

Across from her, Sister Allen sat erect with her eyes shut, as if she could find the peace of a kip in all this racket. Then, the steamer had not rattled her either. Emilie had met the older woman in Southampton when they had embarked with a group of nurses and volunteers in her detachment. She knew little about Sister Allen besides that she was a member of Queen Alexandra's Imperial Military Nursing Service, and had served in South Africa. Emilie supposed that would have made her fearless.

She leaned forward to ask, "Are they all like this, Sister?"

Sister Allen's eyes came open, pale blue and old with experience, despite her forty-some years. Her pointed face was that of a nymph, angular and fair, eyelashes so light they were practically translucent. "All of what?"

"The ambulances. It isn't a terribly comfortable means of travel . . ."

As if to support her theory, the ambulance hit a divot in the road, sending Emilie, Sister Allen, and the other three VADs up off of their seats. Emilie landed hard on her tailbone, though at least the bench was cushioned. She steadied herself and apologized to the young woman beside her for bumping shoulders.

Sister Allen, unfazed, answered, "Some have birds in."

"Pardon?"

"Parakeets and things. Lifts spirits, doesn't it? Birdsong?"

Emilie could not disagree.

The day before, they had crossed on graciously calm seas to Boulogne. Mercifully, Emilie had fallen asleep on the journey, allowing no idle time to imagine German submarines lurking in the depths below. It was only two months ago the RMS *Lusitania* had been torpedoed, killing nearly twelve hundred civilians. The deaths were fresh on everyone's minds.

But after the looming grey of London, France was a colorful respite. Emilie had marveled at the dried sausages hanging in the charcuterie window, and stopped to admire a display of éclairs. *Mamans* in sabots sold herring and eel while children played at their feet, stopping to wave to a line of Tommies marching and singing cheerfully:

> *"Oh! we don't want to lose you but we think you ought to go*
> *For your King and Country both need you so;*

We shall want you and miss you but with all our might and main
We shall cheer you, thank you, kiss you
When you come back again!"

As they strode by shop windows, it had been impossible for Emilie not to gaze longingly at silk blouses and fine hats. It might have been another life when she had dressed so finely, and it was easy to long for such glamour when one was got up in uniform. Soon, the comforts of her old life would be only distant memories, as the ambulance was taking them to No. 16 Stationary—a military base hospital set up entirely under canvas.

Le Tréport was a charming seaside village tucked in at the foot of chalk cliffs, with a long shingled beach and mismatched gabled buildings stretching to see the view. The sea air was fierce and salted, so thick one could almost take a savory bite. The place reminded Emilie of the Yorkshire coast, of Whitby, where she had once stood on the shore and imagined that the world was delicious and kind.

When they arrived at camp, the flap was torn open by a ward sister, who stepped aside as each of them climbed down. As Emilie's boots landed in the dirt, she felt she was properly in the military. Khaki marquees and lines of wooden huts stretched as far as one could see, with tent ropes gripping the ground between them. Duckboards crisscrossed the campus, keeping boots and skirts out of the mud. Despite the beauty surrounding it, there was nothing welcoming about this place. The utilitarian camp had been erected hastily and designed for efficiency, for the militant order with which the War Office would run it.

"Are you quite well?" the sister asked Emilie. "You look a bit green about the gills."

Emilie touched her cheek, which was flushed with warmth. When she had joined up, Emilie had been handed her identity discs and arm brassard and told to memorize a list of DON'TS FOR VADs. One of them came to her now:

DON'T forget you are under Military discipline,—therefore under absolute obedience to all seniors.

"Yes, thank you, Sister," she said.

"We'll get you all a hot meal and a cup of tea." Sister now spoke to the group. "Firstly, I'm to take you to your quarters and then to interview with Matron Frances. Sharpish, ladies, if you please—there is much to see."

Campus was bustling with activity. Orderlies passed with bins of laundry, and medical officers looked up from where they stood chatting in their white coats. Patients, in haphazard combinations of khaki, blues, and pajamas, stood or lounged or leaned about in the sunshine with slinged arms and bandaged heads, smoking cigarettes. A few of the more fortunate men kicked a football back and forth. In the distance, a gramophone could be heard near where cots had been brought out onto the lawn, so lying patients could take the air.

Emilie swallowed hard as she met the eyes of a man standing between crutches on the one leg he had left. She had seen plenty of men in uniform, but it was different to see those who had so lately come through battle, rugged, malnourished, and war-weary. They looked hopeless, some of them. Entirely defeated. They were so close to the battlefield here—their patients would come to them still muddy, still mangled from the quick patches done at Casualty Clearing Stations, many needing more surgery and constant care.

She could not help but think of her boys, wherever they were.

Trained nurses in their crimson-lined capes stopped to observe the latest arrivals, no doubt wary of the VADs' ability to cope with the harsh work. Women like Emilie had only to train for six weeks in first aid courses before entering the wards, while the sisters had spent three years acquiring their skills. It would take great strength to prove to them that the volunteers could make do without their maids, their cooks, and their mothers.

They were all of them from a certain background, VADs. The "voluntary" nature of their work deemed it appropriate in the eyes of their set. Taking money for labor was considered most untoward, but Emilie and her colleagues would be given twenty pounds per annum, and a six-pound uniform allowance. Though she had never much considered money before in her life, Emilie had quickly learned it was too meager a wage to live on properly.

The other VADs would be supplemented by allowances from home, so nobody knew that Emilie was scrounging for every last farthing. Nor would they. It was for that reason she had briefly considered disappearing among the jaundice-faced women in the munitions factories. But she did not wish to build artillery that would cause more destruction. She wanted to mend what had already been broken.

The ward sister gave her tour concisely. Each row of wards was marked by a letter, each tent by a number. It was only minutes before Emilie lost track of them, there were so many. The officers' wards were kept in wooden huts—finer, perhaps, than the marquees, but rough and temporary fixtures that were harder to keep clean, draftier in winter, and hot under tin roofs in summer. Nearby to these were the post office, Red Cross stores, kitchens, and staff mess. Nurses ate separate to the MOs, and the patients, who messed in a marquee.

Finally, they arrived at the neat line of bell tents in which the nurses slept. The VADs were told to pair up at the start, and to Emilie's dismay, they all had made friends along their journey while she was turning ever inward. Her plan to keep to herself had worked thus far—nobody was interested in knowing more about her, and Emilie wanted to keep it that way. She did not want to be underestimated, given her background.

"Dawes," said the ward sister, gesturing for her to follow, "as there's an odd number, you'll be bunking with Clarke. She's been here three weeks, so you'll have help settling in."

Emilie nodded obediently.

"Here we are, then," said the sister, stopping her. "Good day to you, Clarke."

The volunteers were all called by their surnames. Emilie balked each time she heard it, worried it might identify her. But it wasn't the name most people knew her family for.

Clarke was a slight thing, with frizzy auburn hair and freckles across her cheeks and nose. Her smile was wide and naive, with a gap between her front teeth. Emilie was relieved to see that the time at camp had not yet defeated her.

"Welcome home!" Clarke swung out her arms. "Be it ever so humble, as they say. I hope you'll find it cozy enough for the duration. Your things have been brought."

As the ward sister left them to get settled, Clarke lifted the flap.

Emilie's breath hitched to see her new home from home. Naught but a ground sheet lay over the earth—no proper floor or carpet. Her regulation trunk lay at the foot of the camp bed, along with the new kit she had been required to purchase—camp chair, canvas washstand and bucket, tent strap, collapsible lantern, kettle, and roll-up, which contained her eating utensils and a tin opener. Tinned food was all she could look forward to from now on. Under the War Office, they lived on rations.

On the other side, Clarke had put in a great effort to make the space her own. A knitted blanket lay over the foot of her bed, along with several mismatched cushions. Beside it were a stack of crates, topped with family photos in frames brought from home; a vase of fresh flowers; and other knickknacks. Emilie looked up to see a rope, from which Clarke had hung a chintz curtain, dividing the round tent into two semicircle "rooms."

"For privacy," Clarke said. "I think it's pretty, don't you? I've sewn those bolster cushions myself, to make the bed resemble a Chesterfield. Oh—and I could show you how to fashion a dressing table from sugar boxes if you like."

Emilie was too overwhelmed to give it much thought. She was still fixated on the idea that she would be sleeping out of doors, and wondered more about security measures than about housekeeping. She wrung her hands, staring down at the limp pillow, dull white linens, and anemic wool blanket that lay folded on top of the mattress. For the first time in her twenty-two years, she would be expected to make up her own bed.

"Shall I help you?" Clarke asked. "You'll not want to leave it until tonight."

As she bent to take up the linens, Emilie found herself at a loss for words. Where Clarke had family photos, she would have nothing at all to remind her of where she'd come from. It was for the best—of that, Emilie was certain. She had come too far to regret it all now. There had been something painful yet satisfying about leaving England, like the relief of losing a wobbling tooth. It had hurt, and would surely be inflamed for a time. But the sore wound would heal, and was preferable to the constant, stinging pain of anticipation.

Now, though, standing in the reality of what she had done, Emilie had lost her confidence. As Clarke offered her one of the folded sheets, she found she had suddenly forgotten all her lessons of how to lay them.

Clarke's brows turned down in sympathy, and she took the sheet back from Emilie. "Is it all a bit much? Come, I'll show you. If you cannot make a bed tomorrow, the sisters will never let you hear the end of it."

With Clarke at one end, Emilie soon recalled the perfect folds required of a hospital bed, and felt herself grow comfortable again. "Are the sisters as bad as I hear?" she asked.

"They are none too keen that the military has let us come here. They treat us all as if we are flighty little girls always under their feet."

"Not unlike how one is treated at home, then," Emilie muttered under her breath, but Clarke had heard her and chuckled.

Once Emilie's bed was made up with a crisp, military precision, they both stood and straightened their clothes.

"I suppose they are only trying to do their best for the boys, and would rather not have us to look after," Clarke added. "Not to worry;

so long as you do as they say and get all of your work finished on time, the sisters will let you be."

Her assurance was kind, but a knot tightened in Emilie's stomach. She was confident in her mind, but her hands, softened by a lifetime of privilege, were not so keen.

"Now—are you all set to start tomorrow?" Clarke asked. "I find it makes mornings easier if my uniform is laid out for me."

Together, they dug through Emilie's trunk to unpack the essentials. All the while, Emilie remained quiet while Clarke went on about camp life, implored Emilie to call her by her forename, Nancy, and suggested they take the funicular train to town together and buy a few bits and pieces to make Emilie's side feel more homely. Emilie hadn't a spare bob for that, but tentatively agreed.

Later, Nancy led Emilie to the office where she sat across from Matron's desk, wringing her hands in her lap, waiting for her superior to see her surname and raise an eyebrow. Emilie had hoped the Claremonts would avoid a scandal by keeping her disappearance quiet, but she could not help but imagine what might become of her if they decided to pursue her as a thief. But the pepper-haired matron noticed nothing out of the ordinary, and sent Emilie on her way to eat supper. She spotted Sister Allen outside of the nurses' mess. Though they had known each other for only a short time, it comforted Emilie to see a familiar face.

"How are you settling in, Dawes?" Sister Allen asked.

"It is not quite what I imagined."

"I hope you were not expecting the Ritz."

Emilie shook her head. She opened her mouth to speak, but found she did not know how to describe what she *had* imagined. She had never before set foot within a hospital, let alone a military camp. She had an idea of what the Western Front would look like, from newspaper descriptions and photographs, but this was far from the ruin and destruction of that place.

When Emilie didn't reply, Sister Allen asked, "Why did you come here, Dawes?"

This question was much easier to answer.

"I wanted to be here if—" . . . *he fell*, Emilie nearly admitted. Instead, she started again. "I wanted to fight in the war, in the only way a woman is permitted to. We cannot be there to stop the bullets, or take bullets ourselves, but perhaps we can prevent a senseless death from them."

"Then you know why I began my career with the QAIMNS." Sister Allen's lips rose in one of her careful smiles. "Still, I sense you are missing home."

Emilie shook her head, but the truth was, she did miss England. Not the England she'd left behind, but the one she knew before the war, before everything had smashed. She missed Isaac, though she allowed herself to admit it for only a moment before pushing the thought aside.

"I miss it a little," she said.

Sister Allen slid her hands into the pocket of her apron. "When you have patients to look after, it will be easier to forget where you are and remember why you are here."

With the other nurses, they ate a quick meal of weak tea and a curry made from tinned bully beef. The food was tasteless and gristly, but Emilie swallowed it down, knowing there would be no alternative. Each of the VADs would take her turn on kitchen duty, as well as cleaning the nurses' mess, bringing the water, planning the meals, and doing the shopping. Emilie would have liked to opt out of the cookery portion. Laundering, scrubbing, and folding linens suited her. But try as she might, she could never master heating the water to the right temperature to brew tea.

Another lesson rang in Emilie's ears:

DON'T think you can pick and choose your own work at first. Do all that comes your way with your whole heart, and others will soon see what you are best fitted for.

By the time they were dismissed, Emilie was ready to test her camp bed. Upon returning to the tent, she found herself alone. They had only one half day off a week, and this was Nancy's, so her bunkmate was gone to enjoy it.

Emilie clumsily lit the lamp and had the idea of trying the oilstove to boil water for washing. But after struggling to undress in the near-dark, flinching at every voice beyond the canvas, every hoot of an owl, every rumble of a motor, she was so bone-weary that she gave in, collapsing into the stiff bed before even bothering to plait her hair.

Overwhelmed, she swallowed hard over a stone in her throat. This was the farthest afield she had ever been on her own. Nothing was right—not the canvas overhead that rustled in the wind, not the damp scent of the pillow. Lying on top of the blankets and rugs, she listened to the song of crickets and soft murmurs of female voices from neighboring tents. There was no real solitude in this place, yet Emilie felt so completely alone.

A warm tear escaped her eye, sliding over the bridge of her nose to soak into the pillow. Emilie sat up, brushing it away crossly. She had gone through hell to get here, broken her heart several times over, and sacrificed all she had ever known. Why could she not trust that the choices she'd made to get here were the right ones? Why could she not trust *herself*?

Emilie remembered she was still dressed in her uniform, and unbuttoned the neck to reach down between her corset and combination, where she had secreted the envelope. It was warm from her body heat, and softly wrinkled from being stashed there each day since she'd received it. Her name was scrawled across the front in a familiar hand, the tall, jagged strokes reminding her of the man who had written them.

She had made the cut cleanly, thinking it would heal faster, but it still burned and ached, even greater than before. The envelope was still sealed. It was Isaac's last letter to her, and she would never know what it said. She refused to open it.

Leaning off the bed, Emilie removed the glass from her lamp and watched as the envelope turned orange in the light from the flame. Could she do it? Could she erase the last memory she had of him, his last words to her?

Emilie held the corner to the flame, watched it catch.

With a gasp, she realized the madness of what she was doing and threw the envelope to the ground. Frantically, she stamped on it with her foot, all the while trying to contain the urge to sob so that nobody would come running to her rescue. She fell to her knees beside the bed and breathlessly drew the envelope up into her lap to see the damage was minimal.

She could not do it—not yet. She didn't have the strength.

She could not say goodbye to the one person who would have given her the world had it not been turned upside down.

Sixteen

Emilie

Emilie woke with a shock to the muffled sound of chattering female voices. This could not possibly be morning, could it?

The tent was still dark but for Nancy's lamp, low flame, casting shadows across the canvas walls. Nancy herself was not present, though hers was one of the voices outside. Emilie sat up, her head heavy from exhaustion. Between the firmness of her bed, the sleeping sounds of Nancy lying an arm's length away, and the general noises of the wilderness, she had slept in fits and starts and woke more tired than when she had gone to bed.

She reached for her watch with a wince. It was six o'clock in the morning. Emilie could not remember the last time she had seen the early hour. Breakfast was taken at six thirty, to be on duty on the wards at seven. How would she find the time to dress herself and arrange her hair?

Emilie stood to open the flap and was greeted by a fresh, sea-salted morning, the first signs of pale blue morning on the horizon, and the song of the skylark. Emilie could smell coffee being brewed down the line, saw the outline of three VADs gathered within a single tent to share a morning cup. Somebody within the tent squealed, as the others laughed.

"You'll miss breakfast again, missy!" one of them said.

"I would rather an empty stomach and ten more minutes' sleep!"

Another chorus of laughter.

One of the women came toward her, and Emilie's eyes adjusted to see Nancy's smiling face. She was already fully clothed and smelling of coffee.

"Good morning, Emilie. Let us know if you need any help!"

Emilie was not yet capable of more than a thank-you, still dizzy from sleep. Dropping the flap, she hurried to throw her bedclothes into a neat arrangement. Breakfast would not be held for anyone, and her stomach was already grumbling. Seeing her uniform arranged neatly on her trunk made her feel more at ease, though Emilie looked dourly at the corset—she was not skilled at fumbling into it on her own. Her uniform needed to be worn correctly, to display the utmost modesty, purity, and professionalism: the base of which consisted of a blue chambray dress, black stockings, and plain ward shoes.

DON'T forget that when in uniform all members should be immaculately clean, trim and tidy.

Emilie unbuttoned her soiled clothes self-consciously. Never having sisters, she was accustomed to living in her own space, with her own things. What was once a solitary ritual would now be a strange dance on display. She wrinkled her nose as she smelled yesterday's sweat, which had dried under her arms, and noticed the twisted mess of her hair. What she wouldn't give for a thorough wash of it. But there was no time to bathe. She dusted herself under the arms with deodorant powder—the only beauty product the nurses were allowed. She then reached for her fresh cotton combination, and from her throat came a shriek of terror.

Nesting in the folds was what appeared to be a family of earwigs, bustling in and out and up onto her hands with pincers gnashing.

Emilie threw the garment to the floor, climbing onto her bed, which tilted and bucked under her weight. She wanted to flee, but was still bare from head to toe. As tears pricked her eyes, Emilie scratched her arms and legs, sure that she must have been covered with insects.

She could not be crying already! Surely earwigs would not be the worst enemy she should hope to face here.

Voices came from outside, and Emilie covered herself with blankets.

"Emilie?" Nancy called. "Is everything all right? Are you decent?"

"Yes!" Emilie blurted. "I mean—no, I am not decent. But everything is splendid." Oh, but it wasn't. Peering from the bed, she saw earwigs still teeming from her smalls.

"We're off to breakfast!"

Alone again, Emilie wiped her eyes with the back of her hand and forced a deep breath. There was nothing for it—she would need to take up arms against the intruders. Emilie leaned over the bed for her shoes, giving them a good shake upside down before slipping them onto her bare feet. She carefully stood, plucked up the combination with thumb and forefinger, and flung it out through the flap. Only three earwigs were left behind, dashing in opposing directions. More girlish shrieking as Emilie stamped and stamped until each one had met its end.

"That will teach you to insult a woman!"

Denying the clothes that were left out, Emilie dug into her trunk for fresh articles, giving them a thorough once-over before struggling into them. Her uniform required as much care to put on as her finest evening gowns once had, and without Grace, it was not an easy task. She arranged her hair into something vaguely resembling a chignon and stretched one of her white handkerchiefs across her brow, pinning it in the back to form her cap.

One last thing. Emilie dug in the bedclothes for Isaac's sealed letter, smarting at the charred edge before stuffing it under her pillow. Perhaps she was not strong enough to rid herself of it yet, but she could not face the day without it pressed against her heart.

She dipped under the flap, feeling prepared and confident until she spotted two orderlies, fully uniformed in white, standing over something heaped in the grass.

"They're knickers, all right," one said. "See the ruffles? S'pose they don't call it Petticoat Lane for nothing."

"How have they got there?" the other asked.

"Dunno. Reckon one of the girls went for a bit of How's Your Father last night?"

"I fought all that yowlin' were the feral cats!"

A rather unattractive burst of laughter followed, and then each of them did their best impressions of an animal in heat. Emilie was mortified. Normally, she would have been more than willing to abandon a garment in order to reserve her pride, but she had so few of them now and could not afford more.

Fixing a glare, she stomped up to the orderlies and gave each a stiff glare before retrieving her combination from the grass. "Haven't you anything better to do than stand about making obscene suggestions? I've half a mind to tell the wardmaster you've been lingering near the nurses' quarters talking of sex. I must imagine he would be none too thrilled with such untoward behavior."

The cigarette fell from between the lips of the Cockney one, surely not expecting a young lady such as Emilie to forgo euphemism. At once, both men cowered away, murmuring halfhearted apologies as they fled. Lucky for them, Emilie's threat was empty.

DON'T criticise anybody, but do all you can to see that your own bit of work needs no criticism.

Emilie looked down, finding the earwigs had gone in favor of a more natural habitat, and plucked her garment from the grass. Her mother would expire if she knew of any of this. Though as she returned it to her tent, she could not deny the rush in her veins from the outburst, reminding her of the tenacity she had needed to get here in the first.

In the nurses' mess, she sat at a long table with the other VADs, sisters, and Matron, connecting eyes with Sister Allen at the other end. She took notice of the offering; toast and tea was the extent of it. Their meals would be meager compared to what she was used to—

meat and beans for dinner, meat and potatoes for supper, and twice weekly there would be no meat at all, only soup or fish, and puddings would be tasteless without a proper amount of sugar. Each of them were given a rationed two pounds of bread to last two days, and three-quarters of a pound of sugar for a week, so there was no room for indulgence. The tea was weak, but nourishing, and though the toast was spread with margarine rather than real butter, it went down easily.

At seven o'clock, Matron knocked her knuckles on the table and everyone stood to say the Lord's Prayer. With her swift "amen," Emilie pushed in her chair, taking a hasty last bite of her crust before moving along with the stream of women to her ward.

Each sister-in-charge looked after three to four wards in a line, with VADs and orderlies to assist. Each line consisted of up to nine marquees of a certain purpose—medical or surgical—and according to the severity of the cases. Some were close enough together to be connected by tarpaulin tunnels. To stand at the entrance and see twenty beds lined up made Emilie feel there was simply no end to it at all. It was a relief to her that most of the walls were rolled, so the boys could get fresh air and light. Winter promised a different atmosphere.

Emilie was assigned C-line with Sister Allen and two of the other new VADs. She overheard the night nurse saying it would be a slow day—of the hospital's one thousand beds, only two hundred were filled. That was all right by Emilie. She would use the spare time to acclimate.

Now it was time for Emilie to add the final elements of her uniform, tying on an apron with the Red Cross on the chest and pulling up her white oversleeves. As she moved into line with the other volunteers, she caught a look at herself in the reflective glass of a medicine cabinet and was struck still. The woman gazing back was not the Emilie she knew, but someone else. Little wonder the boys had stood taller in their khaki—Emilie felt brave in her apron.

As Sister Allen drew near to give orders, Emilie stuck a finger under her starched collar where it rubbed her neck uncomfortably. The action forced it to spring from its button and she gasped, feeling the sister's eyes on her as she struggled to fasten it back into place.

The sister lifted a light brow. She looked immaculate in her grey uniform and red-trimmed cape. "Dawes, many thanks for introducing our first lesson. We have strict rules and regulations in regards to appearance. If your uniform is incorrect, you will receive a warning, and I will expect not to see you make the same mistake again."

With that, she gave Emilie a pointed look. The other VADs, flushing, quickly checked themselves.

"Nails should be kept short and clean," she went on. "Shoes are always to be changed before entering the ward. You are not to travel any distance from the hospital in clean aprons and sleeves—so always have a spare. No earrings, no jewelry, no ribbons. Paints and scents of any kind are considered a discredit to this organization."

Nods all around.

"Remember, your first three months here are probationary. Should you succeed, you will be given the opportunity to sign on for a period of six months or the duration. Should you fail, you will be thanked and asked to return home. This is a military hospital, run by military personnel on active service. The work you do here is extremely grave, and laziness or disobedience will not be tolerated. You will be expected to look directly into the horrors of war—that means blood and excrement—as well as the bare bodies of male patients . . ."

There was no stopping the heat that fluttered to Emilie's cheeks and neck. Of course, in the back of her mind, she knew such things were unavoidable, but did not expect they would be explained so plainly. She thought of days spent at the sea, of Rhys and Fletcher in swimming costumes. That was as much knowledge as she had of the male anatomy.

"Here, it will be your duty not only to set an example of discipline and perfect steadiness of character, but also to maintain the most courteous relations with those whom you are helping in this great struggle. If these demands do not suit your expectations, I must ask you to kindly remove yourself before we go any further." Sister swept a pale hand toward the flap door.

Nobody moved.

"Very good. Are we all quite ready to begin?"

EMILIE WAS THROWN STRAIGHT into the fray, where in this case, the fray was a battle against infection. Before the patients' wounds were attended to, every surface on the ward had to be dusted, to be swept, to be mopped and scrubbed until it shone. The other girls happily busied themselves—the novelty of such work still fun as a game. Emilie instead struggled to remember her Home Nursing lessons and wished she had not found them so trivial at the time.

The challenges of camp nursing presented themselves immediately. The boarded floors were difficult to sweep, and there were dirt, spent matchsticks, and cigarette ends in every crevice and corner. No plumbing meant fetching water in buckets and warming it on the stove, an arduous task which took a great deal of time. Once she had warm water to mix with cresols, Emilie got to work scrubbing the ward table and benches. Then lockers were to be dusted, and any beds that would be emptied that day needed to be stripped, the frames wiped down and disinfected, then the soiled linens handed off to an orderly.

In an hour, Emilie was already exhausted. To think that so many steps went into cleaning a floor, which would dirty again in minutes!

Emilie moved warily among the beds, not wishing to wake the sleeping soldiers. Nothing could have prepared her for the state of them, lying hopelessly in their pajamas, their faces gaunt and grey or jaundiced, brows sweating with fever, some bandaged so extensively that she could hardly see their faces at all. Others wheezed and coughed, blinking at her through glassy eyes, offering a smile and a "good morning" if they had the strength. Many were missing things—arms, legs, ears, fingers—some of them more than one. In each of them she saw what could become of Isaac if he was fortunate enough to come through the war alive.

And then there was the odor, which Emilie could not ignore through the sharp scent of disinfectant. Their wounds stank of rot, sweet but mousy, lingering with the sour musk of male perspiration, urine, and sick.

Emilie tried to no avail to breathe through her mouth, to concentrate on her work, but all at once it became too much and she stepped away, searching for a cloud of fresh air to breathe. Touching her chin to her chest, she willed her head to stop spinning, and watched the towel in her hand drip onto the floor.

Sister Allen spotted her standing in the center of the ward and floated in her direction. Though Sister allowed the hint of a smile, Emilie was well aware that she was about to be scorned, and tried to right herself as much as she could.

DON'T forget to stand up when seniors come into the ward or room.

"Something the matter, Dawes?" Sister asked.

"No, Sister. I just, I—" The room spun again.

"There, there. You will not be the first VAD I have seen swoon on the job." Emilie looked up to find the sister's smile had deepened. "Then, she'd been assisting in an enterics ward. Do you know what that is?"

Emilie shook her head.

"It is where one treats cases of bowel disease."

Emilie's tongue went sour and she swallowed hard.

"Do you need to sit, Dawes?"

Emilie shook her head again, trying to relax her shoulders from her ears. For heaven's sake, she would not allow herself to drop on her first day! Around her, the ward was coming to life, the men were beginning to converse with one another, to ask for things—water, tea, a jab, a hot water bottle . . .

She could not let them down.

"My apologies, Sister," Emilie said, adjusting her sleeves. "It shall not happen again."

Sister Allen dropped her eyes down to Emilie's shoes and brought them back up. Emilie had never felt so exposed. "I expect not."

Emilie, feeling ashamed, returned to cleaning patients' lockers. She had thought herself so clever; she had thought herself above swooning. What if her family was right? What if she didn't have the fortitude to exist on her own? To support herself? She knew so little, it was humiliating. How could she ever expect to live independently when she had only just learned of the existence and function of disinfectant for cleaning?

WARD CLEAN, THE TIME had come to change into a clean pair of oversleeves and take temperatures, prepare for dressings, ready fomentations, sterilize instruments, and distribute castor oil, aspirin, and other medicines. Though as Emilie began to sort through the cabinet, there was not enough of anything. There was only one syringe to be used in her line, and she went up and down it twice in search of a kidney dish, eventually being handed a well-washed pie tin by another VAD. Clearly, the ingenuity found in the bell tents was reflected in the wards. Leave it to women, Emilie thought, to be expected to make do with the bare minimum, and create ingenious solutions. A man would never have considered a pie tin could be anything but. In fact, a man would never have considered a pie tin at all.

Emilie would have little to do with the dressing itself, which was a relief. That task was reserved for the trained nurses, though she stayed close beside Sister Allen to assist, and soon became so enamored of the woman's skill that she could hardly focus. Sister Allen's hands were a milky extension of her tools, strong and gentle all at once. Emilie watched as Sister performed a marvelous ballet with syringe and saline. She studied Sister—not only the procedures, but the tightened calm in her brow, the tone of voice she used with her patients, the phrases she repeated to each of them: *How are we feeling this morning, Private?* and *We'll discuss that with Doctor* or *You may feel a bit of discomfort.*

Emilie had never met a woman so sure in her knowledge, so commanding in a room of men, even when the medical officer arrived for rounds.

Dressings complete, it was time to bring the patients' dinners from the kitchens, and help those who could not cut their meat or lift a spoon to their lips. Emilie found this task particularly harrowing. Men in her life had always been pillars of strength and poise, the leaders, the strong. To see these men, who as soldiers were the ultimate example of masculinity, unable even to grip a utensil was perhaps the most dismal thing she had ever witnessed. It depressed her, but more than that, it was disquieting. Everything she knew of the world had dramatically been proven false, the fabric of humanity torn into unsewable threads.

After half an hour for her own dinner, Emilie returned to the wards and was instructed to give blanket baths to the lying patients. This was a skill she had learned to mime in her first aid courses, and in her arrogance, expected not to be shocked by. But many of their patients were career soldiers, muscled by years of service, and looked nothing like the boys she knew back at home. When Emilie lifted her first patient's arm, she marveled at the weight of it, the masculine hairs and sinew coiled like vines. As she passed her cloth over a flat, rigid chest, she felt a curious tightness in her core, a familiar quickening of heat. And then she was thinking only of Isaac, even as she washed a foreign body, even as she held her breath to reach under the blanket and run her flannel over the man's hips and pelvis.

As she moved to another bed, she found she was enjoying the opportunity to provide care. Like those who required help cutting their meat, these men, in their great need, had surrendered to her. Women, for once, were relied upon for providing the basic needs of their lives—having the benevolence that the medical officers did not possess. There was something in that notion that prevented her from blushing as she reached beneath a rough wool blanket. Perhaps she'd been only a girl when the war began. Now she was certainly a woman, and like Eve, was freed from her innocence. There was so much more than a kiss, and Emilie wondered if she should ever know what that *more* could truly feel like.

A crash from the other end of the ward startled Emilie from her work. She hadn't noticed the flap had come open, bringing a new lying patient. Emilie whirled in time to watch her fellow VAD flee the ward, looking pale as she had been that morning. For a moment, Emilie didn't move, fearing what could have been so terrible to make the woman have such a reaction. Then she looked at Sister Allen, working with her usual clinical indifference, and knew this was her chance to prove her worth.

Emilie dashed to where Sister had been left standing over the new patient, hands full of soiled bandages with nowhere to put them down. "That kidney dish, please, Dawes," she said.

Emilie grabbed the dish to collect the bandages from her, and took up the dressing tray, turning to have her first look at the man in the bed. The sight took her breath away, and she knew instantly what had upset the other volunteer.

The patient's chin had gone. There was nothing left below his top lip but a horrible black cavern that met up with his throat. He whimpered through the triangular hole where his nose had been, split down the middle by a thin line of cartilage. Eyes bulged white against the red, weeping endlessly.

Sister Allen put her back to the patient and spoke with a soft severity: "The last thing this man needs is to see another person horrified by his appearance. If he lives, there will be no end to them. Assist if you're capable, or fetch an orderly."

Emilie looked again at the man in the bed, trying to picture the face before the whiz-bang, but could not. Had he been a man, or a boy? Handsome or plain? The only way anyone might have recognized him was by his mop of sandy red hair and striking green eyes.

Emilie pressed her dry lips together, regaining composure. "I am at your disposal, Sister."

Relief washed over Sister Allen's face. "He needs to eat. Will you prepare an egg flip?"

The kitchen was full, her peers busy preparing the patients' luncheon. Emilie squeezed past them to the bench and cracked two eggs in a bowl, leaving out the yolks, and began to froth the whites, watching out the window as more stretchers were brought in from ambulances at the center of camp. She added castor sugar and medicinal brandy, surprised at how quickly she was able to recall the recipe. At Sister Allen's side again, she felt a sudden rush of confidence.

"Ready?" Sister asked. Emilie nodded. "Wash well, please."

Feeding the patient required a careful system of rubber tubing that dribbled the egg flip into his mouth, past raw flesh. Every swallow was a chore, and if they poured too quickly, he'd choke. Sister Allen did most of the work while Emilie ensured his wounds were kept clean of drippings. All the while, she held his eyes. They were handsome eyes, deep set and concentrated, and Emilie was glad he still had them, if nothing else.

After they'd bound up the wound, he almost looked a man again, if only his eyes and brow and forehead. Emilie again tried to imagine who he was. Did he have a wife? Would she recognize him? Would his children look upon their father with fear?

A shudder ran through Emilie's body, something foul curling from deep in her stomach. She closed her eyes to steady herself. When she opened them, the private was focused on her and made a gurgling sound in an effort to speak. Her heart broke once more.

God forbid her brother would suffer such devastation and have no one to smile at him.

"You have done so well, pet," Emilie said, holding the man's hand. "We are going to take such good care of you."

Seventeen

Emilie

SEPTEMBER 1915

Each day, Emilie woke newly sore in back, feet, calves, neck, and arms. Every muscle in her body screamed in protest. Sleeping was difficult, for despite the exhaustion, there were a thousand thoughts and fears swirling: Would her patient survive the night? Had she remembered to return the medicine pots to the correct cabinet? What if a convoy arrived in the night? Or an air raid?

Despite this, Emilie woke each morning on time. Dressing became another mindless routine, and in time, she could pin her hair into a chignon with little fuss—though it was often a knotted mess for need of washing. What had shocked Emilie in the first week became commonplace after a month. She could stare down all matter of blood and gore, could give a blanket bath with cool, clinical indifference. She was learning the ins and outs of wound care and treatments for a range of maladies that plagued the soldiers. It rather fascinated her, and she found herself starving for knowledge, asking dozens of questions, watching over Sister Allen's shoulder whenever she was permitted to do so. Sister Allen was different to the other trained nurses—firm, of course, but clearly glad to be shaping a new set of young women who might never have known real labor, and encouraging them to see the satisfaction in doing the difficult.

Emilie certainly did. And perhaps that was why she had come to love her work, despite the aches and hunger and exhaustion. It proved to her that for all the years she swore to her parents that she was more than just a girl in a gown, she had been right. For here, Emilie was doing things she never could have imagined she was capable of. Now, there was hardly a spare moment in the day to do any thinking of home; when on duty, there was only the next patient to be concerned with. For entire hours, she forgot who she was, where she was from, forgot everything besides the war they were fighting.

Lifting the flap of her ward was like entering a void. Sometimes she thought she could stay there forever.

Most of the beds were empty today. Her first patients had long gone to Blighty. It was rare for someone to stay for long at No. 16. The hospital acted as an in-between place, for stabilization before moving down the line to convalescent depots, or home to England.

With such little work to be done, Emilie was granted her first day off. She sat in her camp chair, absorbing what she imagined was the last truly warm day of the year. In her lap was Isaac's unopened letter. She rubbed the pads of her thumbs against the paper he had so lately touched. She had dreamt of Isaac the night before, been so sure they were together again that she woke feeling painfully hollow. Would his face be the same when she saw him again? *If* she did?

Fearing the temptation was too great, Emilie let the envelope fall to the grass at her feet.

Looking up again, she was surprised to see the graceful figure of Sister Allen floating toward her, cape catching in the wind.

"You are looking rather glum, sitting there on your own," she said. "You have not received bad news, I hope?"

Emilie shook her head. It was not uncommon to be crossing campus and stumble upon a member of staff doubled over in grief after receiving a devastating wire. Mercifully, Emilie had not yet been one of them.

"Why are you not off shopping in town with the others?" Sister asked.

Hesitating, Emilie wondered if she ought to give Sister the truth: that she hadn't the spare francs for café au lait and omelets, fabric for chintz curtains, and souvenirs to send home. Nor did she have the energy for them.

"It is too fine a day to waste inside a restaurant," Emilie said.

Suddenly, a great burst of wind came through, cracking the canvas tent and catching the letter at her feet. Emilie leapt from her chair, chasing after it with a mad desperation. How could she have ever thought she could burn it? It was the most precious thing in her possession.

It was Sister Allen who caught it. Emilie's pulse thumped in her ears as Sister looked down at the envelope, reading the name it was addressed to: *Lady* Emilie Dawes. She waited for the woman to lift an eyebrow, to laugh, to tease her, even.

Instead, she handed Emilie the envelope and folded her hands. "I never thanked you properly for helping me that first day. I was impressed by your instincts. I wouldn't have thought a woman of your background could remain so composed."

"On the contrary," Emilie replied, "a woman of my background is brought up to be composed in the face of even the most troubling of circumstances."

Sister's thin lips deepened into a smirk, and Emilie knew she was safe. "I must admit, I do enjoy being proven wrong by a fierce young woman."

Emilie returned the smile. She had improved in the weeks since her first day, and was proud of herself. She only wished her family could be proud of her, too.

"Have you been for a bathe in the sea?" Sister asked.

It was certainly not what Emilie was expecting. "No . . . ?"

"Then do come with me now. Have you got a swimming costume?"

"I—yes. But will the water not be frightfully cold?"

Sister's pale eyes sparkled. "When you've changed clothes, meet me outside the nurses' mess—quick as you can."

There was no refusing her, was there? Though Emilie did grumble to herself as she dressed, wishing she'd had the nerve. When she eventually found Sister Allen waiting for her, she was already out of breath. Sister smiled, perhaps wider than Emilie had ever seen, and announced they would be taking the steps down to the sea.

It was a long walk—Emilie could only be glad they were going down. She didn't ask, but hoped desperately that they would be taking the funicular train back up to the top later on. When they reached the shingle beach, Emilie was panting, hair and face damp with sweat despite the chill. Sister Allen marched them down the beach. Never had Emilie imagined the stony nurse she met in Southampton could be so spirited.

From below, the chalk cliffs looked even more magnificent, standing as battlements in craggy defiance of the waves that crashed upon them. A few other bathers had come to drink the last of the sun, bundled up and lying out on rugs. At the top of the beach, a clutch of French girls in bonnets collected shingles in square wicker baskets, carrying them away on strong shoulders. A lone fisherman in a straw hat waded in the water, his trousers rolled up to his knees.

Where the waves curled and foamed onto the shore, the shingle became more sparse to reveal fine sand. It was there that Sister Allen came to a pause and took a deep breath, grinning at Emilie as though they were coconspirators.

"You do know how to swim, do you not?"

Emilie nodded hesitantly. "I shouldn't like to go too far in."

Sister removed her hat and worked her buttons. "What is it you are so afraid of?"

Emilie opened her mouth to speak, finding she had no answer. It was not the water she was afraid of, nor the cold. So what, then? There was no mother here to scorn her behavior, no peers to gossip behind her back if she should let her hair loose. Her decisions were her own now, and she was unrestricted by the laws of etiquette she grew up with.

If she wanted to splash and dance in the sea, then she should do it. Emilie faced Sister Allen and told her, "I'm not afraid."

"Right. Then, in you come."

Sister dashed ahead and into the surge, leaping over the breakers on long legs. Outside of the wards, out of her uniform, her body was less graceful, movements agile but boyish. She wore no bathing cap, and had unpinned her short copper hair so it flew up in the wind. She was completely unlike the women Emilie knew at home, free of shame and fear. Sister reminded Emilie of the boys at Whitby, tumbling their way past the swells to fall and dive. Would they ever have such summers again?

The water was frigid, and stung Emilie's toes as she waded in. The waves were not large, but strong enough to tug her legs. She hugged herself, shivering as Sister Allen plunged and came up again like a creature of the sea. Sister shook her hair and let out a euphoric cackle that made Emilie laugh in return. As Sister Allen swam back and forth in graceful laps, Emilie squeaked, the cold water reaching the sensitive skin of her stomach. And then, seeing Sister's joy, and knowing how fleeting this moment was, Emilie let her feet slide out from under her and dropped beneath the surface.

At first, the water cut into her, taking her breath, pinching at her skin like a thousand needles. Then, all at once, Emilie's brain accepted the temperature was no true danger, calming against the tide, leaving her heart thumping to know it was still alive.

When she came up, Emilie's lungs were tight, but the air was warm. Sister Allen was near, watching and cheering her on. Emilie pushed her hair out of her eyes, not bothered by the sting of the salt water. Nothing at all of this made sense, but somewhere below, in the ebb of the tide, she found the woman she had always known she was.

They could not withstand the cold for long. Another few minutes, and they were dragging themselves through the water, back up toward the shore, laughing all the while. Emilie couldn't stop, in fact, and found herself shaking with the elation as much as the chill.

"Exhilarating, is it not?" Sister Allen said, draping a towel over Emilie's shoulders. "I was brought up in Cornwall. I find a good plunge always gets the blood pumping."

"I've never felt anything like it." After wiping her face, Emilie returned the towel and began to step into her clothes.

"Well, you will again, if you continue nursing—it's why I do it. Is it something you would consider pursuing?"

Emilie was surprised by the question. Sister Allen knew who she was, now. Knew where she had come from. Could she see that Emilie had stripped herself of that old life? Had come here looking for a new one?

Emilie decided not to answer the question. "I daresay there is little point to making plans in wartime."

Sister chuckled. "Quite right, too. But there will not always be a war on. God help us if there is. In the meantime, we cannot allow ourselves to be consumed by the melancholy of circumstance, even for a few dark years."

Emilie wiped her eyes to meet the sister's, feeling the sting from the salt water stuck to her lashes.

"Acknowledge it, yes," Sister Allen went on. "Cry when it hurts you. Rage, certainly, against the injustice. But laugh, too. And dream of an end. Otherwise, why ought we to carry on?"

"What if I haven't got anything left when the war is over?" Emilie asked.

Sister sighed, planting her hands on her hips. After everything, part of Emilie could still not believe Sister Allen stood before her in a bathing costume, her hair wet.

"The world is vast, dear girl. There is always a fresh stone to turn over."

To display her point, Sister dipped to lift one of the shingles, oval and smooth, the color of amber. She set it, still warm from the sun, in Emilie's hand, and closed her fingers over it.

"Now, then," she said. "Shall we go and find a piping cup of tea?"

When they arrived at camp, it was bustling with activity, the air thick with the odor of petrol and horses. Emilie followed Sister Allen to the office where Matron Frances was standing, orchestrating the staff as they hurried to work.

"Is it a convoy, Matron?"

Matron Frances nodded. "And a large one, at that. There's been some trouble at the front, and we're next for taking in. Everyone is to be on duty immediately."

❧

IT WAS A MAD dash to prepare the wards for new arrivals. Blighty-ward patients were packed up and sent off, freeing beds. Emilie polished the ward tables and stacked them with clean dressings, lotions, drums, and medicines, everything at the ready. Floors were scrubbed, lockers cleaned, linens changed, and dressing boxes organized. Biscuit mattresses were laid on the floor between each bed, nearly doubling the capacity of the ward.

Then there was nothing left to do but change one's apron and wait.

Emilie found herself trembling all over as the bugle sounded, and ambulance motors roared outside. Was it her nerves, or the cold bathe she had taken with Sister Allen earlier? Emilie felt ready to drop. How was she to make it through the day?

Sister Allen appeared by Emilie's side, once again dressed and polished. "Don't look so frightened. You know what needs doing, do you not?"

"Yes, Sister."

"Fine. Chin up, now—there we are."

The flap came open, allowing a slice of cold air, and stretcher-bearers followed. The rumors of gas were true. Walking wounded stepped blindly, clinging to the man in front of them for guidance, their eyes padded with gauze and adhesive plaster. Flesh was red and inflamed with burns; faces were yellowed and gaunt, belonging to weathered old men, not bright British boys. All of them seemed to be gasping for breath, coughing, or vomiting. Some of them spit phlegm and wiped yellow froth from their noses and mouths.

Whether walking or carried, every man was filthy—covered in clay and mud and worse, by the smell, many still wearing their tin helmets. Clothes were tattered or removed entirely; arms were held in haphazard slings; chests were bandaged, blood seeping through to dry and clump in brown stains. Men in "trench slippers" were carried in pickaback fashion by orderlies or one of their peers, clinging to necks with what strength they still possessed. Nearly every man had more than one injury, and the parade of them continued on.

Sister stood at the flap, deciding the severity of each patient's condition and directing the bearers to bring them one way or the other. In minutes, C was so full there was hardly space to turn round. Emilie took deep breaths of air laced with exhaust fumes and sweating horses, blood and infection. For a moment, she could do nothing at all but gape in horror at the carnage, at the misery and terror on the faces of the men.

Finally, like a siren waking her up, Emilie thought of the boys she had been brought up with. She imagined them in pain, calling out, desperate and thirsty, and the thought made her snap to work.

Emilie was suddenly handed full responsibility of the ward. Uniforms had to be off and away; they could not risk the spread of lice through the hospital, and the chlorine still clung to the fabric—even the bronze buttons were tarnished green. As Emilie bent over a bed to remove the clothing, she got a stinging whiff of it herself, oddly sweet and peppery, and turned to cough into her elbow. She breathed more carefully as she continued down the line, collecting bloodied uniforms and washing the worn bodies as best she could until it was time to take the dressings down.

Chest and head cases were abundant. Nearly everyone needed foments and bandaging. Emilie washed the skin with ether soap, and the old, caked bandages softened with sterile water and hydrogen peroxide until they began to fall away. Emilie returned often to one lad whose voice had gone raw from shouting over a bullet wound in his foot. The nerve-heavy hands and feet caused the worst pain. As she checked it, the private eyed her suspiciously.

"I heard the sisters were strict," he said warily, "but you seem all right."

Emilie pulled his blanket up over him. "I certainly am, though you ought to keep a sharp eye on that one."

She nodded behind her, where Sister Allen was charging through the ward with a fresh basin of water. The private offered a weak smile, and Emilie was glad to see it, even at her beloved sister's expense.

"Ta. Never had so much as a bruised elbow, me," he said. "Will I need surgery, you reckon? I don't want to be put out, see. Me mum says people never wake up from it."

His wound was simple, but heavily gangrenous, and he had a fever. If the doctors couldn't get it under control by their means, some of the infected flesh would need to be cut away. Still, Emilie thought it unnecessary to tell him.

"Doctor will have to take a look first of all. Is there anything else I can fetch for you?"

"A glass of water, if it ain't too much trouble."

Emilie nodded and started to go, then took note of a voice in the neighboring bed. She was filled with a visceral memory of home, of Grace in her dressing table mirror, chatting away about the latest fashions. She turned back to the private with the injured foot.

Rather than ask, she leaned over to check his medical ticket once more, removing it from his brass button. She knew there were several

Yorkshire regiments, and many more hospitals where the battalions might have ended up. But she had to be certain.

As Emilie read, her heart skipped a beat. The letters were scrawled hastily, but they were clear enough. She felt outside herself as she read precisely what she had expected to see: *9th KOYLI*. King's Own Yorkshire Light Infantry. Isaac's regiment.

The ticket fell to the ground as Emilie drew a gasping breath.

Eighteen

Emilie

Once she had helped her thirsty patient, Emilie was through the flap door.

Her hands shook at her sides as she hurried her pace toward the officers' ward. She would be scorned if she was seen leaving her post, and in her apron no less. But what if Isaac was not here? How long would it be before she knew if he'd been killed? He did not know where she was—nobody did. She would have to wait until his death was published in the papers.

The door was open to the hut, allowing fresh air in. As Emilie climbed the stairs, an orderly came through with an armful of bloodied bandages. She tried to push past him, but he moved his bulk to block her path.

"Oi, what are you up to?"

Another glance sank Emilie's shoulders. It was the corporal she had scorned outside her bell tent. She was so upset, she nearly shoved into him. Instead, Emilie found her tongue too thick to move this time around.

"Did Matron send you?" he asked.

Emilie shook her head. *Speak, dammit!* What was the matter with her? She had never been more frightened in her life. "I—I need to get inside."

"What for?"

"Please, Corporal—"

"You've got to tell me what you're doin' here, miss. Can't have every Tom, Dick, and Francis—"

"What's all this?" Sister Allen's voice sounded behind them.

Emilie turned so swiftly, she nearly fell from the stairs. Sister was carrying a tray of instruments, perhaps returning it or answering the need of another nurse.

The orderly answered first: "Sorry, Sister. I was asking where she belongs, is all."

Sister Allen's eyes moved to Emilie's face, white as her veil. With her usual lack of urgency, Sister blinked, and a wash of calm brought Emilie to her senses. "I'm looking for my friend. I think he must be here."

"Name?"

"Second Lieutenant Isaac Thurston."

Sister Allen gave nothing away as she gestured for the orderly to step aside and moved past Emilie into the hut. The orderly stomped down the stairs, not bothered enough to see it through. Emilie waited breathlessly for Sister Allen to return. It could have been seconds or an hour—she was not sure—though it was enough time for her to imagine all manner of horrors that might have befallen Isaac, from a broken finger to a severed arm. And what would he say when he saw her? For all she knew, Isaac would only look upon her with disgust.

When Sister finally showed in the doorway, Emilie went giddy and drifted until her hip leaned against the railing. She didn't swim back to the surface until Sister Allen spoke gently.

"He is here, tucked up in bed."

A choking sound ripped out from Emilie's lungs, and she put her hand over her mouth, knowing it would not do to lose herself entirely while on duty.

"Now you will need to breathe," Sister said.

She did, shakily, and searched Sister's face for answers. "What's happened?"

"He's been gassed—quite badly, but no flesh wounds apart from the chemical burns. Look at me; if I see tears I will send you straight back to where you belong."

All at once, Emilie found her courage, swallowing a stone in her throat. Isaac's body was whole—his comely face untouched. There was no denying it now, no turning around. She had to see him. She would risk everything to see him one last time.

"May I go in?"

"You shall have one minute," Sister said. "Following that, you will return to your ward. When and *only* when your work is complete for the day may you return. I will speak to the sister-in-charge so you will be expected. Come."

Sister was up and into the hut. Emilie followed, feeling her vision close to a point. The hut was warm, owing to a sunny afternoon and a tin roof. Here, the beds were spaced far more generously, though most of them were filled. There were screens between each, creating some privacy. Emilie searched back and forth as they went.

When Sister Allen stopped, Emilie did, too, and turned stiffly in the same direction. Though as she gazed down at the man in the bed, she thought Sister had made a mistake. Laid out pale and small under a heap of blankets, Isaac might have been anyone. A thick layer of gauze remained over his eyes, bandages tied round his head to keep them in place. His cheeks were swollen and drenched in sweat, his mouth purple and agape, desperate for air. He wore a mustache now, which grew in a shade redder than his hair.

A rush of memories flooded Emilie's senses, so strong and sudden that a feather could have knocked her over: memories of the final bright days of summer, of warm skin and gentle whispers, of stars and a strange gentleman staring at her.

"The MO believes he must have fallen, or stood his ground," Sister said, pulling Emilie out of her memories. "Most that fled the gas have less severe symptoms, and most of those who could not didn't make it this far."

Flashes of horror reddened Emilie's vision—Isaac writhing in the mud, gasping, fighting for air, drowning on dry land as his lungs filled with liquid and the yellow-green cloud crept farther over him until he disappeared.

"Is he blinded?"

"His eyes are swollen shut, so we don't yet know the severity." Sister gave her the smallest nudge at the center of her back. "One minute."

Emilie approached the bed as a frightened child. She had cared for hundreds of men, most of them in far worse shape, but now she felt as if a single uncalculated movement could worsen Isaac's condition. Of course, he could not see her as she stood beside the bed, but the slightest stiffening of his shoulders indicated he heard the floorboards creaking. Isaac opened his mouth to speak, but only a cough came through, painful and wet. He being too weak to cover his mouth, the yellow phlegm had nowhere to go but down his chin.

In that moment, Emilie could have wept. Instead, she lifted her apron, no stranger to the sight, and used it to clear the mess from his lips and mustache. When she was through, Isaac turned his chin in her direction, breathing audibly and mouthing words he didn't have the wind for. Was he trying to call out for help? To ask where he was? If his men were safe?

In her fear, Emilie could not speak. She was not sure if he would recognize her voice. But if he was blinded for now, perhaps she could slip away and he would never know she'd been. She could keep the cut clean between them, keep her anonymity, keep her new life all her own.

Isaac's neck twitched, and Emilie saw the muscles of his jaw slide tight in pain. She wished desperately that she had a glimpse of his blue eyes, to see more fully that he was alive. She had not even known he'd embarked for the front. The last time they were together, he was still in training at Halton Park, vexed and desperate to be across the channel.

Emilie could feel Sister Allen's presence looming over them, hear the seconds ticking down. Isaac's hand slid over blindly, off his chest and over the mattress. Searching for hers? She crouched beside the bed, and when his fingers closed over her wrist, she knew he was gripping with all the strength he possessed. He may not have known who she was, but he was desperate to know he was not alone. She wanted to throw herself down onto the bed beside him, to cover his body with her own, to warm him and keep him forever.

How had she ever been so cruel to him? How had she thought her own blind ambitions were more important to her life than his friendship?

Sister Allen gestured for Emilie to come along. Nearly as soon as she had left Isaac's bedside, his neck went slack against his pillows. It pained Emilie to leave, but sleep was best for him. Perhaps chlorine was less deadly than mustard gas, but it did irreparable damage to the respiratory system. Even if Isaac made a full recovery, the symptoms would haunt him perhaps for years to come. And what if his eyes never healed?

"Will you be all right, Dawes?" Sister Allen asked, as they hurried back to C-line. "There is still much work to be done."

Emilie nodded, but Sister still looked concerned.

"I take it he is not your relation."

To this, Emilie found the strength to reply. "He is not."

"What does he mean to you, then? This young man?"

Emilie thought she must have already known the answer, by the way Sister was looking at her. Had they built enough trust between them for Emilie to tell her the truth? Or would admitting it smash any chance of her seeing Isaac again before he was gone?

Emilie, feeling faint, swallowed her pride. "He means everything to me, Sister."

She did not know what to expect in Sister Allen's reply, but she was surprised when the nurse cut away suddenly, leaving her standing on her own.

THAT EVENING, EMILIE LEARNED from a talkative private that Isaac's regiment had only just come over a fortnight ago, thrown directly into the trenches. The British had deployed gas that was blown back by the wind into their own men. An utter failure, and just the beginning. There was another convoy on its way, and as the night staff came to relieve Emilie, she saw the look of terror on their sleepy faces.

Sister Allen had kept her promise, for Emilie was admitted to the officers' ward that evening without a hitch. Isaac was asleep when she arrived, and the sister on night duty brought her a stool to sit beside his bed. Emilie was permitted to stay, so long as she did not disturb the other men. Some of them slept, others sat up working endlessly to clear their throats and lungs. Others moaned from the pain of their wounds.

Emilie felt a chill. She dreaded the day she would be assigned night duty. There was something unsettling about the darkness, about witnessing the frightening hours one usually spends in the safe naivety of a dream.

Despite her exhaustion, Emilie was restless and stood to have a look at Isaac's chart. He was labeled DI, or Dangerously Ill, the poison having caused acute congestion of the lungs, swelling and inflammation of the throat. The sister had scrawled below the MO's notes dictating observations from his last round: The patient was to be confined to bed, as severe shortness of breath was plaguing his heart.

As Emilie returned the chart to the foot of the bed, the blankets rustled. In the dim light of his gas lamp, Isaac came awake from a sputter, trembling as his weakened body tried to sit up. The small effort stole his air, and as he sank back against the pillows, Emilie hurried to his side. Some of her patients had perished only hours after being gassed, their hearts simply giving out from the strain. She would not let Isaac die that way.

The sister-in-charge swept toward the sound of her struggling patient. While Emilie slipped her arms under Isaac's shoulders to lift him, Sister fetched an extra pillow to prop him up, and like that he could breathe easier. When Emilie stepped away, her hands were slick with his perspiration—the effort to breathe so enormous for him.

Sister lay a soft, loving hand on Isaac's head. "He should sleep for a time. Will you be all right?"

"Of course—I can manage."

The sister conceded with a curt nod. "I'll leave you to it."

Alone with Isaac, Emilie was struck by the sudden intimacy. She had cared for men of all shapes and sizes, but not Isaac, not like this, lying in bed in the ill-fitting pajamas from the stores, so helpless, so unlike himself. He had once said it would be heaven to be under her care, but now he was here, she wondered if he would be pleased for her to see him in such a state of vulnerability. He hid so often behind smiles and jests. There was none of that now.

Though Emilie couldn't see his eyes, she could tell he had come awake from the struggle. Isaac shifted, once to turn his head, and again to move his arm closer to her side of the bed. Emilie put her hand over his wrist, hoping to provide some comfort. Each small movement took a great deal of energy, and by the time he was settled again, his breaths were shorter and gravelly. She used a damp cloth to wet his lips and was glad, for once, that he could not see the distress on her face. It was all starting to wear—the exhaustion of an endless day, the cries of wounded men, the poisonous gas that was preventing Isaac from speaking to her, and the knowledge of what she had done to him.

She longed, suddenly, to return to Hallesham Park, to the gravel crunching underfoot, to the dogs barking happily in the kennels, to the heady scent of the rose garden in summer, to Fletcher's youthful face reddened by the sun. Emilie could almost hear him taunting her in a game of tennis. She could almost taste the lemonade, feel the wind lifting her skirt—

Isaac's chest rumbled in a cough, breaking her daydream.

"Pl—please?" he croaked, his voice thick and slurred. "Help? I—I can't see—"

The first tear slipped down Emilie's cheek. For so long she had envisaged a postwar reunion, Isaac's handsome face smiling, his strong arms lifting her off the ground as they spun together. She imagined his lips on her neck, the rough wool of his uniform against her cheek, the juniper and tobacco scent of him, his laughter in her ear.

"I can't—" Isaac stopped short, swallowing painfully. *"Je ne peux . . . pas voir . . ."*

Was he so muddled that he did not even know he was with his countrymen? Damn the consequences. Emilie could not keep her lips sealed any longer.

"You're going to be all right, my dear." She leaned closer so he could hear her whisper. "You are safe in a British hospital. There is nothing to fear now."

"May you stay?" A rumbling cough. "Ma'am?"

"I will not leave you, my love. I promise."

Emilie lay her open hand gently over his chest and felt the awful clicking and grinding of his lungs against her palm. Isaac's wrist went limp in her grasp, his chin turned to the ceiling and his lips parted as he slipped out of consciousness. Her aching muscles eased, and she closed her eyes, wishing it all away.

Nineteen

Emilie

Emilie, who had fallen asleep on her stool, sat straight up. She wouldn't have believed such a thing was possible before the war, but she had heard the stories from the men who slept on horses, slept standing, slept with their heads rested on the butts of their rifles. And sure enough, when her eyes came open, she was erect, and there was the sister from the night before. Isaac was still asleep in his bed, heart beating, lungs filling—*thank God.*

"You'll want to trot on," Sister said. "I'm going off duty, and there was a convoy in this morning."

Emilie hurried to the bell tent, her mind racing. Isaac's arrival had knocked her for six, and the lack of sleep made her feel she was in a waking dream. First chance she got, she would write to Lady Thurston, letting her know Isaac was safe. The dowager would have only been sent a wire—enough to stop a much younger woman's heart.

Once she had thrown cool water on her face and dressed in a clean uniform, she lifted the flap to head to C-line and nearly went straight into Sister Allen. In her frantic state, Emilie had forgotten their last meeting entirely, forgotten to worry about what it all had meant. Now, Sister wore her usual neutral expression.

"Good morning, Sister," Emilie said.

"Good morning." Sister Allen studied her, and Emilie instinctively reached up to adjust her collar, forgetting she wore her navy serge coat. "I have just spoken to Sister Lawrence. As she will be specialling Mr. Thurston, she needs a spare pair of hands. I've offered yours."

Emilie thought she had misheard, or else was still dreaming. It was the last thing she had expected to hear from someone who knew her situation.

"I'm to move to the officers' ward?"

"Have you any objection?"

DON'T expect your own particular feelings or likes to be considered. You are but one of many.

Emilie shook her head. "No, Sister."

Sister Allen gave her a curt nod, and stiffly turned her chin in one direction and then the other. There was nobody about—Emilie had long missed breakfast, and the other girls had already gone to their wards. Sister took a step closer, bowing her head.

"It would not be appropriate for you to look after someone for whom you have romantic notions, and so you mustn't allow the day nurse to find out that Mr. Thurston is anything but a stranger to you. Have I made myself clear?"

Emilie felt a rush of nerves. It would be a difficult task, once Isaac was well enough to recognize her. He would wish to talk about what had happened the last time they were together—he would be angry. She would need to ensure a scene was not made on the ward.

"Yes, Sister," Emilie said. "But—" She wet dry lips as the sister waited for her to speak again. "I feel as though I've upset you. That I have let you down—but I do not understand how."

Sister Allen's lashes fluttered, a momentary lapse in her usual poise. "I was not upset with you, dear girl; I was upset with myself for ignoring my better judgment in order to put you and that boy together."

"Why did you do it, then?"

Sister Allen let out a short sigh before speaking quickly and concisely. "When I was young, I fell in love. That person became ill, and I was not permitted to be by their side as they withered away. Now, I did not know if your Mr. Thurston was long for this world, but I found I could not rob you of the right to guide him through it if he was not."

Sister sniffed, and produced a handkerchief to dab her nose. It may have been the cold that made her eyes water, and so Emilie did not try to comfort her. She knew, somehow, that it was better not to acknowledge the sudden fracture in Sister Allen's indifference.

In the blink of an eye, Sister had regained her stoicism and tucked her handkerchief away. "Have you any further pressing questions for me, volunteer?"

Emilie was startled by the sudden harshness of tone. Within Sister Allen were two distinct women—the one in the veil and the one who laughed at the cold and danced in the crashing sea. For a moment, Emilie could not think who Sister reminded her of, and then it dawned on her. Sister Allen was so like Isaac's Captain Ridley.

"No, Sister," Emilie said, and went to work.

~~~

THE WEEK WAS TRYING on all the staff. Stretchers came endlessly to take patients into theatre, and brought them back in time for another to go. Then Sergeant came round with his list of names to leave on the convoy out, so that the next day their beds would be filled again.

The infection in Isaac's lungs became acute bronchitis, and because speaking was still difficult, Emilie decided not to tell him who she was. Physical exertion would only increase the severity of his respiratory damage, and so it was better if he stayed ignorant—stayed calm. Though he suffered no flesh wounds, he required constant care, and Sister Lawrence helped him with washing, changing, eating, and using the bedpan. Emilie was certain he would be relieved to know she did not have a hand in those less dignified activities.

As with all specialled cases, Isaac was kept apart in a side ward for privacy. Emilie saw him only when she went through to assist the sister-in-charge when it came time for medicine. She gave Isaac oxygen for five minutes every four hours. He had aspirin to bring down the fever and help with aches, cough medicine, and inhalations of boiling water and friar's balsam. His eyes were washed out twice daily, finished with lotion. He ate coddled eggs, beef tea, and mash, as meat was too difficult for him to swallow. His burns were dusted with sodium bicarbonate and boracic powder. It pained Emilie to see the red, raised flesh across the whole of his body, and the pain of them every time he moved.

Here were also the stirring feelings Emilie hadn't recognized since her first blanket baths. Until Isaac, she had adapted the cold blindness of a medical professional. Now she couldn't help but note the shape of him, the square chest, the broad shoulders, the hollows of his clavicle, the tendons that wrapped his forearms and hands. Her skin prickled to be touching his, to feel his muscles clench as she powdered his flat stomach, his knobby knees, his narrow thighs.

Did he know? she wondered, when he turned his bandaged eyes to the sound of her voice. Was it the sheer comfort of human contact that made his skin blush, or Emilie's touch? In the night, when Emilie was lying in her camp bed, she thought of him and wondered what would become of his writing if he lost his sight completely.

That was why, on his fifth morning in the ward, Emilie nearly fell to the floor when she entered the side ward to find Sister Lawrence standing over Isaac, smiling wide with a heap of bandages in her hands. When she noticed Emilie, Isaac did, too. His eyes were swollen and moleish, but open and aware.

Emilie's breaths stalled as she stood paralyzed. She dared not look away, despite her worry—it was too precious to hold his gaze for the first time since she had left him in London. Emilie waited for Isaac to stiffen, to frown, to speak her name in bitterness, to reveal to Sister Lawrence what they meant to one another.

Instead, he smiled.

"This is Dawes, sir," Sister Lawrence said when she noticed Emilie. "She has been helping me look after you, and doing a splendid job of it."

She gestured for Emilie to approach the bed, and she did, sliding her ward shoes over the worn floorboards with caution. All the while, Isaac's eyes followed her, miraculously blue as they always were, dark lashes damp from his treatments.

"Good morning, Nurse Dawes," Isaac said groggily, his mustache shifting to reveal the inward slant of his front teeth.

"I shall leave you in Dawes's capable hands whilst I go and fetch the MO," Sister said, and carried the tray of bandages out the door.

Isaac's mouth was weak but clearly upturned. He looked Emilie over from veil to scuffed ward shoes, and her cheeks burned. She had yet to consider how she must look to him, who had never seen her in uniform, and was self-conscious of her covered hair, splotched apron, and matronly frock.

"Remember us in silk?" she asked jestingly.

He held her eyes fiercely. "You have never needed silk."

Emilie was suddenly filled with immense emotion, and the first tear slipped from her eye. She nervously dabbed it with the back of her hand, glad they were not in the main ward among other patients.

"Little sparrow," Isaac whispered. "I am hardly worth all that."

Emilie's body gave in to the enormity of the moment. She crouched beside Isaac's bed to be closer to his eye level, and laid her hand out open on the mattress, hoping he would wish to hold it. She knew she did not deserve this, his smiles or his sweet words, but she was so greedy for his affection she could hardly think of it.

Isaac slowly moved his hand to lay over Emilie's. It was warm and rough, like hers were now. She grasped his back with all her might, as if it was the single thing keeping her from floating away. "You do not look surprised to see me," she said.

"I *can't* see you—not clearly," he replied. "But enough. Like a watercolor picture."

Emilie began to smile, the tired skin on her face tingling with the delicious pleasure of a good stretch. "What is that on your lip, Mr. Thurston?"

He scratched the mustache, and took the moment to cough into his fist. "It's meant to—to make me look severe. Does it?"

"Not a bit."

"Shall I have it off for you?"

"For me, you need only get well."

Isaac took a moment to catch his breath, smile fading. Emilie saw in the set of his jaw there was more than just illness making him wary.

"Did you truly expect I would not recognize your voice?" His lashes flickered down as he used what little strength he had to turn her hand over, to move his thumb over her palm. "That I would not recognize the touch of your hands?"

Her brilliant boy had not lost his gift for eloquence. And though his voice was ragged and strained, it was stronger than she had thought. He had been keeping quiet on purpose.

"Were you hiding from me, Emilie?" he asked.

She let her head hang, watching their hands. "I wanted to be by your side, and I thought if you recognized me you would send me away. Isaac—" She could hardly see him through the blur of tears. "I am ever so sorry for what I've done to you. I don't know why I did it, I don't—"

Isaac squeezed her hand, making her pause to wipe her eyes. It was all too much, too fast, and Emilie felt the weight of the war breaking her at her core. She ought to have been happy—to see Isaac again, to know he did not despise her. But she could only mourn what they had lost, what more they could lose if the world did not change.

"I know why you did it," Isaac said gently between shallow breaths. "I have always understood the way your roaring mind works. What I don't understand is why you thought you needed to do this on your own. Because I—*I* can't do it on my own, Em. I need you." Isaac's eyes swelled with feeling. "Say it was not the money."

"Of course it was not the money, Isaac."

"I thought Fletcher might have convinced you." Emilie's jaw set at the mention of her brother. "Has he written?"

Emilie shook her head. She had not expected Fletcher to go out of his way to find her, given how they had left things. He hated writing letters, in any case, always grumbling over a pile of correspondence he didn't care to attend to.

"I suspect you wouldn't have heard he is in Gallipoli," Isaac said. "His unit ran into some trouble at Suvla Bay."

Emilie stood to busy herself with straightening his bedclothes. She knew of the failed offensive which was talked of often back in August, even so far from where it had happened.

"How do you know that?" she asked.

"We exchange letters now and again."

She furrowed her brow. Why would Fletcher correspond with Isaac, whom he was so eager to cut from her life? "You remain friends?"

"Yes, thanks to you. You ought to send him a note, Em. I know he would want to hear from you. He was injured, you know. A bullet graze—"

Emilie hardened her heart. "We have nothing to say to one another."

"Is that why you ignored my letter? Left the country and told no one your address? Why would you estrange yourself from your beloved brother over our love, only to disappear clean from my life?"

Emilie's hands went to her face. But there was no hiding from Isaac anymore, no burning his letters, no shoving him to the back of her mind. The wound was open and bleeding, and the only thing to do was to tend to it—to wash away the infection and dress it well.

As her arms fell to her sides, she faced Isaac again, remembering to keep her voice low. "I do not know if I can give you what you want from me—not now, or after the war, or in ten years' time. I've made a life for myself here. For *myself*. Do you know what that means to me?"

"I do—"

"And because I want you to be happy, to have the love you dream endlessly of, I want you to carry on seeking it out. If that means leaving me behind, then I shall remain behind."

Isaac blinked into the middle distance. She could hear his strained, wheezing breaths, see his chest stuttering. All this talking was wearing on him, and she would need to put an end to it soon so that he could rest.

"Come here," he said, reaching out for her. And because Isaac always possessed a magnetism made just for her, she went. Here was the intimacy again, the closeness that made her heart race and her skin come alive. Even now, she could not deny it.

Isaac drew her hand into his lap, holding it against his core. "You are all I know of love, Emilie. The love I dream of is yours, and it does not fit inside of a pretty box, but I would take it no other way." He formed a smile for her that shattered all her wretched thoughts. "Now please, for God's sake, agree to write to me. Frankly, I haven't the wind to carry on discussing it."

Emilie felt the broken pieces of her heart finding one another in her chest. She drew Isaac's hand to her mouth and placed a soft kiss on his palm.

BY OCTOBER, THE WARDS quietened once more, and Emilie was finally given back her off-duty hours. She went into Le Tréport for a rare shopping trip. Isaac was improving every day, and he would need a few items for his toilet, good cigarettes, and perhaps a book to keep him occupied on his journey. He would convalesce in France, to be returned to his regiment if his lungs cleared enough to pass a medical exam. For now she still had him, but their time was fleeting.

Emilie brought the new things to the officers' ward to find Isaac sat outside of the hut on a lawn chair. The collar of his greatcoat was up round his ears, and she was glad to see someone had brought him a scarf from the stores. It was colder every day, and the sea air, though nourishing, was damp.

Isaac smiled, and Emilie stopped a few feet from him to admire the pink sheen of health on his handsome features and the way the sun brought out the red in his hair.

"Here's trouble," she said.

Isaac replied in his best cut-glass accent, "I am taking the air."

"It's much too cold for you to be out of bed."

"Nonsense; I've a blanket."

"Sister Lawrence didn't allow this, surely."

"She did. She's taken a liking to me."

Emilie burst out a laugh. "She's old enough to be your mother!"

A wink. "Come—I've been saving this chair for you. If you only knew the lengths . . ."

Emilie laughed, shaking her head. Inside the hut, someone started up a gramophone—"Where Did You Get That Girl?" An old favorite among the men, that made Emilie think of her first weeks nursing, of the moans and cries of pain it did so little to console.

"I am not allowed to fraternize with men, Mr. Thurston," Emilie said.

"Please sit? We haven't much time."

She hesitated, observing the space around them, which was admittedly desolate. Isaac had chosen to sit along the side of the hut, rather than at its front, facing away from the main campus. Most often, when the sun was shining, up-patients took the opportunity to stretch their legs and wander. But there were so few patients now, and it seemed the chill was keeping them indoors with the hot stove and Billy Murray.

So Emilie huffed, ensuring Isaac knew she could not be swayed easily, and sat on the neighboring chair, holding his Dorothy bag of gifts in her lap. "You'll get me a lashing."

With his head resting back, he faced her, eyes squinting in the sun. "Have I not done that already?"

"I went looking for one, didn't I? It was hardly your fault I spotted you first."

Isaac closed his eyes momentarily, caught by the music, and pursed his lips to whistle along with the chorus. *Where did you get that girl? Oh! you lucky devil. Where did you get that girl? Tell me on the level . . .*

"I see the mustache has gone," Emilie said.

One eye came open, the oval mouth she had been admiring twisting with mischief. "I suspected you didn't like it."

"I was beginning to, you know. Then, I won't have to look at you much longer."

It was meant to be a joke, but the notion sobered him and he forgot the music. Despite his better health, there were still dark smudges under his eyes. Had he not been sleeping? Was it the coughing, Emilie wondered, or the anticipation of returning to the front?

"How has it been," he asked, "a life of work?"

She remembered a conversation they'd had in their early days together. Lady Thurston's fortune had all gone, and Isaac had been preparing for a career, a life never intended for a man born of a nobleman.

"It is far more difficult than I could ever have imagined," Emilie answered truthfully. "I see now how my very ignorance was a privilege. Our wealth afforded us the luxury not to think, and it was thoughtless of me to wish it away, when so many people struggle only to feed their babies. Even so, I cannot imagine returning to the life I once knew . . ."

Isaac allowed Emilie's words to rest with him. Part of her expected it was a relief for him to hear this—to imagine a life after the war where wealth would not drive her choices, and therefore not away from him.

"Is that for me?" he asked, pointing to the Dorothy bag.

"Yes, the lot of it. I wanted you to have some good soap, and couldn't send you away with awful ration tobacco. There's a photo of me as well."

It had been a last-minute decision, but she'd seen a line of Tommies outside the studio and decided to duck in. She posed in front of a painted background of a garden, knowing she looked stiff and matronly in her uniform. When she handed the postcard to Isaac, she expected a smile or a jest, but he looked overcome for a moment and slid it wordlessly into his chest pocket.

"Thank you," he said, gravely. "Very much."

Emilie wanted to lighten things again, so gave Isaac a light thump on the arm. "I haven't got one of you, you know."

"I hate having my photograph taken."

"Do you? Well, you must! Just once, for me? Please?"

He slid his eyes to her, looking completely miserable at the idea. She could not understand why. She'd seen photos of him at Lady Thurston's flat, and though a camera could not do him justice, he still looked ethereal.

"I need to ask something of you," Isaac said.

"Anything, if I get my photograph."

"Will you take my notebook? Keep it safe with your things?"

Emilie's smile collapsed. A few days ago, he had asked her to check his locker for his notebook, to ensure that he had not lost it when he fell. It was tattered, but intact, and Isaac had closed his eyes with relief.

"Will you not need it?" Emilie asked.

"If I lose it, that's my novel gone."

"But you'll need it to reference if you're going to write more."

Isaac shook his head. "I would rather have it safe. The rest is in London, in my desk—"

"Isaac—"

"You know how much can be lost when one of us is hit."

Emilie panicked. She did not wish to talk as if Isaac's life was so delicate. But the truth was, men went missing entirely—perhaps because they were truly lost somewhere, but most often because their body lay in the mud, half-buried in rubble, never to be recovered. Emilie heard all the terrible stories of blasts, of men being thrown up into the sky like dolls and not coming down—not in any state that once resembled a person.

She was glad when Isaac's hand found hers, clammy but warm. She drank in the familiarity of his features, the dent in his brow, the glimmer of emotion in his eyes. He let go before anyone could see.

"Take the notebook now, and I will send you the pages as I write them," he said. "Do this for me, please? You are the only person I trust . . ."

"What if *I* lose them?"

The corner of his mouth crept upward. "Then we'll know it was not meant to be read."

This was important to Isaac—perhaps the most important thing in his life. Emilie could not refuse for the limp hope that no more harm would befall him. "Leave them with me."

The music stopped for a moment, and they were left with the skittering of fallen leaves blown across the duckboards. When the gramophone had been cranked again, another Billy Murray record played and his nasally voice flowed out from the ward.

Who are you with tonight, tonight? Oh! Who are you with tonight?
Who is the dreamy peach and creamy vision of sweet delight?

"Has he been writing to you?" Isaac asked, breaking their silence.

Emilie wished he hadn't. Fire licked at her temples, and she moved her attention to her pink, chapped hands. "You need not feel threatened by Rhys Bridgmond."

"Threatened?" Isaac laughed, a disingenuous blast of an English gentleman that dissolved into a cough. "That is not the word I would have chosen."

"No? Which, then, please? Jealous?"

"I am not jealous of Lord Bridgmond. Rather I am . . . *aware of* him mulling about this country, believing you to be his prize should he return."

Emilie set her chin. "When you put words in his mouth, they become your own. Do you really see me as some *thing* which may be won?"

"Emilie, you know that I do not."

"I am unsure that I do. And I cannot understand why you expect he would want anything to do with me after how I treated him."

"No, no, you're right. The man would have to be an imbecile."

Emilie felt the knife twist in her gut. What Isaac implied was true enough; she had betrayed both men the same way, and Isaac had forgiven her. Though what they shared was completely different. She had done more to Rhys than break his heart. She had lied, and stolen from him. No better than a common thief.

"Do you expect they are looking for me?" she asked.

Isaac sank in his chair, raising his shoulders against the cold. "The loss of a ring is inconsequential. The Claremonts have wealth enough to care only for their reputation."

Emilie expected he was right, but was still afraid. One day she would have to return to England to face the consequences, and she would be returning empty-handed.

"Perhaps you are an imbecile for caring for me," she said, which brought a genuine smile to Isaac's face. Despite herself, she noticed a fluttering in her belly that she had not felt since before the war. "I think you are out of sorts, my boy. Where has this hot head come from? Are you sad to leave me? Or only afraid to return to the front?"

"I am not afraid," he said defensively. "I am frustrated that it took so little to send me out of it. I had been in France barely long enough to miss home."

Emilie drew a patient breath. This was the truth she'd been searching for, the words he would not have uttered among the other officers. They were difficult to admit, even in confidence. She would have to be delicate with her response.

"Men were killed on the first day of war. It says nothing of your courage."

"I fell—" Isaac bowed his head in her direction. "When the gas began to burn at my eyes and I was suffocating—I fell to the ground, helpless. I do not even know how I got out, who carried me to safety. My men were dying and I just lay there—"

"It would have been the same if you had been shot."

"—and I haven't so much as a scar to show for it. Our own bloody gas." He shook his head, face pinched in pain. "Blake is dead; I slept beside him only days ago. And they are saying over two hundred killed, wounded, or missing from my battalion alone. I cannot feel pride, not in myself or what was done that day, though I should die before admitting as much to anyone but you."

Emilie tightened her grip on his hand, showing her appreciation for his trust. How many men would confide in a woman the way Isaac did her? Her own brother could not even admit his fears. She was incredibly fortunate. Sharing Isaac's secrets was a privilege.

"This was never going to be easy for you," Emilie said, "no matter what you tell yourself. But you are here, you are breathing, and you have your wits—there is no reason why you should not have another chance to prove yourself. They cannot afford to lose an able body."

Isaac's eyes went far off—goodness knows where. "That is all we are, isn't it? We have signed our bodies over to the government, to be placed and broken and disposed of as it sees fit."

She gripped the arm of his coat, tight enough that he had no choice but to listen. "Take care with your words, Isaac, I beg of you."

Something shifted in his eyes as she stared into them, and a great wash of dread came over her. Here was her beautiful boy, so close she could reach out and feel the warmth of life in his flesh. Soon he would be gone again, only words on a page.

The firmness of his arm in her grasp made her sway. She was suddenly all too aware that she didn't know when she would see him next, *if* she would see him next. How had she left him so easily before? The idea that his perfect face might be torn, or broken, or buried for eternity made Emilie's eyes suddenly fill with tears.

"I love you," she said, "so much it pains me."

When he looked at her, she forgot how to breathe. "Wait for me, then. Promise me you'll wait."

But for all the affection Emilie had for him in that moment, for all the fear, all the passion, all the past and future tears, she could not promise. She could only nod.

Twenty

Emilie

DECEMBER 1915

Come December, Christmas was all anyone could talk of, and the VADs threw themselves into decorating. The members of staff were each in an unofficial competition to outdo the others, stringing up holly berry, evergreen, and mistletoe they'd picked themselves, cutting paper ornaments to string up from the canvas roof, making snow out of cotton wool, and adorning the tables with oranges, pine cones, and whatever else could be found about camp. Patients hung socks from the ends of their beds, and nurses filled them with cigarettes, soap, and chocolate. A fancy dress ball was planned for the staff, and a concert for the boys.

The post office was the busiest it had ever been, with everyone expecting parcels from home, and post taking twice as long to come and go. Emilie had been delighted to see she had a parcel from Isaac, and a few letters. When she saw her brother's handwriting on one of the envelopes, she thought her heart might come to a stop. She stumbled out of the post office, collapsing to a seat on the stairs.

Emilie, do not crumple this letter until you've read it!
I know you will not wish to hear from me, but your dear

Thurston gave me your address, and so you must suffer my letters from now on. Take it up with him if you have any complaints—I shall not scorn you for continuing your correspondence with him. He's a good chap, but you know that well enough. Shame about the rest of it.

I am in Egypt now, if you haven't heard, which I imagine you have not. It is dreadful most of the time. I never thought I could miss Gallipoli, but I long for it now. Did you know, I was grazed by a bullet there? Spent one night in hospital, all the while thinking of our Christmas conversation about scars, and decided this one is quite enough and I should not like more.

The lice are beastly here. I was appalled to learn that the best solution to an infestation is to lie one's uniform out on an anthill and wait for the lice and their eggs to be devoured. One then shakes the ants and is comfortable for a few days before the lice return. The food is often fresh, but bland—one must be careful not to consume flies and sand with one's dinner, though it is inevitable. Some of the men here tried to cook up a flamingo, finding the meat green and tough. I would give anything for a proper Hallesham roast . . .

Emilie looked up from the letter as a group of caroling VADs passed with their oil lamps wrapped with festive red paper. Up-patients flooded out of their wards to investigate, some joining in song, some watching, tired eyes gleaming with reverence.

Fletcher was in *Egypt*. Another world entirely.

She continued reading. Fletcher wrote that the campaign in Gallipoli had been abandoned altogether and pronounced a failure. He did not say so, but Emilie could devise from his tone that he was terribly dejected, having been pulled out of the East after so much work and such heavy loss, only to be sent to another foreign land of extremes. Her heart was so suddenly full for him then that the carolers' song brought a tear to her eye.

Enough for now, duck. If you are still reading this, know that I would appreciate a reply, but will continue sending notes in any case.

                              Your most unfair and evil brother,
                                                Fletcher

Perhaps she could send him something lovely for Christmas, but could not imagine what he needed in such a place, where the days were excruciatingly hot, and the nights so cold and damp that the men woke with frost on their bodies. Emilie wondered if she would be able to send him anything of worth.

When she stood to brush herself off, she was smiling again. Her dear brother. She had not yet lost him.

With Isaac's parcel in hand, Emilie dashed to her ward. The evening before had been her first evening on night duty. She had stumbled groggily into jersey, greatcoat, two pairs of stockings, gum boots, belted mackintosh, mittens, and sou'wester hat only to find she was stuck inside her bell tent, the canvas having shrunk so badly in the rain that the ties were too tight to open. The fight lasted long enough to make her late, and once she finally emerged from her quarters, a gust of wind sent everything up, and the mackintosh was rendered useless.

Tonight, as Emilie arrived for work with wet feet and a damp hem, she discovered the rain had found its way inside. One of the boys was up out of his bed, his pillow already drenched. Emilie groaned and threw off her coat.

"Would it be too much to ask for snow?" Emilie asked as the sister-in-charge, Sister James, came in under the flap.

Sister yanked off her hat, speckling her shoulder with the runoff. "*C'est la guerre.*"

Once Emilie had the patients settled with clean, dry beds, she moved to the stove to warm herself, and open Isaac's parcel. It was a small box, wrapped carefully in brown paper and twine. His note inside read, *For my little sparrow, with love on Christmas.*

Emilie carefully drew away a handkerchief to find a brass box, intricately decorated with swirls and florals and cherubs at the center. It was old, though polished enough to glow in the light from the fire. She gently pulled it out, trying to work out what exactly it was. There was a circular bit in the center of the lid with separate hinges. On the right was a small lever. Curiously, Emilie pulled it, and the center popped up to reveal a delicate automaton bird that at once began flapping and chirping his joyful song.

Her breath was taken as though she had witnessed a miracle. The bird was exquisite, adorned with real feathers of midnight blue, orange, and green, turning back and forth, wings going, beak opening and closing as it sang. The room faded away and Emilie stared in childish wonder, moved by this intricate display of human ingenuity and artistic elegance. When the bird finished and lay back down beneath the lid, she pulled the lever again. The bird leapt up, startling her though she had expected it, and filled her heart with mirth.

A few up-patients had heard the chirping and gathered round to watch as Emilie set the bird going again. It seemed to be the thing they all needed in that bleak winter hour of war—a small reminder of what beauty and wonder was still possible.

There was no more perfect present in the world. Emilie was so very lucky to be in love with Isaac Thurston.

***

"WHAT WOULD YOU GET for a man in Egypt?" Emilie asked Sister Allen.

Sister turned from a display of folding fans. "Oh, I don't know. A parasol?"

They both broke into laughter—Emilie because she had never heard Sister make such a blatant joke—loud enough to draw the eye of the bearded *commerçant*. Turning their backs to him, they leaned over a glass case of bric-a-brac to sober themselves. They had come into Eu for lunch and Christmas shopping.

"I thought you were buying for your Mr. Thurston," Sister said.

"I am. But Fletcher desperately needs cheering." Emilie had explained her rickety relationship with her brother to Sister on the drive to Eu. "You've been stationed in Africa. What would you have liked for Christmas?"

"Perhaps something to remind me of England."

Looking closer at the glass case, Emilie became aware of a display of snuffboxes. Fletcher had collected them as a boy, though long abandoned the hobby. Still, Emilie was drawn to look closer, and spotted one that depicted a scene of a fox hunt, with two men on horseback and three dashing hounds. What could be more British than that?

Emilie bought the snuffbox, shocked by the price, and chastised herself for living so many years without considering the cost of anything.

They went on to browse the market. Eu was a colorful little town, so quintessentially French with narrow streets and mismatched buildings of brick or timber framing, with mansard roofs and shutters. Plenty of merchants had braved the cold to sell in the square to a crowd made up almost entirely of the British military.

Emilie found Sister Allen to be a most pleasant shopping companion. She had a keen eye and pointed to things Emilie might have missed. Emilie tempted her to splurge on fine soaps, but Sister declined, replenishing her stationery instead. They bought as many apples and clementines as they could carry, which everyone would go wild for back at camp.

For a break from the cold, they visited the Collégiale Notre Dame, a magnificent Gothic chapel that excited Sister Allen more than it did Emilie. Sister was overcome with reverence as they strode along in silence, taking in the stained glass and great organ. Emilie had lately acquired a rather complicated relationship with religion, and wondered, after all she had seen in this war and the last, how Sister could gaze upon the cross and feel held.

Emilie left the cathedral ahead of her, needing a moment alone, and sat on the steps, where a pair of boys were playing with a little brown dog. The dog came to sniff her boots, and the boys followed when she stroked the head and spoke to it in French: "*Beau chien, beau chien!*"

The younger, nose red from the cold, stepped up bravely to point at the Red Cross on her coat. "*Une infirmière?*"

"*Oui, très bien.*"

He then lifted his elbow and pointed to it. "*J'ai mal au coude!*"

"*Mon Dieu!*" Emilie furrowed her brow, pretending to have great authority on hurt elbows, and gave his arm a pinch through his worn coat. "*Ce n'est pas cassé.*" It wasn't broken. "*Tu es fort!*" You are strong!

He smiled at the compliment. The older, not to be outdone, proudly held up a cigarette, declaring it was given to him by a British *capitaine*. Emilie gave them both a clementine, hoping to make up for the negligence of her countryman.

As they dashed away together, Emilie felt a twinge of longing for her own brother. Looking around her, she could almost imagine his head on one of the broad sets of khaki shoulders walking down the road. But he was not here. He was so terribly far away.

Sister Allen came out of the church, and they walked the short distance to the Château d'Eu, the royal estate where Louis Philippe twice entertained Queen Victoria. Standing before the brick castle, on the gravel among pristine lawn and meticulous topiary, Emilie moved away from Sister to stand on her own. Hallesham Park was no palace, but it was beautiful and grand, and it had been months since she'd been reminded of its splendor. It had been months, truly, since she'd missed home at all.

By the time Sister lay a soft hand on her back, Emilie was dabbing wet eyes with her mittens. Sister Allen weaved her arm through Emilie's. "Come; let's see you fed."

Unlike many of the girls at camp, Sister Allen did not turn her nose up at French cuisine. At the Hôtel du Commerce, they ate potage and boiled mussels, poached fish in capers and butter sauce, *pommes fondant*, crusty bread with lashings of fresh butter, and apple tart. Emilie ate like a woman who had not seen food in months, and forgot, for a moment, there was a war on.

They lingered over empty plates, drinking strong coffee. Emilie brought out the snuffbox she'd bought for Fletcher. What would he be eating today? Would he be eating at all?

"You are miles away, I think," Sister said, stirring her coffee.

Emilie was. Though the day had been a welcome respite from the realities of the hospital, it had also conjured emotions that were easily set aside when there was work to be done. Idling could be dangerous, and it was why she tended to avoid trips to town—they reminded her too much of life before, and what she had robbed from her life after.

"I'm missing my family. But I fear that things can never be the same between us after the war."

"Why is that?"

Emilie hesitated, reminding herself the woman knew enough about her that a little more would not change her feelings. "I joined the VAD to escape them . . . to discover whether there is a person inside of me before I must give her away to a man."

"Not your writer?"

Emilie shook her head. "My parents forbade me to correspond with him. I ran away because I wanted a different life than my mother planned for me. I wanted to be independent, to learn things, to fall in love."

"And what does she want for you?"

"She wants me to marry the sensible man she's chosen, to stay at home and learn to play piano, to wear fine gowns and pay calls to the right people. She wants me to have *her* life."

Sister Allen removed the spoon from her coffee cup, setting it down in the saucer. "Your mother sounds a strong woman."

"No—no, she is anything but. She is incapable of thinking for herself."

"But does your mother enjoy her life?"

Emilie had never considered it. "I suppose."

"And it is a good life?"

"Yes . . ."

"Then I am certain she must have fought for it, in her way, and now wants to do the same for you."

"But it isn't the life I *want*."

"Ah, there we are." Sister Allen lifted her coffee. "What sort of life are you after?"

Not a year ago, Emilie would have answered that she wanted a life of her own. Some days, she wanted the life she'd had before the war, but with Isaac in Rhys's place. She loved Isaac, and she knew that he would have her without second thoughts. But marrying him would mean losing her family, her home, her brother, forever. With the money all gone, they would need to live differently to how she was accustomed—no extravagance, no jewelry, no motorcars or house parties. But marriage, even to a man she loved, would rob her of some part of herself that she longed to discover. Could love alone be enough to satisfy her?

"I want your life," Emilie answered finally. "I want to be free to do what I like, but— Is it worth it? Is it worth the loneliness?"

Sister Allen's lips pressed together and she turned her head away. There was a tightness in her jaw, in her throat—and emotion Emilie did not recognize in her. Was she angry?

Emilie waited, letting the hum of other people's conversations fill the silence. The waiter came to take the coffee cups, offering more, but Emilie declined. It wasn't until he was gone that Sister Allen looked at her again.

"Why do you ask me about loneliness?" she said.

"Well, you cannot marry, can you? It would mean forfeiting your career. And you don't . . . you don't strike me as the sort of woman who would give it up for anyone."

Sister's thin lips curled into a smile. "I did wish to marry once, when I was your age. Through trial and error, and some heartbreak, I found that my life was nourished not by a man's company, but by the way I live my life. Unfortunately, I cannot advise whether nursing will do the same for you. That is something you must discover on your own."

"But you are lonesome?"

Sister sat straighter, letting out a sigh. "No—I am surrounded always by other women, and patients, and doctors. They are all that I need. You are thinking of Mr. Thurston?"

Emilie hesitated, then nodded. "If I marry him, I will lose my family. If I marry whom my mother has chosen, I will lose myself."

"And if you do not marry at all?"

Emilie swallowed, opening the snuffbox absently to find a few remaining crumbles from the gent who had owned it previously. Truthfully, she could not imagine her life without either Isaac or Rhys. The two futures were different enough, but there seemed to be no third option. Was there a world in which she could have her independence *and* her family? And was there nothing standing in her way but two young men?

Sister reached a hand across the table to set atop hers. "Your life is your own, Emilie." It was the first time Sister had used her Christian name. "Think not of what or whom you will lose; think only of what can be gained if you start living for yourself."

Twenty-One

Emilie

Spring brought warm weather and the sudden ability to forget one was living through a terrible war. The Earth does not realize its inhabitants are at odds, and neither do the birds, the rabbits, the insects, the flowers, the sun. Nature cares little for human squabbles, and thank heaven for it.

Camp was finally dry, so Emilie was able to roll the tent walls to allow the dusty, grassy scent of picnics and garden parties to drift in and out of the ward. Apart from the never-ending need to swat flies from lying patients, the marquees were a far nicer place to be. She picked flowers in the nearby wood whenever she had the afternoon off, keeping bouquets of lilac, laburnum, and chestnut in the mess and on ward tables.

Isaac was writing frequently as ever. He was finding free time, wherever he was, for she began to receive pages of his novel each time the post came through. Before long, she was craving them, sometimes even more than his letters alone. Emilie liked to take Isaac's pages out to the cliffs and read them with Captain Ridley's iron seas as a backdrop.

There was a new depth to his characters, and though his prose was more direct, it was better than it had ever been and deeply poignant. The descriptions were raw and graphic, written in a way that only someone who had seen the like could put into words. There was a sudden realism to every aspect of the story—from the smell of gunpowder, to the blue ring around a fresh bullet wound, to the pain of hunger, to the feeling of thrusting a knife into a human chest. And perhaps that was why the book had gone from an adventure story to a thoughtful reflection on the uselessness of violence. Emilie knew without asking that Isaac had been Captain Ridley, that he had seen his men die and could do nothing to stop it.

Emilie had asked him in her last letter, *How can you still, after all you have been through, write a character who does not fear death?*

His reply had arrived that evening, and she read it in bed by the light of her oil lamp:

There are far worse things to fear than death, he had written. *To die fighting for one's freedom is one of the greatest honors bestowed upon man. So it is not the grave that I am frightened of, rather the thousands and thousands of torturous ways in which life can be drained from a body. I am frightened of the pain of flayed flesh, of the slow bleeding of a severed limb, of being forgotten in a shell hole full of mud and having no voice to shout for help. I fear returning to you as some abominable creature rather than the man you first met in a London ballroom.*

When she finished reading, she folded the letter neatly and tucked it back into its envelope, thinking perhaps she would have preferred to continue imagining that Isaac had no fears at all.

The next letter she opened was from Fletcher.

Duck—

Hot season has arrived. I am rather miserable, murderously angry. Cannot write much, as my hands are in bad shape. The sun bakes equipment so hot that the odd bumped knuckle on leather or metal results in septic burns. Everyone's bandaged like mummies: faces, hands, legs. Flies come round to swarm as if we're already corpses. I don't bother swatting them anymore.

Sweat is everywhere—dribbling endlessly down neck, back, stomach, fingers, hair, thighs, toes. You cannot dry from bathing before more comes along. We are issued two pints of water a day for drinking, chlorine-flavored and boiling from the sun. The third is for washing. I do not register my own odor anymore. I do not remember the scent of cleanliness. Our uniforms are bleached from the sun, our faces burnt like leather. We are permitted to cut our shirtsleeves and trousers to the knee, though it does little to combat the heat and allows for more sand in. You would not recognize your brother, and I hope you will never see me as I am today.

We sleep in holes, digging to find cool earth—it is the only respite. With a canvas over the top, one feels one is in a coffin, buried alive. I don't mind the notion much.

I shall end here. Wrote Mama a happier note, but I daresay you can stomach this. She is too proud to acknowledge you but I always tell her you are well, a brave little thing.

Please keep sending me your lovely letters.

—Fletch

It was often difficult to read letters from Fletcher, who was not one for euphemism. But if he bothered to write of the horrible things he saw, there was good reason. It was difficult for men to commiserate, especially officers, who were pressured to be as stone in the face of anything. She could pray only that her brother would live to see their bright green world again.

Emilie returned to sort through her stack of post, where there were two more letters from Isaac, and a wire from Northampton. Emilie sat up in bed, careful not to wake Nancy on the other side of the curtain. For a moment, she could only stare. It must have been her brother who passed along her address. But had he thought of the consequences? What the Claremonts might like to do now they could find her and prove her guilty of jilting and stealing from their precious heir?

For a moment, Emilie thought to dispose of the wire before anyone else could see it. The idea faded quickly. There was no use in destroying it when there might have been another in Matron's office. She knew the day would come when she would need to face her actions—she just did not think it would come before the war was over.

She opened the envelope and read hastily.

We have had word that my brother is wounded and is currently under the care of No. 32 Stationary. Our family hopes you are able to pay him a call if you know of its location and are near. As yet, we understand little of his condition. We would be most grateful if you could write with news, as it seems Rhys is unable. Let us set aside our grievances momentarily for the sake of an ailing man. My parents would be much obliged.

Sincerely,
Lady Harriet

NO. 32 WAS IN Wimereux, up the coast to the north, and could be got to by train. Matron had been sympathetic, and allowed Emilie to take two days' leave. The wards had been quiet, so they could spare her—along with Sister Allen, who volunteered as chaperone. Word was sent to the matron there, and they were offered beds for the night. In such times, Emilie found most people would bend over backward to ensure a wounded man had a willing visitor. Though she still could not believe the Claremonts had been desperate enough to send her to Rhys's side.

Emilie feared the quick action alluded to the worst. If his wounds were not serious, he would have sent word home by now. Emilie had seen every terrible way a body could be torn open, and dreaded to learn what had happened to Rhys, to see him out of the context she had always known him in. To face him and what she had done.

On the train, Sister Allen tried to get Emilie to eat the apples she had brought for their journey, but Emilie could not stomach a thing. There was a peculiar mixture of emotions tossing around within her. She was glad that the news had not come about Fletcher or Isaac, and ashamed that she had regarded Rhys's life as any less important. She was surprised at how shaken she was, at how much she wanted him to be all right—a man who she had spent so many years wishing away. How could she have been so cruel to him?

A carriage had been sent to collect them at the station. By the time it stopped in front of the matron's office, it was full dark. No. 32 was a Canadian camp hospital, not unlike their own—marquees in neat rows with electric lights strung sparingly between them.

"Good evening, ladies," Matron said, holding up her lamp. "I trust you had no trouble on the journey?"

"No, it was fine, thank you, Matron." Sister Allen was happy to answer, and Emilie let her speak for both of them, anxiously wringing the life out of her gloves. "We do appreciate you accommodating us on such short notice."

"It's our pleasure. May we offer you a hot supper before you go in?"

Sister looked at Emilie, who shook her head.

"I'd just like to see him, please," Emilie said, finding her voice. "Is he . . . ?"

Matron lost her smile and Emilie's stomach dropped to her feet. "He is having a rough time of it, I'm afraid. From what we understand, the billets were badly shelled."

"Is he conscious?" she asked. "Is he speaking?"

Matron exchanged a look with Sister Allen, like Emilie was a child they wanted to hide something from. "There does not seem to be much fight left in him."

Sister reached up and chafed Emilie's back, but she couldn't feel it. She wanted to collapse to the ground, to beat the earth with her fists, to rage and to wail at the injustice of it all. Instead, she stared at the flame in Matron's lamp until the rest of the world fell away.

"Why don't you go on," Sister said. "I'll wait here, unless you'd like me to go with you?"

Emilie shook her head. She wasn't prepared for Sister Allen to know everything.

Matron led Emilie to a line where a VAD with large, round eyes introduced herself as Dupuis. She had been specialling Rhys, and was directed to take Emilie to him, to fetch a stool, and a cup of tea. Emilie declined the drink, though was glad of the rest.

Oftentimes, a ward of moribund cases felt much like a church. It was mostly quiet, with the exception of the odd cough or shuffling of linens, or the dull tap of leather shoes on worn floorboards. The padre spent many of his hours there, dispensing his time between the members of his ever-changing congregation. And the soft voices that disturbed the silence were usually prayers, verses of Scripture, or talk of eternal life.

Conversely, nobody left moribund with a hymn in their ear.

Rhys was boxed in by three standing screens, the light of an oil lamp causing it to glow from within. Men were given privacy in the end.

Dupuis squeezed her arm, a reassurance Emilie wished made her feel stronger. "Take all the time you need. But please, if he speaks, there is a pad of paper on the bedside . . ."

The nurse at a dying man's bedside was expected to record final words. Often they were jumbled and meaningless. Other times, they were worth sending to a grieving family.

Emilie slipped between the screens, setting them together again before becoming overwhelmed by the smell of infection. Rhys's brown eyes were stuck on her, alert though sleepy. But he did not smile, nor say her name. Did he recognize her?

The lamp was low, but Emilie saw the shell had taken one of his legs. A quick glance at his chart revealed that his blood was still badly infected. He had taken fragments in the stomach, a more deadly location even than the head, and the strain on his breathing was obvious.

His face was familiar but pale and gaunt, his light hair stuck down with sweat.

Rhys's head turned slowly to follow Emilie's movement to his bedside. As she sat, his brow furrowed. Had he worked out she was not his nurse? Was he upset to see her? Emilie tried a smile for him, waiting with false hope that he might return it. But though his languid eyes only stared on, they were empty.

"Hello, Rhys." She leaned in to take his clammy hand. "It's your old pal from home. It's Emilie."

His bottom lip hung open. The morphia was doing its job to comfort him.

"Sister . . . ?" he muttered, blinking. "I seem . . . I seem to be slipping . . ."

Emilie brought her other hand up, pressing his between her two palms, rubbing them as if the action might return some life to his body. How terribly small he looked, with the cage over his leg, and the buttons of his top done up under his chin. He had always towered in a room, had always been smiling. She had not taken the time to know him properly—to ask him about his dreams, his ambitions, his fears—and now there was no time left.

"Rhys, darling," Emilie said. "Don't you recognize me? Don't you . . ." A tear slipped out and she dotted it off her nose with her wrist. "Wouldn't you like to say hello to your fiancée?"

Emilie spoke the words in a mad desperation, feeling she had somehow caused this, that if she had only worn his ring and darned socks with Harriet all war, he wouldn't have ended up here. It was senseless, but her logic had gone.

Rhys swallowed hard, having a fair bit of trouble with it, and coughed wetly. When he was through, he blinked, eyes wandering. He flinched as if he'd seen something that startled him.

"I'm in the wrong dugout," he said.

"You're in hospital," Emilie said. "With Emilie. Lady Emilie Dawes of Hallesham Park. Your sister sent me to you. Harriet sent me—"

Rhys blinked and looked at her with wide eyes. "Harriet?"

"Yes, your sister—"

"Dear God," he said. "I—I must tell her . . ."

The tears were coming fast now, and Emilie hiccuped, unable to continue swallowing her emotion. He was gone—gone already, and he would die thinking he was entirely alone.

"I'm sorry, I'm so sorry—" she sputtered. "I was cruel and thoughtless and petty, and I ought not to have done it, to—"

Rhys tugged at her hands, his fingers wiggling in her grasp. She looked up, and there was a new brightness in his eyes, and the wrinkle in his forehead had smoothed. Had he understood? Was he going to forgive her?

"My Emilie," he said.

She gasped, smiling against his knuckles, kissing them with urgency to show him how much she cared. To apologize for everything she'd ever said to hurt him.

"You sound far away." His voice broke as his brows pulled together. Then his gaze moved to a far-off place, beyond the screens, beyond the camp, beyond the Earth. "Emilie?"

"I'm just here, Rhys." She put his hand, cold and clammy, against her face, and held it there. "You see? I'm very close."

"Oh . . . oh yes." He nodded slowly, then took a moment to catch his breath, wheezing horribly from his battered chest. When he mustered some wind again, he said, "Don't go down that end, there . . ."

His hand became weightier against Emilie's cheek. "What end?"

"That end. Suicide Corner . . . Where's Lowry?" His head moved side to side again, struck with panic. "Private Lowry? Where's—"

Emilie sat back as the realization came over her. He had not understood her apology. She would need to have Dupuis fetch the padre, but was too frightened Rhys might be lost in the time it would take her to cross the ward. Emilie shifted, willing her feet to move, but Rhys held on, keeping her back.

"Don't leave," he said. "I'm frightened. Oh God—"

His eyes welled with tears. It became difficult for him to speak after that, with the taxing combination of sniffing back tears and fighting for air. So Emilie stayed, holding tightly to his hand while his body shook for the struggle. Rhys was so young. He'd been so brawny the last time she'd seen him, so cocksure, and bonny. Now it hurt to hear him whimper, to cower before demons which were only in his ailing mind.

Emilie thought of Isaac, wherever he was, and hoped that if he was hurt or dying that he had someone by his side. Sometimes, that was all she *could* hope for.

And that was when they began to crank the air raid siren, an imposing roar that made Emilie put her hands over her ears. On the other side of the canvas walls, she heard frantic movement, voices of soldiers and the nurses who were helping them to shelter. Beyond, the first sounds of danger hummed in the night, far off and threatening approach.

Emilie looked over Rhys, her body filled with panic. A zeppelin raid.

One of the screens rattled aside, giving her a shock. Emilie sat up straight, still holding Rhys's hand, and saw Sister Allen's face come into the light, void of all color. Her lips parted and then closed again, pale lashes fluttering. Her usual serenity had gone.

"Get to the dugout," she said. "Now."

Emilie was dizzy, sitting between Rhys from her past and Sister Allen from her present, neither of them belonging in this place. "What about the men? None of these boys can get out of their beds."

Sister stiffened, hardened her jaw. "This is not our hospital, we are not on duty."

"Then we are to abandon them?"

Before Sister could reply, the screens moved again, this time to reveal Dupuis and the padre.

"I need the two of you"—Sister pointed one finger at Emilie and one to Dupuis—"to go immediately to the dugout. As should you, Father."

The padre brought his Bible up to his chest, gripped between smallish hands. "My place is with my boys."

Sister Allen didn't bother fighting him, instead gave Dupuis a small push in the direction of the flap door. The girl did not protest—the authority of a trained nurse, even a strange one, was enough to make her move. Then Sister stepped forward to take Emilie's arm, but she struggled away, pushing her stool backward until it bumped into Rhys's cot. For all she had done to him in his life, she could not abandon him in death.

"I am not asking you, Dawes," Sister said through her teeth. "On your feet this instant!"

"I'll not leave him. I won't let him die alone."

"Emilie!"

Sister Allen shook her shoulder. But she had already made up her mind. Captain Ridley would never think of abandoning her men, so neither would Emilie.

The padre shuffled forward, crouching beside Rhys. He opened his Bible and began to read softly, his words flowing in memorized rhythm.

Sister Allen was shuffling the privacy screens out of the way. "Help me get these men under their beds, then."

Reluctantly, Emilie left Rhys in the hands of the chaplain, and followed Sister around the ward with a candle. Some of the men were heavy and couldn't much help with moving themselves bodily to the floor, but they managed to get five or six of them under their mattresses before the first shell landed.

Emilie was knelt on the ground. Her breath left for what felt an eternity. The sheer sound of it was monstrous—a wayward *shoo* through the air and then a dull crunch into the earth, the cracking burst and the soft rain of soil. When she finally remembered how to fill her lungs, Emilie did so too quickly, making her head spin. It had to have been quite close.

Somewhere outside the ward there was shouting. Sister Allen dashed through the flap, returning with two men—an orderly and a patient. Emilie couldn't see yet where they'd been hit, but the orderly's white uniform was stained with red handprints. In the darkness, Emilie picked up her lamp and stood, though it did little to cut through the black. The lights had gone out.

Sister Allen guided the men to one of the empty beds beside Rhys. It was the orderly who was bleeding, having taken shrapnel in the leg. The patient he'd been helping had become the carer, and had a few scrapes, but was otherwise not reinjured.

"Dawes, quickly!" Sister shouted, her face coming up to search for Emilie in the darkness. "Find something to keep it straight."

That explained all the blood. He must have been hit close to his femoral artery; they would need to get the leg splinted before it was disturbed. Emilie found a broom and brought it to Sister Allen, who was comforting the orderly as best she could. He was shaking from shock, his face white as the pillow beneath his head. He knew as well as Emilie did the danger of his injury.

Emilie instructed the patient to tear shreds from the bed linens as she held the leg straight and Sister Allen tied the broom in place. Two beds down, she looked to Rhys, who was still moving restlessly. She let out a long sigh of relief—of desperate hope.

Stay alive, she silently willed him. *Stay alive until I can say goodbye.*

"He needs morphia," Sister Allen said. Her sleeves were so drenched they were nearly purple. "He must keep still—"

Another shell, a whistle so loud and sharp Emilie felt it was ripping through her ears. It only grew louder for seconds before it hit. The earth took the shell like a boot to a tree trunk, dull and solid. It burst and the floor shook, and the tent walls, and the beams holding it up.

"*'Because he loves me,' says the Lord*," the padre muttered. "*'I will rescue him.'*"

Sister Allen nodded her head, as if accepting the words, then looked to Emilie with eyes wild. "Forget the morphia—get under a bed now."

"But—"

"Now!"

Emilie looked again to Rhys. She went to the bed, wanting to leave him with a kiss on the forehead. How could it be that she was so calm? She had never triaged a fresh wound before, and her hands were sticky with the orderly's blood. Shells were falling all over, threatening her life. Yet all she could do was be glad that Rhys's head was still warm despite it all.

The next shell was not a whistle or a train but an angry lorry, speeding down a dirt road, kicking up gravel, louder. Emilie turned to see Sister Allen's eyes close, white lashes and freckled lids. A gust blew her cap and her hair, and she fell over Rhys, straddling the bed, folding her arms over his head and her own. There was a rush of air, a great and heavy pressure against her body, and a bang so loud it almost sounded of silence.

Emilie tasted gunpowder on the air and coughed.

There was no way to take a breath, for her air would not go in or out. She gasped and felt around in the dark, ears ringing so loudly it made her nauseous. She tasted grit between her teeth; dust burned her eyes. Emilie struggled to sit up, feeling Rhys's prone form beneath her body. She heard herself cry out, not in pain but in fear.

Isaac. Emilie could not say what made her think of him, but his face filled the space behind her eyes and hot tears cleared the dust away.

Don't let him die like this. Don't let him die . . .

Opening her stinging eyes, Emilie looked down to see Rhys's face impossibly clean. Her head began to hurt, and then her arm, but she was afraid to touch it, having seen the worst of what sharp things could do to a skull. Beneath her, Rhys shivered, and she spoke his name. His eyes came open, bright white in the darkness, and somehow more seeing than before.

"Emilie?" he said. She could hardly hear. "Where've we gone?"

She didn't understand, thinking his head was still not clear. Then she rolled off the bed, her shoes crunching on clumps of rubble, and looked up to see stars.

To her left, the canvas wall was torn apart completely in one place, and in others, only filled with holes. At her feet lay shards of metal and rocks and churned-up earth. In front of her, there should have been walls and beams but there was only a floor. To her right, the canvas from the marquee lay torn and bunched in a heap, a craggy mountain of khaki.

The orderly cried out in pain, the shock having passed. Sister Allen was still huddled over him, somehow keeping pressure on the bleeding wound despite it all. The padre was huddled over in prayer, seemingly unharmed. The patient had also come through in one piece, though he sat on the floor between the beds, knees pulled into his chest, face buried in his arms. Emilie fell to her knees beside him, wrapping her arms around his body that felt too small to be a soldier's, and he leaned his weight into her.

Emilie lost time until the flap came open and another nurse ran in, following closely by a stretcher. They took the wounded orderly, and then someone removed the patient from under Emilie's arm and helped him up and away. A VAD leaned over Rhys's bed—the doe-eyed Dupuis—cleaning his face with a wet towel. Was he still alive?

"Emilie," she heard from above. It was such a faint, tinny sound. Emilie was underwater, with skewed vision and cotton ears. "Dear, you're bleeding."

Sister Allen grasped her shoulder. Her face was cut, a gash from cheekbone to chin. She touched Emilie's head and a sharp sting made her blench.

Emilie's lips wouldn't move properly and her teeth chattered. "Is—is it done?"

"It is done, love."

Laughter bubbled up from deep inside of Emilie, shaking her

bodily. She didn't want to be laughing—she was terrified—but she couldn't make herself stop. Then she was gasping for air, unable to pull it through a throat closing ever tighter. Sister Allen was watching with furrowed brow, two fingers on the pulse at her wrist.

Emilie thought she was dying, or completely mad.

Then everything went black.

—————

EMILIE WOKE TO THE sound of a sputtering motor. She tried to sit up, but her head ached. Her eyes darted about the room—it was day, and she was not in her bell tent. A crisp white sheet was tucked around her shoulders, and she wiggled out, a sharp pain burning her arm. She reached her fingers up to touch gauze under her hairline, though the rest of her face felt all right. She moved her toes and shook out her legs. Her upper arm was bandaged as well.

Emilie realized she was in the sick sisters' ward. The other beds were mostly empty, clean linens folded and resting on top. One woman slept soundly at the other end. A stove warmed the space, and on the other side of the dirty window, camp was busy with activity.

The door opened, allowing a rush of cold air. Sister Allen entered, smiling to see her awake. She removed her coat and laid it over a chair, then came to set her hand on Emilie's brow. "How are you feeling?"

"What—" Emilie's mouth was so dry. She cleared her throat. "What's happened?"

"You were hit—head and arm. No broken bones."

Emilie began to sit up again, and with Sister Allen's help, she managed this time. Apart from the pain in her head, she was exhausted and famished. Sister helped her sip a glass of water.

"Was anyone else hurt?" Emilie asked.

Sister Allen's expression remained unreadable. Years of work as a military nurse had taught her how to conceal her emotions with incredible skill. "Seven enlisted men were rewounded, and a few orderlies were knocked around a bit. Three fatal wounds—two patients and a VAD."

A sob ripped up from Emilie's diaphragm, taking her by surprise. Sister Allen rubbed her back calmly, watching as she fell apart. Meantime, Sister was completely serene, unfazed by the attack and the growing bruise at the inner corner of her eye.

"Would you like some good news?" Sister asked, leaning around to look at Emilie's face. "Your Lord Bridgmond woke this morning and has taken a turn for the better. Doctor is hopeful."

Emilie found it difficult to swallow the information. "I don't understand."

"These things happen, now and again," Sister Allen said. "He's got a fighting spirit, has he?"

Emilie could only nod. As the relief passed through her, dread replaced it. Rhys had not been in his right mind the night before. He had not been able to react properly to her presence or her apology. It would be much different to speak to him today.

"Our splint was a success as well," Sister said. "It held until the boy could be taken to theatre. You acted brilliantly, Dawes. In fact . . ." Sister Allen drew her arm from Emilie's shoulder and took her hand instead. Sister was smiling, though Emilie couldn't manage to match it. "Matron is putting in for us to be decorated. Fancy that!"

Emilie balked. She was so tired, she hardly knew how to react. A medal? For her? Such things were reserved for courageous soldiers who risked their lives in battle. Not nurses. Not *women*. Not someone like her—a liar and a thief.

"If you're feeling well enough, I'll bring you something to eat and then you can go and see your friend," said Sister Allen. "He's been asking for you all morning."

The back of Emilie's throat went dry, but she felt too nauseous to drink more water. It had been one thing to face Rhys when he was on his deathbed, half-asleep and incoherent. Now, she was finding her courage had left her.

"I would prefer it if we just went home," Emilie said, looking at Sister Allen.

The other woman's smile vanished. "I don't understand. You've come all this way, you remained by his side when you could have been killed . . ."

Emilie sat up in bed, wincing at the pain in her head and in her heart. She ought to have told Sister everything. In her heart of hearts, she expected Rhys was kind enough to accept her apology if they could find a way to make amends. But she did not have the energy to find out. To explain to Rhys that she could never love him the way she loved Isaac Thurston.

She had done her duty here, and now it was time to return to work.

Twenty-Two

Audrey

APRIL 2014

Nan had volunteered to help me tame Sparrow Cottage's unruly garden. She was a member of a group of retired women who gathered once a week in the village hall to eat cake, exchange cuttings, and talk plants. They called themselves the Petals, which was fitting. Two of her Petals were pulling weeds along the front path, and Nan was showing me how to prune the boxwood. I was timid with my shears, but she took to the hedges with confidence, snip, snip, snipping to make the overgrowth fall at our feet.

"This place'll be gorgeous when we're through," she said from under her wide-brimmed hat. "Just needs a bit of love, doesn't it?"

I agreed. Once Leslie and I had cleared the larger brush, it was easy to see that someone had once loved working on it, and now that the Petals were here, the haphazard shape was being molded back into a work of art. They volunteered to return as often as needed before the sale, and apparently had made the same offer to Bernard, who'd turned them down years ago. Shame. I had a feeling he'd probably get along with them.

His leg had been healing well when I'd been to see him the day before. The boxes he'd told me about in the pantry had been another dead end. When I brought them back to Leslie's house, I'd found

nothing but recent mail in Gran's name—leaflets from local busi-
nesses, magazines, coupons, and other junk that found her despite the
fact that she had left decades before. Part of me was starting to believe
there was no mystery at all, just a flighty young woman who wanted
to escape a country at war. I reread Gran's letter often, searching for
even the tiniest clue. But I was beginning to think there was nothing
at all in it—nothing in her decision to leave the cottage to me—except
the last few drops of her early memories clinging to the edges of her
mind in those last days.

Jim, who had been left in my care while Leslie was at work, howled
at something in the hedge. An orange cat darted out from underneath
and paused to weave between my legs. I removed my glove and
reached down to scratch under its chin.

"Do you know who this cat belongs to?" I asked Nan.

"Likely it's one of Mrs. Lister's. I've lost count how many she's got
now. Eight . . . ? Nine . . . ?"

Jim came to nose my hand, jealous of the attention the cat was
getting. The cat swatted at his muzzle, and then the two of them were
off, dashing across the yard. Nan lowered her shears to have a chuckle,
and set one fist on her hip.

"You've got a real taste of the good life here, love, haven't you?" she
said, and sighed. "Now, I reckon it's about time for a brew."

I went into the house to get the tea while the Petals put up their
feet outside. I'd come to enjoy the simple motions of filling the kettle
and placing the tea bags as I moved around Gran's kitchen. Leslie had
got the old woodstove running that morning before he left for work,
and I set the kettle on top to boil.

As I waited for the tea to steep, I wandered, brushing crumbs off
the countertop and straightening the plates on the shelves. I had less
than two weeks left here and would need to start clearing out the
inside of the house. In moments like this, the idea was almost too
daunting to consider. Everything seemed important—from the Royal
Doulton figurines to the candles on the dining room table, burnt

halfway down since 1941. Sparrow Cottage was starting to feel like more than a charming place I had been sent to by fate. It was starting to feel like a place I could call home. I hadn't thought about drinking in nearly three days, which for me was significant. Even with all the stress over the house, I had found a state of calm in Yorkshire.

I brought the tea and a packet of chocolate Bourbons out to the Petals, who accepted with smiles and excitable noises. Nan waved me over to sit beside her on an iron bench.

"You make a good, strong cuppa," she said, patting my knee. "Small wonder why me grandson's so keen."

A blush burned my cheeks as the other two grey-haired ladies tittered and pursed their lips. There was nothing Leslie could tell his grandmother to convince her we weren't a couple, and the fact I was living under his roof didn't help the matter. I decided to hide my reddening face in my mug, and didn't comment.

Once we'd had our tea, the sun was setting for the evening. I told the Petals they should head home, but they could come anytime they liked to work on the garden. I walked them to the end of the front path, and Nan stopped to give me a hug before joining the others. She grunted softly in my ear, and I quickly pulled away.

"Are you okay?" I asked.

She laughed at herself, waving me off. "Rheumatism. It's rubbish, getting old. Don't bother with it, love."

"My gran used to say the same thing. Why don't you stay and come back to Leslie's house for dinner?"

"No, no. Me grandson doesn't want me about when he's got a lass round."

"That's not true. He'd love to have you."

"You are good." She took my elbow and gave it a shake. "But I'm happy for him to give my dinners a miss if it means he's found some joy of his own."

"It was hard on him, wasn't it? Losing Gemma?"

Nan nodded. "He's got a big heart, our Leslie, but he can't seem to feel more than one emotion at a time. He were barmy with the grief of it! Imagine if I'd been so out of sorts when me husband died. Who would have done the bloody laundry?"

It sounded like something I'd been told in rehab—that emotion is a spectrum, rather than a state. I had my own struggle with reaching endlessly toward an impossible destination of full happiness. Maybe Leslie and I were more alike than I thought. I wondered, momentarily, if there was room for the spectrum in nursing, or if I would find only the same anxiety as before.

"I haven't seen him this happy in ages, you know," Nan said.

"I don't know if that has anything to do with me," I answered, "but I'd be glad to know it did. Leslie is really special."

That made her beam. "Is he bringing you to the fête next week?"

"What's a fête?"

"Village fair! It's the first of the season; everyone'll be there."

Leslie hadn't mentioned it, but I didn't want to let Nan down, so I told her I wasn't sure what our plans were, and she shuffled off to join the others.

I walked back up to the house with Jim at my heels until he suddenly darted away toward the side of the house. I thought it must have been the cat again, but his bark was different this time. I followed him, hoping there wasn't an intruder on the land, and trudged my way to the drystone wall. Jim had his paws up on the wall; whatever he wanted was on the other side. I found a foothold and climbed up for a better view. It was getting dark, so I couldn't see it at first, but when I heard a strained, wavering bleat, I knew it must have been a sheep.

I hoisted myself up and dropped down on the other side of the wall. The ewe was lying on her side a few feet away. She wasn't moving much, and some patches of wool were darkened with blood. Instinct took the place of common sense, and I ran toward her without thinking of whether or not she could hurt me. But as I approached, she only lifted her head for a brief look before it fell back down to the grass. I dropped to my knees, retrieving my phone from my pocket to call Leslie before realizing it was useless.

"It's okay, baby," I said, struggling to stay calm with Jim barking hysterically behind me. "What happened to you, precious? Did you hurt yourself?"

I tentatively reached toward the ewe. She didn't notice, or else didn't mind that I touched her wool. Her midsection was twitching, but I couldn't see any obvious wounds. I looked around me, noticing it was nearly full dark. How was I going to find help for her? I had no idea which farm she'd come from, or which direction.

There was a rumble in the distance, and I stood to see the headlights of Leslie's Land Rover coming up the hill. I waved my phone over my head so he would see the light. In another minute, he was over the wall, climbing around the overgrowth, face opal in the moonlight. When he reached us, he fell to his knees and placed one hand over the ewe's heaving body. I didn't have to explain that she was hurt.

"How long has she been here?" he asked breathlessly.

"I have no idea; I didn't hear her earlier. Where do you think she came from?"

"She's probably Craig's; his land is on the other side of that fence." Leslie leaned over to look at the ewe's face, and then the opposite way at her tail. "God knows how she got all the way here. I think she must be lambing."

I followed his gaze to the ewe's tail. Now that he mentioned it, I could see where she was dilated, and labor would explain the odd jerking movements her body was making. I moved my phone's light over to the grass beneath her, and sure enough, it was wet with a mixture of blood and other fluids. Beside me, Leslie was already dialing on his phone.

"Something's wrong," he said. "She's going to need help— Er, hey, Craig, it's Leslie Whiting. I think I've found one of your ewes up at Sparrow Cottage . . ."

While he spoke to the shepherd on the phone, I gently stroked the ewe's wool, shushing her softly, wishing there was anything I could do to help her pain. Leslie moved the phone away from his ear for a moment, looking at me.

"Craig isn't at home, but he's on his way." His voice was suddenly lacking its usual confidence. "He thinks the lamb might be stuck, and asked if we could start to help her get it out."

"So one of us has to . . . ?"

In the dim light, I could see the uncertainty on Leslie's face. Clearly, he was no stranger to the sight of a farm animal, but I could tell he was nervous about what came next. Leslie might have been a lot of things, but he wasn't a farmer, or a medical professional.

"Tell me what to do," I said, shrugging out of my jacket.

Leslie watched me with uncertainty as I rolled up my sleeves. "Are you sure?"

I nodded, taking a deep breath. "We can't let her die. And trust me, I've had my hands in far worse places at the hospital."

Leslie pointed my phone light at the ewe's tail. "Right, okay. Craig says to go slowly, and feel for the legs. She's done this before, so you won't frighten her."

Gently, I set my left palm on the ewe's hip, letting her know I was there. Her body began to twitch with another contraction and I waited it out, knowing it would make things more difficult. When she was through, I gathered my courage and slid my hand inside.

At first, I felt nothing at all besides slime and warmth. Then, when I was nearly wrist deep, my fingers brushed something hard.

"I got it!" I said, trying to keep still in my excitement. "I feel a leg."

Leslie leaned closer, and I could hear Craig's voice speaking in his ear. "Both legs?"

I took my time, feeling again. "No—no, just the one."

Leslie paused again, listening on the phone. I kept my hand perfectly still, waiting for instruction. "The other leg is stuck back behind it," he said. "You're going to need to push the lamb gently back into the womb so there's space enough for the other leg to come forward."

I did as I was instructed, wincing in concentration as the muscles in the ewe's body worked to get the baby out. This time, when she pushed, two legs came forward and I wrapped my hand firmly around the pair.

"I have them. I have them both! She's pushing!"

By then, I no longer needed instruction, and worked with the ewe's natural instincts. She pushed, and I pulled, and in a matter of seconds, a little head emerged, then the rest of the body slid out onto the grass.

Beside me, Leslie made an excited noise not unlike the ones I'd heard him make while watching a Leeds United game. He had his free hand on his head, and was grinning.

"You absolute star!" he said, reaching over to rub my back. "Well done, flower."

My body was trembling with the rush of adrenaline. "What now?"

"Right." He shifted back on his knees. "See if you can clear the mouth, then bring the lamb here so the mother can lick."

I did as I was told. The lamb was lanky and long-legged, about the size of a cat and yellow with fluid. I gently swiped at the nose and mouth, clearing what I could, and moved it over the grass to lay beside its mother's head.

"She might reject it," Leslie said, still holding the phone to his ear. "Craig says after a struggle like that, they don't always want to be mothers."

My heart raced as we waited to see what would happen. The baby wasn't moving but for a twitch of the ear, still stunned by the trauma of birth and the greatness of the cold new world surrounding it. The mother nudged her head forward, sniffing, sniffing, and then, with another moment of hesitation, opened her mouth and began to lick.

Leslie and I both sighed, our eyes meeting as smiles spread across our faces. He said goodbye to Craig, hung up the phone, and let it drop to the grass. I was giggling again, high on this small miracle we had both witnessed. Leslie wrapped one arm around me and drew me close to him, and while I held my dirty hand out and away, he pressed his lips against my temple. I turned to look at him, and that time his lips found my own. It was brief, broken up by both of our smiles, but it was enough to set all my nerve endings on fire.

I didn't have time to think about what the kiss meant, or didn't mean, as another pair of headlights flickered up the road. Craig had arrived to bring his ewe and new lamb home.

Twenty-Three

Audrey

"That was *amazing*," I said, locking the door as we left Sparrow Cottage. The shepherd had long gone with the ewe and new lamb, and I had cleaned myself up in the kitchen. "Seriously, I have never experienced anything so magical. Craig said I can go by and see the lamb once he's all cleaned up tomorrow, and he promised me some of the yarn his wife spins with their wool."

Leslie smiled at me as we made our way toward his car, Jim between us. The evening had been such a whirlwind that he and I had hardly got a word in. I thought he was being unusually quiet, but expected it was just my imagination.

"You were brilliant, mate," he said. "Honestly—I don't know how you were so calm."

"Maybe I should have been a veterinarian? Or a shepherdess." I chuckled, though the idea sounded rather romantic to me. "You're so lucky you live in a place like this, where you can rely on your neighbor to rescue a lost sheep."

He opened the passenger door for me to get in, which was not an unusual gesture for him. But something felt different this time; there was an awareness between our bodies as I moved past his, a magnetism that made Leslie lean in. I turned to face him, and he left his hand resting on the top of the door to keep me framed in his view.

"I believe it were you who did the rescuing," he said.

"Well, I *am* Craig's neighbor. For now at least."

Leslie's eyes creased handsomely. Looking up at him, I thought about what Nan had told me earlier, thought about the soft warmth of his lips on mine, as brief as it had been. One of us was going to have to acknowledge it, and I thought Leslie was too polite.

So I said, "You kissed me."

Leslie licked his lip, as if acknowledging the memory. "I'm sorry, Auds, I was caught up in the moment . . ."

"Could you do it again?" I saw the tension leave his face, replaced with something between bewilderment and relief. "It's just that the amniotic fluid on my hand kind of detracted from the experience the first time."

Leslie studied my face, as if searching for confirmation that what I said was what I really wanted. It was—I wanted nothing more than to brush my hand through his hair and taste his mouth again. But I knew where his hesitation came from. He hadn't been in a relationship since Gemma, and I was on unstable ground, prepared to leave him forever in less than two weeks.

I took a step forward, hoping to encourage him. And then, all at once, he lost his resolve. His hand came down from the top of the door, landing on my waist, drawing me even closer to him until our chests met. When he kissed me, it was softer than before, more patient, more calculated, and I let my mouth fall open, let my weight collapse into his strength. His kiss was everything I had hoped for and more—it was strong and satisfying.

When my hand closed around his hair, I quickly dropped my chin and pulled away. I tried to catch my breath, feeling Leslie everywhere, from the tips of my fingers to the depths of my core. The world had shifted, as if I'd been underwater and had come up to take a deep breath. My eyes had been closed, and when I opened them, Leslie was still looking at me, waiting for me to speak. But I didn't know what to say. I could see myself sinking further, all the way into Leslie. And that frightened me.

"I have to stay here," I blurted. "At Sparrow. Tonight."

Leslie cocked his head, blinking rapidly as he tried to find words. "On your own?"

I nodded, ducking away from the car so I had some more room to breathe, to move my thoughts away from Leslie's hands, his chest, his lips . . .

"There's some stuff I want to look through." I was pulling this out of thin air, anything to create an excuse not to go home with him. If I went home with him, I knew the temptation would be too great. But I didn't want to tell him that. "I think I'll just stay the night, if that's okay?"

"I ain't holding you hostage."

I laughed nervously. "Right. Well . . ."

"Er . . . just a sec." Leslie went to the back of the Land Rover to open the trunk, and pulled out a wool blanket. "I keep this for emergencies. You probably won't want to use bedding that's been sitting in dust since 1941."

"No, you're right." I took the blanket and hugged it against my chest. "Thank you."

He scratched his beard. "Are you sure about this? I could pop round the house and grab your pillow? You haven't even got a mobile to call for help if anything goes amiss."

I almost kissed him again for using the word *amiss*. "I'll be fine, I promise."

He didn't look convinced. "At least take Jim with you."

I accepted, if only to appease him. From the doorway, I watched Leslie drive away, wondering what the hell I was doing. I was tired and starving, and needed a shower. But I knew myself—I knew how weak my self-control was, knew how much I wanted Leslie. This was safer, at least for the moment. Tomorrow I could decide whether or not I could handle another night with him.

Inside, I set the kettle to boil, not knowing what else to do. Luck-ily, there were some remnants from the last lunch Leslie and I had eaten here—a Pot Noodle, a packet of Wotsits, chocolate buttons, and to feign nutrition, a pair of apples. I poured the boiling water into the instant noodles and wandered into the lounge. Jim happily settled on the couch, clearly undeterred by dust mites, and I sat in the wooden rocking chair by the hearth. I blew on my soup. This was going to be a long night if I didn't find some way to occupy myself. The pub was open for another four hours, and there was nobody here to stop me from walking out the door.

Good thing I had an entire house worth of junk to sort through.

Once I'd finished my dinner, I went room to room scouring over the surface level of items with Jim poking his head in wherever he could. Sparrow Cottage was packed with all the things you would expect to find in a 1940s family home—balls of yarn and sewing pat-terns, long-expired canned foods and kitchen tools that had become obsolete, half-empty bottles of detergent and shampoo, hundreds of books, magazines, and crinkled bills. Set so perfectly like a movie set, it was easy to forget that someone had actually lived in the rooms, had shoved children's toys and shoes under the bed, had listened to rec-ords, had cluttered drawers with paper clips and rubber bands, adver-tisements for Brylcreem and packets of seeds for carrots, potatoes, and cabbage.

After two hours, I lost interest in the value of an eighty-year-old shaving kit, and tossed it into the garbage pile with a twinge of re-sentment. The Smiths had clearly not been living with the kind of wealth Lady Emilie had left behind. There were no precious pearls or jewelry to save, no antiques that couldn't be bought for a pound out of someone's car boot. And so most of their belongings would have to be thrown out. Anything nice enough to pass along, I set to one side for an estate sale. It was the best solution, I'd decided. Selling some of the furniture would not only take the burden off me, but allow some of the Smiths' things to have a second life.

When the clock struck eleven, I knew that meant Keys was no longer serving, and the village shop was closed. I could relax in the knowledge that any alcohol was barred from me. I was bone-tired from working in the garden all day, and so I brought the chocolate buttons and Leslie's blanket up to Gran's room. After testing the decades-old mattress, I decided it was probably best to stick to the floor, and spread the blanket out. Jim nestled in beside me with a flop and a sigh, clearly ready for bed.

I lay still, staring at the ceiling and thinking of the kiss. It was ridiculous. I was lying in my grandmother's childhood bedroom, and yet, the only thing my brain would allow me to focus on was how strong Leslie's thumb had been, pressing into my waist, and the sound of his frustrated pants as his mouth opened to my tongue.

I groaned, disturbing the dog. Why did I have to make every single thing that much harder for myself?

With a huff, I turned over on my side. Beneath me, one of the floorboards creaked and buckled. Curious, I rolled one way, then the other, making it squeal. I wasn't going to be able to sleep in this particular spot, or the sound was going to drive me crazy. I sat up to move the blanket aside and saw that the edge of the board was sticking up. In the moonlight, I felt along the edge, picking at it with my fingernails, and the whole board came right up and out.

For a second, all I could do was marvel at the odds of it. Then I set the board aside and turned on my phone to peer inside the rectangular space in the floor. There was definitely something in there, something somebody had wanted to keep hidden. I pulled it out, setting it closer to the window so I could see it in the moonlight—a tin box, like the ones they used here for cake or biscuits. It had a garden scene painted across it, the colors faded and the corners rusting away. My hands shook as I gripped the lid and forced it open.

On top were newspaper clippings, one talking about a private convalescent hospital established in the Northampton home of the Duke of Claremont during the Second World War. Somebody had underlined the name of the house in red ink. The next was from the same era, with a short paragraph about Lady Harriet, praising her charity efforts that carried on in London despite the danger of air raids. Seeing the familiar names made my breaths come quicker.

Beneath the clippings, I came across a train schedule, two of the times circled, and a notebook filled with notes that seemed to be irrelevant to the rest of it—math problems and history lessons. Beyond the homework was a page of frantically scrawled lines—a telephone number for a hotel in London and directions for how to get there from Victoria Station. The next page had been completely torn out.

I thumbed through the rest of the notebook, but found nothing on its pages. There were a few bits of paper tucked within that looked to have been from a letter, torn up so I could read only a few words here and there:

> *have broken my heart more times than*
> *want nothing to do with the child*
> *born of your deliberate betrayal of*
> *not see you again*

The words were clearly written in anger, and I could not blame whoever had read them for tearing them up. Another paper, this one fully intact, was tucked within the back cover, and I pulled it out, unfolding it with a painful pounding of my heart. In my hand was my grandmother's birth certificate. Dorothy, a baby girl born September 9, 1917, to Lady Emilie Bridgmond, formerly Dawes, and Lord Rhys Bridgmond.

A chill made me look around the room, finding Jim still asleep on the blanket. This meant that Gran certainly was the daughter of Lord Bridgmond, and that her mother had taken her away from him. Away from her true family, to Sparrow Cottage. That explained why Gran had always told us she was the daughter of a lord, but why keep the certificate hidden here? Why not bring it with her to America?

There was one thing left in the bottom of the tin: a letter. I brought it to the bedside, turning on the lamp to read.

7 February 1941

Dear Miss Smith,

I must admit, your letter did come as a shock. I expected your mother would not have told you about us, not after what happened, and your surname proves as much. She created a rift between our families, which until her deception were allies for centuries, and her brother, your uncle, shamed us, and his country, beyond words. There is much to be explained about what occurred during the last war, none of which I would dare put into writing. But if your mother refuses to give you the truth, someone ought to. Therefore, you must come to me in London. I hold no grudge against you as the innocent party, and shall welcome you as a friend. Send word of your departure, and I shall ensure a car is at the station to fetch you.

Sincerely,
Lady Harriet Pomfrey

I stood to put everything back into the tin and whipped the blanket off the floor, sticking all of it under my arm.

"Come, Jim," I said, and hurried downstairs. "We're going home."

THE HOUSE WAS DARK and quiet when I unlocked the door and pushed in. But I was consumed by this new knowledge, still shaking from head to toe with the thought of what it all meant. I had to share it with someone; I had to talk it out. Poor Leslie happened to be the only person available.

I knocked on his bedroom door softly, hoping not to startle him.

Light filled the cracks around the door, and I heard him padding across the floor, hesitating before opening. He wasn't surprised to see me—who else would it have been?—but he had a look of sleepy bewilderment and a line across his cheek from his pillow.

"I know how this looks," I said. "I just need to show you something."

He blinked a few times and ran a hand over his face before speaking slowly. "Will I need to put on trousers?"

"That would probably be best."

While he dressed, I brought the tin down to the kitchen and laid everything out on the table. It was overwhelming to see it all beneath the bright lights, to see the age, where the letter had been handled, read over and over. Poor Gran. Could it be that Emilie never told her of her true parentage? Had Gran put the clues together herself?

Leslie came plodding down the steps, wearing a sweatshirt, zipped up over his bare chest, and a pair of thick-rimmed glasses. When his eyes caught on the table, they finally cleared. "Where did you find all this?"

"Under a floorboard." He gave me a look of disbelief. "I'm serious. Gran was hiding this from her parents."

Leslie slowly drew out the chair opposite to me, and sat heavily, running a hand through his mess of hair. Squinting through his glasses, he first took up the letter from Lady Harriet, the fold still crisp in the heavy stationery. Then he moved to the birth certificate, and the shreds of paper that could only have been from a letter. But from whom? I wondered, as Leslie pinched his bottom lip thoughtfully. And had the child in question been Gran herself? I couldn't imagine how much it would hurt to see those words. No wonder she wanted to run away.

"What d'you reckon?" Leslie asked.

It was hard for me to speak at first through the lump that had developed in my throat. I couldn't believe how close I had gotten to this mystery, how much it was weighing on me emotionally. I would have given anything to have Gran by my side, to put her soft arm around me and tell me everything was going to be all right.

"Emilie wasn't the woman I hoped she was. My grandmother was torn away from her father, from her family, and was kept hidden from them out here. She probably wasn't even aware that her father had died all those years ago. She wasn't even given permission to grieve."

"You don't know that for certain."

"Why else would Lady Harriet have written all those things? She obviously thought the truth was important, or else she wouldn't have invited Gran to go and visit her in London during the Blitz." My words came faster and faster. "Maybe she helped her escape—maybe Lady Harriet is the reason Gran got away. She thought it was best for her lost niece to run . . ."

Leslie didn't comment, only listened, and by the time I ran out of breath, he reached over to take my hand across the table. I held his back, too emotional to think about what it meant, or remember how I'd fled from him so abruptly after our kiss. He didn't deserve that, and I regretted the impulsivity of having followed him home.

"It isn't the right time to tell you this," he said, "but my brother rang me tonight about what he found in the Archives. I think it would explain what Harriet says about Emilie's brother's shame."

I braced myself, squeezing his hand. "I guess I should hear it."

"In the war, he was court-martialed for cowardice," Leslie explained gently, pulling me back as I began to slip away from him. "He was executed in 1916. I'm so sorry, Auds . . ."

Then I did slip out of his grasp and he let me go. My hand fell to my lap as I let the information wash over me. That explained why his name had not been on the monument in the village he was raised in, why his name was forgotten from history. It was likely another reason Emilie had broken away from her past and kept it all secret.

"I thought Gran sent me here to preserve her good memories," I said, feeling I was drifting underwater, "but I don't think there were any. What if she left it all behind for good reason and I'm doing the wrong thing by trying to rescue it?"

"That doesn't explain why she's kept it all these years. If it meant nothing to her, why not sell, or leave it to crumble and rot?"

It was a valid question that I didn't have an answer for. I took up the letter shreds again, comparing the handwriting to Lady Harriet's. Though the penmanship was careful on both of them, they were clearly not from the same person. So who had written these words?

want nothing to do with the child

born of your deliberate betrayal

I thought of Mr. Smith, the reclusive Great War vet with a stutter who gave my grandmother his surname. Had she convinced him that Gran was his child? Was her betrayal of their relationship, or of his trust? Did Gran see these words and think the only man she'd known as her father had decided to reject her after so many years?

"Whatever happened here," Leslie said, "she lived a long, happy life in America."

I knew he was right, but somehow couldn't allow myself to nod. I looked up at Leslie, seeking comfort in the familiar soft features of his face. The glasses made him look less like a rugged builder and more like the amateur historian he was. I hadn't even known he wore contacts. It reminded me of how little we knew about each other, and some sensibility floated back to the surface of my mind.

"I'm sorry I woke you," I said. "It's just that I let all of this get to me, and I . . . I *really* need a meeting and I doubt we're likely to find one at midnight in the middle of nowhere."

"I haven't got any booze in the house." That much was a relief. Leslie sat back, rubbing the tops of his thighs, lids heavy with exhaustion. "Shall we see what's on telly?"

And that was it. Leslie knew I couldn't be alone, and that was enough for him to give up the sleep he most certainly needed. There was only one other person in the world who would have done that for me, and I knew she would be glad to know I had stumbled across this man in the place of her birth.

We sat on the couch with Jim at our feet, and Leslie flipped channels until he landed on an old sitcom wherein Rowan Atkinson and Hugh Laurie bumbled around what looked to be a World War One dugout. He set down the remote and settled farther down onto the couch, letting his legs open so his knee was resting against mine.

I watched in silence for a while, comforted by the familiar sound of laugh tracks, and the soft light flickering in the dark room. I hadn't expected to laugh so hard at something set during the war, but I did, and turned to Leslie hoping to share it. But he had already fallen asleep, his head fallen back, his lips parted. I reached up to carefully slide his glasses from his face. He had clearly had a long day; the touch hadn't disturbed him in the slightest.

Feeling safe and comfortable, I wriggled to a lower seat and rested my head gently on his shoulder, enjoying the slow rise and fall of his breaths. It was enough to have him there, waking or sleeping, to know he was in the fight alongside me—this woman he had just met. Leslie was different from anyone else I'd known before, and different from anyone else I was likely to meet.

Thoughts of Gran trickled back to me as I sat idle. In the morning I would call Patrick and urge him to help me get the house on the market as soon as possible. Gran had left me the heavy burden of her turbulent past, and I would clear it all away so she could rest in peace.

Twenty-Four

Emilie
LE TRÉPORT, FRANCE
SUMMER 1916

28 June 1916

My love,

I am not sure how much I am permitted to say, but I will write what I can, and you have probably heard of the rest. All officers have been pulled back from leave, and word arrived a few days ago of another great push. What irony that these offensives should always come in spring, when nature is renewing herself from the shriveled death of winter to the green promise of life.

Very few work parties over the last week, as the men were given ample time to rest. We arrived yesterday in the trenches and our artillery was at it all night. The enemy replied with H.E. and shrapnel—these are mortars filled with nails, screws, scrap metal, anything they can find that will do damage. Between checking sentries, I got hardly a wink, the noise and fear jolting me awake every other minute.

Orders came that double rum be issued this afternoon, and it was looking like "over the top." Then, suddenly, the attack had been postponed. I felt no relief at the news, Em; I feel rather like I could jump out of my skin. You know my fears, so I shall not repeat them, but there is a weight on my chest today heavier than I have ever had. I look around me at these young, careworn faces and cannot help but mourn them already.

Do you know that wildflowers have grown in no-man's-land? The first time I noticed it through a periscope, it was all I could do not to stand up on the fire step to confirm that my eyes had not deceived me. Though there they were, blooming right out of the black sludge and ash. Red poppies dusting the landscape like a flush smudge on a pavement chalk drawing, up and over the carnage, the death, the rotten soil. They grew where dead men fell and were never recovered. They grew despite it all, and that, my love, is the most beautiful thing I have lived to see. I imagine they will all be gone in a few days' time, and plenty of our men with them.

There will be much work for you in the coming weeks, so do be strong, but also think of me when you can. I am no poet—you know that more than most. But you also know, I hope, that my love for you is too great for words. I pray that I be granted the chance to prove it to you with my life.

Please see that Lady Thurston is not alone in the end.

Yours, as ever,
Isaac

BENEATH THE TREES, EMILIE found a sort of oblivion. She set her head on the moss of a root, lying flat against the soil. At one with the earth, she surrendered to the insects, embracing the tickle of a ladybird landing on her cheek, the cold, wet slug inching up her finger. She became nothing, and no one, a part of the landscape. The sun found her in droplets between the leaves, the ground embraced her, morphed to the contours of her body. The birds sang fearlessly; a creature rustled in the brush. Life was everywhere—moving about her, beneath her, above her, through her.

Emilie and the woodland had become great friends. She went alone and lost herself, thinking of Isaac as if her voice might find him on the battlefield. It wasn't so much a prayer—she did not believe anyone was listening. But she felt, somehow, if she gave herself to the Earth for an hour, dug her fingers into the dirt, planted her sweet thoughts in the permafrost, fate might smile on her boy. It felt like holding on, clinging to a world that was spinning out of control.

She returned to camp through a meadow, picking cornflowers, poppies, chicory, orchids, and sweet violet. A Frenchwoman was selling apples on the road. Emilie hadn't brought francs, but offered to exchange for one of her orchids. When she bit into the fruit, the flesh was warm from the sun.

"*Bonne chance*," Emilie said.

Upon returning to the camp, she put her flowers in spent food tins. Nobody suspected there was any more to her wanders than a simple hunt for beauty. But she needed her time away. She yearned for it, watched the seconds tick down, the anticipation making her skin crawl.

She had been awarded the Military Medal for helping in saving an orderly's life, for protecting the patients who lay beside Rhys. Everyone wanted to talk about the fateful evening, everyone wanted the story. She wanted only to put it behind her. Rhys had not written, and she did not hear again from Lady Harriet. Perhaps what she did for him was enough to grant her clemency for her actions, though it did nothing to alleviate the guilt. She had abandoned him yet again, and no medal could convince her to believe she was anything but rotten.

Another convoy was in any moment—seven hundred men in all. How could there be any left? Emilie wondered, as she passed an ambulance full of patients for evacuation. Summer was dragging along, stifling and relentless, and it seemed no end would come to the mess at the front. They had five new sisters, and more new VADs than she'd bothered to count, and they still did not have enough help. Emilie could only hope they didn't run out of bandages or splints or morphia.

She was with Sister Allen in A-Surgical now. Sister saw her come through the flap and called her over with a nod of her head, hands plunged in a basin of soapy water.

"Anything from your lieutenant today?" she asked.

Emilie shook her head. She had been waiting three weeks to hear from Isaac, and had not heard from her brother since he told her he had left Egypt and was headed here, to the Western Front, to the chaos.

"The beds are in a right state." Sister reached for a towel to dry her hands. "We'll be full in an hour, and I don't want any new patients on dirty linens."

Emilie did not require further instruction. It had been a month since the offensive began, and the staff had found a mindless rhythm. There was no time to consider things that were once urgently important; a dirty floor mattered little if there was nowhere clean for a wounded man to lie down. A dressing station had been set up for the walking wounded so that the wards could remain clear for stretchers if they ran out of beds. And they had, more than once. Though it was often enough that a man was brought to theatre and did not return.

Emilie made quick work of the beds, but stretcher-bearers came through the flap before she could finish. At once, the ward was full, loud with voices moaning, crying out, calling for a lost friend, for a sister, for a glass of water. Emilie had thought she'd seen everything of this war, but nothing compared to the look of these men, their blood-spattered faces, their clay-covered hair, the vacant look in their eyes as if all hope had been lost. Any walkers stumbled in, looking ready to drop anywhere and sleep. More stretchers came, until there was hardly a line to walk through the ward.

"No more," Sister said, pointing through the flap. "Line them up outside and tell an orderly to fetch blankets and mackintosh sheets."

There were men from a variety of regiments, Canadians and New

Zealanders among their own boys. With every face Emilie wiped clean, she hoped to see her brother. Every wound she unearthed from a muddied, blood-caked uniform, she imagined on Isaac's body. What if he hadn't written because he was paralyzed in a hospital? Or his ambulance had been run off the road? Or he was shivering at the bottom of a shell hole?

But there was no time to linger on thoughts of Isaac. There was no time to chat, to jest, to give nicknames, to light cigarettes. There was only time to move—move bodies in, move bodies to theatre, move bodies out so that more could be brought. Emilie had not learned a single name that afternoon, had not even registered the faces of the men she was helping. It made her ill, and she longed for the gentle humanity of her first days in France.

Sister Allen ordered her outside, to look after the overflow of men lying outdoors. Going through the flap, Emilie squinted in the sun, watching in awe for a moment at the state of camp. On a long bench, six soldiers sat side by side, with only three legs between them. Orderlies and VADs ran between wards, carrying dressing trays, bandaging bowls, linens, uniforms, pillows, water. Matron was coming out of one of the surgical theatres, blood all down her front.

At Emilie's feet was a queue of bodies all the way down to the end of the line. Some of them lay on stretchers, others on biscuits, a few on nothing but a rubber sheet, with coats and jackets lying over them, or blankets shared between two or three. One of them was wailing for help—"*I'm dying! I'm dying!*"—his voice raw, but Emilie could not pick him out among the sea of brown and red.

She stood staring uselessly, her body heavy from exhaustion, her skin itching from the pooling sweat under her uniform. Where even to begin? She had nothing—not even a cloth to wipe a sweaty brow— only the pair of scissors, pencil, and safety pins she was required to carry with her at all times in the pocket of her apron.

Emilie dropped onto her knees next to the first stretcher, hands trembling as she began to unbutton the man's shirt. It wasn't until she had got it all the way off and checked the bandage on his neck that she realized he was already dead.

The air went out of her. Emilie bowed her head, and her body followed, lying over the dead man's bare chest. His flesh was warm, still with the musk of a man and the faint scent of the rum he'd had before going over the top. Emilie wanted to cry, but there was no moisture left within her body. She clung to this stranger as if he were her brother, as if he were Isaac, wondering how many hours he had lain on the ground, set aside and forgotten. Wondering if she might have saved him if she'd come a minute sooner.

Someone's hands settled on her shoulders. Emilie ignored them at first, leaning farther into the lost boy. But the hands were strong, and eventually she was pulled to sit up. It was the orderly she had come to know as Corporal Martin. He smelled terrible and his hair and uniform were drenched through. Lord, it was hot, and the sun relentless.

"He's gone, is he?" Martin asked.

She could only nod.

"Let us take him, love. Let us get him cleaned up."

There was another orderly behind him, waiting with a sheet to lay over the dead man's face. It was the right thing to do—to get the body up out of the dirt, to clean him and wrap him so that he could be returned to the ground. There were piles of them now, waiting for free hands to dig their graves behind the camp, and mark them with a simple wooden cross.

Martin pulled Emilie the rest of the way to her feet, and she stumbled forward. There were more bodies, living ones, more lives that could yet be spared.

"Dawes? You all right to carry on?"

She did not answer, only fell to her knees beside her next patient.

EMILIE DID NOT COME off duty until nine o'clock. They had moved some of the men into the mess and recreation tents, anywhere there was room. Feeding them all was a challenge, and she was glad she was not on housekeeping duty. Though perhaps seeing the relief on a man's face to be given hot food was better than the anguish of the wards.

Emilie ate her portion of boiled mutton hastily, not tasting it. She wanted to get back to the bell tent, to scrub the blood from underneath her fingernails, and fall into bed. She had been promised the next day off, and planned a swim in the ocean. She needed the oblivion of floating underwater.

After her meal, she stopped at the post office. As ever, it was a busy place, though it had become strangely silent. In the past weeks, there had been more bad news than ever before, and word from home became a dreaded concept.

Nothing from Isaac. Emilie could only be disappointed for a breath, for Fletcher had written. She went out into the night, finding a quiet place to sit alone, and tore open the letter. He was alive—or at least had been recently.

30 July 1916

Dear sister,

I am well today. I feel better than I have all war—peaceful and content.

I have seen my bullet. The dream was as vivid as any I have had, and I know what I saw belongs to me. I used to fear death, you know. When the other men wrinkled their chins and drank themselves to courage, I shook in the darkness. But I have no fear now that I know how it shall end. There will be no pain, I assure you, so do not cry for me. I have put on this uniform and done what I was bid.

In some ways, I am glad it will happen here in France, where so many of our countrymen have fallen in this war. I should not like to have been buried in Egypt, in the sand, so very far from home. Here, I can almost imagine I am in England, with the larks and the poppies, the patchwork fields. Shame to see such beauty burnt away,

torn into. They think we don't know, but how could we not see? We
have watered the fields with our blood; we have dug our own graves.

I love you, brave little duck. I believe, as I always have done,
that you are the better of us, and deserve the life you want. Go to
Mama, for she will weep, and I suspect Papa will mourn the
bloodline.

Look after yourself, Em. The world is so big and not at all as we
thought.

Your brother,
Fletcher

SISTER ALLEN HAD NOT been expecting her. When Emilie
shouted through the flap of the bell tent she shared with Sister Cole,
two beds creaked, and only one head popped out. She was in her
nightdress, hair braided over one shoulder. The look in her eye would
have sparked fear in the colonel himself.

"I hope you have a good explanation for disturbing me at this
hour," she said.

It was not even ten o'clock, but they'd all been working nonstop
since dawn.

Emilie put Fletcher's letter in Sister's hands. It was stained with
her tears, smudged where she tried desperately to wipe them away.

"What does it mean?" Emilie asked, before Sister would have had
the chance to finish the first line. "What is he talking of? A bullet?
My God, I have to find him—I have to—"

Sister lifted one hand to silence her. She read quickly, and Emilie
saw the discomfort in her eyes, recognized it as it matched her own.
Fletcher had never written a letter so coherent, so fully formed. There
was not a single jest, not a single complaint. And the bullet—the bullet could have meant anything at all, yet all Emilie could think about

was the private in Isaac's platoon who had taken off his shoe, set his rifle under his chin, and pulled the trigger with his bare toe.

Fletcher could not do that to himself. Could he?

Sister Allen took a deep breath, folding the letter and putting it back in Emilie's hands.

"Write to him now, and get it out with the morning post," she said. "Tell him you are concerned and that you love him. Tell him to go to medical if he is unwell."

"There isn't time! It won't reach him for days; he could be dead by then."

"Then go to the wire office."

Emilie was shaking her head. Telegrams were expensive, and how long would it take to find him? Nothing would do—nothing. Emilie had no idea where her brother was and she had no power to help him. To stop whatever it was that was going on inside his head.

She stared deeply into Sister Allen's eyes. Sister always knew what to do; she always had an answer. Why now was she silent?

"Perhaps it was only a dream," Sister said. "Perhaps it was the *rum*."

Emilie covered her face with her hand. She was so weary, she could have collapsed and slept right there, under the stars. She regretted everything. What a stupid little girl she was for running away from home, from her family, thinking she was strong enough to face a war on her own.

"Go and get some rest, Emilie," Sister said, pinching her shoulder. "Let this dreadful day pass."

～

A WEEK PASSED QUICKLY, all days the same. Out would go the stable patients, and in would come more. Emilie developed a welcome numbness. She was too busy to think about Isaac or Fletcher; there were too many wounds to linger on the gravity of any one in particular.

The fighting went on, and no end in sight. Another set of VADs came over from England, and Frenchwomen were hired to take over the kitchens. There were German prisoners in one of the wards, set apart from Tommies. Emilie wrote to Isaac and Fletcher, expecting no reply. If it was too dangerous to carry out wounded, to bring rations to the trenches, how could she expect the post to be delivered? But she could not leave them with nothing. In the hopes that one last letter might reach them before they met their end, she wrote with fervor. She wrote only of love. She wrote to please be brave. Please come through it. Please get home.

She returned to work each morning with mad urgency. To help was the only thing that could distract her worried mind. To distract from the thought that any day, any minute, she would receive the dreaded wire that would bring her to her knees.

But instead, she received a letter that was postmarked Hallesham, Yorkshire.

Emilie had left it sitting on her bedside while she worked, while she ate her supper, while she washed the sweat and grime out of her hair for the first time in two weeks. And then, just before bed, she tore it open to face whatever news had come from her parents.

10 August 1916

Dear Emilie,

I am so sorry to be giving you this news by post, but you will need to know. Please take care as you read further, as this will be a shock.

Your brother was killed earlier this week. We were told by telegram that Fletcher was court-martialed for misbehaving before the enemy in such a manner as to show cowardice. He was found guilty and sentenced to death. He was executed on the morning of 9 August.

We have not yet spoken of this great shame to anyone, though it will come out soon enough. Pray do not share the manner of Fletcher's

Twenty-Five

Emilie

Emilie was on the train the next morning, and set sail for Southampton. A family crisis was at the top of a short list of excuses which could facilitate immediate leave. Obeying her father's instruction, Emilie told no one what had happened to Fletcher, only that he had died and her family needed her at home.

The journey was agony—all of those idle hours for her mind to turn the news over and over in her head, to imagine what action had got Fletcher court-martialed, how he must have felt as he waited alone in a cell to die. There would have been a padre with him. Fletcher would have loathed hearing the empty Scripture read aloud.

Emilie needed not use her imagination for the next bit. Once, an Irish patient in one of the neighboring wards had arrived with a bullet wound in his face, and had been stabilized over the course of three days, only to be court-martialed and collected for judgment. His wound was self-inflicted. His life had been saved only to be taken by other means. In the days following the drama, everyone chatted endlessly about the boy—some thought he was a disgrace, a coward. Others felt it was one of the saddest deaths they'd heard of.

By then Emilie had learned precisely how it was done. Men found guilty of cowardice were taken out of doors where they could be made an example of. They were blindfolded and bound to a stake. A white square of fabric was pinned over their heart as the target, and a firing squad made up of their own brothers-in-arms finished the job.

By the time Emilie reached English soil, she had such a clear image of Fletcher meeting his end that she could have convinced herself she'd been there. She felt a piece of her burn up, ashes flaking away until nothing remained. She was empty; a shell. Her brother, her best friend, the dancing flame that lit Hallesham Park, was gone. He died alone, and worst of all, he died in shame. In years to come, they would remember the names of thousands who had fallen, but not his. His name would be muddied, crumpled up, and tossed away. Forgotten.

Emilie was sure that nothing had changed at Hallesham, but it looked entirely different to her now. The size of it was no longer opulent, but garish. The windows were all dark, the front steps blackened by lichen, the ivy overgrown, crawling up the pillars, consuming the manor.

Let it, she thought. Let the whole place shrivel like a corpse. Let the flowers wilt, let the grass yellow, let the trees die and fall their leaves for the last time. Hallesham Park had lost its heir apparent and ought never again be a place of life, of music, of glee.

When she stepped out of the motor, Emilie had opened the door for herself, forgetting the chauffeur. O'Henry scurried around the car, kicking up gravel. He was too old to go to war, and so here he remained, driving her parents to and from—where? Were there still soirees in wartime? Were there regattas and afternoon teas?

O'Henry appeared astounded that Emilie had working hands, and watched in awe as she shut the door as easily as she had opened it. Rendered useless, he folded his gloved hands in front of him and offered what might have been a sympathetic smile. Emilie wondered if the staff knew the truth.

As Emilie might have guessed, her parents were not present to welcome her at the door. Instead, the butler, Nelson, pristine as ever in his livery, and Grace. It was strange to see her again after more than a year away. Emilie's memory had caught her differently—a dull slip of a thing. But she was strong and quietly elegant, with a pretty pug nose and sharp cheekbones.

Emilie searched their eyes for some indication that they knew the truth. Nelson would have collected the wire to bring to Papa, but neither were wearing black brassards. Emilie had fashioned her own from a pair of stockings before leaving camp.

"Welcome home, milady," Grace said, and curtsied. "Shall I take your things?"

Emilie blinked, rethinking the question. It had been so long since she was waited on. She looked down at her serge coat, not yet wanting to let go of the Red Cross on her breast. She feared how she would stand up straight without her armor.

But Emilie removed it, and her felt hat to place in the maid's arms. She smoothed her skirt, standing before the two of them as if awaiting instruction. She did not feel like a lady of the house—not even like a guest of equal rank. Her old life was entirely foreign to her.

"Lord Ashwood requests that you lunch with him in the Venice Dining Room." Nelson's voice was its usual clipped monotone, giving nothing away. "Will you require refreshment?"

Emilie couldn't remember the last time she had eaten. Her stomach might have gone with her heart and lungs. "No, thank you. Where is Lady Ashwood?"

Nelson's throat twitched as he swallowed. "Her ladyship is poorly this evening."

Emilie took that to mean her mother's doors were currently closed to visitors.

"Your room is ready for you, milady." This was Grace, eager to please. "I've brought some of your clothes out of mothballs and given them a wash. Shall I draw you a hot bath?"

Emilie shook her head. She wanted nothing. She wanted to *be* nothing.

As she drifted emotionless through the upstairs corridor, she half noticed some of the portraits and furniture covered in dust sheets, and thought of her mother lying abed, perhaps with the back of her hand resting across her brow. She was of a generation of women who could be entirely consumed by a tragedy, could wallow endlessly for days and nights. Lady Ashwood had the privilege to commit herself to bed, to think of nothing but her sorrow, while maids fed her, washed her, dressed her, kept her house.

Emilie knew many women who had learned their cousins and brothers and sweethearts were killed or missing, and had gone right on working with hardly a tear. There was no time for crying on active service. There was only another life to be saving.

So which woman would Emilie be? She considered this as she stepped into her plush bedroom, the very pinkness of it making her nauseous. Now she was home again, she had no chores, no duties, no reason to rise in the morning or go to sleep at night. She could assume the same prone position as her mother, let her tears soak the pillow until Grace came to replace it with a dry one.

But Emilie denied herself the soft embrace of her bed, going instead to the window, where she sat and peered out at the Yorkshire fog. It was there that the image of Fletcher returned, the blindfold over his eyes, the burn of the rope binding his wrists, his dimpled mouth bent with fear.

Or perhaps he had no fear at all. Perhaps he had got precisely what he had wanted. His bullet. An end to the pain and exhaustion.

A knock came to the door. Emilie's consciousness rose to the surface of a dark pool.

"Milady?" Grace's muffled voice behind the door. "Are you ready to dress for luncheon?"

Dress? Emilie was already dressed, in a simple but clean wool skirt and cotton sailor blouse. There was mud on the hem from the road, but her father would hardly notice. What need was there to dirty more clothes?

"Lady Emilie?"

The name grated. Emilie clenched her jaw and stood to open the door. For a moment, she longed to be in the maid's place with an apron, a cap, and a job to do.

"Thank you, Grace; I shall be wearing this."

"Shall I do your hair, milady?"

Emilie had no idea what she looked like. There was a time when the dressing table was the first place she went when entering the bed-room, anxious to check her face, her clothes, her hair. No wonder Grace was so befuddled. How many times had Emilie called on her in a single day to change into another dress, to ensure she appeared to be effortlessly flawless?

The thought made Emilie think of Fletcher. He hated to be alone; he hated waiting. He used to linger in her room while she readied for dinner, sprawled across the bed in his evening clothes, or leaning against the bedpost with a drink he'd poured in secret.

Emilie's eyes filled with tears before she could steel herself. He was gone, her big brother, her lighthouse, her rock. He was dead, his body buried far from home.

Emilie shut the door in Grace's face, poor girl. She did not want the maid to see her when the sob she had been pressing down into her gut for days finally escaped.

PAPA STOOD WHEN EMILIE entered the Venice Dining Room. It was the smaller of the two, and she imagined the Marseille Dining Room was under dust sheets for the duration. Some of their peers had volunteered their country houses to be used as convalescent hospitals and military depots. Walking across the parquet floors, Emilie began to imagine the mahogany furniture away, the windows open, beds lining the walls, and the smell of men.

"Emilie." Papa held her eyes, daring not to look down at her trav-eling clothes. "How was your crossing?"

They were not a family for physical affection, but Emilie expected that, despite their uncivil parting, he might come to take her hands, put a kiss on her cheek, to share in the terrible loss they had both suffered. There was no indication at all of his bereavement.

"Where is Mama?" she asked.

Papa cleared his throat. He was heavier—his face fuller where his chin met his neck, his tummy stretching outward under his waistcoat. Her father was sat at home in his castle, getting fat while their boys withered away, skeletal by the time they reached her care. His eyes were not red from crying, but ringed with purple from lack of sleep.

"Your mother will not be joining us this afternoon. Shall we sit?"

"But I've come here for her. You asked me to come home to comfort *her*."

"And you will—"

"When?"

Papa seemed flustered by her lack of restraint. He looked behind him, as if to ensure his chair was still there, and then sat in it with a huff. "She is not ready to see you as yet. You broke her heart when you left—you humiliated the both of us."

Fatigued, Emilie glanced at the window. The groundskeeper was on the drive, raking the gravel that had been disturbed by her arrival. The scent of roasted fish wafted into the room as Nelson entered, followed by Grace and another parlor maid with the first course. Emilie remembered that Fletcher had ensured one of the footmen, Henry, for his servant. Was the batman still alive? Did he see the act that incriminated her brother?

The maids paused, seeing that Emilie was still standing in the middle of the room. Papa cleared his throat again—it was wet, sounding like he was fighting a chest cold.

"Please sit, Emilie. You must be hungry . . ."

"May I see the papers, please?"

He hesitated. "What papers?"

"The telegrams, the letters. Whatever they sent. There must have been some further details, some explanation."

Her father's brow darkened, and he slid his eyes to the maids, indicating that this was not a discussion for this particular moment. But Emilie had not come home for small talk; she had not come to pretend everything was all right.

"Come and eat," Papa said. "We will discuss this later."

"No—I am not hungry. Please show me the papers, or tell me where they are."

"Emilie, you will mind your tongue."

She closed her eyes, feeling her blood rise. It was one thing to obey the orders of a sister-in-charge, to silently accept a task that was less than desirable because it was her duty. But Emilie could not bear to be belittled by her own father. Not now she knew her worth.

"Your son, Fletcher, is dead," she said.

The words drew all the air from the room. Nelson opened the baize door, and the maids filed out with their trays.

"I need not be reminded," said Papa once they were gone.

"I think you do. You are not even in mourning clothes, and Mama will not show herself. This is not the home of a grieving family."

He looked at the table, studying his water glass. Instead of reaching for a drink, his fingers drummed on the table inelegantly.

"I left my job where I was caring for wounded and dying soldiers to come here. I do not have time to discuss anything besides the matter of Fletcher's death. *Where* are the papers?"

All of a sudden, her father's iron restraint fell away. Emilie could not remember the last time she had seen him angry, if she ever had done in her lifetime. Now the flaring of his nostrils, the unshifting fury in his eyes made her take a step backward.

"Do not speak that name in my house," he said.

Her next breath shook, lungs snatched tight. "I'm sorry?"

Papa tossed his napkin on the table, standing so abruptly that the silverware and china rattled. He buttoned his jacket and dropped his hands to his sides.

"Your brother acted dishonorably. He was a coward, a traitor to his country, and has brought shame upon our family and my title. And so, that boy's name is not to be spoken in my presence or in this house. Have I made myself clear?"

Emilie was so stunned, so sickened, that it took a moment to organize her thoughts. That *boy*? A phrase that had always been Papa's way of belittling any man he thought was beneath him. It was the only way he would refer to Isaac. But his own son? Who fought a war and so lately had died? How could he renounce his heir without a moment's hesitation?

Emilie was shaking her head. It did not seem that any words in the English language could describe her disappointment in her father. "If you truly mean what you say, then I shall take my things and leave here tonight."

"You shall do no such thing; your family needs you *here*."

"My family, you say? No—*my* family would not be so terribly cruel and ignorant. Not to their own." She lifted her chin to stare down his eyes. "*Fletcher* was my family, and Fletcher is dead."

"You cannot understand the gravity of what he has done."

"Can I not?" Her voice escalated. "Can I not, after spending a year nursing men who have seen devastating combat and suffered unconscionable mental and physical distress, understand why one might be compelled to run away?"

Papa dropped his chin to rub his brow. It astounded her to think that once, she would not have dreamt of talking back to Papa. That she would not have raised her opinion. Now she would stand there all day battling with him if he had the strength. Though he was already beginning his retreat. Better to end a debate than lose it.

"If you shall not be eating," he said, "you are excused."

"I may go, if I should like to, but I should not. I should like to see the papers."

Emilie could not be sure if he ceded because of what she'd said, or only to silence her. The reasoning made no difference. She followed Papa to his study, thinking immediately of the last time she'd entered the room, when he told her there was no possibility that the Baron Thurston's bastard could have any interest in her beyond a dowry.

Papa opened a series of drawers, rummaging through papers. Part of her was astonished he had not thrown the wire into the fire, watched it burn while flames of rage reflected in his eyes. Part of her wondered how he could have lost it so easily—the most important telegram he would ever receive.

He grumbled. Tossed a pile of letters onto the desk. "You will learn nothing I have not already told you." Emilie closed in to take it, but he put his hand down atop them. "We have accepted this news with dignity, and had best put it behind us. It would not be wise to inquire. Any further correspondence could be seen as a challenge to the court's decision."

"If I don't know what happened to Fletcher, how can I be sure the court's decision was right?"

"You would dare dispute the judgment of our army's commander-in-chief?"

"Field Marshal Haig has not seen what I have seen."

Papa was clearly astounded she knew the man's name and rank, and that was why she had said it. "If I give these to you, you must promise me that you will read them, and let that be the end of this."

"Forgive me, Papa. I cannot."

What would happen next? Would he tear the documents in half? Would he take this moment to finally burn them?

"You may have them under one condition," he said, holding his eyes away. "We have had a letter from Bridgmond. He has offered to forgive all and have you, given what you did for him at Wimereux."

Emilie was struck dumb. She had had no idea that her parents knew of the bombardment—that they were still in contact with the Claremonts after what had happened. How could they still agree to have her in the family after everything?

"Rhys is convalescing at Howick Hall," Papa went on. "You have been there for a ball, do you remember it?"

Emilie ignored the question. "What does Mama say about this?"

"She agrees that this is the only way to mend what has been broken. Go there tomorrow, let the man propose to you again, and then it is done. Yours and your mother's future will be secure, and the public will forget all of this in time."

"Forget *all of this* . . . Forget my brother was ever alive?"

Papa leaned forward in his chair, offering her the papers. "It is what he wanted, is it not? To see his sister married to his most trusted friend?"

Twenty-Six

Emilie

Emilie woke in the grey light of morning feeling she was in the wrong place. The pillow smelled wrong, the bedclothes too plush, the room too silent. She sat up, feeling terribly alone not to see her bunkmate, feeling suffocated not to hear birdsong.

She went immediately to the windows and threw them open.

As she moved to pull the cord that rang for her maid, Emilie felt the crush of guilt in her belly. She hadn't the energy to argue any longer with Papa, and her mother was still refusing to see her. Without promising what she would say to Rhys, Emilie agreed to visit him. At the least, she owed him an apology, and she needed to know about Fletcher.

So Emilie sat still as Grace smiled at her in the mirror, dressing her hair. She moved mechanically as the maid got her into a smart silk traveling suit in a light shade of mauve—two seasons out of fashion, but pretty enough.

Mama had phoned Lady Grey at Howick Hall, and a motor was sent to collect Emilie at the station. She did not remember her last visit well, but there was a familiarity to the look of the place. Did all country houses not look the same? With their gravel drives and topiaries, their Roman columns and symmetrical windows? Though pulling up, Emilie noticed those windows were open, as was the front door, and there were soldiers in their blues, sitting out on the lawn, in deck chairs, on the front steps. A light game of football was being played to one side, which paused for the men to gawk as the motor approached.

Emilie's heart filled with gladness. This was something familiar. Seeing those boys felt more like coming home.

She stepped out onto the gravel, feeling the eyes follow as she went up to the door. Some women might have been nervous to climb those stairs, where their ankles passed the lustful glances of several men who had not seen women in some time. But this didn't frighten Emilie. She wished she'd been wearing her Red Cross so they would know she was among the ranks looking after them. In fact, some of her old patients might even have been lurking about.

Inside were more men, and the glorious smell of cigarettes and antiseptic. The hall was used as a recreation area—a few uniformed officers were smoking and playing cards. Beyond that, Emilie could hear the chatter and scuffle of hospital work, but the matron intercepted her before she could explore further.

"Lady Emilie, I presume. We've been expecting you. For Lord Bridgmond, correct?"

Emilie had not expected to be recognized so easily. But rather than waste more time, she confirmed.

Matron led Emilie through what was a ballroom, now a hospital ward. Some of the Tommies were still bedbound, in splints or with bandaged heads. A few of them looked fresh from the front. They must have been running out of room at the base hospitals. The VADs scurrying about made Emilie long to pin on her cap again. One of the older ladies of the house was floating up and down the aisle in an evening gown, apparently trying to cheer the boys.

They went out a set of doors to the back gardens. A gramophone had been brought out and set on the stone banister, playing "There's a Long, Long Trail." Emilie couldn't help but smile to see them all, knowing they were here rather than in the mess on the Somme. Isaac's face appeared in her mind and she tried to shake it away. She didn't want to think about him now.

"Lord Bridgmond will be down beside the fountain," Matron said. "He likes to be brought there in the afternoon, when the weather holds—it calms him."

Emilie paused, tilting her head to look at the matron from under the brim of her hat. She had never known Rhys to be anything but completely poised. "Is he in need of calming?"

Matron had begun to step away, but returned, dipping her head. "I'm afraid he's developed a bit of a temper. I daresay it's the pain in his leg, making him so cross."

Emilie nodded. The symptom was not unfamiliar to her.

The fountain was just at the bottom of the Italian garden. She spotted Rhys straightaway, his light hair catching the sunlight. He was sat in an invalid chair in full uniform. He didn't see her approaching, for his head was leaned back, eyes closed.

"I beg your pardon, sir," she said, "is there a Lord Bridgmond about?"

Rhys's mouth stretched into a smile and his eyes came open. He did look well—fuller faced and rested. The sun had brought out the freckles on his lips, always looking like he'd been eating a piece of parkin and hadn't yet brushed away the crumbs.

"Lady Emilie." He reached past the arm of his chair. "It was ever so good of you to come."

So she would not be met in anger, then. Feeling more at ease, Emilie removed her glove before taking his hand. "You look bright-eyed. They must be looking after you properly."

"Howick is not a terrible place to recover, is it? Though I suppose I have played my last game of rugby. I shall become terribly lazy, now."

Rhys's trouser leg was rolled and pinned above where his knee had been. Soon he would be fitted for a prosthetic, though it did pain Emilie to think her friend should never run again. Instead, she could be thankful that Rhys need not worry over losing his ability to work, and would have the best medical treatment money could buy.

"It's odd," Rhys went on. "I can still wiggle the toes that aren't there, and the foot hurts rather terribly."

"I'm dreadfully sorry, Rhys."

A flush crept round his ears. "I have my life, do I not? Seems ungrateful to grieve. Sit, please. Just there." Rhys indicated the edge of the pool and Emilie obliged. "I must offer my deepest condolences. Fletcher was always a great—great friend—"

His voice then closed and the sound got trapped. He raised his fist as if to cover his mouth for a cough, and Emilie noticed the pain pinching at the corners of his eyes. Pain, she thought, in his heart this time.

"Damn him," Rhys eventually choked out, moving his hand to grip the arm of his chair. "Damn the whole show if it's capable of bringing such a man to his knees."

As Rhys's face broke into a sob, Emilie felt a gripping at her throat, not expecting to see such a turn of emotion over her brother. She turned her head away to give him his privacy, as she did for all her patients who wept.

Rhys found his composure again after a few wavering breaths, and his tears were replaced with a timid, sighing laugh. "Forgive me—it's the first I've spoke of him since."

Emilie found a smile. "Please don't apologize," she said. "I could never have imagined his war would end the way it did. Nor how the reactions of my parents would make them strangers to me."

"They are devastated, I imagine."

"They are like everyone else." Emilie stared down into the reflecting pool, dotted with lilies. She dropped one lazy finger into the warm water and drew a figure of eight. "I did not think you would ever wish to see me again."

"You saved my life."

"You are misremembering."

"You *protected* me. And if I had not remembered, I would have known anyway. That is the sort of person you are, Emilie." He reached in her direction, palm up, but she could not bring herself to touch him again. "Please, let us forget the past. Too much has happened since; we have both grown up . . ."

Emilie looked down at her lap, and Rhys sighed.

"I suppose your mother must have told you why I've invited you here," he said, and went into his chest pocket for his cigarette case. "I certainly do not wish to bully you into the thing. I just thought"—he lifted out a cigarette, settling it between two fingers—"it is the one thing I can offer you to ease this burden. To ensure Fletcher can rest peacefully knowing you want for nothing."

Emilie watched him cup his hand around the cigarette to light it with a match, then closed her eyes. So much had happened since the last time he had asked for her hand. She had learned that there was much more to life than anything she had previously imagined. She had met dozens of interesting men and women who proved how small her old world was. She was no more ready to discuss a marriage with Rhys than she had been before the war.

"I am so sorry," she said. "Another man has my heart."

His face remained as stone. Emilie's words came as no surprise to him, and if he was hurt, he didn't show it. "Isaac Thurston."

"I did not plan to fall in love with him."

Rhys simpered. "When has love ever gone to plan?"

Emilie couldn't help but smile back. She had always imagined Rhys's heart to be more of a muscle than a vessel for true feeling. She'd been wrong. "You will be much happier with someone who adores you the way you deserve to be. Life is not to be wasted on sensibility—surely you see that now?"

Rhys did not look convinced. "What will your family make of it?"

"I shall lose them."

"And will it have been worth it? Haven't you lost enough, Emilie?"

She sent her eyes away, out into the sunny afternoon. Nearer the house, the song changed to "By the Beautiful Sea." One of the Tommies stood from the step and began to sing along, giving a performance for the VAD serving tea, and the other men cheered and laughed. It was a common picture of hospital life, and wrenched her heart. She had found impossible joy in such a dark period in history. But could she do it forever?

"Will you tell me why?" Emilie asked.

Rhys tapped away his ash. "Why I still wish to marry you? Or why I still love you?"

Emilie swallowed, taken aback by his response. She felt so incredibly small. She wanted to lean back, let herself fall into the water, and sink to the silted bottom of the fountain.

"I may not have been myself that evening," Rhys said, "but I remember you throwing yourself over me before the blast. I remember you by my side until the end."

"That is why you love me?"

"No. No, I loved you long before that. I've loved you since we were children—always. Since the day we met, when Fletcher and I poked fun at that dimple in your chin and you called me a rotten louse. I do suppose you were right . . ."

Emilie touched her chin at the unlocking of this forgotten memory. She had always assumed he felt the same complacency as she had. He was shy, and too mannerly to flirt, even if he'd wanted to. Had that been why she'd gravitated to Isaac? Because he was bold in a way that matched her own nerve?

"Struck you dumb, have I?" Rhys said.

"I imagined you've been politely enduring me all these years."

He chuckled, and the sound reminded her of the seaside. "I saw, as we got older, that there were other things—other *people*—taking your attention, and I knew if I stepped in your way you would come to despise me. Instead, I—I tried to be loyal to you in hope that eventually, I could take your attention as well."

Slowly, and with a wince, Rhys reached into his chest pocket. Emilie knew what it was before he held it out—the shotgun shell cap he had once gifted her, collected from her own gun. The brass winked in the sunshine, and Emilie marveled at how many miles it had traveled, how many tragedies it had survived.

She reached out her hand, and he spilled it into her palm, covering it with his own. Poor chap; his were sweating badly. Emilie pocketed the shell and retrieved her handkerchief. With a nurse's care, she began to wipe Rhys's hands dry, unsteady as they were—whether from the familiar tremors of shell shock, or from her touch alone, Emilie did not know.

Rhys had been a part of her life for all the years she could remember vividly, hers and her brother's constant friend. He was comfort, nostalgia. However, when she looked at him she did not see a man to love properly, in the way a good wife must.

A life with Rhys would perhaps not be the one of passion and romance that she had envisaged. But it would be a good life, a comfortable life, and she would not go unloved. She remembered her brother's words from the day they parted in London, *You wish to marry him for freedom, do you not? . . . You will be bound just the same.*

She had not believed Fletcher then, that marrying Isaac would end her independence in the same way it would if she married Rhys. Now, she wondered if perhaps he was right. She did not think she could bear a life alone like Sister Allen's. And though she was estranged from her parents, she did not wish to lose them entirely. Could marrying Rhys convince them to look again at Fletcher's situation, to forgive their daughter *and* their son?

"If I marry you," she said, "you will be touched by the scandal."

Rhys removed the cigarette from his mouth and exhaled a thin stream of smoke. "I expect I shall whilst the war is on. But eventually, people will forget. They will know me for my service, and you for doing your bit. My family has a good reputation; all can be wiped clean with time."

Emilie took her hand from Rhys, folding it elegantly with the other like she had been taught when she was a girl. "I cannot say if I shall marry Isaac Thurston. But I do know that I cannot return to the life I once lived. Not having learned what I am capable of."

To her surprise, his expression lightened. "You were always an enigma to me. But I daresay I am beginning to understand. My offer shall remain open. You need only say the word."

Twenty-Seven

Audrey
APRIL 2014

I woke on the couch with a tartan blanket draped over me. My head was at the end of the couch where Leslie had fallen asleep the night before. I sat up, feeling disoriented. Jim wasn't anywhere under my feet, so he must have been with Leslie.

In the kitchen, I found his note on the fridge: *Gone to work. Phone when you're up.*

That meant I had the whole day to spend on my own, preparing the estate sale. I found his phone number in my contacts while I put two slices of bread in the toaster, and leaned on the counter while the phone rang.

He answered quickly. "All right? How'd you sleep?"

"Great, actually. What's up?"

A power saw started up in the background, and there was a pause as Leslie moved farther away from it. "Just wanted to check you were okay this morning."

I hadn't had much time to consider it myself. Gran's research was still spread across the kitchen table, and I glanced at it warily. But the majority of the shock had passed. "I'm hanging in there, thanks."

"Good, I'm glad. Hey—if you're up to it, would you like to go to the fête with me tomorrow aft? It's this ridiculous fair on the village green, but everyone expects me to be there."

I smiled as my toast popped up, and quickly moved it onto a plate before I could burn myself. I thought Leslie was downplaying the whole thing, unwilling to admit that this ridiculous fair was probably something he enjoyed very much and looked forward to.

"Sure, sounds fun." I moved to the fridge for the jam. "I was thinking of doing a sale at Sparrow to try and get rid of some of the clutter before Patrick takes pictures for the listing. Do you think we could do that on Sunday?"

"We'll bring the lot to sell at the fête. I'll ring the organizer and get you put down for a booth. She owes me a favor."

"Who doesn't?"

Leslie chuckled into the phone as someone shouted near him. "I've got to dash. Speak later?"

"Bye, Les."

"Cheers."

I felt a little twinge of regret as the line cut off. Last night, I hadn't been thinking of leaving Leslie, only of being nearer to him because of how much better it made me feel. We still hadn't had a proper conversation about the kiss, but I imagined it was in our near future.

I checked my emails while eating breakfast. One had come through from Beth the day before, and I sent a quick reply that I was going ahead with listing the cottage for sale and would be home soon.

I opened my browser to the web page of flights I'd kept open for several days, putting off the task of choosing what day to leave. Maybe it was the disillusionment of Sparrow Cottage's magic, or my fear of what was going on between Leslie and me, but something made me finally add my credit card details and book my flight for Monday.

There. The worst was over. I was going home, no matter what my heart or head would tell me in the next few days. I would apply for my license renewal and find a new position. Maybe at a smaller hospital, somewhere nobody knew me. I'd start going to meetings regularly; I'd find a sponsor. I knew I was capable now, I just had to believe it.

When I walked up the road toward Sparrow that afternoon, I saw it with new eyes. I imagined the pain Gran felt when she discovered her mother had been lying to her, the confusion she must have experienced learning she had a completely different life as a baby. A different father. A *true* father, whom she had never had the chance to meet before he passed. Opening the front door, I was heavy with Gran's grief and my own. I was mourning the loss of a dream. Sparrow had felt like a home to me; I'd lost yet another.

I had thought, given these realizations, that setting aside items for sale would not hurt. But it did. Each time I blew the dust from a porcelain figure, or wrapped a Wedgwood plate in newspaper, I couldn't help but think of the conversations that must have been had in this room. The whispers they heard behind closed doors. If only the walls could talk.

I'd been kneeling on the floor of the snug, sorting through horse medallions, when I heard a knock on the door. I stood quickly, hoping it might be Leslie surprising me early. But Namita was on the other side with a clipboard.

"Don't tell me you organize the fête," I said.

"Just on the committee." She winked. "I have you down for a booth, but I thought I'd come round and see what you've got so I can ensure you've enough space. If you encroach on Mrs. Darlington's jam, I'll be hung and quartered."

"She sounds a bit scary for a woman who makes jam."

"Her bark is worse than her bite, but I'd rather not have either."

I opened the door wider and motioned for her to come in. Namita was struck for a moment as we stepped into the foyer, gazing around at pictures and sconces and rugs and plant stands. "I always wondered what the inside of this place looked like. It's pretty, ain't it? Like something off of a costume drama."

I led her through to the snug, where I had the majority of the items in boxes already. She crouched to peer in, moving aside some of the newspaper for a better look.

"The pensioners are gonna pop their clogs when they see this." Namita let the lid on one of the boxes fall closed and stood. "I guarantee it'll all go by end of day."

"Good." I folded my arms, stepping back. "It would cost more than it's worth to ship it all back to New Jersey."

Namita's face fell a little. "You are going back, then?"

"There'll be no reason for me to stay once Sparrow sells."

And she didn't know the rest of it. But I wasn't interested in getting into the particulars.

We both went silent for a moment. It was going to be hard to leave Namita, like it would be to leave Leslie, and Nan, and Bernard. Home seemed so far away, and intimidating. Where would I even go when I returned? Crash on my sister's couch while I searched for a job? The idea made me put my hand in my pocket to clutch the military medal I still kept there. I'd put it in that morning after last night's close call. Sometimes staying sober for a few hours was no easier than staying sober for a year.

"I reckon one booth will be enough," Namita said, rescuing me from a tailspin. "Can I help you get things sorted? I don't open Keys until noon."

"That would be great. I need to pack up the books. I was thinking of bundling them—three for a pound?"

Namita clearly hadn't noticed the books lining the wall when we'd come in. She spun on her heel and let out a little gasp, probably rethinking her estimation on the size of the sale. "Reet, I'm moving in." She skimmed her fingers over the spines. "Can you imagine? Putting your feet up beside the fire, pouring yourself a nip of scotch, taking up a good book?"

She let out a dreamy sigh while I began to take the books down from the shelves to fill the boxes I'd left out for them.

"Take whatever you like," I said. "Consider it payment for your help."

"You haven't got any Brontës, have you? I've a mate with a birthday coming up who would give her eyeteeth for a vintage copy of *Jane Eyre*."

"If I do, they're all yours."

We filled the boxes with what books were in good enough condition to sell, and Namita ended with an armful she had chosen for herself. I made her promise to stop by the booth on Saturday to say hello, knowing it would probably be the last time I saw her before leaving. I didn't tell her that.

She paused at the door when I walked her out, gazing around the front garden, which, thanks to the Petals, was looking almost intentional.

"There's something special about this old place, isn't there?" Namita said, hugging the books to her chest. "It's a sort of feeling, like— I don't know. Like in the pit of your stomach. Like coming home to a warm house after a long night and flicking the lights on." She broke into a grin. "Blimey, listen to me. What am I like?"

I smiled, even as she rolled her eyes. I couldn't lie. Despite myself, despite what I knew in my head, my heart was still in these halls.

"You're right. There is something . . ."

And as I said it, I got the feeling someone was looking at me from behind. But when I glanced over my shoulder, the foyer was empty.

I GOT A FEW odd glances as I brought boxes to the three tables that comprised my booth. Luckily, Leslie was behind me, and wary frowns smoothed to warm grins. He had that effect on people in the village, particularly the older women. I started to unpack books while he stopped to chat with Mrs. Darlington. Her jam booth *was* rather close to mine, so I was glad he was taking the time to explain what we were up to. I'd buy some of her jam to bring home to Beth, who loved a good farmers' market. That morning, I found a text from her from the night before, saying she was proud of what I'd done, and was surprised by how much it affected me.

It was early yet, but most of the fête had already been set up. The village green sat beside the stone church, which provided an idyllic backdrop. There was a bandstand and tea tent at one end, both strung with Union Jack bunting. At the other end were booths where locals were arranging their wares for sale—honey, cakes, jewelry, artwork, and other handmade goods. There was an area for the vegetable competition, another for a dog show, and a few typical fair games like ring toss and bottle knockdown. I noticed Namita with her clipboard, pointing and helping to arrange the festivities. More people would be pouring in soon, when the band would start up and children would perform their maypole dance, signifying the beginning of fête season.

My booth's first table was laid fully with books, and already drawing some attention from passersby. I knelt to open the next box, which was full of other objects—a silver hand mirror, a carriage clock, a pair of sewing scissors shaped like a swan, a brass makeup powder container. This would only make a small dent, but at least it was a start. Patrick suggested going forward with the estate sale to clear the rest of it, and I'd agreed, asking him to make the arrangements. In a few weeks' time, Sparrow Cottage would be empty, and I would be too far away to think about it.

Jim appeared beside me, sniffing noisily in my ear before giving me a wet lick that made me laugh. I looked up to see Leslie on the other end of the leash. He set down a box he'd been carrying under one arm, and pushed his hair behind his ears. "That's the last of them, I think."

"Is Jim going to be in the dog show?" I said, standing.

"Just a spectator this year."

Behind Leslie, I noticed Mrs. Darlington and another lady tittering over a new bottle of Pimm's. The latter put a finger to her lips and poured into a plastic cup.

"Do people drink at this thing?" I asked.

Leslie lifted a shoulder. "It's not strictly allowed, but pretty much inevitable once the pub opens. Is that okay?"

I nodded. I couldn't stay out of the world in order to remain sober. If I needed to get away from it, Leslie's house wasn't far.

"Everything looks so nice in the sunshine." I turned a porcelain whippet to face the front of the table. "Think any of this is worth a small fortune?"

"You never know." Leslie smiled. "Listen: normally all the proceeds from sales go back into the village, but as you aren't local, I've had a word with Namita and she's said you can pocket any money you make today."

My gaze moved across the green, to Nan catching up with one of the Petals. They both waved at me when they noticed me staring, and I waved back. "No, it should go to the village."

"You sure? They weren't exactly accepting of your family."

"They've been pretty accepting of *me*. That's all that matters."

I bumped my shoulder against his, hoping he could tell I was including him. But there was a distance to the way he smiled back. It was the same distance he'd been using in our conversations, in the way he kept his eyes from holding mine for more than a fraction of a second. Maybe it was self-preservation, and I was being unfair to him.

It was as good a time as any to tell him I was leaving.

"Hey, Les—?"

"Oh, I do fancy a white elephant, me!" It was Bernard's neighbor with the broken loo. She clapped her hands together. "And it's a bumper crop! How much for the toast rack, lovey?"

I lifted the ceramic toast rack to hand to her, silently saying goodbye to the little hens painted on either side. "Name your price."

She gave me a five-pound note, which I thought was generous. But I supposed it was all going to feed back into more carnivals and garden parties she would surely enjoy.

"And what of this? Oh, it's darling . . ."

The woman had picked up a small brass box—perhaps for jewelry or makeup. She turned it over a few times, inspecting the cherub design on the outside, and then suddenly the top flipped open and a little bird came out of it. She gasped, and laughed, but I couldn't return the smile, so rapt by what I was seeing. I surely must have seen the box before when I was packing up, but never thought to look any closer at it. It was beautiful.

"I must have it," the woman said, when the bird had finished singing and retreated back into the box. "What about a tenner?"

"No," I answered, surprised at how quickly the word came out. "Sorry—it isn't for sale."

I couldn't explain it, but something in my gut told me not to give it away. Not this. The woman handed it back to me and I slipped it into my bag.

By then, there were several more browsers—new faces, and some I recognized. Leslie stayed on one side of the U-shaped table, and I stayed on the other, peddling items until my pockets were heavy with coins. With each sale, it got easier to say goodbye to the items I'd come to associate with Sparrow, and before long, I was too busy to think. I dashed between customers, haggling with people who knew far more about antiques than me, and accepting samples of shortbread biscuits and lemon drizzle cake from the other sellers.

I didn't notice Bernard wandering between the tables until he approached me, holding a carriage clock under his arm. He no longer needed his cane, and some of the color had returned to his cheeks. I was glad my treatments had worked.

"Bernard, hi!" I said, wiping some sweat from my brow. "You're looking good. Oh, that's far too much—"

He was holding a twenty-pound note toward me. "This is a fine piece, this, and still works. I had it serviced two years ago."

"Then it should be yours," I pushed, putting my hands in my pockets so I couldn't take the money. "I'm glad you came. It must be strange seeing all of this stuff where it doesn't belong."

Bernard swept his eyes over what was left of the sale, and looked wary. Of course, he'd spent his lifetime at Sparrow. It probably hurt him far worse than it did me.

"Some townie'll gut it, I reckon," he grumbled.

My heart broke—for Bernard, for Gran, for the house that was so precious despite its history. "You sound like Leslie," I said. "You should have seen him when the estate agent recommended an open floor plan . . ." I turned to bring Leslie into the conversation, but he had suddenly disappeared. I spotted him a few feet away, lifting some kind of enormous squash for an older gentleman at the vegetable competition.

"Anyway . . ." Behind Bernard, a few other customers were waiting to pay for their items. "It was nice to see you out and about."

"Er . . ." He scratched his head, looking anywhere but at my eyes. "I had something I wanted to tell ya—"

A lady appeared at my arm, clearly unwilling to wait any longer. I held up a finger to Bernard as politely as I could, and took the woman's pound coin for an armful of books. I didn't have time to question the amount—I wanted to get back to Bernard. But another customer was on my left, and then another, and by the time I returned, he was gone.

I crouched beside Jim, who was panting happily from a prone position at the back of the booth. I fed him what was left of the shortbread sample, and emptied the money in my pockets into the paper bag they'd come in. My tables were nearly empty, and part of me wished I could run across the village green and retrieve all the items. But I felt lighter, too, and hoped again that I had done the right thing.

Leslie was returning as I stood up. The crowd had thinned in favor of watching the maypole dance, and I was glad for the break. Maybe I could find Bernard and ask him about what he'd wanted to tell me. But I felt Leslie's eyes burning into me, noticed the tightness in his shoulders that hadn't rested all day, and knew he had to come first.

"Do you want to take a walk?"

He nodded in a knowing way that told me he knew exactly why

I'd asked him. He left Jim with Mrs. Darlington, and we walked in silence away from the village green, stopping on the squat stone bridge that stretched across the River Rye. Leslie leaned over the edge with his hands in his pockets, watching the water trip over rocks. Birds sang overhead, and in the distance, the band fired up with a classic, "God Save the Queen."

Suddenly, I'd lost all my confidence, standing with my back to the river, looking across the meadow where green hills rolled up toward the horizon, kissing the clouds. Home would seem so bland, now that I knew the beauty that existed elsewhere.

Beside me, Leslie turned so we were shoulder to shoulder. He had a handsome profile, a rare, natural stoicism in brow and pout that softened the instant he laughed. But now, the moment was too taut with unspoken words.

"You've been quiet today," I said. "Something on your mind?"

Then the stoicism did melt away, but his smile was wry and humorless. He crossed his arms loosely, keeping his gaze across the river. "Honestly? Yeah. You." When I didn't answer, he turned his chin, and I felt a wobble in my knees as our eyes met. "What are we doing, Auds? You run off on your own, only to return and wake me in the dead of night. What the hell is going on?"

I curled into myself meekly, even knowing he was right. "I shouldn't have asked you to kiss me. I'm sorry—"

"You shouldn't have? Why? Because you didn't mean it, or because it wasn't what you were expecting?"

"It isn't that. I wanted the kiss—I wanted *more*. But . . ." I reached into my pocket and pulled out the medal, turning it over in my hands. Leslie noticed, and when I lifted my chin, his had fallen to stare at it. "I just freaked out, okay? I said I'm sorry."

Leslie shook his head slowly. "I've been trying to follow your lead, to be respectful of your boundaries, given your situation. But I've given you all of me, because I care about you, and I'm not getting owt in return. And I don't mean sex, I mean *anything*."

His brows bent in a wounded expression that made me hate myself for hurting him. But at the same time, my defenses were rising, whether I wanted them to or not. The great, inexplicable urge to protect myself from pain ignored all evidence that this man clearly wanted only good for me.

"I don't know what you want, Leslie. I know you're Mr. Commitment—"

"That's not fair."

"—but I'm only visiting here, you knew that. What did you expect would happen between us?"

"I thought, as anyone does when they meet someone they fancy, that we could work it out. Now I see you're unwilling to try, or to even take me seriously."

"I'm not like you, okay? I don't have everything figured out. I've never been in a real relationship, let alone a marriage. I can't just jump in with both feet."

"Did I say anything about marriage? Jesus—all I'm asking for is a yes or a no. Do I have a chance or not?"

Before I could reply, his phone rang in his pocket and he drew it out to squint at the screen. It was only a few seconds, but it was long enough for me to consider what I'd said, to consider Leslie and what he was asking of me. I was being irrational, I knew that, and still I couldn't figure out how to let my guard down.

Leslie stuck his phone back into his pocket, having silenced the ring, and looked at me expectantly. I wasn't getting out of this without giving him an answer. I had to face what I had done to him, decide what I wanted for myself. And what I wanted, in the depths of my heart, which I usually ignored, was for Leslie to wrap his arms around me and hold me while the rest of the world kept spinning rapidly around us. But there was no way for it to work.

"I want to be with you," I said slowly, "but I *can't*. I can't stay here."

"Why not?"

"Because eventually, I will drink, and I will pull you down with me, and I refuse to do that to you after everything you've been through."

The answer surprised him as much as it did me. The words were true, and cut through me as they left my body. They were the real reason I was so hesitant. My own sobriety mattered to me, but not as much as Leslie's did. He deserved the happiness he'd fought for, the life he'd built for himself, and I wasn't willing to be responsible for stripping that away from him.

Leslie blinked as his mouth came open. When he spoke, he strung the words together with careful patience. "It is not for you to decide what I can and cannot handle. I would not be standing here with you if I didn't think I was capable of maintaining control over my own bloody weaknesses." He sighed, dropping his head. "Maybe I had it all wrong . . ."

His phone rang again and he cursed under his breath, drawing it out of his pocket without answering. "It's a work emergency; I've got to go."

I nodded, pressing my lips together. I couldn't blame him for finding any excuse to abandon this conversation.

"Can I give you a lift back to the house?" he asked.

"No. Just go."

Leslie didn't hesitate. Standing alone on the bridge, I allowed myself to watch him break into a jog back up the street, knowing it would be the last time I'd see him.

Twenty-Eight

Emilie

LE TRÉPORT, FRANCE

SEPTEMBER 1916

Papa had been truthful; there were no further details about Fletcher's conviction in the papers he'd shared. But there was something about holding them, seeing the typed blue ink and the signatures of the men who turned him over that made it all feel like more of a reality. Upon returning to work, Emilie began writing to the War Office and Fletcher's commanding officers, asking for any information they could provide. She procured Henry's address from Grace, hoping his servant was a witness.

Emilie tried to write to Isaac with the news, but could not find the right words. The wound was still too fresh—she needed to gather her thoughts.

There was no time to linger on her own woes—it was back into the fray. In the first few days, Emilie found it difficult to adjust to camp life. But the comforts of home soon faded in her mind, and she returned to thinking of little besides the next convoy.

Sister Allen watched her closely. Emilie often felt her eyes, but didn't meet them. Sister knew something was wrong, and perhaps she assumed it was only Emilie's grief. She wanted to tell Sister every secret she was keeping but couldn't. She wanted to keep her head down, to work, to think it through on her own.

At the end of her first week back, Sister Allen came through the flap while Emilie was specialling a young private with lockjaw. Emilie hadn't been watching the clock, but after a glance, saw it was nearly her time to pop out for a quick snack lunch.

An orderly came in to take over for the time she would be away.

"Meet me outside when you're through," Sister said. "I've found something of yours."

Emilie's breath caught. As usual, Sister Allen gave nothing away in her expression, and was gone before Emilie could question. What could it possibly be? Had a parcel arrived with Fletcher's effects? Had someone come to speak to her about him?

She quickly finished her work and left her patient in the care of the orderly. The afternoon sun stung her eyes as she went under the flap, looking back and forth for Sister Allen. She felt like she had a swarm of bees trapped inside her body, buzzing one way, then the other.

Eventually she found Sister lingering near one of the flap openings, conversing with an officer. Sister turned first, her expression unreadable. Then the officer, removing his cap and running a hand through his auburn hair.

The air left Emilie's lungs as she ran forward, thinking of nothing except throwing her arms around Isaac's neck. She met him with reckless force, but he caught her, embracing her so tightly her ribs cracked. Pressing her tears into his neck, she breathed him in, savoring the solidness of him and the beat of his heart against her chest.

"I'm sorry," he was whispering, his lips against her ear. "I'm so sorry, Emilie."

In another breath, her mind began to catch up with her body. Emilie unraveled herself and slid back to a flat foot. She couldn't help but take Isaac's face in her hands, to study every angle of it until she was sure he was real, he was here, he was well.

"You do love your surprises, don't you?" she said.

"We've been in Manin for physical training, so I begged the afternoon off. I wrote ahead, but had no answer."

Emilie dropped her hands from his face to quickly dry her cheeks.

"Emilie?" Sister Allen was standing just beside them. "Why don't you take Mr. Thurston for a walk to the cliffs? And do be discreet."

Emilie tugged Isaac by the sleeve, steering him through campus as quickly as she could without breaking into a run. Once they were far enough away, she slipped her hand into his, and they did not say another word until the tents were in the distance behind them.

Isaac released her hand when they reached the cliffs, stepping closer and closer to the edge. Here, the grasses grew to knee height, dancing on the sea breeze. Isaac's hair blew free, and for a moment, he was captured by the view—the crystal water, the sand below, the chalk cliffs in the distance. Emilie admired the shape of him, his familiar silhouette against blue skies.

The sea was churning fiercely below, and a storm was black on the horizon, making the chalk cliffs stand out in sharp contrast.

Emilie unpinned her cap and put it in her pocket, letting the wind cool her brow. Folding her arms, she waited patiently until Isaac pivoted and walked back to where she stood, his head down, his shoulders hunched. He kicked at the grass. Clearly, there was something on his mind, some greater reason he had come.

"Your Sister Allen tells me you've been given the Military Medal," he said. "Not worth mentioning?"

"It was an accident."

"How is one accidentally gallant?"

"I wasn't meant to be there at all. I was only there to . . . to be with Rhys."

Isaac gave nothing away, though his eyes were so intense and magnetic that she thought for certain he would kiss her then and there. Instead, after some time, he looked away.

"I reckon you have me beat. Shall I send you back to the trenches in my place?"

Emilie knew then that the slump in his shoulders was the guilt he wrote so often about. The sense that he was somehow failing his men and his country, that he hadn't proven himself the way he'd hoped. "I could never do what you do," she said.

"You certainly could. I'll happily admit women have got the real backbone."

She slid her hands into his. The skin was cracked and rough with dry patches, and though the rest of him appeared immaculately clean, there was dirt in the fine lines of his knuckles. That was when she noticed the cuff of his jacket peeking out from his greatcoat sleeve, with a second star.

"You've been promoted," she said.

He did not meet her eyes straightaway, but kept them squinting on the horizon. "We've lost half of our officers since July."

"Half?"

"Very nearly."

Emilie shivered, though the information should not have come as a shock after all the men she'd seen at the hospital, and how many they'd buried. When she saw the shine of a tear on the corner of Isaac's eye, Emilie pulled him to face her.

"What's happened, Isaac?"

He shook his head and pressed his finger and thumb to his eyes. Emilie took his elbow to draw it down and away, and had to touch his face to bring it level with hers. All at once he seemed to lose his resolve, and took a strong hold of her so suddenly she let out a gasp. But there was a tenderness behind the urgency, and his expression was falling further with each tight breath. When his words finally tumbled out, they were shaky and grizzled by the emotion in his voice, and Emilie's heart broke for him.

"I needed to get away," he said. "I needed to see you. I feel I am coming upon my time and I'm—I'm so afraid. I'm so tired . . ."

Emilie drew his head down to her shoulder, holding him as fiercely as she could.

"Please, please don't say such things," she said, smoothing his hair. "We must hope, or else there is no point in going on . . ."

In lieu of a response, Isaac gripped her shoulders ever tighter, clinging to her as if she were the very thing keeping him from floating away on the wind. The poor man, and all those that stood beside him in the terrors of the Somme. How would they ever find peace again after what they had seen and done?

"Go away with me," Isaac said, his lips pressed to her ear. "Please, Em; we can align our leaves—go home, or go south—it doesn't matter. Allow me to have one night with you in case it is my last."

The words shocked Emilie, making her ashamed of her prudishness. A *night*, he had said, all on their own and far away from parents and chaperones. And what would he expect of her? Would she give him what he wanted, should he ask for it? She felt a stirring in her core, and almost as if he could feel it, too, Isaac pressed his mouth against the sensitive flesh beneath her ear, making her hairs stand on end. What if he was right, and they were only afforded one last chance to be together? Would she regret it for the rest of her life if she declined? She could not deny that she held the same fear as Isaac did— that his time would come. It could happen so easily. One half step in the wrong direction, and a bullet could be his.

She drew away, needing to clear her thoughts without the distraction of his lips. Closing her eyes, she thought of Rhys's offer, thought of the desperation in her father's voice, of her mother, hiding away in her grief. She thought of Fletcher's grave, wherever it was, of his fear. Of Isaac's fear. Her lids fluttered open to find Isaac staring deliberately at her mouth, which quivered as she formed her answer.

"All right, Mr. Thurston. Where am I to meet you?"

~~~

ISAAC'S LEAVE WOULD NOT come through until December. Emilie begged only two days off. Thankfully, because their staff had recently grown in numbers, Matron could spare her.

They met at the station in Boulogne and continued south, to a small town they hoped was far enough away from the front line that they would not be recognized. The weather was slightly milder than it was in Le Tréport, away from the damp sea air. Here, the stone buildings were short with tiled roofs and white shutters on the windows. They found a little inn that, from the outside, appeared to be a family home, with a line of laundry drying in the garden. When Isaac rang the bell, a small woman answered with a balk, taking in his uniform. He spoke sweetly in French to her, and it was enough to make her soften her shoulders and wave them in. Dark beams hung low over the foyer, with clay tiles and modest curtains.

The innkeeper brought them up the stairs to a corridor loud with shuffling, conversation, and a baby's cry flooding out from under the doors. She unlocked one of them to reveal a small room with a window, fireplace, iron bed, and vanity. Once they were inside, Emilie noticed another door propped open. Inside was a toilet and a small bathtub.

"*De l'eau froide,*" the woman said from the corridor. "*Je vais en apporter chaude.*"

Running water, it appeared, though not heated. Still, it was a luxury for the rural countryside, and a maid would bring hot water for a bath. The woman explained that this was her only room with an indoor lavatory, and apologized for the noise—she was housing refugees who had fled German occupation in the north.

"*Bon travail, madame,*" Isaac told her, and she nodded and left.

Unraveling her scarf, Emilie watched Isaac slump against the dressing table, head bowed. What a familiar image this had become—the bone-weary young officer collapsing now he was out from under the eyes of his CO and his men. No need to look brave now, no need to stand tall.

Emilie went to him, lifting his face to see her smile. He rested his hands heavily on her hips, touching his forehead to hers. What had been weighing on him that last time they'd seen each other had not gone. She had thought it might be the time to tell him about Rhys's offer of marriage, but she would keep it to herself, not wanting to risk him wilting any further.

"We have waited ever so long to be here," she said. "Won't you be glad?"

Emilie raked a hand through his hair and he leaned into her hand, closing his eyes at the sensation. She should have been prepared for the changes in him, but they were still a shock.

"I don't believe I've done the right thing by asking this of you," he said.

"Have you changed your mind?"

"No—no, it's just—" His voice cracked in the way that a much younger man's might. "I have spent my entire life aiming to be a better man than my father."

Of course he would be thinking of his father, who thought nothing of making love to a woman he should never consider marrying, and abandoning his child when it came.

Emilie curled herself around him, drawing his head to her chest. "You are nothing like your father, Isaac. I have come here because I love you—it is my choice, not yours. If you think me incapable of making my own rash decisions, you don't know me at all."

That finally made his mouth crack into a smile, and he chuckled. "You are something, Lady Emilie."

"Something good, I hope." She began to push his coat off his shoulders. "Wouldn't you like to lie down for a while? You are no use to me this groggy."

To this, he could not refuse. He slunk to the bed, and began removing his boots. Around that time, the maid knocked and Emilie let her in to lay the fire. When she was gone, and the room was beginning to warm, Isaac stood to undo his Sam Browne belt, facing the window.

Emilie sat on the bed, testing the mattress. Not good at all, but she supposed it would feel comfortable compared to her camp bed, and whatever unusual place Isaac had slept in the last billet. Isaac got out of his jacket, laying it over one of the chairs, and worked the knot from his tie. Then he was out of his shirt and Emilie's face fell.

She crawled over to stand from the bed and touched the thin, pale skin on his back where vertebrae protruded from his spine. He was covered in little pink dots left behind by biting lice. She ought not to have been surprised, having seen the wasted state of so many of her patients. But it was shocking to see Isaac this way, when he had money enough to buy full meals in restaurants when he had time off, or be sent parcels from home.

"What have I done?" he asked, in good humor.

"Forgotten to eat, apparently." She turned him by the arm to see his front, collar and hip bones framing the inward curve of his torso.

"You are off duty, Nurse Dawes."

"Not anymore. I am going this instant to get us some food."

"Em—" He tried to grab at her but she was halfway to her coat. "I am quite all right."

She wrapped her scarf around her neck and reached for her hat. "Then you will be rather well when I'm finished with you. Don't let the fire go out."

⚜

EMILIE BORROWED A BASKET from the innkeeper and returned half an hour later when it was filled with cheese, saucisson, fresh bread, fig jam, and a cheap bottle of wine. All was quiet when she pushed open the door, and shut it gently behind her. She set the basket down on the table to get out of her coat.

Isaac was lying on his back, peacefully asleep. The bedclothes had been pushed down to his waist, and she was able to admire the shape of him. He had his head to one side, the tendons of his neck taut as they angled toward his chest. His ribs expanded with every slow breath.

Emilie wanted badly to kiss him awake. Instead, she went into the bathroom to wash up. She removed her blouse, skirt, and petticoat, leaving them draped over the edge of the tub. She released a few pins from her hair so half of it touched her shoulders. In the mirror, she saw a different girl to the one who had waltzed with Isaac Thurston. She was older, the cheeks more severe, the eyes sadder, the skin dull. She looked like her mother.

She applied perfumed powder and brushed her finger over her lips to make them pink.

Returning to the room, Emilie found herself in nothing but her underthings and alone with a man. The thrill of it took her by surprise. The creak of the bedstead caused Isaac to stir, and when his eyes opened to see her, he smiled sleepily, reached one hand up to touch the ends of her hair. She thought he might comment on the reduced length. Instead he sat up to put his fingers through it.

"I've never seen it loose," he said.

So he hadn't. Emilie removed the last few pins so it fell around her face. Isaac noticed her bare shoulders under the straps of her chemise. His eyes trailed across her chest, over her arms, lazily but with intention. Her skin burned. She could not keep her hands off him any longer.

The skin of his chest was hot from sleep. He had silken hairs there, growing sparsely across his breastbone. Emilie's heart quickened. She kissed him so suddenly their teeth knocked, and he made a sound in her mouth. As she moved over him he winced and retreated, putting both hands behind him to rest his weight on.

Turning red, Emilie shifted to a seat on the other side of the bed. "Am I too eager?" she asked. He laughed, finding it amusing how little she understood. She began to regret not confiding in Sister Allen. "I haven't ever done this, you know."

Isaac sat forward, and the blanket slid off the side of his hips, revealing the curve of his bottom and dimple in the thigh. "Neither have I, *you know*. I'm bloody nervous."

"*You?* You are the man—you aren't meant to be nervous."

"So says who?"

"Me. Shall we lie down?"

He flopped down onto his side, and Emilie lay facing him. He touched one of the hooks on her corset and began picking at it with his nail, like a flake of paint that would easily come away. Apparently he was too timid to ask for it off.

Emilie put her hand over his, moving it to where she'd tied the laces round the front. He worked through the knot slowly, then pulled the ends until the laces were loose.

When she sat up, he followed, both reaching for the first hook. She let him have a go, and after a puff of laughter, he managed to undo it, and then the next, and the next, sneaking kisses in between. It fell off, landing somewhere behind Emilie. Underneath, he found her cotton combination and a dozen more buttons. He threw his head back, and they were both laughing.

"Now you understand the pains we women take in dressing. At least we've saved time on your end."

They both looked down to find that the blanket had fallen away entirely from Isaac's groin. He quickly replaced it, red-faced but smiling. "Always thinking ahead, me."

Emilie giggled. She loved him ever so much.

She suggested wine to shake the nerves, and he agreed. There were no glasses, so they drank from the bottle—something Emilie had never done before. The drink did its job to loosen the tension, and once they got into the food, Emilie forgot she was nearly naked, that Isaac was, that it had become dark outside.

Their hands began to explore each other freely. Emilie unfastened her garters and rolled her stockings off so Isaac could brush his hand from her ankle to knee, making her muscles tighten and release. She lay back, reaching out to him, drawing his shoulders down to kiss him. She untied the top of her combination and he fumbled until he could move the straps from her shoulders and tug the bodice down below her belly.

Emilie felt the sudden cold and pinched her eyes shut, as if to hide from her own exposure. Above her somewhere, Isaac's breaths had become hurried, blowing hot against her face and chest. He dropped kisses along her collarbone, soft and slightly unsure, then pursed his lips around her nipple, which made her back arch.

He kissed her closed lids and drew a finger down her nose, making her eyes open. "Who are you hiding from, little sparrow?"

All at once, Emilie's eyes smarted, and before she could stop them, two tears slipped over her temples and into the pillow. Did anyone in the world know her better? She touched Isaac's face, admiring the beautiful curves for the millionth time. How did she ever think she could be content without him?

Isaac moved onto one elbow, his other hand on Emilie's ribs. Without a corset in the way, the sensation was almost too much to bear. She wanted to lean into his hand, to absorb it, to have every inch of his skin touching hers.

"Do you want to stop?" he asked.

Emilie shook her head, blinking her eyes dry. She pushed at her combination, kicking until the drawers fell past her feet, bunched at the bottom of the bed. Isaac was up again on both elbows, knee between her legs. She pulled his hips down, gasping at the sheer need of her own body that she did not yet fully understand.

She could feel him under the blankets, feel that his body wanted hers in return. He kissed her and leaned over to the bedside table where he had left a French letter. He knew well what happened to babies born of affairs, and she had heard stories of women sent away.

Then they were nose to nose again, breathing the same wine-laced air.

"Are you sure it's what you want?" he asked one last time.

"I've wanted this for a very long time."

Like a spell, her words melted Isaac's hesitance away.

It was slow, and tender, clumsy at times, but wonderful. When they were through, Isaac was trembling, and let his weight rest against her. Emilie held him close as he kissed the side of her face, pawing at her tangle of hair, making tiny, breathy sounds like a dying man. It was not pain in his face, but rapture and need, a need for her, and that made her want to weep.

"Are you all right?" he whispered. "Emilie—?"

Isaac drew her face to his, pressing their heads together. Emilie was crying again—there was nothing she could do to stop it. She felt sorry that he must have thought she was hurt, but she wasn't, not physically. It was only her heart that was shattered beyond repair. For now that she finally knew she could make her choice, she feared the war would make it for her.

Twenty-Nine

Emilie

Emilie was nearly asleep when the noises came. They sounded at first, like a dog whining for his dinner. For a moment she thought the window had come open, that the sound came from somewhere below. Then Isaac began to tremble, his shoulders gone rigid, his head tucked closer to the pillow to hide from something bearing down on him.

Emilie forgot every lesson she had ever learned, her heart bypassing her logic. She slipped across the bed so she was flush with Isaac's back, wrapping her arms around him from behind. He was too deep into the dream to notice, his flesh cold and damp. As he flinched and shuffled, the sheets wound tighter around them. She pressed her nose to his neck, offering gentle coos suited for an infant. She wished desperately to be with him wherever he was, to put her body between Isaac and what dangers he was seeing in a place she was barred from. There was no bandage for night terrors; there was no tablet to cure a wounded mind.

When the dream ended, Isaac's body went stiff, and then suddenly slack. Emilie could tell he was awake by the irregular movements of his breath, but he did not say a word, nor turn to face her. He only slipped out of her arms to stand. She watched him move through the darkness, disappearing into the bathroom. As she shifted, a dull tenderness became apparent between her legs, a physical memory of what they had done. In another moment, Emilie felt her body coming alive again.

He returned a moment later, smelling of lavender soap. He lit a cigarette on the candle's flame and sat beside Emilie. She nudged herself closer, laid a hand on his stomach. When he removed it and shifted away, she knew something was wrong.

"Was it a nightmare?" she asked.

He showed no indication that he had heard, only ashed his cigarette and took another drag. It wasn't until he stifled it that he even looked at her. Something made Emilie sit up, no longer conscious of the difference between clothed and unclothed. Isaac looked ghostly in the night, pale skin glowing, eyes dark holes in an expressionless face.

"I need to tell you something about Fletcher."

Emilie's heart stuttered. "What?"

"I was with him before he died."

The cold took Emilie all at once, and her body began to shiver violently. She pulled the sheet over her, clinging to it for comfort. This must have been why Isaac had been so distraught when he came to her at the hospital.

"I intended to tell you when I saw you last," he said, "but then I lost my way."

"It doesn't matter. Tell me now."

"I don't wish to upset you."

Emilie blinked slowly, her nerve crumbling. "I've already lost my brother. Nothing you say can hurt me worse than that."

Isaac drew his knees to his chest. "My company was rebuilding in the support trenches. One doesn't expect visitors there—nobody volunteers to go down the line—but it was a quieter day than most. I was helping organize the ration party." He paused for a breath. "I didn't recognize him at first; his face was tanned and lean. He was the last person I expected to slap me on the shoulder."

The image made Emilie smile, and Isaac allowed the hint of one, too.

"At first, all was well. He wanted me to tell him what we were up to, so I toured him down the line, showed him where some of the walls had come down. I told him a story—" He scratched his brow thoughtfully. "One of the men had been digging in the mud and hit a smear of red—thought it was a body, but it was only a tin of raspberry jam. Fletcher had a good laugh. But it was wrong, his laugh . . . it sounded wrong."

Emilie swallowed, trying to keep herself steady.

"We went into the dugout and I started a brew. Fletcher wouldn't stop talking; I hardly got a word in. Something about the water, how it tasted so badly of oil from the barrels it was kept in. Nothing out of the ordinary—every man moans of the same. He asked for something stronger, so I put a nip of rum in our cups before the tea.

"That was when he started to shift. He began talking of that last summer we spent together, how good a friend I was, how much fun we'd had. He started talking of you." Isaac's eyes came up, heavy with sympathy. "There's no point in me going on about everything he said, but he told me to steer clear. He got violent, Em, so suddenly. He stood, and he pushed me into the corner, and he made me admit to him that marrying Bridgmond was the right thing for you, that marrying me would be ruinous."

He looked terribly hurt and Emilie wanted to comfort him. But she couldn't move. It felt as if he was telling her one of his fictional stories. This was not her brother, this was a stranger, a character in a book.

"I told him everything he wanted to hear. He had me by the collar, and I had one eye on the door. If anyone walked in, we were both for it. But I let him have it out—let him shove me as much as he needed to. I understand what that feels like, to lose your humanity, to fight against the barbarous thing inside you. I thought that was what he needed to come round. After a moment, Fletcher's grip on me loosened and he leaned into me, into some strange embrace. And he began weeping."

Emilie's hand went to her mouth. She had not seen her brother drop a tear since they were children. She could not imagine him in full uniform, surrounded by an army, crying like a child. The war must have truly broken him.

"He said—" Isaac paused. "He said, over and over, *I can't go back. I can't do it anymore. I'm so tired. They can't make me go back.* I tried to calm him gently, tried to get him to breathe, to stop talking. When that didn't work, I said, *Do you want them to hear you? Do you want to be shot for a fucking coward?*"

The word shook them both, like a phantom in the room.

"And he stopped. Whatever had snapped went back into place. Fletcher turned without another word . . . and I—" Isaac's face fell into his hand, his next words muffled. "I was so afraid of what he might do, that I went after him. I followed him back up the line for nearly an hour—"

"Did anyone see you leave your post?" Emilie asked, grasping his wrist. "Isaac, they'll shoot you the way they did him!"

"I returned before anyone knew I was gone. But I lost Fletcher, and I never saw him again."

Emilie was so overcome, she could do nothing but stare. The story proved what she suspected—that Fletcher was not well. He went to Isaac, not for her sake, but for his own. He knew of all the men he could confide in, Isaac was the one who would not pass judgment. And in the end, that man used the word *coward*.

"I couldn't help thinking I put the idea in his head," Isaac said. "I wanted to take him to the medic. I didn't want to hurt him—I was trying to protect him—"

"I know."

"He loved you so much, Em."

She stood, moving to the dressing table where her valise sat open. Inside there was a stack of letters tied together with twine, the same letters she had brought to her mother in hopes of proving Fletcher's instability. On top was the last—his bullet.

The floor creaked as Isaac approached her from behind. "What are you doing?"

"Have you got a match?"

Without questioning, he fetched one from the bedside where he kept his cigarette case, and held it out to her. She crept to the hearth, wary of the families sleeping in neighboring rooms, and lowered herself to her knees. She kissed the letter, as if kissing her dead brother goodbye for the last time, and struck the match against the floorboards.

The letter quickly caught, and Emilie watched the flame devour Fletcher's damning words.

Thirty

image decorative separator

Audrey

APRIL 2014

Abandoning the fête, I returned to Leslie's house soon after he left. I wanted to take advantage of his absence to pack up my things. I could survive my last two nights in England sleeping at Sparrow Cottage, packing up what was left of it, and be out of Leslie's way.

Our argument left me feeling unsteady, and more confused than angry. I didn't think he had the right to expect something from me in return for his friendship, but I knew that I had not been subtle with my feelings for him. We were both at fault, but I felt I carried the lion's share of blame for thinking there would be a clean end to my time in Langswick. Leslie deserved better than what I had given him, but in the end, there wasn't time to consider. I had to stop clinging to this place as if it would somehow bring my grandmother back to me. Gran was gone, and I had to move on. She wouldn't have wanted me to linger so long in mourning.

As I was zipping up my backpack, my phone rang across the room. The sound was sudden, and I'd gone so long without it that my chest jolted. I stood to check the screen, expecting it might have been Leslie with a halfhearted apology, but it was an unknown UK number. Maybe the airline was calling about my flight.

I sat on the bed and answered. "Hi, this is Audrey?"

"Audrey, yes, hello. This is Meredith Pomfrey." The woman's dialect was crisp, English RP, and I didn't recognize it, but the depth of it spoke of her age. "I was given your number by Patricia Whiting. I hope you don't mind that I've telephoned; my daughter suggested I write an email instead, but I've never got on with computers."

She was a friend of Leslie's nan, then. "I don't mind at all. Can I help you with something?"

"I thought I might be able to help you, actually. I believe your great-grandmother was married to my Uncle Rhys."

My heart leapt in my chest. "Your uncle was Lord Bridgmond?"

"The very same. My daughter volunteers with the National Trust, and a friend of hers connected me to Patricia. You may remember meeting him at Hallesham Park?"

She could only be talking about the steward whom Nan had been so eager to talk more in depth with. I stood straight up from the bed and began to pace the room. "Yes—um, thank you so much for calling. I didn't know any of the family were still around . . ."

Meredith chuckled, a light rhythm despite the crackle of age in her throat. "There are a few of us still clinging to life."

I cringed. "I apologize; I didn't mean it that way."

"No, of course you didn't. Now, from what I hear, you would like to know a bit more about Lady Emilie?"

Now my cheeks burned with shame. "I'm so sorry your uncle suffered so badly after the war. I can't believe Emilie was insensitive enough to leave him over it—especially given she'd been a VAD. I had no idea she had been so cold."

"I'm afraid I must contradict you, my dear," said Meredith. "It was *my* family who were cold. They took a chance, allowing the marriage to go forward after the bother with her brother, and when Emilie did not embrace her role the way they'd hoped, they made her days rather miserable, or so I've been told. They believed she was becoming too obsessed with her baby, refusing to give leave to the nurse to look after her, so once she was weaned, they kept her from seeing the child at all."

I stopped pacing and leaned against the windowsill. It was difficult to change my mind, after everything I'd learned. But if this was true, and they hadn't allowed Emilie to see her baby, it would certainly justify her running away to Sparrow.

"I found a letter from your aunt—Lady Harriet?—to my grandmother, implying that Emilie had betrayed her husband, but she invited Gran to visit her so they could speak in person."

"Well, she had betrayed him, but that was long before the vows were read."

Her bluntness threw me, but I quickly regained my footing. "Do you know what happened?"

"The story goes that she had been carrying on with a chap she met before the war. Whether or not this is true, or simply petty gossip, one cannot say for certain. After Emilie left, they kept appearances, told everyone the baby had died and that Emilie went mad with grief and was sent away to convalesce." Meredith paused to allow another stiff laugh. "What great lengths the well-born would go to for a clean reputation, I say."

That explained why Gran hadn't been listed as Lord Bridgmond's descendent on the internet. I went cold thinking about it. They mustn't have expected Emilie would ever return after running away. "Wouldn't Bridgmond have been heartbroken to know he'd never see his daughter again?"

"That is the rub, you see. I did not introduce myself as your cousin, because Emilie admitted outright that the baby was not his."

I pressed the phone closer to my ear as if I hadn't heard her correctly. But before I could ask her to repeat herself or explain, she went on, "Little wonder why Lady Emilie was in such a rush to marry Uncle, but there it is. A marriage of convenience, though so many were in those days. Desperate times, they most certainly were."

"So—so my gran's father wasn't a lord?" I struggled to formulate my words, and forgot to censor myself. "Her father was whomever Emilie was sleeping with during the war?"

"To put it plainly, yes, I suppose he was."

"Do you know his name?"

"He was a baron's son, and if I understand correctly, illegitimate, which meant much more in those days than it does now. He was called Isaac Thurston."

I covered my mouth to prevent Meredith hearing the shrillness of my immediate reaction. Emilie had reunited with the romantic young man who had written her the letter I'd first found in the VAD uniform. And he had been my great-grandfather. Which meant that Emilie hadn't been keeping Gran from her true family, and if she'd been lying to Gran about her parentage, perhaps it was because she thought Mr. Smith would be a better father.

"Are you there, dear?"

"Yes—sorry, I'm just digesting all this."

"I imagine it is quite a lot to process, so I will leave you to it. But I don't wish for you to think ill of your great-grandmother. People married for all sorts of reasons back then, not all of them the right ones. I am mostly disillusioned about my ancestors—but it was a terrible war, and humans are fragile creatures, aren't they? And she came back, in the end, to say goodbye."

"She did?"

"A few times before his death. He wrote to her when his health declined, and I suppose she felt some sort of duty to him. Perhaps it was the nurse in her, I don't know." I heard the shrug in her voice. "He was not terribly kind after the war, my uncle, but he was remembered so fondly. Such a shame . . ."

Meredith's voice drifted off. She knew firsthand how unfair war could be; no wonder she didn't hold a grudge.

"Before I let you go, I have one more question," I said, thinking again of Gran.

"Go on."

"Do you know if my grandmother ever made it to London to meet with your Aunt Harriet?"

"I'm sorry, my dear—I haven't the slightest."

Before hanging up, I thanked her, and she promised her daughter would email a few old photos they had found. I sat on the bed again to catch my breath, staring at my backpack. Minutes ago, I was ready to leave Langswick, thinking it was best to erase Gran's painful memories forever. Now everything had changed. Emilie had protected Gran fiercely all along, had done only what she thought was right. Whether Gran knew that or not, I still wasn't sure. But the last pieces of the family were in my hands, and I couldn't throw them away before I knew the truth. I couldn't let them be lost to history the way Emilie's family was. The key to everything, I somehow knew, was Isaac Thurston. I couldn't leave England before I figured out how he was tied to my grandmother.

There was one last place I had yet to look. Leaving my backpack behind, I went out to the garden, where I knew Leslie kept his spare toolbox.

~

I WENT STRAIGHT UP the stairs to the smallest bedroom, used as an office. There, I dropped the toolbox on the floor with a *thunk*, and took a look at my options.

Hammer? Pliers? Saw?

There was a small crowbar and a rubber mallet. That would do.

Silently apologizing to the antique mahogany, I set the crowbar against the lock on the first drawer and drew back the mallet. I didn't think twice as I let it fall. There was a mad urgency compelling me forward, convincing me that what I needed was inside. I brought the mallet down again, feeling the reverberation through my wrist to my elbow. I went again, and again, until the brass began to give way, and the lock was too broken to hold itself together.

Falling to my knees, I used the crowbar to pull at the drawer until it came sliding out, falling in front of me. I shuffled to one side, pulling it into my lap and cursing as a splinter dug into the pad of my thumb. Inside was a stack of thick white typed pages printed from a typewriter. There were several, some poetry, others prose—pages and pages of what looked to me to be a full story, perhaps about the war. But the writing was dense, and jumbled, and it was difficult to follow. In the center of the pile, what had to have been a cover page read *On Seas of Iron by Isaac Thurston*.

So my great-grandfather was a writer. But what was his work doing here?

I put the papers aside to work on the next drawer, finding bills, and some old checks paid to George Smith. Then I ripped out the bottom drawer, accidentally breaking it into four pieces, which lay sadly on the rug. Inside were letters, most still in their envelopes. One in particular caught my eye, an official form letter that was certainly much older than me.

My heart dropped as I began to read the typed letters:

It is my painful duty to inform you that a report has been received from the War Office notifying the death of—

Beneath, the man's number, rank, regiment, and other details had been filled in hastily by hand.

Lieutenant Isaac Thurston
9th KOYLI
with B.E.F. France 9th of April 1917
Killed in Action

I sank back to a seat on the floor, letting the letter fall from my hands. Though he would have been long dead had he survived the war, my great-grandfather's passing hit me as if it had happened yesterday. Emilie had married Lord Bridgmond not because of his money or status, but because she was single and pregnant, and the father of her child was dead. Where else was she to turn, in the middle of a war?

I sighed, looking over the mess I had made. There were no answers left at Sparrow Cottage, at least none that ended the story the way I had wanted it to.

I stood, and took the walk back to Leslie's house to collect my things. He still hadn't returned, but I moved quickly, not wishing to cross paths with him when he inevitably did. As I splashed cool water on my face at the sink, my phone lit up. A text from Patrick.

Great news! I've just had an offer on the cottage!

It's pretty strong, I think we should take it. Give me a ring when you can.

Congratulations!

Thirty-One

Emilie

"Madam, it is my painful duty to inform you that a report has been received from the War Office notifying the death of Lieutenant I. Thurston Jones of the 9th Battalion King's Own Yorkshire Light Infantry which occurred on the 9th of April 1917. The report is in effect that he has been killed in action. By His Majesty's command I am to forward . . ."

Sister Allen continued to read, but Emilie stopped listening. She felt she was underwater, sitting on the seafloor, the current pushing her lightly back and forth. Her labored breathing made her head spin and she leaned into the lightness. Leaned into the sensation of anything at all beside the wrenching pain in her core. All at once, Emilie's body abandoned her and she collapsed to the mud outside the nurses' quarters, legs becoming twisted in her skirt.

Sister Allen crouched beside her. She had asked Sister to open the letter from the War Office, to read the words she could not bear to see on her own. She put an arm around Emilie, smelling of rose hip and antiseptic. "You must stand, my love."

But Emilie was already imagining Isaac dead, a cold, greying body in a field of blood and mire. The rats would have him, or the worms, if he was lucky enough to be buried properly. His beautiful eyes closed forever. His beautiful voice silenced. His words cut off for eternity.

What words he would have brought into peacetime—what brilliance and empathy this damnable war had wasted.

Emilie was sick in the mud.

Sister responded as any nurse would, chafing her back while waiting for more bile to rise. When Emilie was through, Sister wiped her mouth with her apron and bowed to look into her face. "Emilie? May I stand you up?"

She was strong, Sister Allen, pulling Emilie effortlessly to her feet. Then those feet began to move of their own volition. Emilie did not register the direction in which they were headed, nor the bell tents coming into view, nor the flap lifted or the softness of the mattress she was lowered onto. Sister worked with expert care, removing her soiled coat and dress, using warm water to wipe her face. The wire was placed beside her, where she could see it from the pillow. The tears returned as she read the words again. *Killed in action* . . .

Sister Allen sat on the ground, petting her shoulder. "He did not die in hospital, and so his pain was brief."

A lie, if a kind one. A man could lie for hours in a battlefield, his chest laid open for the crows. He could shout until his throat was sore, bleeding out into the soil, watering the poppies. If Isaac was killed in action, then he died alone.

"Is there anyone I can write to for you?" Sister asked.

Emilie shook her head. There was no one. Lady Thurston had passed away in her sleep shortly after Isaac visited her on his last leave—that was why Emilie had been listed as next of kin at all. She had been glad, then, that the dowager had seen her grandson one last time. Perhaps it had been for the best that she did not live to receive his death notice. Were they together somewhere? Emilie wondered. With Isaac's mother? She could no longer be sure a heaven existed from a God so cruel.

"You need to eat something," Sister said, standing. "I shall bring your dinner here, and then you can get some sleep. Let's get you out of your corset—"

Sister's hands went to the ties and Emilie caught them, digging her fingers into the other woman's knuckles. Sister furrowed her pale brows, making no indication that Emilie was hurting her.

It would have been better to tell her calmly that Emilie was all right to undress herself, that she could go on, back to work. But now Sister had seen the panic in Emilie's eyes. There was no hiding anything from Sister Allen.

"Emilie?"

She released Sister's hands, sitting up in bed. The blood rushed from her head, making her dizzy. When her eyes cleared, Sister was still watching her closely, waiting for her to give something away. "You need not be afraid, dear girl. I am a woman, same as you."

Emilie hesitated, looking down at the floor. She could not hide it much longer. Eventually, the corset would not be enough; her shape would be completely altered. Perhaps it was better to tell her now.

Emilie's eyes filled with tears as she began to undo the hooks, letting her corset fall away. She could not help but sigh at the relief of having it off from under her sore breasts. They were foreign to her, swelling over her belly, which was now hard and protruding enough to make Sister Allen cover her mouth.

"My sweet girl. What have you done?"

To Emilie's surprise, Sister sat again on the bed, putting her arms around her and the baby that was growing inside. She smoothed Emilie's hair and kissed her head, shushing and rocking as Emilie continued to fall apart.

"On my last leave," Emilie answered shakily. "I went away with Isaac."

Emilie felt the air go slowly out of her lungs and quickly return. She was meant to hold Isaac's published novel in her hands, to adore the look of humble achievement on his face. They were meant to grow old and soft together. She was meant to spend eternity smoothing the worry between his brows. Oh, why had she not married him that very morning? Why had she thought she had needed so much time when there was so little to be had?

"How long ago was that?" Sister asked. "Three or four months?"

Emilie nodded. "We used a preventative, I thought . . . The first time. I don't—I don't know when it happened." Her head fell against Sister's shoulder. "I haven't told him. He's—he's gone and now he'll never know. Oh God—"

Sister sat with Emilie until she had cried all the tears she had left, until she was so exhausted that she went limp. Then she helped Emilie lie back down, pulled the blanket over her. Sister lit the lantern and got the stove going to boil water for tea. She sat again beside Emilie while the tea was brewing.

"Roll onto your back, please," she said. Emilie did. Then she began feeling around her belly with open hands, pressing gently into the sides. She lifted the blanket to look at Emilie's ankles. "We might have a heartbeat at this stage—I'll bring a stethoscope tomorrow, and you can have a listen. Any symptoms beside the nausea? That should pass in a few weeks."

Emilie could not believe her ears. Where was her dressing down? Where was her shaming? "How do you know that?"

"My older sister is a midwife."

Emilie saw pride in her eyes. No wonder she became a nurse herself.

"My chest hurts," she replied, "and my back, a little."

"All normal." Sister got her tucked under the blankets again.

Emilie struggled to sit up. There was a small part of her that was relieved to share the secret. She had written a note to Isaac—written around the truth of it in a way that only he would understand, to avoid being found out by censors. She had imagined the way his eyes would have glistened with tears to know he would be a father, because she knew, most certainly, that it would have been good news to him. But the letter remained in her trunk, unsent.

"I am sorry," Emilie said, adjusting the straps of her combination.

"I wanted to stay through the war. I wanted to be here at the end of it. I never imagined I would be a mother, never truly wished to be."

"I suspect you have not yet written to your parents?"

"It would do no good; I won't be allowed home this way."

"Well, unfortunately, you will not be allowed to stay here either." Sister stood to fetch her tea, and placed it carefully in her hands. "Is there somewhere else you can go? Anywhere safe?"

Emilie looked down into her tea, weak and black. She didn't think she could go to a mother-and-baby home on her own, nor could she afford it. Without the Thurstons' flat to run to, she was rid of options. She hadn't the money to live on her own, and would not be able to work in her state, if she could find any with such little experience.

Emilie did not allow herself to feel remorse. She had wanted independence, and she had got it. Her damnable pride had led her to beggary.

There was only one option, she knew. The notion made Emilie set her tea down and bend double, worrying she might be sick again. She remembered something her brother told her once, something that had sounded so archaic. Now, she knew it to be the truth.

War is war. We do what we must in order to survive.

"Rhys proposed to me last year, after Fletcher's death," Emilie said to her feet. "I know without a doubt that he will have me, so long as he does not find out I'm with child until after the wedding."

Sister stood to pace. She paused, momentarily, to part the flap with two fingers, checking for nearby ears, Emilie imagined. Surely Sister was thinking the same as Emilie. Would a man, unlearned in medicine, recognize her condition? Emilie put her hand on her belly. It was likely Rhys had never seen a woman without her clothes, certainly never Emilie except with a corset forming an unnatural curve to her figure. It was a risk, perhaps, but in Emilie's mind, it was the only way to provide for her child without damaging her reputation even further.

"How will you bear it?" Sister asked.

That was the other thing. In order for Emilie to convince Rhys the child was his, she would need to lay with him on their wedding night, to ensure the marriage was consummated properly. The thought made her shiver, but this time no tears followed.

"For Isaac's child, I can bear anything."

Sister came swiftly to sit at Emilie's side and lowered her voice. "You will need to marry as soon as possible, and explain away why the baby has come early. It happens all the time, but your baby, God willing, will come into the world after nine months of growth. The doctor will have reason to speculate, to talk to your husband—"

"Not if baby is delivered by a midwife." In moments like these, Emilie saw how much her older brother's mischief had been bred in her, too. "Would your sister stay silent for me?"

Sister Allen sent her eyes to the roof of the tent, then back to Emilie. "You will be the death of me, Emilie Dawes. I shall get your things together whilst you go to the wire office and send word to your Lord Bridgmond. He will need to begin arranging your wedding immediately."

IT WAS MORE DIFFICULT than Emilie imagined, saying goodbye to her temporary home of No. 16 Stationary. In some ways, the years she spent there were the best of her life. For a while, she had lived her dream, and in so doing learned more about herself than she ever would have at Hallesham Park.

Before she left, Emilie visited the last places she'd been with Isaac. He was everywhere, all around her, prickling her skin, tickling her ears on the wind. She did not know if she would ever return to France, but as Isaac would never leave it, she would have to say goodbye to him—what was left of his physical being—forever. She had hoped to get word from the War Office of his burial location, but such things took time that she did not possess.

When she kissed Sister Allen on the cheek and left camp, it felt like she was leaving half of herself behind. The remaining half crossed the channel, arrived in Northampton, and was collected at the village station to be deposited at Folcroft Abbey. Rhys greeted her in the great hall, standing tall on a prosthetic leg. He opened one arm, the other leaning on a cane, and pressed his lips against her ear. It was the first time Emilie had felt his lips, and when the tears began to fall, she pressed her mouth into a smile.

"Would you look at me!" she said, pointedly wiping her tears. "It is just so good to see you on your feet again."

Rhys seemed to believe the tears were for him, and so she had succeeded in her first lie. There would be many more to come.

They were married the next morning at the parish church, with the Claremonts and the Ashwoods as witnesses. A small breakfast was held afterward at Folcroft, and Emilie was glad not to have to return to Hallesham Park. She smiled for her parents, for the duke, for her new husband, and remained staid as the maid helped her dress for bed and called her Lady Bridgmond. She allowed herself to be bathed and powdered, to be trussed up and left alone to drape herself over plush pillows. She beckoned Rhys with small kisses, undressed him slowly, paid no mind to the abrupt end of his leg, and carefully removed his prosthetic for him. When his breaths came quicker, she braced herself for what must be done. He was shy and gentle, quick and to the point, but content to be in her arms.

Emilie closed her eyes and thought of Isaac.

Afterward, she watched Rhys fall asleep, and then watched him shudder when night terrors disturbed him, and then watched him stand from her bed, take up his cane, and leave her for his own. Would he never sleep a night beside her? she wondered. Or had he sensed she was lying to him? Had he seen the curve of her belly and suspected?

She rolled over, pressing her face against the pillow he had been using, hoping the male smell of him would bring Isaac back to her. But it was wrong—peppery and sharp—not Isaac at all. Then she cried tears she didn't think she had left.

The next morning, Fletcher's effects arrived from the War Office—sent to Emilie according to the orders he had left in his pay book: *Anything of worth I leave to Emilie*, as if he knew his parents would turn their backs on him. He had left a sum of money, as well. This she kept secret from her parents, from her husband, along with what little remained of her wages from France. Perhaps one day she would need it.

Rhys returned each night that week, either eager for an heir, or eager for Emilie, whom he claimed to have loved all his life. Sister Allen told her to wait to tell him until her cycle was due to return, and when she did, Rhys was all smiles. A baby! *His* baby! And she knew her little plan had succeeded. There was much fanfare from the duke and duchess, much excitement from her new sisters-in-law. Rhys no longer came to her bed, and so left alone again, Emilie recovered the little brass box from under the bed, pulled the lever, and sent the tiny bird singing for Isaac's child.

She did so every night until her darling girl was born with her father's eyes.

Rhys had returned to the room once baby Dottie had been cleaned and nestled in her mother's arms. He leaned over, pecking Emilie's temple lovingly, and pinched Dorothy's tiny hand in his. "Blue eyes, eh? How curious."

Emilie had held her breath, until the midwife chuckled at the foot of the bed where she was packing her kit. She looked most like her sister when she smiled.

"Do not get attached to those beauties, my lord," she had said. "Most babies are born with blue, but they darken in time."

Emilie did not know if this was truth or fiction, but was glad she could trust the woman just as well as she trusted her younger sister. The midwife had explained away the early birth, the size of the baby, making Lord Bridgmond believe it was all normal. Emilie knew the women would talk among themselves, but her husband, ignorant in his maleness, had accepted it easily.

In any case, Emilie paid her husband little mind, for in her arms was the flesh of Isaac Thurston—the navy eyes, the bent brow, the oval mouth. She could have wept for how much she wished for him to see her, but instead she cooed and cuddled, happy for the first time since that dreaded wire.

Rhys brought on a nurse, but Emilie often hid away from the stern woman, greedy of her time spent with Dorothy. Her daughter grew at an alarming speed, got up to walk one day while Emilie was looking out the window. After that, there was no stopping her, no preventing curtains from being pulled or glass animals to be swatted off low tables. There was a reason, Emilie found, that children were confined to the soft safety of a nursery. But she could not bear to be parted from Dottie, not even for an hour while she had her bath. Instead, she bathed in shallow water with baby splashing in her lap, took meals in her room and fed baby from the same plate, to the Claremonts' dismay.

Even Rhys was growing weary of the behavior, but he scorned her only in the evenings, when he came to her bed with other things in mind and ended up too tired following their row. Emilie never backed down. She would rather be alone with her child.

When Dorothy cried, Emilie thought it would bring the roof off the house. Emilie bounced her on her hip, rubbed her back, changed her, gave her baths, gave her milk, but nothing worked. Dorothy cried until her voice was hoarse, until the effort of her own misery put her to sleep. What on earth was she so upset about? It was as if she knew there was something important missing in her life, something she knew she would never get back.

On the eleventh hour of the eleventh day of the eleventh month, the war ended with fanfare, but Emilie hardly noticed. She cared little to celebrate its end when the existence of it had taken so much from her. That very night, Emilie was lying on her side in the bed, Dorothy wailing on her back. She leaned over baby, at the verge of tears herself, wishing she could take away whatever was paining her.

Emilie sat up suddenly, gazing around the room as if there might be something, anything within the four walls that could stop it.

That was when she remembered the singing bird, forgotten since there was an infant to care for. She brought it to the bed, wiping her own tears with her sleeve. The bird had once soothed writhing soldiers in their beds, brought childish smiles to the faces of the sternest sisters. Perhaps the magic could bring peace now.

After a deep breath, Emilie pulled the lever.

The bird sang as clearly as he had the first time. Wings flapped as he joyfully chirped for all to hear. She was so distracted by her memories that she hadn't noticed Dorothy was silent.

Exhausted, Emilie lay down beside her, careful not to stir the mattress. She gave baby a soft kiss on the forehead, nuzzled her nose into her hair and whispered: "Thank you, Papa."

It was then that Rhys entered in his dressing gown, smelling of cigars. Emilie set the baby back into the cradle and tried to silence the bird, but it was too late. Rhys had seen, and though he said nothing, he gave Emilie a pointed scorn and then, after leaning over the bassinet to kiss Dorothy on the head, decided against his marital obligations and retreated to his own rooms.

Thirty-Two

Emilie

She could not have been certain whether Rhys had recognized the trinket or had heard her loving words through a crack in the door. But the next morning when Emilie woke and leaned over to smile at baby Dorothy the way she did each morning, the bassinet was empty.

She stifled a cry and threw her covers off to leap out of bed. At first, all sense was replaced with a rush of madness over her missing child. Emilie bent to check under the bed, opened her wardrobe, flew to the window to ensure it was latched. Dorothy was not here—stolen in the night while Emilie lay ignorant in her sleep. But of course, she was not stolen. She was *taken*. By Lord Bridgmond or the nurse, Emilie could not be sure.

Donning her dressing gown, Emilie took a sharp right out of her rooms. Her bare feet thudded on the carpet in the corridor as she made her way to the nursery door, which was locked. By then, tears were streaming down her cheeks, and a deep ache of fear had coiled its way round Emilie's heart. Her baby was within the nursery, safe, by all means, but wailing for her mother. How many hours had she been in there? Frightened and alone with the strange nurse who knew nothing of the child's needs? Emilie banged her fist against the door, but it was no use. The nurse was no doubt sworn to keep that door locked, and by the time Emilie's throat was raw from shouting for

Dorothy, Lady Harriet had come to draw her sister-in-law back to bed.

"Don't you see, the exhaustion of motherhood has made you ill," Harriet said, guiding Emilie to bed more roughly than what may have been considered kind. "What you need is a long rest, and some quiet. Doctor will be here later to look in on you."

"I don't require a doctor," Emilie stammered, as Harriet pressed her cold hand against her forehead, forcing her to lay it on the pillow. "I need my baby—my child. I need to feed her; she's frightened—"

Lady Harriet shushed her, and drew up the bedclothes. "You need *rest*, dear sister. The nurse will take perfect care of Dorothy. It is what she is paid for, after all . . ."

Emilie suddenly sat up, pushing with all her might until Harriet stumbled away, eyes widening at her sister-in-law's brass. But it was too late, for Rhys was standing in the doorway, watching the whole scene, and he possessed the authority and might to ensure Emilie did not leave her rooms that day. Or the next. Or the remainder of the week.

The doctor said it was nervous depression, exhaustion, and hysteria, all brought on by her pregnancy. Emilie was suddenly an invalid in the eyes of the Claremonts, and her tears satisfied them. She paced her room, weeping as her breasts became engorged and the pain of them grew unbearable, weeping when the pain stopped, knowing her milk had gone.

Perhaps they were right. Perhaps she was mad.

Influenza took Emilie's father in March 1919, caught from his valet before breakfast, to kill him before midnight that evening. His funeral was Emilie's first outing in months, as she was confined to the short walks in the garden she was prescribed for her ailments. She stood beside her mother at the grave, feeling numb, speaking not a word as people she once laughed with gave her their condolences.

After dinner that night, she was permitted to stay up with Rhys for a digestif, watching the fire play on his brown eyes, noticing the sheer pain in them. He drank for it, more and more as the pain increased. It made him mean—the pain, the drink, or the shell shock, Emilie did not know for certain. But for a moment, she felt only sorry for him, and with that ounce of empathy, she knelt before his chair and took his hand.

"Please, may I see my baby?" she asked. Not *ours*. Not his. "For an hour a day, or just a few moments. I cannot even watch her play in the gardens from my window—"

Rhys looked down at her as if she were a beggar woman, one fist resting against his mouth. She waited, pleading and smiling sickly, until he slid her hand from his and she knew for certain that he had tumbled to the truth.

"You are hysterical, Emilie. Go to bed." And he turned his face back to the fire.

With mindless obedience, Emilie lifted herself off the ground, pivoting from the heat of the hearth to be engulfed by the cool darkness of the corridor.

~~~~~~

ON HER TWENTY-SIXTH BIRTHDAY, Emilie woke as she normally did, alone, to lie idle and pluck at the flaring wound of loss. She found herself like lead, unable to even lift her head, for she had reached an age that Isaac would never see. The notion somehow made his death more solid. From a possibility only granted by death, he was now her junior. Forever twenty-three and beautiful. A tear slipped from Emilie's eye, soaking into the pillow. She had thought she had cried her last tear for Isaac, but it seemed she had one left. She longed for Dorothy—to look into Isaac's eyes, to smell the sweetness in her silken hair.

Emilie sat at her breakfast table alone, as always, pushing the food round on her plate. When she lifted her napkin, she was surprised to see a tattered copy of Byron beneath it on the tray, one that was once Emilie's favorite. Grace must have smuggled it in for her, a treat for her birthday. Emilie had been barred from reading any books apart from the Holy Bible, the doctor claiming they might upset her further. She thanked her lucky stars she had brought on Grace as her lady's maid: her only friend most days.

Thinking of Isaac, Emilie opened to the first page. She was reminded of those first moments of their friendship, of his stories, of his fidgeting, of his dreadful dancing. Briefly, Emilie's lips quirked. How had she forgotten? Isaac wasn't lost; not completely. She had the haphazard pages of his novel tucked under her bed, still smeared with mud from an Arras trench.

After locking her door, Emilie carefully knelt on the carpet to lay them out, reading each page to determine the order. Emilie was captivated once more by Captain Ridley and the power she possessed over her own life and ship of knaves. Such freedom and disregard for propriety and convention. Like the author, Emilie thought, and found herself smiling once more.

It was hours before she came up for air, and by then she knew Isaac's novel was incomplete. The climax was messy, written in notes, rather than narrative. Poor Isaac had probably stolen a brief moment of solitude to put down the words while bombardments went on all around him. She could see the trembling of his hand in his writing, his bones shaking with the impact. What had it been like in his final moments? she wondered. Was he afraid? Or did he not even see the reaper behind him?

Emilie sat on her haunches, remembering how frightened Isaac was to be forgotten. Perhaps his legacy could live on, if only through Captain Ridley.

Emilie's grief had eaten her alive, leaving her spineless. She would not fall any deeper into the illness the Claremonts had invented for her. If she wanted to finish Isaac's book for him, if she wanted to type it and send it to publishers, she could not remain here. If she ever hoped to hold her baby again, for Dorothy to know her true father, there was only one option.

Emilie had run away before, not so terribly long ago. Why could she not do it again now?

It was Grace, again, who helped her. The maid agreed to secret away clothing from the laundry, one pair of stockings at a time, to fill a valise she had brought to the servants' hall, pretending it needed mending. Emilie, in turn, stashed other things away beneath her mattress—the jewelry that could be sold for train tickets and lodgings, items for her toilet, and her old VAD uniform. She would go in June, when the rain eased and the weather was warm. Grace would come in the dead of night, would fetch the baby from the nursery using the butler's own key, would meet Emilie in the garden with her valise.

When the night finally came, Emilie remained awake until the wee hour they had chosen, and fumbled as she dressed herself in her traveling suit. The corridor was so dark, but she dared not bring a candle, instead felt along the wallpaper until she came to the stairs. She worried Grace would not wake in time, or would disturb the nurse to sound an alarm. But as Emilie quietly closed the terrace doors behind her and looked out into the misty air of night, Grace's pretty face shone in the moonlight, pressed lovingly to Dorothy's.

Emilie could not stop the gasp that escaped from her throat as she fled over the gravel to take Dottie in her arms, to feel the beautiful weight of her, to smell the lavender from her bath, and notice the length of her chubby arms and legs. How she had grown since they had been apart! And to her relief, the baby knew her mother, grasped on to Emilie's lapel with her tiny round hand, and wept softly with her face tucked under Mama's jaw.

Grace touched her arm, acknowledging the time. Emilie shifted Dottie to one hip, silently thankful for the strength she had acquired from nursing, and took the valise in her other hand. She leaned forward to place a kiss on Grace's cheek, pressed her lips against her ear.

"Thank you, my dear friend."

Grace kissed Emilie's cheek in turn. "Be well, milady."

Emilie made it as far as the gate before her arms grew weary, but there was no stopping her—there was only a forward march, forever, if that's what it took. She would not stop until she was far away, until she was alone with her baby, until she was free.

But as she set down the valise to open the gate, she noticed a motorcar idling on the other side of the dirt road, the headlights shining on the morning mist. It was Rhys's car, undeniably, the same Vauxhall Prince Henry that Fletcher had purchased when it came on market. Britain's fastest car, and though Rhys could not drive it himself any longer, he frequently went motoring with his father or chauffeur. One of them was surely behind the wheel now.

For a moment, Emilie was frozen with fear. Ought she to turn round? Return to the house, place baby back in the nursery, and climb into her own bed? Would it quell the anger that was surely building within her husband, would it convince the Claremonts not to scorn her?

Dorothy wriggled in Emilie's arms, and she looked down at the baby. Her little eyelashes were stuck in star points, her dark curls glittering with dewdrops of mist. She was, as ever, the most beautiful thing Emilie had ever laid eyes on, and more like her father each day. Her arms tightened around her child, and Emilie swore to herself that whatever happened, she would die before anyone took her daughter away from her again.

The door opened, and Rhys's broad figure ducked out, straightening as his cane was set on the ground. Blinded by the headlights, Emilie could not see his expression, but could devise from his posture that he was tensed.

"How did you know?" she asked.

"I saw the girl from my window, waiting for you with the baby," he shouted over the stalled motor. "If you recall, I don't sleep much any longer."

Emilie cursed her own thoughtlessness, driving her heels into the ground, and pressed Dorothy's head safely against her neck.

"I am leaving you," she said evenly. "Tell your family whatever you like, but I will not live another day under your roof."

Rhys did not move so much as a finger. "Let us return to the house so we can talk this through properly. Perhaps we can arrange for you to see the child more often—"

Emilie bent for the valise and began to walk. Without looking up, she strode past the motor, toward the first wink of dawn peeking up from over the River Nene. The light gave her hope, and she imagined that, when she reached it, she would remember what carelessness felt like. She would see the face of her love again.

But her elbow was caught. The valise fell to the ground, Dorothy wailed, and Emilie curled herself around the baby. It was the chauffeur who had snatched her on behalf of Lord Bridgmond, who approached stiffly, favoring his left leg.

"Unhand me this instant," Emilie said, wrenching uselessly. "You are hurting my arm— For God's sake, you'll hurt the baby!"

Rhys could take no more, and waved for the chauffeur to release her. He obeyed, stepping away, but keeping his shoulders square for a fight. Emilie would give him one, if it came to that. She had dealt with soldiers his size in France.

"Give the baby to Findlay," Rhys said.

"Not on your life."

"Then give her to me, and Findlay will escort you back to the house."

Something primal awoke in Emilie, the need to protect her young, and she felt suddenly murderous. "I shall be going nowhere at all with either of you."

Rhys huffed, reaching over to pet Dorothy's cheek. She did not pay him any mind, too distracted by her mother's lace collar. Her indifference enraged him even more, and he began to grab at the baby's middle, shaking her for attention. Emilie pivoted away from him, bracing the baby's head with her hand, wondering if it was worth the risk to run.

"You are frightening her," Emilie said.

"Do you think I know not how to hold my own child?"

"You know nothing about this child, not how to hold her or how to love her. How could you tear her away from me? When she was not yet weaned?"

"You were becoming too attached to the child."

"I am her *mother*."

"And I am her father."

Emilie tasted her tears as she opened her mouth to shout. "No, you are not!"

She closed her eyes, waiting to be struck for her words. But Rhys did not move—did not utter a single word. When her lids fluttered open, she saw Rhys look down at Dorothy, study the inherited features that did not belong to him, the blue eyes that were bright as ever.

"I ought to have known," he said, frighteningly calm. "I ought to have known that the bastard was no better than his father."

Rhys pivoted away slowly, and with a nod to the chauffeur, returned to the motor. The tires ground against the dirt road, and Emilie watched the car slowly move away from her, blinking as the headlights crossed her face. In her arms, Dorothy giggled, and Emilie turned to see what had taken the baby's attention.

Oblivious to the danger of the moment, Dottie had spotted the morning's first bird, hopping along the side of the road, pecking for his breakfast. Emilie smiled to see her daughter's eyes alight, and as the grey of dawn crept over them like a warm quilt, she saw that the bird was a little sparrow.

Mama had once said that a woman's intellect could not be found in books. Emilie had scoffed at the time, but in that moment she finally understood. Women were not encouraged with books, nor offered education, and so paved their own roads, learned for themselves how best to move through a world that would pin them down. That road was different for every girl, every woman—some selected, others granted. But there was no road that was right or wrong, so long as she used her intellect to make her own choices along the way.

They waited for the first train to Yorkshire. It did not matter where precisely they were headed, nor what Emilie would do when they arrived. The war was over, and so was her life as she had always known it.

While Dorothy napped on the bench beside her, Emilie reached into her pocket, pulling out a smooth pebble from a shingled beach in the north of France.

The world is vast, dear girl. There is always a fresh stone to turn over.

Thirty-Three

Audrey

APRIL 2014

I didn't want to talk to Patrick in person about the sale; I didn't want to think about the buyer signing a contract that would take ownership of Gran's house.

So once again, I ran away from my grief.

It had taken one phone call to exchange my departing flight from Manchester to Heathrow. I wasn't going to leave the country before taking one last look for information on the people of my grandmother's past. Meredith's daughter had emailed photos as promised. Lady Harriet and Lady Emilie had sat for a photograph in wicker chairs, wearing draping white tea gowns. Lord Bridgmond, tall and brawny and imposing, had posed beside Emilie's brother in front of the Gothic arches of Oxford University. There was even one of my grandmother as a doughy baby in a lacy gown and bonnet, posing stiffly beside Emilie.

I was surprised to have recognized Fletcher's face from the frame above the mantel at Sparrow. Emilie hadn't forgotten him, not even when his country had. She had kept his image in pride of place, unashamed. That frame was one of the few things I kept from Sparrow, along with the VAD uniform and singing bird.

I'd left a simple note for Leslie before leaving: *I'm so glad I met you, but I have to go home.* On the train to London, I'd worked on my crocheting to keep my emotions at bay. This time they were not for Gran, but for Leslie. I wished I had been willing to fight for him the way he was willing to fight for me.

London was too loud and grey after the quiet of the Yorkshire countryside. I had never been, and was sure I would have enjoyed the city in other circumstances. Now, it served as a gateway between Sparrow Cottage, the place I had grown to love, and home, the place I feared. After arriving at King's Cross, I found the closest hotel to sleep off the emotion of the day. I didn't bother connecting my phone to the Wi-Fi; tomorrow I would call Beth, tell her I was on my way home. I would call Patrick, tell him to move forward with the sale. But I wanted to be long gone by then.

In the morning, I connected in a café while sipping a cappuccino, and answered a text from Namita.

Where'd you run off to, love? it read. **Bernard is here asking for you.**

That tugged at my heartstrings enough for me to answer.

In London. Trying to piece together a few things before I leave.

Tell Bernard I'm sorry I missed him.

Then it was onto the District line and to the National Archives. The imposing concrete building sat on the River Thames. The interior reminded me of something out of a superhero film—utilitarian, yet sleek and modern, like a library without books. After speaking to the woman at the front desk, I was given a pass to view the War Office records, and was led to a computer where I could see all of the digitized documents.

The first name I searched was Lord Fletcher Kinsley, Emilie's brother, thinking I'd find him under his title. There he was, just as Leslie's brother had found him, court-martialed for cowardice, and tried in haste, and like many others in his position, without legal representation. It was his word against that of his superior officer. I went cold, reading the warrant for his death sentence, the date and time he was to be executed before his peers, and made an example of, all of this during one of the most deadly battles of the First World War.

Next, I found Isaac Thurston's service record, and his death. I knew, of course, that he'd been killed in battle, but the confirmation still made me wilt. Looking further, I found a transcript attached to his name, another court proceeding. Lieutenant I. Thurston had also been court-martialed, and gone to trial for desertion, but a decision was not made. Instead, he was sent into battle a few days later and lost his life to a bullet in the head.

I sat back in my chair, my mind spinning. Could he have learned of Emilie's pregnancy? Was the reason enough to leave his post, risking execution and humiliation?

Meredith's story was all the confirmation I needed to understand why Emilie had married Lord Bridgmond after Isaac's death, but not why she had ended up at Sparrow. But why, when she'd left, did she lie to Gran, telling her that Mr. Smith was her true father? Was she ashamed that her beloved Isaac had also been court-martialed? But then why celebrate her brother?

"Can I help you find anything?" I looked up to see one of the members of staff looking over my shoulder—a salt-and-pepper-haired man in a tweed jacket who might have been a history professor in another life. "Only, you look overwhelmed."

"One of my ancestors was shot for cowardice during the First World War. He was forgotten entirely by his family, left off the memorial in the village where he grew up."

The man nodded, folding his hands behind his back. "A common story, indeed. But are you aware they've been pardoned?"

I sat up straighter. "No . . . I had no idea about any of this before I started researching my heritage."

He smiled and removed his thick-rimmed glasses. "In 2006, the British defence secretary pardoned all three hundred six men who were executed in the First World War. A controversial decision, to be sure, but it brought comfort to many families who had evidence that their man was suffering from shell shock."

I thanked him for the information, though it didn't give me much comfort. Perhaps I would appreciate it someday, but I was too close to Fletcher's story at that point, too wounded.

Before I left, I searched one last name—the VAD Lady Emilie Dawes, surprised to find she was awarded the Military Medal. Breathless, I reached in the pocket of my jeans and pulled out the very prize that was handed to her all those years ago, tears pricking the corner of my eyes. The record stated the medal was for showing conspicuous gallantry and devotion to duty during an attack on 32 Stationary hospital on May 20, 1916. She left active service in 1917, and I was willing to bet it was because she discovered she was pregnant with my grandmother. She left, after all she'd been through, and made a new life for herself—just like Gran had. Like Leslie had. Like I could, if only I had their courage.

Emilie's medal was heavy and warm in my palm. I'd never felt more connected to my family, to the women who made me who I was. I smiled, thinking how excited my own mother would have been to know them, too. I remembered what Gran had said in her letter: *It is never too late to start again.*

I knew, then, what she had been trying to tell me. Why she had sent me here at all. She wanted me to see another country, to learn new words, hear the accents, and laugh with people I'd never expected to meet. She wanted to show me that there was more to life than just the little world I was born into. I was not my success, or my past decisions. I was not my job, or my addiction. I was filled with far more passion than what I once had for nursing, and that passion could lead me to greater happiness, if only I allowed myself to follow my heart.

It is never too late . . .

I left the Archives feeling surprisingly buoyant. The sky was bright compared to the dark room I'd been researching in, and I took a deep breath of spring air. Crossing the walkway that led over the Thames, I tried to appreciate where I was and all that I'd learned. I still didn't know exactly why Gran had left England, but that was okay. *Why* she did it was no longer important to me. What was important was that she *had* done it, and found a new life she was proud of. A tear rolled from each eye, and I let them linger on my cheeks, too distracted by what I saw to wipe them away. Across the walkway, leaning against the metal railing, was Leslie.

I stood staring at him as if he was a figment of my imagination until he peeled himself off the railing and stuck his hands in his pockets before approaching me, a lopsided grin on his face.

"Now, then," he said.

"What are you doing here?"

Leslie's eyes, turned the color of toffee in the sun, shifted toward the building. "I heard it's a pleasant place to spend an afternoon."

When I slapped him on the arm, he laughed, revealing a full smile that nearly knocked me over. "Namita told me you were in London. I figured this is where I'd find you."

Without thinking, I fell into his arms. The air swirled, lifting Leslie's scent toward me—wood shavings and expensive cologne from London. He was impossible. A person I couldn't have imagined if I hadn't sat beside him in a crowded pub.

Leslie spoke against my ear, sending shivers down my spine: "Why did you run off like that, flower?"

I shook my head against his shoulder. "Sparrow sold yesterday. I wasn't prepared for it to happen that quickly—I thought I was ready but I'm not. I don't want to leave it. I don't want to leave *you*. And then I freaked out and said all those stupid things to you at the fête."

Leslie pulled away gently, placing a hand on my cheek to lift my face. I was crying fully by then, but there was nowhere to hide anymore. He thumbed away a few of my tears and kissed my lips ever so briefly. Ours was a whirlwind romance, the kind of thing I could never believe happened in real life. But standing there in his arms, with the sun twinkling off the river and the birdsong overhead, I could believe anything was possible.

"Patrick didn't tell you who the buyer is?" he asked.

I sniffed, shaking my head. "I've been ignoring his calls and texts. I'm worried if I get too overwhelmed, I'll want to drink, and I thought it best to just go home—"

"You *are* home, Audrey."

I frowned, confused by the twinkle in his eye. "What are you talking about?"

His hands slid down to my hips, creating some space between us as he leaned back against the railing. The wind blew a strand of his hair forward, and he pushed it behind his ear, mouth fixed in a pensive line. Then he looked down at me again, and the twinkle returned.

"I bought it, Auds."

My grip tightened on his shoulders as the floor began to sway. "Bought what?"

"I bought Sparrow Cottage. I'm sorry, but I had to. It belongs with you."

"You—" I stumbled, trying to find the right words while my lungs were refusing to fill and empty. "You bought it for *me*?"

Leslie chuckled, shaking his head. "No, I bought it for the village. You know how desperate we are for more places for tourists to stay, and the local business could use the additional revenue. I've plans to convert the outbuildings into suites."

"You're going to make it a bed-and-breakfast?"

"And I want you to run it."

I tried to step away, but Leslie kept a firm grip on me. My heart was telling me to be glad that Sparrow was in the hands of someone who appreciated it, someone who would keep it the way it was meant to be. My mind was fighting with logic, reminding me of my responsibilities at home, of the life I would be leaving behind.

"I don't know anything about running a bed-and-breakfast," I said.

"No, but Namita does, and you know people. As soon as you softened old Bernard's heart, I knew you would be perfect as the face of it. I took a chance and made an offer, hoping you would forgive me for not telling you first."

"But—" I almost couldn't think of any reason to argue. I wanted to stay. I wanted to live at Sparrow Cottage, to tell people about the Smiths, to wake up in Yorkshire every day. Maybe wake up next to Leslie. I wanted a new life, and this could be the one. "But there's the matter of citizenship. And I can't get into anything serious until I know I can handle it without drinking."

"I know." Leslie's voice was soft, and calm, like he knew we could handle it. Knew *I* could handle it. "But for now, just stay a few more days. Look at the proposals I've drawn up, help me make the plans. We'll sort the rest in time, I promise. I think you'll find I'm a patient man, and if you don't mind me saying, you're worth the wait."

Before he could say more, I was kissing the smirk off his lips, fully and deeply, for anyone to see, dizzy with love for him, and this place, for the possibilities of a life in the village where Gran had grown up. For once, I set the future aside and lingered in the present. I was happy here; I was at peace here. I couldn't say that about anywhere else. The details didn't matter. It was like Leslie said—I was finally home.

SPARROW COTTAGE LOOKED EVEN better upon returning to it that evening. It was the warmest day since I'd arrived, and the windows, freshly cleaned, glinted in the sun, and all the flowers, now tamed by the capable gardening hands of the Petals, were all in bloom. With Leslie standing at the front door with Jim by his side, I had a perfect picture of how idyllic my life could be if only I let go of the past, and I suddenly understood why Lady Emilie Dawes had come here.

On the drive from London, as I finished the scarf I was crocheting, I told Leslie everything I knew about my great-grandmother, and he agreed, she had made the right decisions. As he had. He wore the scarf now, folded double and draped over his neck, despite the warm evening. I used it to draw him to me for a kiss.

Namita's car pulled up as I met Leslie at the door, and we both waved. She came running up the path, squealing for all the village to hear, holding up a bottle I hoped wasn't champagne, and an armful of books.

"Look at my lovely partners standing in front of our fabulous place of business!" She rushed a kiss on each of our cheeks. "I swear I'm not pissed, I'm just excited. Nonalcoholic!"

She raised the bottle of sparkling juice, and I offered to take it out of her hands as Leslie gestured her through the door. We filed into the kitchen, and Namita set down her stack of books. They were the ones she had taken from the study.

"Figured they should stay where they belong," she said. "Now that I'll be here every day, I'll have plenty of time to appreciate them."

"Who will run Keys now?" I asked, leaning against the counter.

"My parents run the inn, and to be honest, they'll be glad to be rid of me. I love the pub, but there was no way I was passing up the chance to work here."

I couldn't disagree. I was going to miss being a nurse, miss the rush of hospital work, miss the patients and the satisfaction of making them well. But Leslie was right—I could care for people here, and tell every guest the history of my family. I could keep their memory alive, and that could be just as fulfilling. I didn't have to go back to a hospital, a place that would only remind me of how I had let myself down. I could start fresh.

"Can you believe I've been keeping this secret for a fortnight?" Namita asked, bustling about the kitchen looking for glasses. "I nearly let it slip three times when I was helping you clear up the other day!"

I looked at Leslie, who was opening the bottle with forced concentration. "If you'd been planning it that long, why didn't you just tell me?"

He began pouring the juice into wineglasses Namita had found. "I wanted to—honestly—but I was afraid of frightening you off. I didn't want you to think I was keeping you close just so I could buy it from under you."

"But you knew I was desperate to sell it anyway."

"And I really wish I could have put your mind at ease." He reached out to draw me closer to him with one hand on the small of my back. "But I wanted *this* more."

I felt the emphasis of his words in my toes, and pecked a short kiss on his lips. "I didn't exactly make my feelings clear at the fête."

"No, you didn't." He smiled and brushed my hair behind my ear. "Nan told me to go for it anyhow."

"Nan is very wise."

Our faces leaned in again, but stopped when Namita clapped her hands. "I honestly hate to break this up, but I think it's chuffin' well time for a toast."

Leslie lifted his glass. "Right. What have you got?"

While they began to piece together a meaningful toast between bouts of laughter, I absently read through the titles of the books Namita had returned. She had found her copy of *Jane Eyre*, along with a few other novels I didn't recognize. One of the books was a tattered hardback, with classic fabric binding and gold letters. I had to read the title twice before I could believe what I was seeing. *On Seas of Iron*.

Holding my breath, I opened the cover to the title page, looking for an author's name. Below the title, it was there, clear as day: George Smith.

I didn't allow myself to get excited. Smith was perhaps the most common surname in the English language. It could have been a coincidence. But as Namita and Leslie toasted their juice with a *clink*, I flipped to the middle of the book and saw another familiar name. Captain Ridley.

"Oh my God," I said aloud, paying no mind to whether or not anyone heard me. Frantically, I flipped back to the copyright page, seeing the book was published in 1919. "Oh my God!"

Leslie appeared at my shoulder, and Namita was the first to ask. "What have I missed?"

I looked at Leslie and began to laugh. It wasn't funny, per se, but it was too perfect, too simple, too obvious. I might have cried if I wasn't hysterical.

"Mr. Smith is Isaac Thurston."

In a flurry of excitement, I ran upstairs to find the desk still lying in pieces from when I had broken it open. I brought the manuscript pages back down to the kitchen and laid them out for Leslie and Namita to see. The title clearly said *On Seas of Iron by Isaac Thurston*, and paging through, I found the mention of Captain Ridley. It couldn't have been anyone else.

When we found the dedication page in the book, all was confirmed.

For my little sparrow.

"I don't understand," Leslie said. "You said he was killed in action."

I shrugged, still smiling. "We don't have the full story. But if anyone does—"

"—it's Bernard."

IT WASN'T UNLIKE HIS generation to withhold a story for so long. Even Leslie said his grandfather hadn't told anyone he'd been a POW in World War II until he was on his deathbed. I couldn't begrudge Bernard for keeping his secrets all this time, especially if Gran had asked him to. But I was so close now, there was no way I was going to let him keep it any longer.

Leaving Leslie and Namita at Sparrow, I took the Land Rover to Bernard's house and knocked enthusiastically, remembering all the times I'd done it before. I had *On Seas of Iron* tucked under my arm, ready to show him, hoping to prompt the memories to come flooding back.

When he came to the door, looking bright-eyed as I'd ever seen him, I nearly threw my arms around him before remembering who we were, and instead gave a small wave. "I'm sorry I didn't get to talk with you at the fête. But I have something to show you."

With his usual skepticism, Bernard gave me a once-over, then grumbled and opened the door wider. "Come in, then, flower."

We made two cups of tea, and then he led me to the back garden, which was mature and lush, a wonderland I would have liked to explore if I had the time. Instead, we sat at an iron café table on a patch of gravel. Bernard huffed into his seat, tipping his face into the sun for a moment before addressing me again.

"What is it that you've come for?"

"I found this today." I slid the book toward him. "Mr. Smith wrote it, didn't he?"

Bernard didn't have to open the book—he must have recognized it instantly. When he nodded, guilt pinched his brow, but I wasn't upset he hadn't told me sooner.

"What happened to the Smiths?" I asked, carefully as the first day I'd met him. "I think they must have died before Gran left Sparrow, but you're the only person who would know. You're the last person she spoke to . . ."

I was patient. I waited while Bernard looked out into his garden, maybe trying to remember, maybe deciding whether or not to tell me. I sipped my tea, savored the perfect weather, allowed myself to enjoy what wonderful things had already happened that day. And then the old man let out a long, wheezing sigh.

"She were married to someone else," he said, with a tone of defeat. "Mrs. Smith. She called herself that, but she were still married to that lord whatsit."

"Bridgmond." I knew much of this, but didn't want to cut in.

"Aye. She and Smith were never wed. When Dottie found her

birth certificate, she was inconsolable—thought her whole life had been a lie."

Poor Gran. I could imagine how confusing it all would have been, especially with a war on in the background. "Is that why she left? She was upset with her parents?"

Bernard's hand fell from his mug, pressing flat against the table. "Dottie wanted to meet the lord's sister," he said, "who she thought were her aunt. Her mum refused to speak of the past, and Dottie wanted to hear the other side of the story. One night, she fled to London to meet with the lady, and her parents went after her." Bernard paused, drawing a shaking breath. "They were killed—both of them—in the bombings. When Dottie found out, she blamed herself, and the pain of it were too much. She'd a pen friend in America who agreed to take her in. She made me promise never to speak of it, and then I—I never saw her again."

Bernard's lip wobbled and his head bowed. I moved my chair closer to his, took his hand, and to my surprise, he squeezed it back. I didn't know how I would ever thank him for all he'd done for Gran, for us. But I was certainly going to try.

"You cared a lot about her, didn't you?"

He produced a handkerchief from his pocket and patted his nose before nodding. "I were just a lad, but I loved her. I loved her dearly."

We sat together, silently letting the story wash over us. It hurt to know Emilie and Isaac had come through a war, only to be killed in another. They had not grown old together, but they *had* been together, and I supposed that was more than I could say for many of their generation. It made me appreciate life all the more, the simplicity of the time I was living in.

"Did she ever find out who her real father was?" I asked.

Instead of answering, Bernard drew slowly to his feet and went into the house without a word. I remained in my chair, hoping he would return, and when he did, breathed a sigh of relief. He sat again, and set a sealed envelope atop *On Seas of Iron*.

"This were left for her, when her parents left for London," Bernard said, pointing to the envelope. "It must have fallen to the floor before she saw it. I only found it after she were gone."

My heart broke as I lifted the sealed envelope, and instantly recognized the handwriting as Isaac Thurston's. He had written *To my darling daughter* on the outside. I had no right to open it, to read what would have been his final words to Gran. But I needed to complete the story for her. I needed to complete the story for myself.

Before I could open it, Bernard cleared his throat. His eyes were watery, full of emotion I didn't know he was capable of.

"You do her proud, flower," he said.

I couldn't imagine higher praise.

With a smile to thank Bernard, I opened the envelope and the hairs on my arms stood up on their ends. A breeze blew over the garden, filling my senses with the scent of lavender, and a sparrow landed on a nearby perch, calling to me with urgency.

With that as a sign that Gran was with me, I unfolded the letter and read.

My beloved Dorothy,

I hoped one day to tell you this story face-to-face, but as you well know, conversation has not been a talent of mine since the war. Your mother is sat beside me as I write this, and shall tell me the words that I have no doubt forgotten. That was always your favorite game as a girl, wasn't it? Your laughter made me forget my frustrations, perhaps saved me from dwelling on what the war took from me. It took a great deal, but it also gave you to me, and so I shall never regret those years.

You have heard about those years, here and there, but I have neglected to tell you how my war ended. I wanted to wait until you were old enough to understand, for it is not so simple as you have been led to believe. We have told you about your Uncle Fletcher, but not that he came to me shortly before he died. Not that I followed him up the line, hoping to prevent him from hurting himself. Not that the captain saw me leave my post, kept the information tucked away for months until he could take no more of me. I was a bit difficult to get on with in those days, you see, speaking my modern ideas too loudly. In any case, I was taken to court and could not argue their case. I had gone after Fletcher, who had already been found guilty. I had deserted, and even though I returned, I was deserving of the punishment.

There was a push coming, and the court's decision was postponed. Too few officers remained, and I was needed on the front lines. I was shot in the shoulder, knocked in the head. One of my men must have seen the blood running over my ears, for my death was recorded as a head wound. I woke in a French hospital, rattled that I could not remember my own name. My identity discs had been lost, and so they called me Smith, and a nurse suggested George, after the king. When my true name finally became clear to me, I also recalled the court martial, the penalty for desertion. I feigned oblivion, allowed myself to be called Smith, returned to Blighty, and was invalided out of the army as a free man. When I found your mother again, I met you, beautiful girl, and told her everything. She promised to protect me, as she had you, here at Sparrow Cottage.

The war is long over now, and I don't believe I am in any danger of being found out. Isaac Thurston is dead, but he is your father, Dorothy. Lord Bridgmond was a good man, and he provided for you while I was away. But it's my blood that runs through you, my color in your eyes, my dimple between your brows. I have done wrong in my life, and I have lied to you, but I hope that you can forgive me the way your mother has.

We love you with all of our hearts, and we are coming to bring you home.

With all my love,
Your father

Epilogue

There was a beauty in the calm serenity of morning chores—the strength in her fingertips, the rhythm in each pull, the drumming of milk in her pail. The weather was cooling off after a particularly hot summer, and she found herself smiling absently at the gooseflesh on her forearms. Autumn was Emilie's favorite time of year.

Suddenly, the dogs sounded off from across the yard, making a frightful racket. She cursed as the cow kicked the pail of milk, sending it across her boots. With a sigh, she abandoned the milking and spotted little Dorothy toddling after the dogs toward the front of the house. She never would have thought a baby could move so fast on stubby legs.

Emilie hastened her pace, leaving the barn to cut across the garden, which needed seeing to, but she quite liked the wild nature of it. So different to the sculpted gardens of her youth. Birds called from the trees nearby, a pair of larks leaping and flying across to the nest she knew they were keeping under the nursery window. They went up, and Emilie watched them dance together in the sky before disappearing into the tree once more.

The dogs were still going when Emilie turned the corner. It was not a bark for rabbits or squirrels, but the one reserved for the rare occasion when they were out of doors to see the postman or the grocer, trying desperately to protect their domain from the smiling intruders. Emilie could finally see Dottie up ahead, bent over the lavender that lined the flagstone path. She loved to brush her little hands across the stalks, once Emilie showed her how it could scare up the soothing scent that reminded her of bath time. She smiled and moved her attention to the end of the path, where the three dogs were circling their victim.

The man must have been passing, or had gotten turned around; no one from the village came this far up the road. He wore simple linen trousers and a flat cap pulled down over his eyes. From afar, she could not make out the words, but he was certainly talking to the dogs, and whatever he was saying had quietened them.

On instinct, Emilie scooped Dorothy into her arms and made her way down the path, lifting two fingers to her lips to whistle for the dogs. One of them looked up, the others still enamored with the new smells of a stranger.

"For heaven's sake," she said, "let the poor man be! Enough, chaps. Here!"

Two of them trotted in her direction, then past, having caught some other, more thrilling trail to follow. The last still wiggled at the knees of the man at the end of the path. Emilie approached him from behind, sighing as though excitable dogs were the sole problem in the world. Why had she bothered with them anyway? Was it not enough that she was running a small holding on her own, without these little terrors making such chaos?

"I am terribly sorry, sir," she said. "They are pests, these dogs, but clearly rather good for security. Have you lost your way?"

The man turned, at the same time lifting his cap from his head. Emilie's eyes took a moment to focus, or so she thought, for what she was seeing was certainly a trick of the mind. But the hair was the same, the nose, the eyes, and when he spoke with a familiar voice, Emilie fell to the grass.

Beneath her, the earth was swaying. Dottie had landed firmly in her lap, giggling about the silliness of Mama's sudden drop. She grabbed at Emilie's necklace and she let her tug it, holding baby close to her chest. The sun blocked Emilie's vision until the man went to a knee in front of her and she could see more clearly the curve of his jaw beneath his beard, the wear of war.

"Emilie . . ."

Tears were coming steadily now, and it was difficult to breathe. She was shaking all over, and it began to worry Dorothy. She let go of Emilie's necklace and tucked her face into her mother's neck.

"Steady, now . . ." he said.

When he grasped her arm, Emilie flinched. She stared down at the impossible hand, not a scratch on it, and waited until the heat of his palm soaked through to her flesh.

"It cannot be."

A smile grew slowly across Isaac's face, even more handsome than her memory had kept it. He wore no tie, or else had abandoned it in the heat of the walk from the train station. His jaw was covered in thick, reddish whiskers, his hair pushed back from his forehead.

Isaac's hand moved up and down on Emilie's arm, raising the hairs on the back of her neck. "Forgive me for—for giving you a shock. I—I ought to have written."

Emilie reached out to touch the firmness of his shoulder, and he waited patiently while she squeezed it tight and then withdrew. There was so much she wanted to say, but she could not remember how to speak. A large part of her still expected she had fallen and hit her head, or drifted to sleep while reading in the garden. Either way, she hoped never to wake.

"Isaac?" she murmured. "You were dead. They told me—"

"If you'll allow me, I have much to explain." His face pinched as his eyes began to glisten with moisture. His grip on Emilie's arm tightened and she savored the physicality of it. She had heard of dead men returning, but never allowed herself to hope that Isaac would be one of them. His eyes floated down to the child in her arms. He tilted his head. "You—you're a mother, Emilie?"

She nodded, staring into his face.

When he exhaled, a tear beaded down his cheek, breaking in his whiskers. His mouth remained open, his shoulders rising and falling with the increasing speed of his breaths. "Who—?"

The word broke, and he bowed his head, swiping his hand down his nose and chin. Emilie put her hand on Dorothy's dark head, noticing how the strange man had finally caught her attention. She watched Isaac's movements with two fingers in her mouth.

"Isaac?" Emilie said, suddenly stronger. "This is your daughter."

His face came up, flushed and damp. "Mine—? My girl?"

Emilie nodded, cupping Isaac's cheek with one hand to feel the slick of his tears. His back shook as he finally allowed a hushed sob. His face fell to his hands and Emilie put her fingers through his hair—soft and real. He leaned into her touch, moved toward her onto his other knee, and then his lips found Emilie's, clumsy and eager, and feeling exactly right.

She was finding it difficult to breathe again, seeing the baby's face so close to her father's, realizing all at once that she was not dreaming—that Isaac was here, with open eyes, open lungs, and beating heart. Isaac was alive, and was going to be with her for the rest of their lives. Their long, long lives.

Dorothy, finally finding her voice, stared at Isaac while speaking to Emilie, "Who is that, Mama?"

Emilie hugged Dorothy to her, kissed her on one chubby cheek. "That's your papa, my love. He has finally come home."

Isaac was smiling again, staring at the marvel that was his daughter, too shy yet to reach out. Overhead, the larks were dancing nearby, and Emilie looked up at the sky, still blue, still hanging where it was meant to be. She half expected it to fall and shatter, to break this miraculous scene into a million pieces. How could she be so lucky?

"Shall we stand you up?" Isaac asked.

After a breath of hesitation, Isaac slipped his hands under Dorothy's arms and stood with her, then offered Emilie a hand. She climbed to her feet, head spinning, and went straight into Isaac's chest. Dottie met her eyes and giggled, then turned to watch the dogs over Isaac's shoulder, happy as can be.

"How did you find me?" Emilie asked.

Isaac swallowed twice before finding his words, which had seemingly got stuck in the back of his throat. "An old friend of yours recognized me in London. She said you had returned to Yorkshire and would be glad to see me . . ." He glanced around them, at the stables, at the cottage, at the sheep grazing nearby. "You live on a farm, Emilie."

She smiled. "I do."

"You have cows."

"I have."

Dorothy lifted her head. "The cow is called Chicken!" She giggled, and Isaac's brows raised in amusement. "I named the cow."

"Chicken, is it? My . . . And have you named the dogs as well?"

Dorothy nodded. "They're my dogs." She pointed at them, counting as Mama had taught her. "One . . . two . . . three . . ."

"What a clever girl you are. Like your mother . . ." Isaac then looked to Emilie, hand firm on her back. He struggled to find the next word, as if it was stuck on the back of his tongue. "How did you do all this?"

"Fletcher put some money by for me. Apparently, he thought I may do something silly like run off on my own."

"Not you, Lady Emilie." Isaac dropped a kiss on her head. "Madwoman."

Emilie stared into his eyes, weary, but just the same as they had always been, and for a moment, she didn't wish to know how Isaac had got there—only that he had arrived. He looked down at Dorothy, who had returned to staring at him, and pinched her belly. She giggled and writhed, and, finally warmed to the stranger, tried her new word. "Papa! Pa-*pa*, it tickles!"

Tears began to fall again from Emilie's eyes and she wrapped her arms around the both of them. The three fit so perfectly together.

Suddenly, the last four years no longer mattered: the pain, the struggle, the endless dark days. Wars ended like everything else. Theirs would, too, one day. Until then, they had each other.

Author's Note

Researching the First World War, particularly the lives of British nurses, has been a passion of mine for several years. While I took care to ensure this book depicted the time period accurately, I acknowledge that there are no doubt errors made unknowingly. Therefore, I'd like to point out a few liberties I purposely took in the name of plot.

During the war, letters home were read and heavily censored by commanding officers. Classified information was blacked out, but so were the gruesome details of life in the trenches, in order to keep the public from learning of the conditions. Much of what Fletcher and Isaac shared with Emilie in their letters would have been censored, but I chose to include them, as it was the only way I could provide a glimpse into their experiences.

I decided to accelerate Emilie's training to become a VAD in order to keep the story moving. Likely she would have had to serve in a hospital in England before going to France. VADs were required to be at least twenty-three years old to serve overseas, which Emilie is not when she goes abroad. However, in a time when many people did not have birth certificates, it was not uncommon for volunteers to lie about their ages—which is why something like 250,000 recruits in World War One were under eighteen.

It was also unlikely that Emilie would have stayed in the same place during the war. Tented hospitals could be periodically moved or taken over by, for example, the American Red Cross, causing the staff to be relocated. No. 16 Stationary and the other camps mentioned in the book are fictional and not meant to represent the actual hospitals numbered as such.

VADs were indeed given a list of DON'Ts, along with a letter from Katharine Furse, who led the first Voluntary Aid Detachment sent to France. I want to acknowledge that I used some of these words in Sister Allen's dialogue when she greets Emilie and the other new recruits.

The ins and outs of life in active service I learned from a handful of diaries written by real-life VADs. I used these documents to learn their schedules, their tasks, their slang, and the types of wounds they treated, and to understand their thoughts and feelings about what was going on around them. We are very fortunate that these courageous women, and so many other eyewitnesses, took the time to carefully document the war. Below, I've recommended a few of my favorite books.

- *Your Daughter Fanny: The War Letters of Frances Cluett, VAD*, edited by Bill Rompkey and Bert Riggs
- *A Volunteer Nurse at the Western Front* by Olive Dent
- *Dorothea's War: A First World War Nurse Tells Her Story* by Dorothea Crewdson
- *Testament of Youth* by Vera Brittain

Acknowledgments

This book is the most difficult thing I have ever had to write. It tested me mentally and emotionally, and there were times I thought I would never see it completed. So I must first and foremost thank my incredible agent, Abby Saul, who is the reason *The Forgotten Cottage* has made it into your hands. Thank you, Abby, for all the work you put into this book (in all its many forms), for the encouragement, for your kindness, and for hearing me cry over the phone. I am so lucky to have you in my corner.

Thank you also to my brilliant editor, Kerry Donovan, who was so patient and never stopped believing in this ever-evolving story. I'm so grateful for my entire team at Berkley—Fareeda Bullert, Tina Joell, and Mary Baker—for their tireless work.

Enormous thanks to my good friend and critique partner, Rick Danforth, who graciously read this book many times and helped to ensure I did justice to North Yorkshire and its lovely residents. I still owe you a beer!

Thank you to the Berkletes for your friendship and support, with special thanks to my Upstate New York pal and dog-walking companion, Elizabeth Everett.

I'm so appreciative of my family—Mom, Dad, and Christopher—for believing in me, cheering me on, and listening to me ramble about World War One for, like, six years. It truly means the world to me that you are so invested in my work, despite the ups and downs. I love you all, and I'm incredibly fortunate to have such a strong support system.

A million hugs and kisses to my dog, Isla, who provided much-needed emotional support over the last year and is the reason I get up every morning.

And finally, thank you to everyone who bought my debut novel, said kind things about it, and spread the word about this one. I am so sincerely grateful for your readership.

THE
FORGOTTEN
COTTAGE

Courtney Ellis

Discussion Questions

1. Audrey first feels kinship with Emilie after finding her nurse uniform. Apart from their shared experience with this work, what other parallels are drawn between Audrey and her great-grandmother?

2. There are many women who influence Emilie in her journey: her mother, Lady Thurston, Sister Allen, and even Isaac's fictional character, Captain Ridley. What do you think is the most important lesson she learns from each of them? What women have influenced your own life?

3. Isaac's novel plays a key role in helping Audrey discover her family's history. Why do you think the book was so important to both Isaac and Emilie that they brought it through war together?

4. Emilie's life as a VAD in the war is vastly different from her life at home. What do you think are some of the lessons she learns in France that help her to become the woman she is at the end of the novel?

5. In France, Emilie gravitates toward Sister Allen, rather than her bunkmate or the other VADs closer to her age. Why do you think that friendship means so much to her?

6. Leslie believes that Audrey's skills as a nurse can be applied to a different path in life, should she choose one. Where do you see this sentiment being proven in the story? Do you think Audrey could have reached her goal without these skills?

7. When Audrey begins to explore Yorkshire, she feels a connection to the county that makes it feel like home. Have you ever felt this way about a place, whether it be a country, a house, or a city?

8. Much of Isaac's and Fletcher's perspectives of war are only shown through their letters to Emilie. Today, preserved correspondence such as theirs as well as diaries and memoirs help us to better understand historical events. With diaries and letter writing falling out of relevance these days, do you think future historians will struggle to study our time? How might the internet and social media play a similar role?

9. If, like Audrey, you could suddenly inherit a mysterious home from a relative, where would you hope for it to be located? What type of home would be most thrilling for you to discover? Where would you start to uncover its secrets?

Keep reading for a preview of

AT SUMMER'S END

by Courtney Ellis, available now!

It didn't take much to excite the neighbors—only a little feature in the *Times* accompanying a photograph of my painting, the winner of an art contest put on by the Royal British Legion. Four years on, there were still plenty of funds needing to be raised for veterans of the Great War.

My painting had received first prize. I delighted in the opportunity to parade the crimson ribbon before my family, but the true victory was having my name in print. It was my name shortened, but no matter. Everyone who saw the feature would think Bertie Preston a man. Or so I hoped. For who would commission a painting from an unknown female artist?

Our neighbor Mrs. Lemm would, and after seeing the article, did. My very first.

On a Tuesday afternoon, I completed the portrait of her Yorkshire terrier, Duchess, and accepted annuity of four shillings, sixpence. The amount made no difference to me; I was only pleased to be paid for my work at last. It was only four shillings, sixpence, but it was four shillings, sixpence closer to a room in London and a life of my own.

Unmarried at twenty-eight, one might resolve to consider oneself a sad and lonely spinster. Only I wasn't sad, or lonely. I rather enjoyed an empty room with an easel in it.

After leaving Mrs. Lemm's house, I used my earnings to buy a bunch of peonies. It was while I was out that the earl's letter arrived.

Our maid Jane didn't come to the door, so I set down my easel, hung my cloche on the rack, and went through to the parlor, where I was accosted by the odor of wood glue. My father had lately taken the hobby of building model boats, which he then sailed on the local pond of an afternoon. Now he sat at a table once reserved for games of bridge, painting tiny strokes on his toy boat's hull. Painting! *My* father! Who, as a retired banker, was a man of numbers and not creativity. I never knew my parents to engage in the arts, which was why I'd been under their scorn since adolescence for lacking focus on anything apart from painting.

Mother came through from the kitchen, where she was surely bullying our cook about the state of dinner. Neither of them had noticed my arrival, so I announced, "Peonies!" and held the bunch in Mother's direction. "Won't they be lovely?"

Her mouth was permanently downturned, but the creases deepened at the sight of the flowers. "Oh, Bertie, you know your father's hay fever is the devil in June. Do put them outdoors."

Father peered over wire spectacles balanced on the end of his nose. "No, no bother to me, surely."

"I'll not have you bedridden over a few measly blooms. Please, Bertie?"

On cue, Father sneezed. I sent my eyes skyward and trudged back to the foyer, swung the door open, and tossed the flower bunch—which I'd spent a hard-earned penny on—to the front path. How remarkable the glue odor should have no effect whatsoever on Father's lungs.

Back in the parlor, Mother leaned over his shoulder, watching him tinker. "How does Mrs. Lemm do, Bertie?"

"Well," I answered. "Charming as always. I had a lovely time." I shrank to the window seat and pinched a piece of my newly chopped bob. A smudge of paint clung to my thumb, the rusty shade of a terrier's whiskers.

"So good of her to have you, wasn't it? She knows how much you enjoy doing your paintings." Here, Mother implied I wasn't an artist at all, but a hobbyist like my father. "Mrs. Flynn called by earlier; she'd seen the *Times* and wanted to have a look at the prize painting. You remember her boy John was killed on the Somme?—poor lamb burst into tears."

My painting, entitled *Something for the Pain*, had begun as a sketch I'd done whilst serving in the Voluntary Aid Detachment, stationed near the Western Front. It captured a nursing sister in her grey uniform and veil, lending her strength to a soldier patient outside a tented ward. They'd been chatting about lice—*Ever 'old a fag to one and 'eard them poppin', Sister?*—and hadn't known I was drawing them.

Drawing had been my way to cope with the horrors I saw in my wartime career. I tried to capture the lovely moments in between, the now blurred memories of friendship and warmth between nurse and soldier, between men and women stuck in the worst of what the world had seen. Perhaps I ought to have been documenting the worst of it—the pain and torn flesh and mud. But in the end, I couldn't decide which was more important to remember, so I chose what caught my eye. One day it was the look of utter exhaustion on the face of the walking wounded, another, the beaming smile of a freckled VAD serving weak tea and dog biscuits.

"I remember John," I said. "Living in London, was he not?"

Mother nodded solemnly. "Left behind a wife and baby girl, God rest him." She selected an envelope from her pile and handed it to Father. "One from Violet, dear."

Violet was one of my two elder sisters. Father took it eagerly, setting his paintbrush aside.

We were similar, Father and I. In retirement, he worked ardently on his boats to keep busy, as I had done with the Red Cross in war.

When armistice came, I hardly wished to leave my post. In peacetime, I was redundant, merely a single woman with no purpose or use. When the men returned, all were quick to forget what worth their women had.

"For you, Bertie."

I looked up from my thoughts. Mother held out a letter, eyes elsewhere. I stood to collect the envelope, turning it over and over as I paced the airless room. All windows were to be shut in summer months. Hay fever, of course.

It was postmarked Braemore, Wiltshire. I didn't recognize the hand, though my heart quickened all the same. For the letter was addressed to Mr. Bertie Preston.

Mister.

I tore open the envelope and removed a single, crisp bit of stationery. At the top was an embossed golden crest, and the words EARL OF WAKEFORD, CASTLE BRAEMORE.

"Good Lord!" I blurted.

Mother sighed, lifted her weary face. "Honestly, dear, you know I dislike you speaking so harshly."

I ignored her, began to pace. There was absolutely no reason I should have had a letter from a nobleman. I'd never met a lord, much less an earl. Or maybe I'd nursed one? An officer, perhaps? No; I certainly would not have forgot that.

I took a deep breath and read.

Dear Mr. Preston,

I am seeking to commission an artist for several paintings of my Wiltshire estate, Castle Braemore. As an admirer of your work, I would be delighted if you would be my guest at Braemore for the summer months to gather the inspiration necessary for your process. If you should accept the undertaking, please enclose with your response a

*list of materials you shall require, which will be provided upon your
arrival.*

   I eagerly await your reply.

                                                         Sincerely,
                                                         Wakeford

My cheeks set flame. The room spun. I was not a woman who
swooned—I'd been elbow deep in blood during the war and hadn't
batted an eyelash—but now I thought my knees might give out. I ran
to the window and threw it open.

Mother scoffed. "Bertie, what on earth—?"

Father stood, scraping back his chair. "Fantastic news, everyone—
Violet's expecting a third!"

I thrust my head out the window and took a gulp of summer evening air, the letter crumpled under my hand on the windowsill. Behind me, my parents embraced, delighted to be grandparents yet
again. My sisters were really rather good at producing children, and
with Heather widowed and me hopeless, Violet was their champion.

Old news. For I had a commission! A real one!

I plucked a petunia from the flower box and brought my head back
indoors, shutting the window with force. When I turned, my parents
had gone. I could hear Father chatting to the operator in the other
room, telephoning Violet to congratulate her. The letter shook in my
hands.

Someone—a bloody earl!—wanted me to paint for him. For
money. This had been my goal when entering the contest. But how
could I ever have expected such a commission? An earl might display
my paintings where his titled friends could see. It wouldn't be long
before more commissions came through and I had the income for a
solo show, to submit a piece for entry in the Royal Academy Summer
Exhibition, to rent a flat with a view of Hyde Park.

Now I certainly *was* going to faint. I sat down in a nearby chair to save myself the fall and put the petunia under my nose to breathe the warm sweetness.

I was finally on my way.

～

NOT WANTING TO FOLLOW up Violet's news too closely, I waited until dinner to give mine. As I settled in opposite Mother, I flapped the letter, beaming so hard my cheeks ached, waiting for someone to ask about it. Jane came forward with the tureen under her arm, offering me an odd glance as carrot and ginger soup was ladled into my bowl.

Father said to Mother, "We'll stop with Violet and Henry at the weekend. She'll be wanting you."

As ever, neither of them were paying me any attention at all. So I said, "I've had an exciting letter."

Eyes remained on soup. Mother sipped. "How nice. From whom?"

"Why, it came directly from the Earl of—" I had to read again; I'd forgot his name. "The Earl of Wakeford!"

Bless Jane, the only body to react, dropping the lid onto the tureen. Mother sent her a scowl before turning to me. "I do love you, but all this jesting can be so wearing."

"It isn't a jest!" I made to hand her the note, then changed my mind and gave it to Father. He set down his spoon and pushed his spectacles up his nose.

I watched his eyes dart back and forth as Mother waited impatiently, breathing more audibly than before, every exhale a sigh. Was there not more in life to be excited by than babies?

"'I am seeking to commission an artist for several paintings of my Wiltshire estate, Castle Braemore,'" Father read aloud. "A castle, Bertie?"

I could hardly sit still for how excited I was. "Indeed. And I to be the artist. I've already sent my reply, accepting."

Mother blinked rapidly and snatched the letter from Father's hand. She read it herself, mouthing the words, then tossed it down beside her soup. "His lordship writes to a *Mr.* Bertie Preston. It is all a mistake; you must write again immediately to set it right. A telegraph. Jane?"

"Naturally, it's a mistake," I said, shooting the maid a warning glance as she came forward. "A mistake I've been hoping someone might make. Nobody wishes to commission a painting from a woman, Mother, hence why I entered the contest as Bertie and not Alberta."

"And I suppose you mean to resemble a man as well?"

"Oh, for heaven's sake, it isn't *that* short." I self-consciously fluffed my bob. "Will you not be glad for me?"

Father played a tattoo on the table with his fingers. "You ought to have discussed this with us before responding."

I shrank in my chair. Father was my supporter. He had gifted me my first set of brushes. He'd given me permission to join the VAD in 1915, to accept a post abroad. Now I saw doubt in his eyes. He viewed my painting as my mother did—an *accomplishment* only. Something to show a young man to prove I was a woman of substance.

"This is a real opportunity," I said, "to prove myself, to make a name—"

"It isn't *your* name, Alberta!" Mother clapped her hand down on the table, rattling the china. "You cannot allow this man to carry on believing you're someone you are not."

"It was his mistake. He may turn me away if he likes, but I shan't forfeit the chance."

"At any rate, we cannot in good conscience allow you to stop at this strange man's home without a chaperone. Have you heard of this Wakeford, George?"

Father shook his head. "His lordship's note is rather brief . . ."

Mother gave an arrogant nod. "I've always been of the mind that a man of such few words has something to hide."

I sat up again to reach for the letter. "I'm more than sure he's an old, married chap."

"With unmarried sons, we may assume."

"Did I not stand over the beds of hundreds of men during the war, and return unscathed?"

Her face was unmoving. "I shall not allow it."

"I'm a grown woman; I don't require your permission."

"Yet you require our allowance." Mother was proud of her response, chin lifted. "Your father will not pay the train fare. Will you, George?"

Father shifted in his seat. His eyes drifted to the letter, now in my hands. I could tell he wished he'd held it longer, further dissected Wakeford's words to find a viable reason why I should be permitted to go. This time, however, he would not defend me. Whether it was my mother's glare, or some deeper belief that I was undeserving of the commission, I wasn't sure.

He lifted his spoon and said, "I'm sorry, Bertie."

The room hushed to scraping spoons and the sucking of soup. I stared at my plate, thinking of Violet and her swelling belly, sitting to dinner in Hertfordshire with her stodgy husband. Violet was the ideal daughter, everything I was meant to be but could not imagine emulating.

"With thanks to Mrs. Lemm, I've my own money now," I said, a calm threat. Surely, if they knew I was to go it alone, they would not withdraw their support.

It had worked on my father, at least. He set down his spoon again with a sigh, taking the moment to knead at his forehead. "Perhaps you will wait until I've written to the fellow . . ."

"How am I to be taken as a professional if my father writes ahead of me?"

Mother inserted, "You are *not* a professional."

"I may yet be!" I heard the pitch of my voice change and tried to steady myself. How could I explain to them that I felt my very life was at stake? "You know this is all I have ever worked towards. I've spent my years not looking for a husband, not building a family, but *painting*. I am nothing without it, and if I stay here, nothing I shall remain."

"If that's how you feel," said Mother, "then I have failed you."

My desperation boiled to the surface, reddening my vision. There was no use arguing, that was clear. "I shall take the train to Braemore soon as I have word from Lord Wakeford. I would prefer to go with my parents' blessing, but I see now it is too much to ask."

I pushed back to stand, making a show of dropping my napkin on the table and moving in my chair. In reality, I was stalling—waiting for one or both of them to see sense, to see that their youngest daughter was upset, and move to make amends.

But it was no good. Mother's eyes welled with tears, her face crumpled, and Father began to mumble words of reassurance as he set his hand over hers. My own resolve weakened as Mother took a shaking breath.

"If you leave this house against our word"—she blotted a tear with the back of her hand—"do not expect to have a place here when you return."

I drew in my lips to keep them from trembling. It no longer mattered how many years I'd spent dreaming of the day I would leave home—the notion, come so immediately and in anger, was terrifying. I was a girl again, watching timidly as the other children played, not as yet willing to abandon the comfort of Mother's hand in mine.

"Mummy, please don't say that—" At this, she turned her head as to avoid my eyes. "Surely you don't mean it?"

I looked to Father for help, but he had nothing to say. If he wouldn't defend me, then we were no longer allies.

It was difficult to speak through the lump in my throat, but I managed a curt "Very well."

As I left them, I tried to remember that their response did not diminish my success. I had done it. I had earned a commission on my

Photo by Kelly Gleason

COURTNEY ELLIS is the author of *At Summer's End*. After obtaining her BA in English and creative writing, she went on to pursue a career in publishing. She lives in Upstate New York with her rescue dog.

CONNECT ONLINE

Courtney-Ellis.com

🐦 CEllisWriter

📷 CourtneyEllisAuthor

f CourtneyEllisAuthor

Ready to find
your next great read?

Let us help.

Visit prh.com/nextread